# THE ORC OUTCAST'S MATE

## ORC MATES OF FAEDA
### BOOK TWO

AURORA WINTERS

ISBN: 978-1-963552-07-2

# CONTENT WARNINGS

All content warnings can be viewed on Aurora Winters's website at www.AuroraWintersRomance.com/ books/content-warnings.

# PRONUNCIATION GUIDE

I want to preface by saying that however you want to pronounce the characters and locations in my novels is absolutely fine by me. But if you would like to know how I read them in my own head, I have a pronunciation guide on my website here:

https://www.aurorawintersromance.com/books/pronunciation-guide

# CHAPTER
# ONE

*MIRANDA*

Violent heat strangled her throat and lodged in her chest. She couldn't move. Couldn't squirm. Metal caged around her, and in a frenzy, she squealed and panicked.

The metal cage held her down. Her shoulders, her back, her neck. Everything burned. She fought hard, twisting her arms, but they were caught against her sides. Her legs twitched and cramped.

She was wedged, muscles straining, bones cracking under the pressure. Her fingernails scraped against the metal, snapping, and tearing. The blood only made her scrambling more desperate.

She was stuck. In the vent.

The blinding prick of daylight a few dozen yards away burned her retinas. It was so bright.

But she couldn't get out. She couldn't break free.

The air vent caught her in its grip.

She would die here, agonizingly, slowly. She wailed and

snapped and fought until her body felt broken. Her toes were curled, calves blistering, and mind racing.

She couldn't get out! *She couldn't get out!*

"Miranda!"

Someone screamed her name. She froze. She looked toward the light. The escape that was so close but impossibly far. Her lips were chapped, and her tongue swelled.

"Miranda, come—"

An earth-shattering roar cut the words off.

The blistering agony of her eardrums rupturing slammed her. The quaking of the ground shook her out of her sanity. Dragged her back to Earth again.

She was in the vault. In the black. Reliving those terrifying moments, she'd spent locked up behind Blackridge Bank's thick security door. Surrounded by the clanging of deposit boxes and the stink of metal. The rumbling shook, and the ceiling rained dust onto her face, into her eyes. She breathed in rubble and hacked for air.

The bombing went on for *so long*. Hours trapped underground, just waiting for her boss to come back. Just wondering if he was even still *alive*.

She'd pleaded for any gods from any of the hundreds of religions to make the horrible boom's *stop*.

Then it did, and she was alone in the silence. It rang around her, trembled in her guts. She'd screamed until her throat was tattered, just to hear something outside that agony of brutal *silence*.

She'd fumbled along the wall in the dark. Skating her hands around the boxes to find some means of escape. And she'd found it. A tiny vent near the bottom of one corner. Its grate had flung open, broken loose from the shaking of the ground. She could feel cool air coming through and saw an impossibly dim glimmer of light at the end.

She'd grappled with the horror of it. With the terror of what she must do. She'd paced and shivered and tried not to even look at it. It was too *small*. She'd never make it through that tiny pipe.

And it mocked her. Jeered at her. Wailed that it was the only escape.

Her desperation grew too high.

"Miranda! Come back!"

She couldn't. She couldn't get *out*.

Burning and panicking, she'd crawled inside the vent. Shoved her body where it couldn't fit. The metal that was supposed to make it easy for her to slide only made it impossible to gain traction.

Her clothes caught on a jutting screw. It tore into her side and her blood dripped.

She was stuck. Trapped. The walls were pressing down. *Down.*

"You are not trapped, Miranda!"

But she was. This was the end. Another explosion roared around her. Her consciousness winked out for one blissful moment.

And then she was burning. Screaming. Pleading. The metal heated until she felt like she was being cooked alive. Her stomach rolled.

A burst of cold air hit her face.

She gasped, breathing it in. Something in the taste was familiar. Comforting.

Another gust. She heaved. Gripped tight to warm, soft flesh. Not metal. Skin.

"Come back. I beg you."

Growling. Soothing growling. Her eyes unclouded, and the tunnel faded.

"Come back." Hands stroked her hair, her neck, her cheeks. He exhaled gently against her face again. Air whistled across her overheated flesh. "Come back, Miranda."

"I-I'm trapped," she whimpered.

"Not anymore." Govek gripped her fingers, right over the nails that should have been missing. They were gone a second ago.

"You're in the goblin mines. On Faeda, not Earth." He pressed her hand to the cool, rough texture of the wall. "With me. You are not alone. I will not leave you alone."

His green eyes were glowing in the darkness as she stroked that wonderful rock surface. It abraded her fingers but soothed her agony.

"There are no bank vaults on Faeda," Govek said, stumbling slightly on the foreign words. "No bombs. No quaking and destruction. No small vents."

She shivered, clinging to his shoulders, and tucked her head into his fragrant neck. Spicy and clean. Nothing like it existed on Earth.

Her voice tore at her vocal cords, as if she'd been screaming. "But there is war."

Govek's grip tightened, and she relished it. The hold of his strong arms about her torso. Uneven pressure that gave when she squirmed against it.

This was Govek, the orc, not the air vent. She really was out.

Her throat closed and her eyes burned. "Earth is gone. We killed it. We killed our planet."

She heard him gulp.

"We fought over *everything*—gods, politics, food, and

water. Oh, Govek, there was *nothing* left. It was just ash and burned trees. Rubble, scorching heat, and poison. It's gone and there's no bringing it back."

He cradled her, crouched on a hard stone floor. The darkness closed in around her and he breathed another gust of air onto her face. Her shoulders relaxed, slumping.

"Faeda is not Earth, Miranda," Govek assured her, stroking his hands in gentle waves down her hair and back. "Our world was built by the might of the Fades and is protected by sentinels."

"And humans are destroying it."

His body grew tense, his movements stilled, and his breathing caught in his throat.

Miranda sobbed, because he didn't deny it.

How could she have been inexplicably saved from the death of her own planet, only to be forced to relive that agony on another? It wasn't fair. What had she done to deserve this?

"It isn't your fault, Miranda," Govek whispered as if he was reading her mind.

She choked out a half laugh, half sob. "How do you know? If it's not my fault, then why am I the only one left? There were twenty-two *billion* humans on Earth, Govek. And I didn't see one. Single. Body. I walked for *days*. Where did they go? How is it possible? Why am I still alive? Why didn't I die with them?"

She must have been in hysterics because Govek started to rock her slightly. The motion helped her to breathe.

"The only living things I saw were those fucking dogs that chased me down and kept me moving and herded me to the ocean—oh, god, Govek. The ocean was *gone*. Dried up. I *can't*—"

"I have you, Miranda," Govek vowed, continuing to rock,

to squeeze, and to exhale his cool breath against her face. His life soaked into her frame and dragged her back to sanity.

"I don't even know how I got out of that vent." Her voice was a high sob against the cords of his neck. "I was stuck and then I wasn't. I was burning and then I was healed. I was starving and parched and *poisoned,* but I survived. We don't have *magic* on Earth, Govek. How am I still *alive? Why am I alive?*

"And then I just . . . I just went to the *ocean.* I don't even remember half of it. There are blanks spots. Missing pieces of time. It's all spotty and distorted. Rotting dogs herded me and signposts guided me and there were cars. Strange cars that somehow survived the explosion and had food and water and . . . oh god, Govek, why didn't I go back? I should have gone back to find them. I should have known they wouldn't be at the ocean."

"Who?" Govek asked.

"My *babies.*" Miranda's voice cracked, breaking under the weight of the horrors she was speaking. Her mind blistered from the agony. Her eyes flooded. "Oh god. *I left them.* I should have gone back, Govek. I should have gone to make sure they hadn't . . . that they weren't . . . what if they *needed* me? What if they were crying, and I didn't even bother to—Oh god. I *can't—*"

Miranda gasped on her sobs. She vented her confusion and sorrow and *guilt* all over Govek's chest as he breathed gently against her hair. His heart was steady under her ear, anchoring her to him.

"You said that you cannot remember some of your final moments on Earth?"

She swallowed hard but still couldn't find her voice, so she nodded against his shoulder.

Her thoughts scampered right over themselves trying to remember *exactly* what had taken place.

She remembered being in the vent, being trapped. It had been so brutally *hot*.

And then she'd been walking near the edge of New Seattle. Or what she assumed was the edge of it. She saw the lit-up road sign pointing her toward the ocean. Forty-two miles.

She'd turned back and had seen the destruction of her city. The vision shot agony through her even now. Making her want to curl in on herself. To wail until all her breath was gone.

She'd wanted to go back to search for survivors. She'd almost gone back. She'd stepped toward it. And then . . .

And then what?

She couldn't remember.

There had been a bright flash. And she was further along. Near the car where she'd found the gym bag and workout clothes. She'd raided it. She'd administered the radiation boosters and switched out her clothing and drank the water and ate the granola bars and packed up and prepared to go *back*.

She'd wanted to go back to help. To find her babies. She was set. Ready.

And then the dogs arrived, and she'd *ran*.

And things got hazy again. A blur of chaos and destruction, of broken pavement and stale air, of heat and dust and *pain*.

And those *fucking road signs*. They shouldn't have been working. Why were they working if no one was ahead of her fixing them? Why were they leading her to an ocean that had already burned up?

Why did she believe, to the deepest part of her soul, that her *babies* had had something to do with those signs? It didn't make sense.

Nothing made sense.

"You should not blame yourself for things you are not certain of, Miranda."

Govek's words wrenched her back to the present, and she took a deep breath as he slowly continued. "You did what you needed to in order to survive. So too would they. You do not know that you could have saved them. Or that they were not somehow saved by other means. You made it here and survived. So too could they. Allow your guilt to ebb."

Her body jolted with shock.

Could . . . could they have lived?

"Could they be here on Faeda?"

Govek's body went tense at her question.

"Do you think they could have, Govek? Do you think they could be here on Faeda somewhere? Do you think we could find them?"

How would they go about doing that? How big *was* Faeda?

It didn't matter. She'd search to the ends of this world to find her babies if they were here.

Were they here?

Desperation made her rational thoughts hazy and her gut twisted, gnawing at the corners of her mind, eating away all logic at how impossible the odds of them being here on Faeda were.

*She'd* made it here. Why couldn't they?

Her stomach twisted with anticipation. "If they're here, they need me, Govek. I have to find them."

"I . . ." Govek's voice broke, betraying the truth that he would have no idea how to find her babies if they were here. He'd already told her that these lands were war torn. Ravaged. It would be difficult enough to travel to his cousin's home. Finding toddlers from another planet was out of the question.

And yet, "You told me of an orc seer. Do you think the seer

would know? Would he know if they were here and where they are now?"

Govek's chest was so tight it felt like iron under her palms. She heard him swallow hard. "He . . . could. His power is immeasurable. If the Fades will him to know, then he will."

Miranda's head burst at the idea. What if she could find out what happened to them? What if they could be reunited? What if she *hadn't* been the only one to survive?

What if . . . what if they were dropped into the icy forests of Faeda too?

What if they were lost, and hungry, and cold, and crying.

Crying for *her*.

*They needed her.*

She hadn't gone back for them on Earth. *She hadn't gone back.*

She wouldn't make that same mistake again.

Hot tears coursed down her cheeks. "I have to find them."

"Then we must get to Baelrok Forge and speak with the seer. But first we must escape this goblin mine," Govek said. "Rest easy, Miranda. I will carry you through."

New hope rose warm in her chest and spread through her limbs.

She would find them. With Govek's help, she *would*.

She wanted to thank him, but words didn't seem like enough. She wasn't sure anything she ever did would be enough.

"I can see five things," Govek said.

Miranda tensed as Govek got to his feet, rising to begin walking in the complete darkness. Black but for one thing. Her eyes snapped to his face, the sight finally registering. "Your eyes are glowing. They glow green?"

He blinked. Cutting off all the light for the split of a

second. She tensed, wanting to order him not to blink again, but she knew that was unfair.

"You hadn't noticed?"

She shook her head. Touched his cheek. "I didn't. It's kinda neat." The glow widened and her lips twitched. "I had toys on Earth that glowed in the dark like that."

His eyes went even wider. "I hate to disappoint but my cock does not share this feature."

Her breath hitched, and she managed a half laugh. "Oh god. Not *that* kind of toy. I meant as a kid . . ." His gaze softened and her tension softened too. At least until her throat closed up and her eyes started to prickle and hot tears coursed down her cheeks again.

Earth was gone.

She clenched her fists and ground her teeth together, shoving the thoughts to the back of her mind. Back so far they couldn't hurt anymore.

"My eyes can count toward one of the things."

"What do you mean?" She sniffled, rubbing at her face. She wanted to stop crying, but her body fervently disobeyed.

Govek's steps were steady as he continued. "I can see intricate columns lining our path, arches above our heads, smooth stone floors, and dust that proves this place has been abandoned for a long while."

"Where are we?"

"Inside the goblin mine. And we must be quick, so none find us here before we make our escape."

"How long?" she gulped. "How long until we're out?"

"Not long," he assured her softly. His breath rustled her hair again. "Four things I can hear."

"How do you know about this exercise?"

There was a brief silence. Another blink. "I was not

unconscious when you were bringing me water to wash out the poison on that first day we met. Only paralyzed."

"What? Are you serious?" For one breathless moment, she was struck dumb and then all the memories of sitting next to him babbling while he *died* slammed into her. "Oh god! I'm so so sorry."

His chest quivered and rumbled, and she realized that he was trying to withhold laughter. She wanted to hear it. Let it drown out what remained of her horrors. "I can't believe it. You must have thought I was a complete idiot."

"I did think you might have been insane."

"I guess this event confirmed that for you," she mumbled, clinging to him a little tighter.

He hummed. "I'm still not sure. I need more time with you before coming to a proper judgment."

"You really want me to stick around? Even though I'm probably crazy?"

"Yes, Miranda." His voice was solid and sweet. "I want nothing more than that."

Her chest swelled, and her pulse quickened. She found his lips in the dark and gave him a lingering kiss that flooded her with warmth.

When she broke away, his voice was tinged with pleasure, and it made her want to weep for a completely different reason. "Performing the taste portion early, are you?"

That got a laugh out of her. The sound felt raw and vibrant in the darkness. She hugged him close again, pressing her cheek to his.

Then he huffed a harsh breath and continued moving. "We cannot falter here."

Miranda wasn't going to argue with that. The darkness was oppressive and even with Govek's strong hands around her, she

11

couldn't help but feel the terrifying weight of the cavern closing in.

"Fades willing, we will not be found."

Miranda shivered, and in response, Govek dipped to the left. He uncurled one of her arms to stretch out and touch the rock wall. Her hand dragged gently along the dusty surface. The dips and grooves showed patterns were carved into the walls. A harsh contrast to the smooth metallic surface in her nightmares. Every minute or so Govek would shift outward, and her fingers would swell around one of the round columns he'd described.

Her mind worked back over Govek's words from before the tornado had descended on them. It felt like a lifetime ago. "Do *you* think the Fades created humans on Earth too? That they left Faeda and went to my planet next?"

"I am no seer. I have no skills to divine with the Fades outside of humble communions to their force."

"But . . ."

"I . . . believe that it was the Fades who saved you. Guided you to our lands. Kept you safe in your own," he swallowed thickly. His voice became a whisper. "Gave you to me."

She met his eyes again, and the steady hope she saw rocked her.

"I believe they imprinted you on me."

Her brow furrowed. "Imprint? What does that mean?"

His eyes skittered away. She thought she heard him gulp. "It . . . can mean many things. And I swear to you that through all, I will be at your side, Miranda. Until you no longer wish to be near me."

Miranda exhaled sharply, gut knotting, "I think you'll regret that. I feel like I've brought you almost nothing but problems and with how my luck has been, it's probable that we'll both end up at the bottom of a cliff somewhere."

"Far better to fall from a cliff with you than to face peril alone," Govek said, his voice suddenly echoing.

Miranda tensed. "Where are we?"

"Crossroads," Govek said softly. "I will try to scent the way. Stay quiet. We cannot afford to be found here."

"What would happen . . .?" She shivered. "What would happen if the goblins found us?"

"Entering each other's realms without consent is against Fade law and they would be in their right to seek retribution."

"Retribution?" she questioned. He didn't answer, and the look on his face assured her she didn't want to know. "I thought orcs were friends with goblins?"

"They are usually," he said glumly. "But we have had no contact for decades."

Miranda sputtered, trying to stay quiet even as panic rose in her voice. "If it was that big a deal, why did they make their lock so easy to break?"

Govek paused in his stride, his bright eyes blinking. She held her breath as he took in her words.

And then he *laughed*. A raw chuckle that started from deep in his stomach and bubbled into his chest. It rolled over Miranda like a hot blanket fresh from the dryer.

"You are quite right, woman." He shook his head. "Fuck, I was so tense I didn't . . ." he paused and adjusted Miranda into a more comfortable position. "They left it under the type of lock an orc or sylph could easily release."

She could hear the confusion in his tone. "Maybe they want you in here?" Miranda asked, relaxing further now that Govek was.

"Perhaps." He did not seem completely convinced.

Miranda settled into him again, touching her fingers back to the wall. Letting it soothe her almost as much as Govek's thundering heart did.

"Though I suppose that does mean . . ." He adjusted her to sit in the crook of one arm, and before she could question him, brightness flooded her eyes. Blinding her.

She gasped, rapidly adjusting to sudden light. Govek had somehow lit a torch. He'd taken it from a metal holder on the wall nearest them. A half dozen or so sat, unlit, along the same surface.

Miranda's mouth gaped as she took in the area for the first time and registered that it was far more intricate than her fingers had let on. The walls were carved stone, chiseled with detailed geometric patterns. The ceilings were high and broken up by massive, rounded archways. The floor was so smooth it glimmered even under the thin layer of dust. Everything was in varied hues of gray or brown, accentuating the gorgeous architecture.

But for as beautiful as it was, it was also clearly abandoned. Cobwebs arched from every corner and dust covered the surfaces. The stale air and stillness was almost oppressive.

They were indeed at a crossroads. Govek continued from the hall into a hexagon-shaped room with arched doorways on each wall. They all pitched into blackness after only a few feet, and not a single one appeared welcoming.

Govek slowly set her down. She resisted the urge to cling and demand he pick her up again. "I'll need to scent each passage to determine which has the closest escape."

She nodded, letting him walk a few paces away from her before skittering to follow. She didn't want to be outside the torchlight. She was about to ask Govek if he could light her one too when she stepped closer to one of the doorways.

A shivering warmth soothed her. Her skin tingled with goosebumps, her hair stood on end, and her knotted stomach eased.

Miranda gasped, drawing Govek's instant attention, but she barely heard him when he demanded to know what was wrong.

She took another tentative step. It was like dipping into a hot tub, warm, relaxing, and comforting. She inhaled and even the air felt different, more fulfilling, like it was saturated with oxygen and laced with caffeine.

Govek gripped her arm hard and pulled her into him. "Miranda, what is it? Tell me."

"Nothing's . . . uh, nothing's wrong. It just feels *good* over there." She gestured to the opening. "I don't know how to describe it. It's like . . . tingly and warm."

"Wait here," Govek demanded before moving past the threshold. She barely managed not to run after the light as he strode down a few paces. She watched his back tense as he came to an instant halt.

"It's . . . the Great Rove Tree."

"What's the Great Rove Tree?"

He recovered much faster from the sensations than she did. His gruff expression returned, and he gestured for her to come to him. "One of the Fades great relics. It stands at the center of my clan and its roots tangle out and into other trees for many leagues. Those roots must begin here. You can feel it?"

"Yeah," she said, slowly moving into his arms. The sensation had dulled a little now. Or maybe she was getting used to it. She closed her eyes, wishing it would come back stronger. "It feels good."

"The humans of Faeda cannot sense the magic within the Fades relics."

She blinked up at Govek and put a hand to his chest. "They can't?" He shook his head. "Then why can I?"

"I know not." His voice was clipped. "May I carry you?"

She supposed she would just have to be comfortable not knowing. "Yeah. Can I hold the torch?" Govek nodded, handing it to her, then lifted her up and tucked her back into his warmth. The combination of the tingling and Govek's strength had her feeling almost drowsy. She tightly gripped the torch's wooden handle.

"We will go this way," Govek said, continuing down the hall without preamble. "I can scent fresh air ahead."

"How far?" Even with the light, Miranda was ready to be out of the tunnel.

"Not far."

Miranda clung to him a little tighter. "And then we'll just stop off at your former clan. Rove Wood Clan, right?"

"Yes."

"And from there, we go to your cousin's forge. Where the seer is."

"Yes."

"How far away is it?"

"Half a moon."

Miranda snorted. "Half a moon? How long is half a moon?"

His wide green eyes blinked. "Around fifteen days."

"Fifteen days." Didn't sound *too* far, but through war-torn lands . . . through icy winter chill . . . fricking *tornadoes*. "Do you think the tornado is still out there?"

"You called it that before." Govek adjusted her, examined her face carefully. "You have seen them?"

"Not personally, but Earth had them."

He hummed quietly. "I have heard tales of these from my cousin. They call them Fade Storms or Fade Wrath. According to him, the orc overlords' lands are blighted by them, but they have not made it over the mountains to our half of the continent. Until now."

"Oh, that's just *wonderful.*"

"Do you know of any way to prevent them?"

She shook her head. "No. Even on Earth, they were difficult to track. There was some advanced tech that could manage it, but I could never replicate it here." She considered, "Though I guess I do know the warning signs of them. Hail, strange clouds, green-colored sky . . ."

Govek nodded slowly, lost in thought.

She scratched at the base of his skull. "Tell me what you're thinking."

"I am thinking that the Fades brought you here as a miracle."

She frowned. "What do you mean by miracle? You think they brought me here to do something? Like stop the storms?" She had no idea how she could do that. The idea made her gut clench.

He must have heard the tremor in her voice because he instantly cut in. "I do not believe they would make demands from you rashly, Miranda. The Fades are not so ruthless. And only they can see the future. Well, them and the seers they tell the future to, I suppose."

She took a deep breath. "And to get to the seer, we have to travel to your cousin's forge. Govek . . . are we really going to rob your former clan for supplies?"

He went tense under her.

"Govek," she said threateningly, and he let out a long, heavy sigh.

"All will be well, Miranda. I will remain at your side to

protect you while we travel. I will remain at your side for *all* that you do."

Miranda shifted, guilt knotting in her gut. She owed Govek so much at this point and judging by what lay before them, she knew this was only the beginning. It would take her a lifetime to pay him back.

But Govek's softened features and steady gait helped to soothe her turmoil into determination. Going to Baelrok meant she could find her babies and find out if they were here on Faeda.

Waiting for her to find them. Crying for help.

Her throat closed.

"We're here," Govek said, stopping at a section of the wall that didn't appear any different from the others. Miranda adjusted the torch for a better look. "I will set you down. Stay behind me while I check."

She nodded, breathless. Govek put both hands on the stone surface and though she couldn't see the magic pooling off him, she knew what he did was working because a seam—the outline of a door—appeared in the rock face.

He pushed slightly, and it scraped open. The thick rock was a foot or more deep. It felt like he would never break through the darkness.

And then a slit of light glimmered, and the forest appeared.

Relief tumbled through her as a tiny sliver of sunlight fluttered across her face. She almost went to her knees.

There was no storm, no wind at all. The daylight was striking and vivid. Govek forced the door open a few more inches and opened his mouth, scenting the air.

Then he nodded, took her torch, and gestured her out into the light.

She scrambled, scraping her hands on the stone frame, and burst into the sunlit forest.

She breathed the clean, sweet air deep into her lungs so fast it made her dizzy. The trees were dazzling in colors—oranges, reds, and yellows. The ferns were bright green, the leaf barren bushes seemed lively with their sharp brown twigs jutting every which way. Even the harsh chill on her cheeks was welcome.

The door shut behind them with a loud crunch, and it disappeared into the rock hillside. There were patches of moss that grew over the top of the seam, hiding it completely.

Miranda tipped her head up to the sky, blue and flourishing in the sunlight. She wanted to laugh, to cry, to forget everything that had happened in that miserable mine.

And yet, not forget a single moment.

She turned to Govek, who was still standing stoically, watching her tensely. A smile tugged at her lips and only then did he relax.

"How am I going to repay you?" she asked, almost to herself, and Govek's head tilted, his green eyes blinked, and he shifted.

"Just remain with me, Miranda."

She raised her brows. "I owe you much more than that." She sidled up to him. "And I want to stay with you. I'm so grateful—"

She broke off when his expression softened. His mouth went wide in a smile. Her heart thundered in her chest. She would have to find a way to make him smile more often because—dang!—happiness looked good on him.

Miranda bridged the gap between them, took both his hands in hers, and pulled him down. "Thank you, Govek. Really."

He hesitated and then bent, allowing her to kiss his forehead, his nose, his lips.

He tasted like the forest, rich and heady. Comfortable and strong. She trailed her hands up his arms to wrap around his neck, and he cupped both palms under her ass, lifting her off the ground. She beamed against his lips.

He shuddered and broke away and Miranda was overcome with the desire to teach him how to kiss properly.

"We can't here," he said. She huffed with disappointment, and he explained. "There are too many keen predators in the Rove Woods. Too many threats. I must stay alert to protect you."

Oh. She couldn't think of anything worse than being attacked while getting it on. She gulped. "Okay."

Displeasure must have been clear in her tone because he chuckled. "I swear when we reach my dwelling at Rove Wood Clan, I will make it up to you."

"How far?" she asked.

"It is a two-day journey to my clan," Govek said, adjusting her carefully in his arms. She was beginning to feel like she belonged there. "Are you ready?"

She put her arm around his neck, letting his warmth soak into her, and smiled at his relaxed features.

"Yes," she said. "I'm ready."

# TWO

*GOVEK*

H e could feel her eyes on him, and it drew him to unhelpful distraction.

The evening air was thick with incoming frost, the breeze brisk in the trees. The pattering sound of falling leaves helped to cover Govek's silent steps as he made his way toward the elk he stalked.

And further from Miranda.

She was fine. Her honeyed scent curled around his head and beckoned him, making him long to return to where she was seated on a rock.

Blast him for a fool. He never should have let her watch him hunt like this. He curled his claws, gritted his sharp teeth, and hid away the brutal, dangerous parts of himself that he would soon put on display to hunt one of these massive creatures.

Miranda wanted to *watch* because she did not fear him.

But would that change after she witnessed him take down an elk as tall as he was and twice his weight?

Govek shook his head. He needed to concentrate, or the elk would notice him and flee. Their presence was a gift from the Fades, and he did not want to waste it.

He picked up his pace, narrowing his eyes on the elk as they grazed on the sweet grass at the edge of a stream. He could only see five. They were half concealed behind barren trees and evergreen bushes, tails twitching, ears flicking, black eyes clear.

Only five. Back when Govek was a youth, there had been herds of nearly a hundred roaming the Rove Woods, basking in the flourishing of the Great Rove Tree. Healthy and abundant.

Gone now.

Govek drew nearer still, careful not to crack twigs under his feet or crunch leaves with his toes. He would be careful with this kill, too. Careful, quick, and clean.

He heard Miranda's breath on the wind. Her honeyed scent curled thicker. Her smile radiated through his mind's eye. Her imprint on him thrummed warmth into his chest.

The wind picked up suddenly and red leaves billowed around him. He used the droning noise to cover a few extra rapid steps. Almost there.

A branch snapped under his foot.

The elk jolted to attention.

"Fuck." He leaped toward the nearest—a young cow, quick as a dart. But not fast enough. Her powerful legs thrust away from his position. But Govek's aim was true, and he landed on the back of the cow, putting his entire weight into it.

But she didn't crumble.

Fuck.

He yelped as the animal began to buck and bolt.

Govek clung to her hide, sinking his claws deep into her shoulders to keep his grip. He bounced and rolled and struggled to stay on.

Laughter swept in on the wind, and warmth bloomed in his gut, even as irritation burst behind his eyes.

Miranda was laughing at him.

He gained a stroke of luck as the elk lifted her neck. He took a risk and released his hold, hands shooting toward her head.

His seat slipped. He tightened his legs around her middle but still plummeted.

The elk fell with him.

He grappled but caught her neck in his massive hands and snapped it clean on the way down.

She perished in an instant. Falling with a hard thud to the leaf covered ground. Her light brown coat was stark against the red foliage. His green flesh was just as stark as he pushed her body off his legs.

Govek placed a hand to her hide as she worked through her final spasms, hoping Miranda would not arrive to see them. It was a clean death but for the few punctures to her shoulders. He wondered if he could cover them up somehow even as he wiped his claws clean.

Too late. Miranda hurried in, brown wavy hair bouncing around her head. His gut twisted, and he turned in a last effort to block her view.

But his woman's eyes were already on the animal, wide and stunning. Red lips, pink cheeks.

"Wow, he's beautiful." Miranda said, hazelnut eyes still on the elk.

"She." Govek corrected quietly, attempting to memorize

her reverent expression and tone. He'd witnessed her delight often these last two days and would never grow tired of it.

"*She*." Miranda shot him a wry smile. "Can I touch her?"

Govek blinked, "Yes."

His woman knelt down next to the elk's head. The cloak he'd made for her pooling in the damp leaves. Her slender fingers stroked the animal's neck and stopped short of touching the blood covered punctures at the shoulder.

"She's amazing. Not as soft as I expected. Almost wiry. It's really thick and long too. Is it always this thick or is it only because winter is coming on?"

"Because of winter." Govek said, working to finish cleaning his claws with some of the damp leaves.

"It's too bad she had to die, though." Her tone was soft as she stroked the animal again. "Even if it is for us to eat."

Govek's gut twisted as he dropped the blood-soaked leaves and kicked foliage over the top to hide them. Most in Rove Wood Clan shared her sentiment. They viewed his hunting as an awful sin, especially since there were so few large game left in the Rove Woods. He heard their whispers, knew they thought he hunted to quell his violent urges. They thought him an abomination who *enjoyed* the act of killing. An ill-Faded mistake whose magic was tainted by vicious anger.

And in many ways, they were right. No matter how hard he tried, he could never fully control his temper. Eventually, his patience always broke, and he lashed out against them.

He would not let Miranda see that side of him. He could not let her witness him losing control. He would keep her away from the members of the clan. Keep her safe. She needed a *break*, and so did he.

He was exhausted from the last three nights. He'd only allowed himself to fall into a shallow sleep so he could stay vigilant, so he could protect her from harm. His woman. Miranda.

Fades, it had only been three nights since they had met, but it felt like a lifetime had passed.

He would have a lifetime with her still—away from these woods and his brethren who despised him.

In a day or two, they would go. They would leave these blessed woods and make a new life outside them.

His gut screamed a warning, pulsing dread into the back of his mind. His heels dug into the damp ground as if trying to root him to the spot.

Root him to the Great Rove Tree.

He kicked his feet and pushed the sensation away. Ignoring it.

Miranda cast him a warm smile that was in such contrast to the darkness of his thoughts that he could only blink. "Sorry I laughed when she was bucking you around. It just looked so funny. It didn't hurt you, did it?"

"I'm fine," he said, tension softening.

She shot him a grin. "I guess you would be, huh? You're plenty strong enough to handle the bucking of a female."

Amusement burst from his lips in a snort. "Blast! The things you say, woman."

"You know you love it." She grinned, standing up again. He gulped as she turned and took his hand in hers, barely sheathing his claws in time. "Though I guess my quips *still* aren't enough incentive to, I dunno, take *me* for a ride?"

Govek's blood pooled deliciously, heating in his groin and cueing him up in an instant.

"No, Miranda. There are—"

"Too many predators. I know, I know." She muttered, sliding her hands up his arms.

25

The disappointment in her tone forced him to scowl. "I touched you last night, woman. Was that not enough?"

"Of course, it wasn't. You wouldn't let me touch back." She mumbled, blooming more heat in his cock. "Plus, we were tied to a tree branch fifteen feet in the air with my back to your chest, so I couldn't even *see* you. Or move."

"You moved plenty." His voice was a rumble. Fuck, she would do him in with this talk.

She hummed under her breath and soothed her hands along the sides of his face. Going up on her toes. She smelled like bliss made real and her heat was intoxicating.

Govek resisted.

There were no predators near, but he could still smell them on the wind. He could not risk her safety. She was far too precious.

"We must move on, Miranda. We are very close to the clan now."

Even the mention of it made his gut clench. He hoisted the elk up onto his shoulders to distract from the fact that Rove Wood Clan was just through the next grove. He could nearly smell the smoke on the breeze.

Two days. Three at most. Then he and Miranda would be gone from Rove Wood. They only needed to rest and raid the storeroom for supplies.

It would be fine.

"Govek?"

Miranda's brow was furrowed, and her lips were pursed. He should tell her. Speak on his troubles, but the words locked in his throat every time.

How could he even begin to tell this woman what he truly was? Of all the vile reasons his clan despised him. Of all the horrid things he'd done in anger. Mistakes he could never make right.

He was so desperate to win her, and she would never again look upon him with gentleness after she discovered what he was. A beast that could not control his destructive magic. A dread to all in his clan. A danger to her.

"Let's move on," Govek said. "The faster we get you to my home, the faster we can be gone."

"Gone to Karthoc's forge," Miranda said, almost to herself. "How many days of food is this elk? Will it last that long?"

"It will," Govek said. "Though we will need to stop at the butchery in Rove Wood Clan for preservation magics." If he worked through the night and used enough tinctures, he could get the meat dry in time.

"We'll stop at the butchery first. It won't take me long."

Miranda kept pace beside him. Moving in tandem with his stride. She nestled close despite the dead animal he lugged on his shoulders, and he relished the clean scent of her.

"What if your cousin doesn't like me?"

"I hope he doesn't," Govek grumbled.

Miranda slapped his arm, and he could not help quirking a smile at her gall. She'd been growing brave around him. He begged the Fades to help that bravery maintain.

"So, you've got a jealous streak, then?" Miranda asked.

"All orcs are possessive of their women."

"Oh, so *that's* why you don't want to let anyone in your clan know we're here? Cause you want to keep me all to yourself?"

"Exactly." He tensed, throat tight. It wasn't a *lie,* but it wasn't the full truth, either.

Miranda shot him a wry look, seeing through him so easily it left him a little breathless. "For real though, why *don't* you want to make our presence known? Do you *really* think it's a good idea to rob them and run?"

Govek growled low. She'd brought up her reservations constantly during the last two days they had traveled. "I will not argue with you over this again, Miranda. We will stay away from the orcs of Rove Wood and that is the end of it."

His woman huffed irritably but relented. "Fine, fine. I suppose I won't complain over a few more days of solitude with you. And you have no reason to be jealous. I'm not a cheater. One sexy, randy orc is all I need."

She stroked his cheek again and his irritation dimmed, replaced by the gentle lulling thunder of her imprint in his chest.

"But if we *do* end up getting caught, don't worry. I've got years of experience wrangling toddlers under my belt. If I can handle endless rampages around the playground, I can handle a bunch of men acting like jealous children."

"We aren't going to get caught," Govek said. "And these are not men, they are orcs."

"If I can handle you, then I can handle them."

He slid his gaze to hers. "You think you have me handled, do you?"

His chest nearly burst with pleasure as a mischievous grin widened her lips. "Oh, I absolutely think I have you handled, Govek."

"I'd like you to prove your words," he said before he could consider that he might regret this taunting.

He barely had time to gulp before her warm fingers slid up his thigh and grazed firmly against his cock, still semi-hard from all the teasing. More like torture.

"Handled well enough for you?" Her fingertips grazed over the head of his cock and his mind went deliciously blank.

"*Fuck.*"

"Are you—" She broke off, eyes widening, fingers retreating. He shivered from the loss. "What . . . is that?"

Still half gone, Govek glanced ahead and his gut pinched.

They had arrived in Rove Wood Clan.

Or the outskirts of it, at least. One of the vacant tree homes nestled at the furthest edge of the clan was before them, half hidden by trees. The back door was outlined and the window next to it was dark.

It was fine. These homes on the northern side were too far away for any members of the clan to scent him. He could not even smell the fire from the hall at the center of the clan, which was where everyone should be at the moment.

At the hall, eating and enjoying the company of their brethren.

Govek clutched at the elk.

"Is that . . . that can't possibly be . . ."

He looked down at his woman, who had picked up the pace to approach the vacant dwelling.

"It *is*. Govek that house is carved into a tree. A *living* tree. How is that tree so big? There's no way. That must be like fifty trees put together, right? Where's the top of it. I can't even see it up there?"

"It is one tree," Govek said, forcing himself to relax in the face of Miranda's excitement.

"That's *amazing*! Is your house in a tree too? How did those trees even get that big? They must be thousands of years old. Wow! I can't even believe it. It looks pretty dark. Is someone living in there right now?"

"That one is vacant."

"Can we go in?"

"Not now. We must go to the butchery. My home is also in a tree. I will let you explore when we arrive."

"Man, I'm not sure what I want to do first. You or the exploring."

He huffed a laugh. Her smile was like the warmth of the summer sun, filling him up with light even as they breached the boundary of Rove Wood Clan.

She poked his side. "Tell me more about the trees. And is your clan pretty big?"

"The clan boasts around three hundred. The dwellings are indeed ancient and the trees they are carved from were created from the first five generations of the Great Rove Tree. A blessing from the Fades. It imbues all orcs born under it with magical gifts and bleeds prosperity into the whole of the Rove Woods."

"I remember that from the map you showed me last night. You said the tree roots spread magic all the way to the goblin mines we were in, and that's what I felt, right? Why I got all warm and tingly?"

"Yes," he said, still a little unsettled that she could feel it. No other humans on Faeda could. That was one of the ways the Rove Woods had stayed hidden for so long. "The clan itself is built under the canopy of the Great Rove Tree. We've just crossed under it. Can . . . you feel that?"

Being surrounded top and bottom by the Great Rove Tree was usually a might overwhelming for orcs, though Govek had long grown used to it from so many trips back and forth to hunt. The warmth blooming in his chest tingled to the tips of his toes and fingers. The sensation would fade once his body grew accustomed to the intensity of the Fade magic enveloping him.

Miranda looked up, though he knew she couldn't see the

canopy of the Great Rove Tree through the darkness. "I . . . don't feel much different."

He nodded, confusion burrowing deeper in his gut.

"We won't come across any more blighted animals while we're in the boundary of the clan, will we?" Miranda asked, obviously wary.

"Not in the clan, but there could be some roaming around close by." As a hunter, Govek had often been the one to cull the rotting, vicious animals.

"They're awful," Miranda said, forcing his brows up. "They're the reason I haven't had any good dick for two days."

"*Fades*, woman, do you think of nothing else?" His fingers twitched to pull her against him.

"Course not." Miranda said, though her eyes skittered off into the woods. "I don't *want* to think about anything else."

Govek gulped. Guilty that he'd brought this on. He knew her teasing helped distract from the horrors lurking in her mind. She'd suffered multiple nightmares the night prior. She had thrashed and screamed so often that it scared off any animals that might have made a meal of her.

They scared him too. He did not know how to aid her.

"So, the orc seer, you're sure he'll be at your cousin's place? Would kinda suck if we traveled for two weeks only to find out he's somewhere else."

"He will be there. Our overlord ordered him to serve Warlord Karthoc. Only the overlord can command the will of a seer."

"He could have left if he wanted though . . . right?" Miranda's nervous eyes went back to his and he wished that he wasn't carrying an elk so he could hold her instead.

"He would not have," Govek said, though truthfully, he didn't know. "And if he did, it does not matter. If you want to find him, then I will help you do so. We will travel any lengths to reach him."

"I do," Miranda said softly, looking away again. "I *do* want to find him. I have to."

Govek swallowed. "Have you . . . remembered any of the things you forgot from your time on Earth?"

He hated asking. He knew the memories she had were haunting and the ones she had lost were likely more horrific.

"No. I still don't know how I survived and if anyone else made it here . . ." Miranda squared her shoulders, and her pace grew fast. "But I'm going to find out. I'll find them."

They lapsed into silence, moving quickly until they finally happened upon their destination.

"That's it," Govek said, pointing to the large tree before them which housed the butchery.

How many times had he entered this place hopeful and left dejected?

No matter how important, hunting was still the savage act of slaughtering the Fades precious animals. With so many beasts blighted, there was no honor in killing those that were healthy.

And then, in spite, his clan tossed those precious animals to novice butchers who slashed up the meat, so it cooked poorly and uneven. Mocking Govek's efforts.

His hands clenched the elk. He wouldn't leave this kill behind. It was his. His and Miranda's. It would sustain them on their journey to their new life.

"The butchery is also in a tree?" Miranda's gait grew bouncy with excitement.

His lips tugged into a light grin. "Yes."

He led Miranda around to the back entrance, where he knew a window was carved. Inside, the butchery was dark and cold. He could scent none of the clansmen within. He thanked the Fades for that.

"I will be quick, Miranda."

"What? You can't leave me out here."

"There are no predators around. You will be fine."

"But I want to see inside!"

Govek sighed. "No, Miranda."

"Oh, but *please*, Govek. I swear I'll be super quiet. I just want to check it out for a minute."

He gritted his teeth.

She snaked a hand up his thigh again. "I'll make it up to you."

He shuddered hard. "Fine, but no lingering. I only need to grab the tinctures."

"Yay!"

She went up on her toes and his gut pitched with delight. Leaning in he allowed her to place her warm lips to his.

Blast, she was so soft and divine. He wanted more.

No lingering.

Breaking off the kiss, Govek pushed open the door and guided Miranda into the space he knew so well.

The room smelled clean and fresh. No hints of blood or death, as usual. The magic used to preserve the meat also suspended any unwanted aromas.

Govek went to the candle left on the wall and struck it up with his magic. The dim light illuminated the large space of which only a quarter was used. There used to be a dozen or more hunters of large game in Rove Wood Clan, but now Govek was the only one, so most of the countertops and hooks for butchering were left abandoned.

But he would be hunter for them no longer. A smug satisfaction pooled in his throat.

On the shelves on the left, he could see a few hares and turkey, which had been caught with traps, wrapped and ready for butchering. Five massive barrels of fish lined the wall beside them, sealed with magical wax to prevent spoiling for a whole season.

To the right were hooks and enchanted blankets where the larger chunks of meat could be hung and wrapped. The cloth prevented spoiling for several days and Govek decided he should wrap the elk in one.

"Wow," Miranda said, moving into the room. He watched her longer than he should have. "I've never been in a butchery before. All our animals on Earth were grown on farms and slaughtered in bulk. What's in there?"

"Fish." Govek said, moving to the counter and slinging the elk down heavily so he could tie its legs.

"That's a lot of fish. Orcs must really like fish."

"Fish are plentiful in the springs. So much so that fishing regularly is necessary, or they would be overrun." He tied the front and back legs of the elk tight and hoisted it up to one of the hooks dangling from the ceiling.

Miranda continued moving around the room as he wrapped up the elk in one of the largest preservation cloths. Her fingers lingered over the countertops, which were carved from the tree itself. "This is amazing. It's like they worked with the grains of the wood."

"They did," he said. "The magic requires a collaboration with nature. Trying to bend Faeda to our own will always ends in failure."

Miranda stroked the ring of the tree she'd been focusing on. The orc who had created this place many hundreds of years prior had followed the lines and carved it into a decorative edge around the top of the cabinetry. Govek knew how difficult that act was, as he had done it with his own home.

His chest swelled with the anticipation of showing it to her.

"What are you doing?" Miranda was close now. Her hand touched his arm.

"It must be covered or the preservation will not hold."

"You put my present wrapping to shame," Miranda complimented. She doled them out to him so readily and he lapped them up like the starving wretch he was.

She was so close, right up next to him. And his arms were no longer busy holding the elk.

"Hmm," Miranda said as she caught his lusty gaze. "What are you thinking about?"

"Ravishing you."

"Ravishing me, huh? Right now?"

Fuck, he shouldn't give in. He needed to get her back to his home.

But then her hands came up around his neck and he leaned down. Her breasts pressed into his chest. "Or maybe I should ravish you first?"

She slanted her hot, delicious mouth over his. Her plump lips teased between his tusks.

*Blast*, she felt so fucking good. Tasted exquisite. Better than the finest mead and sweeter than the honey scent she constantly drowned him in.

She forced all reason right out of his brain. His hands clamped firm on her ass and lifted her off the ground, and she laughed into his mouth. He swallowed the sound and trembled for more.

"Govek?"

He and his woman both snapped to attention at the voice.

The orc voice.

*Fuck!*

Govek quickly set Miranda down and pushed her behind him, but he was far too late.

Rogeth stood there. Chest puffed as if that might bring him half a head taller so he could stand eye to eye with Govek. His green skin was flushed dark and his brow knitted into a menacing glare that spiked dangerous anger through Govek's chest. Rogeth tucked his jaw up tight, but the muscle in his cheek twitched as if he wanted to bare his fangs.

Fuck, Govek had forgotten he still had his jaw lowered and his teeth on display. He quickly brought his lower jaw up around his top teeth to hide them. He didn't want to threaten or fight this male. Especially not in front of Miranda.

"Who is that, Govek?" Rogeth asked, stepping closer. Govek's muscles flexed. He was the lead butcher, so he had some muscle, but not nearly enough. Govek could take him out quickly.

*Calm.* Govek breathed heavily as he stared down the younger orc. *See reason.*

It was easier to grasp as Miranda touched his arm, soothed his flesh.

"Well, I guess that ruins our plans to stay hidden," Miranda whispered to him. Her expression was more than a little smug, and his stomach dropped down to his feet.

Fuck, *fuck.* What was he going to do? His fists balled, and he considered knocking Rogeth unconscious so they could escape.

But what would Miranda think of him then?

He would lose her.

"She's one of the women from Estwill? You actually made it?" Rogeth said, his eyes widening on Miranda.

"She is mine." Fuck, should he just pick her up and flee?

But to where? Now that they knew he was here with her, they would come for him.

There was nowhere safe to go.

"Rogeth, who are you talking to?"

A female voice this time.

Blast his luck.

Maythra and Savrah appeared in the doorway. Two of the human women of Rove Wood Clan.

And his precious mate nearly crumbled.

"Oh my god," Miranda breathed, stepping toward them. "You . . . you're . . ."

"What is going on here?" Maythra demanded, her sharp steel eyes skewering Govek. Her gray hair was tight in a neat bun and her attire was equally well kept. She was one of the oldest in the clan. Wise and powerful and immensely disapproving of Govek.

She'd been one of his mother's closest friends and despised him for worthy reasons.

Savrah lingered behind her, her large brown eyes unsettling Govek. She'd always been wary of him, more so than most of the women, but she also *watched* him rather than averting her gaze and scurrying away like the others.

Govek tensed as Miranda took another quick step forward. His stomach dropped and his blood went cold.

"Come here, dear," Maythra said, waving Miranda forward.

And his precious woman rushed into her arms.

Miranda collapsed against the human. Maythra's larger frame dwarfed her smaller one. The elder woman hugged her tight and Govek's claws dug deep into his palms, stinging brutally.

"Where are the other women, Govek? You were supposed to bring five from Estwill. What have you done with them?"

Maythra demanded, even as she patted and soothed Miranda's back.

Govek could not find his words. Fades be fucked. This was the worst possible scenario. His eyes fixed on Miranda's trembling form, wanting nothing more than to yank her back into his embrace and flee to the Rove Woods.

Where she would surely perish in the harsh winter elements. *Fuck.*

"You abandoned them, didn't you?" Maythra gasped, her expression pale and horror-stricken.

"We will go to Chief Ergoth *now*," Rogeth said, puffing his chest higher. "You will explain there, Govek."

"Yes, yes, that's right." Maythra gently stroked Miranda's hair. "And this woman will come with me." Maythra tightened her hold.

Miranda tried to move out of Maythra's grip. "Gosh, sorry. Uh—"

"Let her go!" Fury burst in Govek's gut. Rogeth instantly stepped between Govek and Miranda and Govek's mind blistered with rage. Anger built in his chest like a tight fist. The Fades light grew menacing in his mind's eye.

His magic was going to spiral. He couldn't control it.

"All right! That's enough. Let me go!"

Miranda pushed away from Maythra and came back to Govek's side so quickly he could hardly process it. His whole body snapped as his fury was snuffed out, the light of the Fades dimmed away.

Miranda's soft hands clasped around his, and he began to tremble. Working for calm, he tucked his claws in tighter to protect his precious woman from them.

He couldn't hurt her. He had to gain control.

It was almost startling how easily that goal was met with

Miranda at his side. The tingling force of his magic dimmed to make way for the thrum of Miranda's imprint, pulsing sweetly at the center of his chest.

"Easy there, tough guy," Miranda said softly, then she looked to the others. "I'm not from Estwill. Govek found me in the woods and saved me, brought me here."

Rogeth had his eyes slightly averted and Savrah's face was bright red.

"What did he do to your *clothes*?" Maythra asked.

Govek snapped to attention and forced Miranda's cloak shut. Fuck, he'd forgotten she was wearing scraps. Her legs were bare, and the neckline of the shirt was mercilessly low since it was cut for his large frame. He should have given her his pants before they breached the edge of Rove Wood Clan.

But then he would have been naked aside from his cloak.

"Oh shoot." Miranda laughed and his blood cooled further. "Uh, yeah. We've been through it."

"Come with me, dear," Maythra said, reaching out to Miranda again.

"Maythra, be careful," Rogeth said but hesitated to touch the older woman.

"Don't worry, my child." Maythra soothed the male before her sharp gray eyes skewered Govek. "Govek may be many things, but he wouldn't be so unwise as to attack *me*." She regarded Miranda. "But it's clear he is out of control. Please, come this way, dearest. I would hate to see you hurt."

"Govek's not going to hurt me."

"Savrah, go and fetch our chief," Maythra said, turning away from Miranda. "Tell him what is transpiring here and bring other orcs to aid us."

*Fuck,* there really was no way out of this now.

"Hold on! Just stop." Miranda's shout brought Maythra back around. "Govek's not going to hurt me or anyone. Right?"

Miranda rose her brows at him, and he barely managed a swift nod. She was back with him, tucked into his side. His rational thoughts were catching back up.

"Right," Miranda said. "This is all a misunderstanding. You just surprised us. That's all."

"I believe your head is muddled," Maythra said. "I am unsure what has transpired between you and Govek but—"

"The only thing that transpired is that he saved me. I was lost in the woods, and he helped me."

"Even so," Rogeth said, standing tall again. "He must report to Chief Ergoth. Why have you come to the butchery before making your presence known? Why are you trying to hide her?"

"He isn't . . . I mean . . ." Miranda looked up at him, chewed her lip.

Govek finally found his voice. "I took down an elk."

The three of them all looked to where it now hung in its cloth behind Govek, and he took that moment to really think through this catastrophe.

There was no way he would be able to hide Miranda now. His plan would have to change.

"You took down an elk in front of her?" Rogeth asked, clearly aghast.

"He did." Miranda's voice was bright with excitement, and it soothed him further. "It was—"

"Are you hurt anywhere?" Maythra asked, reaching her hands toward Miranda again, and to Govek's relief, Miranda did not rejoin her.

"I'm perfectly healthy," Miranda held up a hand to ward Maythra off. "Govek took very good care of me."

"Then why did he take your clothes?"

"He didn't take my clothes. They just . . . got kinda lost. There was a storm and some of them were already tattered from traveling around and—"

"You cannot take her into the hall in this state, Govek," Maythra said, waving Miranda off again. "But *you* must go. Now. Our good chief will be furious if he discovers you have crossed into the borders of our clan without making your presence known to him. Go with Rogeth to the hall and we will take Miranda."

"I'm not leaving Govek," Miranda said. Her tight grip on his arm allowed him to finally work for reason.

Maythra was right. He could *not* take her to the hall. Not with so many orc eyes to see her half naked. But taking her back to his home now would, at best, result in a brawl with Rogeth. At worst, Maythra would go to the hall for aid, tell them what had transpired here, and a group of orcs would come to drag Miranda away from him by force.

That horror would spiral his anger out of control. His fury was rising at the very thought of it. He would lose himself.

And her.

He could not allow that to happen. He could not allow his turbulent emotions to rage out of control. He had to stay calm, and the only way to do that was to keep *Miranda* calm.

Which meant he had to leave her willingly. Convince her to do the same.

"Come, you can trust us."

"No, thanks," Miranda muttered dryly.

"You should go with them," Govek said, earning surprised looks from everyone in the room.

"Are you serious?" Miranda asked, tightening her grip on his arm.

Govek hid his pleasure that she mistrusted them, but cleaved to him. "I must go to address the chief. And I will not take you there in this state."

The idea of other orcs seeing her half naked made his blood boil.

Calm. *Calm.*

"I'm not leaving you, Govek."

"There will be many orcs. Many eyes."

"I don't care."

"You're barely *dressed*, Miranda." Govek gripped her upper arm tight. "My control is in tatters as it is. I *can't* let them see you."

"Yes, dear, the hall is no place for a newcomer." Maythra stepped forward again, extended her hand out to them.

Govek took a hard breath and loosened his grip on her arm.

"Govek?" Her worried gaze pierced him and made his chest ache.

"They will not harm you, Miranda." Of that, he could be certain. "And the sooner I go to address the chief, the sooner I can return to you."

"At your house?" Miranda confirmed.

"Yes."

"You don't have to stay with him—" Maythra cut in.

Govek shot her a hard look and, thankfully, the woman went silent. "You will take her to my home. Nowhere else. You will bring clothing to her there."

Even if they took Miranda elsewhere, he would find her. If she was in danger, he would know. The imprint thrummed its assurance in his chest. Warm and strong.

"You try to give a woman of this clan orders, Govek?" Maythra asked, eyes narrowed. Govek gritted his teeth.

He may have been Chief Ergoth's son, but the power and

authority that came from that position had never been allotted to him.

But this was for Miranda's safety. He swallowed his pride and it thudded into his stomach like a burning lump of coal. "She is tired from the journey and needs rest. I ask that you take her to my home. *Please.*"

"I want to go to Govek's home," Miranda said clearly.

"Fine," Maythra agreed—far too easily for Govek's liking.

"Govek, are you *sure* it will be all right?" Miranda searched his face, clearly withholding a million questions.

He should have answered them long ago. He should have known that keeping his presence a secret would not be possible. Even for a short time.

He'd been a desperate fool, and now he would pay the price for it.

"They will not harm you, Miranda. You are precious." Her shoulders sagged, but she nodded. He lowered his voice further, dipping in to speak into her ear. "If you call me by name, I will hear it and come to you."

She shivered a little. "You'll hear me even if I'm far away? Is that magic?"

"The imprint," he told her and she moved back to look at him, obviously wanting to ask what exactly the imprint was. But now was not the time. "I will be only a few moments. Eat any food you wish and draw up a bath."

"Like hell am I having a bath without you," she mumbled and delight soaked him. She tugged at his cloak until he leaned down to her level. "Be quick. No detours."

"No detours," he breathed as she plucked a kiss to his chin. Then he looked to the others. "Do not let her dally in the cold."

"Of course not," Maythra said, waving Miranda over. Miranda reluctantly joined her.

Govek nearly lost his resolve as Miranda disappeared out the door and into the night with little more than a quick wave.

Then he turned his full attention to Rogeth, searing the male through with the intensity of his glower. Rogeth flinched, stepping away, and Govek snarled.

"You got your fucking way, now take me to my father."

# CHAPTER
# THREE

*GOVEK*

"I cannot believe you stole that woman."

Rogeth's clipped tone punctured Govek's thoughts and had him curling his claws to hide them, pulling his lower jaw higher to conceal his teeth. The ache of this effort throbbed in his jaw like an old, bitter enemy returned to mock him.

Every step he took away from Miranda made Govek want to turn back. Like a tether hooked deep in his chest, pulling him toward her, growing tauter with every step.

"Chief Ergoth is going to be furious. What about the other women? Did you abandon them somewhere? Or did you never go to fetch them at all?"

Govek maintained his silence. There was no point in arguing. No one would believe his words. It wasn't worth the energy. He wanted to concentrate on addressing his father and then get back to Miranda as quickly as possible.

"You know how precious those women are to us. With only Oakwall for conquests, how could you not . . ."

Govek turned his attention away from the male's irritating blather and looked off into the woods. He and Miranda being found changed nothing, really. Gathering supplies might be more of a challenge with the clan breathing down his neck, but he and Miranda would still leave in two days' time. They would still go to Karthoc. He would explain this to his father now and all here would be glad to see him gone.

A breeze picked up in the autumn trees, raining leaves down onto the path before them. The trees swayed and moaned, and for one shuddering moment, Govek was struck with the gut driven urge to remain in Rove Wood. To return to the goblin mines with Miranda and take their chances weathering the winter, just so he would not have to leave this place.

He may not have been well blessed by the Fades, but he was still one of their creations. And their Great Tree beckoned him just as it did all orcs.

Govek took another deep breath and froze.

"Is Warlord Karthoc here?"

Rogeth faltered in his step.

Govek released his jaw to scent the air. The pungent odor of orc warriors wafted in on the breeze, growing thicker with every gust. Blood and sweat and thick oiled leather.

Govek turned on his heel and walked toward it.

"Govek, stop! I order you to—"

"You *what?*" Govek shot the male a withering look. Although he was universally disliked among the clan, although their opinions of him were wretched and he avoided them like the blight, none of them had ever dared to *order* him to do something.

He was the chief's son after all. Born from the blood of Rove Wood's leader, Ergoth and his beloved mate, Corine.

Corine, who was blessed to carry and raise a prodigy like Tavggol for six blissful years.

Then cursed with the horror of giving birth to Govek. And that bliss ended.

Because of him.

His body shuddered and his fists clenched until his claws cut deep and his guts churned up as he pushed that pressing truth to the back of his mind.

Being born was his first crime, and there was nothing he could do to undo it.

He was an outcast before *anything* else. Had always been an outcast and would always be. At least in *this* clan.

Govek turned away from Rogeth's stunned expression and began to march toward the warrior camp he'd scented.

"I-It is your responsibility to report to the chief immediately upon your arrival to Rove Wood," Rogeth argued, following behind, though he made no move to stop Govek by force.

"I am to report to the highest authority in the clan. That is my cousin. Or are you trying to argue that Chief Ergoth is *above* our warlord?"

Rogeth scowled, unable to argue with that logic. "I'll be going to the hall. Expect our chief to join you."

Govek snorted. He expected nothing less.

He continued on the trail, following the scent of the orcs to the western most point of Rove Wood Clan. The smoke from their fires grew thick and he could hear their voices on the wind long before he saw the first beige leather tops of their tents.

Karthoc's warriors were well accustomed to making camp. They traveled often to aid anywhere orcs were being threatened or attacked by the Waking Order. Many clans outside Rove

Wood had been razed, and many lives had been lost but the horrors would have been far worse without Karthoc's strong leadership and cunning battle strategies.

Govek had always been in awe of his cousin's vigor. He hoped he would not prove to be a burden to the warlord after he joined Baelrok Forge.

As he entered the camp, many of the warriors—burly males, thick with muscle and covered in scars—were busy pitching tents and building fires. Their sharp rows of teeth were on full display and Govek was tempted to uncover his own. Warriors did not abide by the tradition of hiding one's more dangerous attributes.

But Govek was not a warrior, so he kept his jaw tucked up.

Most of them looked up as he passed. A few offered him a nod in greeting, but none approached, save one.

Brovdir.

Govek's younger cousin looked well but for the many pale-green scars along his hide. The male was nearly as tall as Govek, but leaner and swifter. He was one of Karthoc's fiercest but bore the title with little arrogance.

Of course, it was hard to boast about one's accomplishments when you could barely speak. Brovdir had suffered a horrible wound across his neck in his youth that had cut through his ability to talk. His raspy voice grew tired after a few words.

So, when the male greeted him with no more than a strong pat to the back and a nod, Govek did not urge him for chatter. "Brovdir, I am glad to see you looking well. Can you take me to the warlord?"

Brovdir nodded and guided Govek through the camp. He recognized a few of the orcs from his travel to Clairton, but was glad they all turned back to their duties without wanting to speak.

"How long have you been here?"

"This afternoon," Brovdir replied raggedly.

So soon. What were the odds? Govek wondered if the Fades were smiling on him after all. Traveling with a band of fifty orc warriors would be far safer for Miranda.

Brovdir whistled shrill just as Govek saw Karthoc up ahead. His cousin was chatting with another warrior and looked up. His deep scowl and square features were striking, even in the growing twilight.

Then his dark eyes widened as he saw Govek, and he let out a laugh that struck Govek a little dumb. Karthoc stormed over as Brovdir, patted his shoulder, nodded, and returned to the camp. To an area where a few burly orcs were placing logs into a large circle.

"Govek! Fades be all." Karthoc clapped Govek hard across the back. "Chief Ergoth told me you'd gone to get women from Estwill, of all vile places. What the fuck were you even *thinking*? How did you make it out of there unscathed?"

"I never went. I knew it was folly to even try."

"Of course, you did. No kin of mine would be stupid enough to try to break through Estwill without a full legion," Karthoc said with a shake of Govek's shoulder. His grin was wide enough to split his face clean in half.

Miranda's opinion of leaving one's teeth uncovered rang in his mind.

*"Honestly, you look way better with your jaw in the right spot."*

His gut warmed, and he lowered his jaw back into the right place.

"Come, let's share a meal. We caught so many fish in your springs our blood will smell of it before our time in these woods is done."

Karthoc kept a firm grip on Govek's shoulder as he guided him toward the large bonfire at the center of the camp.

"What are they doing?" Govek asked, watching as Brovdir carried a massive fallen log out of the woods. The ground shook with the weight as he dropped it into the circle. Others came to help shear off the remaining limbs with their claws and smooth it out, so no sharp edges were visible.

"Building a challenge arena." Karthoc said casually, and Govek was struck once again by the differences between Rove Wood and all other orc clans.

"Have you ever been challenged?" Karthoc asked, dark green brows raised, and Govek shook his head. "What the fuck does Ergoth even do when there is strife among his males?"

"Judgments," Govek said, unable to keep the bitterness from his tone.

"Judgments," Karthoc muttered. "That's right. You haven't been in one recently, have you?"

Govek's brow furrowed, wondering just what his cousin was getting at. "Not recently."

After Tavggol's death, he had kept himself away from the clan, stayed in the woods or in his home on the outskirts. One couldn't stand accused in a judgment if they had no contact with other orcs.

Though he'd half expected Yerina or one of her friends to bring one about eventually. Take the rumors she'd spread about him after he'd refused to see her again to his father to get revenge.

But she hadn't. *Yet.*

"I thought perhaps Ergoth sending you to Estwill was some sort of extreme punishment."

"No." Some punishments he'd endured over his life had been extreme, but not *that* extreme. "Being sent to Estwill to retrieve the women was meant to be an honor."

Karthoc scoffed and spat upon the ground. "An *honor*? It is an *honor* to be slaughtered?"

"I do not believe Chief Ergoth understood how bad off Estwill truly was—is," Govek replied.

"How could he not know? Is he so blind to how Faeda has fallen?"

"We have no contact with any outside the Rove Woods besides the warriors you send to fetch tinctures."

"Not even to get women? I've seen a few here already." Karthoc lowered his voice, "You can't tell me they *all* came from that single village here in the Rove Woods."

"They are all from Oakwall Village, yes." Oakwall had been trade partners with Rove Wood Clan for centuries and was cut off from all outside humans.

"Lower your voice," Karthoc muttered, looking around at his warriors. "I don't want my warriors knowing about it or they'll fight to death over who gets to visit."

Govek nodded. He couldn't imagine Chief Ergoth would be keen on the warriors visiting Oakwall either. The peaceful trade between Oakwall and Rove Wood Clan was the only reason their communities could survive without ever leaving these woods.

The humans of Oakwall flinched when Rove orcs bellowed and bared their fangs, he couldn't imagine how they might react to one of Karthoc's battle scarred warriors.

As if to prove Govek's thoughts correct, a thunderous roar

sounded. Govek jerked, glancing toward the arena, which was still being created, and found that two males were engaged in bloody carnage. One slugged the other in the nose and blood sprayed in an arc.

Karthoc barely glanced at the battle. "So, you really think Ergoth didn't *know* what he was doing when he ordered you to your death?"

Govek's gut twisted, and his hands balled, and he took a few cleansing breaths of the crisp autumn evening. Now that time and distance had softened the order, Govek could see reason. Think logically. Put himself in his father's place. "I know he didn't."

Karthoc narrowed his eyes. "So, you're saying you didn't even *try* to tell him that Estwill is their main stronghold this side of the Wyin Mountains?"

"I did." Govek recalled the last meeting he had with his father. In the hall. In front of his clan. Where Govek had tried to impart how going to Estwill would lead to his death more swiftly than any other act.

But his father had not listened. Not when he had missives from Govek's mother, who supposedly lived in Estwill, claiming that she had five young, fertile women wanting to join Rove Wood Clan and play conquest to orcs.

*"I know your mother's hand better than any other. Corine was my mate for seven years until you were born."*

"I believe the hope that Corine might return to be his mate blinded him," Govek managed to say even as the memory of the clan's haunting silence descended on him. Of their piercing eyes as they watched him walk his death march.

Perhaps his father was too consumed by grief to think, but the rest of the orcs should have known. And not *one* of them rose to stand on his behalf.

Govek no longer wanted *anything* to do with them. "I was not going to Estwill. I was going to travel to *you*. To finally take you up on your offer to join your clan at Baelrok."

Karthoc's brow furrowed deep. "Is that . . . so?"

"Yes. With Tavggol gone, there is nothing holding me here."

"Hmm." Karthoc muttered looking back to the still fighting orcs. Each blow cracked like thunder. "Tell me, Govek, are you still able to conjure magic?"

Govek's stomach twisted. Was his cousin changing his mind about inviting him? Had Karthoc decided that he and his cursed magic were too dangerous to live among his warriors after all?

But he could not lie. "I . . . can."

Karthoc nodded and his face relaxed, and Govek wanted to sigh with relief. "I am making an announcement at your hall tomorrow after the morning meal. You will be there."

"Yes, Warlord—"

"Govek! My son."

Govek turned, chest tight, and saw his father moving toward him through the camp with opulent purple robes billowing around him. His slender arms were outstretched, and his white hair was tight in neat braids.

"My son!"

Ergoth threw his arms around Govek and he jolted, a sweltering zing of shock shot down his limbs and froze him to the spot.

His mind reeled at the oddity of being touched by his father. He could not recall a time Chief Ergoth had *ever* done so for any reason.

"My son, you have returned alive and successful!"

"Chief," Govek managed, though the greeting came out strangled. His tongue tasted sour.

"Let me look at you." Ergoth released him and Govek took a breath. "Let me see that you are well. Are you harmed? Since this afternoon when Karthoc told me of how atrocious Estwill was, I've been in utter ruin thinking that I had sent you to your death. By Fades, Govek, tell me, how do you fair? Do you have any injuries?"

"He's fine as you can see," Karthoc said, standing back to watch the uncomfortable exchange.

Ergoth continued his examination, embracing Govek quickly again and babbling about how well he looked. Govek could not for the life of him recall his father ever greeting him with such exuberance before, especially not in such a public place. All of Karthoc's warriors were watching.

It made Govek's skin break out into prickling discomfort. His hands balled into fists and his jaw clenched tight, covering his teeth.

He'd longed for his father's approval all his life. He should be grateful for it now. But instead, he wanted the male to get off him.

"You are certain you are well? You were not attacked on the way to Estwill?"

Govek resisted the urge to step back, to put distance between him and his father. "I was attacked by a boar. One that was blighted. It had spikes tied to its tusks that were laced with goblin poison."

"Goblin poison?" Karthoc exclaimed. "Fuck the Fades, how did you survive *that*? And who did it?"

"It must have been humans," Ergoth said, finally stepping away. Govek breathed a quiet sigh of relief. "Oh, the horror. I cannot believe I nearly sent you to your death."

"Calm down, Ergoth," Karthoc snapped. "Goblins went underground more than two decades ago and took all their magic with them. Govek, do you know how humans could have gotten it?"

"No."

"Those Waking Order wretches must have stolen it," Ergoth said. "And does it matter? My son was nearly *killed*."

"So worried now when it was *you*, uncle, who sent him to his doom."

"Yes, and I will regret that decision every day for the remainder of my life." Govek's father said with such earnestness that Govek blinked.

"I'm sure." Karthoc snorted.

His father skewered Karthoc with a glower. "Govek, you have done well. Rogeth says that you managed to bring a woman here despite not making it to Estwill."

"A woman?" Karthoc said with far too much interest and Govek's claws instantly burst from his hands. "You didn't mention a woman."

"She is mine," Govek rumbled.

"What do you mean she is yours?" Chief Ergoth said slowly. "You rescued her, did you not? Brought her here to live? You cannot claim possession over her, Govek. That isn't our way."

Govek gritted his teeth. Of course, he would not force Miranda to do anything, but blast. His infernal imprint was screaming at him to drag his woman to his home and bar all the doors.

"Rogeth says she is with Maythra now. I will tell her to bring this newcomer to the hall. She can mingle with her new clan while you rest at home."

Have Miranda mingle with other orcs at the hall while he was forced to remain in isolation on the outskirts? Fuck no.

"Miranda stays with me," Govek snarled.

His father's brow furrowed. "Govek, control yourself. She should be allowed to come to the hall if she wants to."

"Fuck all, why are we even bothering with this?" Karthoc said, waving a hand. "Govek is the one who brought her here, so clearly she is his conquest."

Ergoth narrowed his eyes. "That isn't how we do things in Rove Wood, my young nephew. Your warriors may cart women around like property, but the orcs of Rove do not. Every woman here in our clan, in Oakwall, or outside it, is her own being deserving of respect."

"I never said they don't get *respect*. And of course, they are not our property. But Govek clearly feels for her and what point is there going to your hall unless she is there to meet other orcs? Orcs shouldn't be trying to steal women away from each other."

"The fact that you think they *can* be stolen insinuates that you regard them as property and not beings with their own sovereignty." Chief Ergoth lifted his head high.

"You twist my words, Ergoth. Orcs no longer fight for their women as we did in the past. The woman has control over who she plays conquest to. She can choose to belong to any she sees fit."

"Exactly," Chief Ergoth said with a quick nod. "So, Govek, Miranda will come to the hall tonight, meet others and have a meal. So that if or when she decides to play conquest, it can be an informed choice rather than one made only out of desperation. Rogeth told me she was lost in the woods. Poor thing. She must have been terrified."

Govek gritted his teeth, his claws sunk into his palms. Of

*course,* Miranda hadn't chosen to be with him out of desperation. Of course, she hadn't given herself to him only because he was her only option.

Right?

His guts were in tatters.

And then Karthoc leaned in a little toward Govek, sucked a breath in, before bellowing out a laugh. "Not so terrified she wouldn't take Govek here into her bed."

Ergoth's scowled deepened, accentuating the sharp lines on his forehead and darkening his eyes. "Nephew, that is unseemly. How dare you insinuate something so crude."

"You can smell her on him, can't you? She's clearly been all over him. Multiple times judging by the strength," Karthoc said and Govek could not decide if he was affronted on Miranda's behalf or relieved this truth was so apparent. "Is she pregnant?"

"No," Govek said in an instant before his father could think any worse of him. "She's been through a trial. I brought her here expecting nothing from her in return."

"But you *still* took advantage of her vulnerability?" Chief Ergoth asked coldly.

"No vulnerability smells like *that,* Ergoth," Karthoc snapped. "She was wanting, clearly. Or have you never had a hot, willing woman before? Perhaps you don't know the scent of it?"

Ergoth's face grew dark and his gold eyes bulged, and Govek clenched his fists so hard that he could feel the warm, wet blood trickle between his fingers.

"I know better than any, my young nephew. Far better than you. Corine *worshipped*—" Ergoth sucked in a breath, shook his head as if trying to dispel his fury. "This is pointless. I relent. But Govek, I trust you wouldn't hold this woman against her will. If she would like to come to the hall for a meal, you will allow her."

"Yes," Govek responded. He already knew that trying to take command would ruin things where women were concerned. He would give Miranda any boon she wished if it meant she stayed at his side.

Hopefully, for tonight, his home and everything in it would be enough.

"Now, if you will excuse me, I am weary from all the interrogations we have suffered this day." Ergoth looked pointedly at Karthoc.

"I only wanted to know why you would send Govek to his doom, *uncle*. He is your only living son, after all. I would have thought you would treat him better."

"It is not I who dismisses his worth. After all, how many of your messages mention him even in passing?"

Karthoc scowled.

"Exactly. It is clear that your only care is for the healing tinctures my clan provides you. And that is fine, since they are winning you the war and saving your warriors' lives. My conjurers gladly turn their hands black to keep your legions safe. But do not, in your arrogance, assume that my clan's only worth is to keep up with your ruthless demands. We few orcs born under this Rove Tree are the only ones the Fades blessed with magic, and you best not forget that fact."

With that, Ergoth turned on his heel and disappeared back into the woods, back to the hall, and Govek felt all the tension in him evaporate as exhaustion took its place.

"It is not my arrogance that is the problem," Karthoc said, his dark eyes following Ergoth. "The whole lot think themselves superior only because they conjure magic. But tell me this, who would have held back the forces at the base of

Mount Rayvol? Who would have ended the siege at the Blur-ang River? Who would have prevented the *burning* of the very Rove Woods these orcs hold dear if not my warriors?"

Govek understood his elder cousin's words, but his eyes were trained to Karthoc's own brother, who was still working on smoothing the logs. To the numerous scars and marks covering Brovdir's hulking frame. To the deep slashed scar along his neck that carried the proof that without Rove Woods healing tinctures, most of their warriors would have perished long ago.

"Magic is only as powerful and *useful* as the beings who wield it," Karthoc said. "How did you survive goblin poison? Was it your magic?"

"No." The question betrayed how little Karthoc truly knew about conjuring. "My conquest saved me with water from the Spring of the Fades."

"This woman you found, from where does she herald?"

"She was lost in the woods." Govek was uncertain how much of Miranda's past to give.

"Did she give you a name?"

"Miranda."

"Miranda of…?"

Earth. "I'm not sure."

"How did she know about the spring's effects?"

"I told her. I managed that much before I collapsed, and we were close enough for her to accomplish it."

"Fucking odd," Karthoc said, looking back to his warriors. Govek was well aware that most of them had tried and failed to find conquests. "Most humans would rather skewer you through and steal your wares. Take your hospitality and leave you nothing but dark yearnings in return."

Govek narrowed his eyes, trying to work through his cousin's double meaning.

"Enough of this. We will be taking some time here to regroup. The Waking Order is planning something. I suspect a siege on Baelrok will be their next move, but it would be foolhardy of them to attempt it so close to winter." Karthoc crossed his bulky arms and looked off toward a large black tent near the edge of the clearing. "My seer says time with the Spring of the Fades under your Great Rove Tree might reveal their intent. I don't have much hope. These day's he can barely divine his own ass in the privy."

Govek's jaw slacked with shock. "Seer Evythiken is with you?"

"Yes, though it only serves to slow us down. Blind fool can barely handle the travel on a good day. He's constantly plagued with visions from the Fades and can barely concentrate on anything else. Sometimes he can hardly walk. I would order him to be carried if I had the power."

Govek gritted his teeth. The seer wasn't well? What did that mean for Miranda and her longing to have Evythiken divine for her?

"Why? You want to ask him something?"

Govek was unwilling to mention Miranda's plans. "I only wondered if he might know a place free from the war."

Karthoc looked away, toward the camp, toward his brother. His brows furrowed and his concern was plain to see. "Evythiken does know a place and the blind fool thinks that we *all* should . . ."

Govek startled. He hadn't expected that response. "Should what?"

Karthoc waved him off. "The seer's mind is muddled and raw. He is in constant agony from the onslaught the Fades force

60

upon him. He can hardly eat and move, let alone divine the will of our creators. It was no wonder the overlord dismissed him from his fold."

Govek's eyes widened. He hadn't known that Evythiken had been dismissed from the overlord's council. He'd assumed the powerful seer had been reassigned to help Karthoc.

"Most of his babbles are fucking rave dung," Karthoc muttered before changing the topic. "This wears on me. Tell me, instead, of your woman, Govek?"

Govek bristled, jaw unhinging, claws slicking out. Fuck his instincts and his inability to control them.

Karthoc, in all his too observant ways, rose his brows in shock. "For fuck's sake, how did you get imprinted on her so wretched fast?"

"How can you tell?" Govek asked. To his knowledge, there were no outward signs of imprinting.

"I have my ways," Karthoc said, obtusely. "But you've only been gone a handful of nights. You barely smell of her. I've never seen an imprint hit so quick."

Govek had no response for that. Imprints typically occurred over the course of many seasons, even years. It had taken two seasons for Yerina's to firm within him, and even then, it had not been nearly as deep as Miranda's was now.

Karthoc continued. "Brovdir has had many women flee him. All within my forge have. I was just pondering that she may have been a lost conquest."

"She isn't," Govek snarled. "She is mine and smells of no other male."

"For fuck's sake. That isn't what I meant," Karthoc said, his amusement growing even higher. Govek couldn't decide if he wanted to rage at the male or let his tension ebb. "I only thought to warn any fools thinking to challenge you for her.

I've seen your battle rage, Govek, how your magic-laced blows could render even the mightiest to pieces, and I have no desire to lose good warriors to your prowess."

Govek's blood simmered under the weight of Karthoc's words. Govek had lived with the dreaded knowledge of his brutality for far longer than Clairton, but the events there had pushed the truth into the light. He could no longer hide away in Rove Wood and pretend he wasn't the dangerous wretch his brethren knew him to be.

It was only a matter of fucking time before Miranda was informed of it. Dread stirred so thick he couldn't swallow.

"Let's get you to her, then." Karthoc made his way out of the camp. "I'm eager to see the woman who can put up with your wretched ass."

The insult was eased with a smirk that did nothing to quell Govek's dread. He wanted to tell Karthoc to fuck off. To get back to his own business. To stay far away from his mate until Govek could fully win her.

*"When she decides to play conquest, it can be an informed choice rather than one made only out of desperation."*

His stomach rolled.

They met no others on the paths as they walked. All of the Rove Wood orcs were likely making merry in the hall, and would continue to until late in the night, enjoying their meat and mead as though Karthoc and his warriors were not even here.

The silence was easy between him and his cousin, but Govek was glad this night was done so he could spend the rest of it with Miranda in his secluded home on the outskirts. Alone.

He *would* find boons to prove to her he was the right choice.

And then her honeyed scent wafted toward him.

From the opposite direction of his home.

"Fuck," Govek said, turning the exact direction he didn't wish to go. Further into the clan.

"What?" Karthoc said, but Govek ignored him and went to find his wayward mate.

# FOUR

*MIRANDA*

"So, you *are* taking me to Govek's home, right?" Miranda asked. Her initial joy at seeing humans for the first time had dimmed substantially, and the fact that these were complete strangers was daunting.

Strangers who had a pretty negative opinion of Govek.

"We will only stop at Viravia's home for a moment to fetch clothes. Govek's dwelling is much further out, and her house is on the way. Unless you would like to see the healer," Maythra said, her sharp eyes glinting in the torchlight. She was bigger boned than Miranda, probably in her sixties.

"I don't need a healer. And I want to go to Govek's home." Govek had kept them moving at a brisk clip, but she felt perfectly healthy. Like living on Faeda was rejuvenating, camping out on frosty nights, eating nothing but roasted fish and the occasional late autumn berry, getting lost in the beauty of this new world.

It was so easy to forget everything when she was around Govek. The destruction of Earth. All the death.

Miranda gulped and pushed the memories deep. Away. "I can't believe you built your houses *into* the trees. It's really amazing. I've never seen anything like it."

Savrah, a young woman close to Miranda's age of twenty-four with light brown hair and even lighter eyes, finally found her voice. "It is, isn't it? I've lived here for a whole season now and I still marvel at it."

"They are a marvel," Maythra said, sweeping her hand toward one of the nearer dwellings. Firelight flickered through the carved-out windows and Miranda could see a table and chairs within, but no occupants. "There are many homes without owners, Miranda. I would be glad to find you one to stay in while you are here."

"Govek's home will be fine. Thank you."

"You're safe now," Maythra insisted. "He can't hurt you anymore. We can protect you."

"I don't need protecting from Govek and he didn't hurt me." Miranda tried to keep the snap from her tone but wasn't very successful.

"Then what happened to your clothing?" Maythra asked with narrowed eyes.

Miranda hesitated, unsure how to answer. Her first set of clothes had been irradiated and left behind on Earth, more was abandoned next to the spring since it was too worn out and dirty to use, Govek had ripped up others in haste she couldn't blame him for, and the rest . . . got sucked up by a tornado.

"Where are you from?" Savrah asked. "Govek found you? Where?"

"In the woods. I'm really not sure where. I was . . . I guess you could say I was lost? There were dogs . . ."

Her throat closed up despite herself. It was so hard to talk about Earth, but these were humans. *Humans!* She wanted to talk to them. For a moment she thought she might never see another human again.

She'd known Govek's plan to stay away from his clan probably would fall through. She'd prepared herself to talk about this. And yet, now the time had come, and *nothing* would come out.

"What village are you from?" Savrah asked.

"I . . ." Miranda swallowed.

Maythra's hot gaze struck Miranda again. "You are safe now, dear. You are past the pain."

Miranda's stomach twisted. "I wish that were true."

"It is true. We can offer you support. We *all* have painful pasts. The Waking Order and their war has touched us even here," Maythra said, her pace slowing slightly as she examined Miranda. "You wouldn't have to do with the war would you, dear? Could that be why you are fleeing your home?"

Miranda gulped, voice thick. "I am fleeing war."

She could feel Earth's destruction in her veins. See it every time she closed her eyes. Smell the char, feel the blistering heat, hear the dogs howling.

Her gut rolled.

The bank she'd been trapped inside when the bombs hit was three miles away from the Riverside Daycare but still, she should have gone back to check. To help. To look for them.

Her babies.

The little toddlers she'd cared for almost every day. With their endless chatter and constant energy. She could feel their warm bodies in her arms. Smell their sweetness. Her throat closed.

She'd abandoned them. She'd left them to die. She should have died with them.

*Breathe.*

She did, sucking in cold air through her clenched teeth.

They might have made it. Her babies and their parents could have been the ones that lit the road signs to the ocean. They could have fallen off the cliff into Faeda just like her.

Her memories were hazy and distorted. Hope burned in her chest like a blazing fire, consuming all logic.

And she let it.

"Miranda, what is wrong?"

Miranda jolted back into the woods, surrounded by massive trees with houses built into them and lanterns on top of birch trunks and rough dirt paths lined by dense forest so thick and dark and growing more ominous as the light of day faded to night.

The two strange women regarded her with skeptical brows and pursed lips. Both in cloaks like the one Govek had given her and cotton dresses with long sleeves and high collars. They looked warm. Miranda shivered. There was chill deep in her bones but not from the incoming winter.

Maythra stepped forward and tugged Miranda's cloak closed. "Come then. I can see you've been through a trial."

Miranda nodded, following mutely. Her chest was too tight to form words.

They led her toward a truly massive tree. So big that Miranda could hardly fathom it was real. Its trunk was as thick as a convenience store, and it stretched up so high that Miranda couldn't see the top before it disappeared into the darkness.

The overwhelming scent of sage and lavender grew thick as they drew near the doorway. Three steps led to a little porch and bright light flooded out the windows flanking it.

Maythra knocked solidly.

"Why are you knocking?" Miranda asked. "Isn't this Go—"

The door swung open flooding the stoop with laughter and light.

The woman who answered the door was likely in her late twenties with blonde hair and sharp features. Her smile was easy when she looked at Maythra but froze solid when her eyes found Miranda.

Miranda froze too.

This clearly wasn't Govek's house.

"Hello, Beleda. Is Viravia well enough for a new visitor?" Maythra asked, trying to look passed the blonde woman.

"You were supposed to take me to—"

"*New* visitor?" The voice within was so sweet and high Miranda wondered how it could be real.

The woman who came into view behind the blonde was *stunning*. She had long dark hair, bright blue eyes, and pale skin that accentuated plump red lips.

Her smile was bright when she saw Savrah but it was struck from her face when she made eye contact with Miranda. "Who is—"

"Govek has returned," Maythra said steadily. "With a woman, but none from Estwill."

Their eyes engulfed their faces. Miranda felt like a zoo animal.

"C-come in, come in. By Fades," the beautiful woman said, and Miranda was jostled inside before she could fight it. The warmth of the house pulled her in almost as hard as the woman behind her pushed.

Maybe she could stay for a couple minutes.

The woman called her attention back with a smile, but Miranda couldn't pull her gaze from the woman's lower body.

She was heavily pregnant. Judging by things she was likely due any day.

Was . . . it an orc baby?

It had to be, right? Govek had said no human men lived in the clan. Only women. Miranda's thoughts ping-ponged around in her brain, emotions like yearning and excitement competing for space. Her hands clenched as she resisted the urge to pepper the woman with questions. How many children were in the Rove Wood Clan? Was pregnancy different with an orc baby? Would any of the parents need a babysitter?

Did she deserve to watch children after she couldn't even save her babies on Earth? Bile burned the back of her throat and her enthusiasm waned.

"Welcome, please have a seat over here. I'm Viravia." The gorgeous woman gestured toward a table and Miranda pried her gaze away only to freeze all over again.

The butchery was one thing, but this home was something else entirely. It was hard to put a time period on the dwelling. Some things looked modern, like the cushioned chairs and couch flanking the fireplace and the ornate rugs on the floor. But others looked far less so. Namely the lack of appliances visible in the kitchen space.

If you could call it a kitchen. There were two cabinets carved out of the tree and a single countertop. A cast iron oven, so small that the kettle sitting on top almost dwarfed it, sat in a nook near the back. The large window to the left had a bowl cut out of a pedestal beneath it that Miranda assumed was a sink, but she couldn't see a tap.

Govek had told her they had magic that worked the same way as indoor plumbing but now, seeing this, she wasn't sure she believed him. Or maybe Viravia's home just didn't have the magic that Govek's did?

Her gaze found the stairwell next. It wrapped around the outermost part of the trunk and worked with the natural rings of the tree. There was another large window halfway to the second floor and a branch had grown up from the railing, arching toward the sunlight, tiny orange leaves covered its branches.

Miranda was still pondering the oddity of having to rake leaves *inside* your house when a throat cleared, and her attention was drawn back to the four women.

Viravia regarded her with a stunning smile that drew Miranda in despite her reservations.

"What is your name?" Viravia asked, gesturing toward the table again. The base of the table was attached the floor—or rather the *tree*—with six chairs around it.

"Her name is Miranda," Maythra answered curtly, not even bothering to glance Miranda's way before sitting down at the table.

"I think she can answer for herself, Maythra," Viravia said, but the older woman ignored her.

"It is Miranda. It's good to meet you." Miranda tried to force a smile. "I was told you had clothing I could borrow?"

"Oh, of co—" Viravia's eyes went wide as she glanced down Miranda's body. "What— uh . . . where are your . . .?"

"Govek—"

"It's just been a crazy couple of days. Luckily, Govek was kind enough to loan me what he had."

"Where did he find you?" The blonde woman, Beleda, asked, eyes fixed to Miranda's body.

"I was lost in the woods."

"How did you—"

"Why don't we let her settle in first, Beleda? Come sit here, Miranda, and I'll get you some of my pre-baby clothing."

Miranda couldn't help herself as she followed Viravia toward one of the chairs at the kitchen table. "How far along are you?" The final two women followed suit.

"Only one more moon now," the woman said, rubbing her belly tenderly. The gentle expression on Viravia's face had Miranda's tension softening.

One moon. From what Govek had told her, that meant Viravia only had thirty more days or so. Miranda wondered how long orc gestation was. If the pregnancies had the same side effects as a human one.

What did a tiny orc baby look like? Green with little black tipped nails and pointed ears?

Adorable.

Viravia broke Miranda's musing, "Wait here, and I'll fetch the clothes from my room. Beleda, could you make more tea?"

"O-Of course," the blonde said before rushing into the tiny kitchen.

"I'll go get them, Viravia. You should be taking precautions with Tavggol's son," Maythra said, moving to intercept Viravia's ascent up the steps.

Viravia's expression flattened. "I can handle my own staircase, Maythra."

"It is the heir to the clan you carry," Maythra said, looking pointedly at Miranda. Miranda tensed. "His protection and wellbeing are the concern of all in this clan."

Viravia shot her a glare and pointedly went to the stairs, going up with a slight waddle and no further issue. She disappeared into the upper floor.

"That woman," Maythra muttered darkly, returning to her seat.

Heir to the clan, huh? Miranda wondered who the father was. If the orc was going to show up here soon.

"Do you like sage, Miranda?" Savrah asked, a slight warble to her voice. "Viravia has wonderful sage tea."

"Uh, yeah. Sure." Sage *tea*?

"She also makes wonderful soaps too," Savrah said.

Oh wow. That didn't make the tea sound better.

"She used to do more crafts before she got pregnant and before . . . well . . ." Savrah's face paled, and she went quiet.

"Yes, it's all been a trial since the tragedy. Things are still so uncertain," Maythra said.

"Uncertain?" Miranda asked, unable to help herself.

"Miranda," Beleda interjected then, standing pensively with the empty kettle still in her hand. "Are you Govek's conquest?"

All eyes were on her in an instant and Miranda thought their weight might sink her down into the floor. Bury her alive.

"I mean . . . I don't plan to have his child anytime soon if that is what you are asking," Miranda said. Of course, she wasn't. They'd *just* met.

And . . . did she even deserve to have a baby after abandoning her babies on Earth?

*Stop.*

She took a deep breath, pushing the horrors away.

"Well, that is a relief," Maythra said.

Beleda went back to fixing up the tea and Savrah sagged in her seat. Miranda glanced between them. "Why is that a relief, Maythra?"

She'd thought the woman might dodge the question but instead she narrowed her sharp gray eyes and Miranda felt stuck right through. "You must have not been with him long if you have to ask."

"Maybe I haven't known him as long as *you*, but I've been alone with him for days and he's done nothing to make me think he wouldn't be a good father."

Maythra's mouth curled almost in disgust and Miranda's spine straightened. "If that is the case, then he must have you perfectly beguiled."

Miranda huffed out a disbelieving laugh. Just where did this woman get off?

"Miranda," Maythra's voice went lower. "Heed my warning. Do not remain with that male. Do not tie yourself to him. I have lived in this clan for more than fifty years. I have seen *everything* that male has done. You would do well to take my advice."

"Take what advice, Maythra?" Viravia asked, coming back down the steps. Savrah got up quickly to take the bundle of clothing from Viravia's hands.

"You needn't worry." Maythra said, with a wave. "Govek and Miranda aren't planning any children."

"I was gone a moment, and you are already asking her about such personal matters?"

"I would think Govek's decision to bear a son would be of particular importance to *you,* Viravia."

"We shouldn't be discussing such things so soon after Miranda has arrived. We should be making her comfortable and helping her settle in. Miranda, let me show you to the washroom."

Miranda wasn't sure if she would rather get dressed or shake all these women until they explained what was going on. She took the clothes Savrah handed her and followed Viravia across the living space toward a door in the corner.

"Take your time," Viravia said, pushing open the door. Inside the torches were already lit. Miranda entered, and the door clicked shut behind her.

The space was exactly what Miranda would have expected from a rustic bathroom. A rather large wooden tub sat near the back. It didn't have a faucet and Miranda hated to think how much time it would take to boil water to fill it. There was a sink on a pedestal off to the left and a toilet that—thankfully!— appeared to be made from ceramic rather than wood.

It was clean and cozy from the light from a few torches flickering on the wall above the sink and Miranda found herself lingering, trying to get her bearings.

This was fine. Everything was *fine*.

Leaving the clothing on the side table near the door, she used the toilet, which had an old-fashioned rope pull to flush, but she couldn't figure out how the sink worked to wash her hands. It was wood like the tub and didn't have a faucet either, but they must use water with it because the smooth shiny surface was scattered with little droplets.

She went to try on Viravia's clothing. The cotton was rough and had buttons down the front. The long sleeves and high neck resembled those of the other woman. It would be nice and warm. The fit looked about right.

She set down the clothes for a moment and pinched the bridge of her nose as anxiety twisted up her gut.

She absolutely should have asked Govek a million questions about his clan *before* they arrived here. But there was no point beating herself up about that now.

Miranda yanked off the cloak and shirt and pulled the gray dress on over her head. The cotton was a little scratchy, and the dang thing hung baggy around her breasts and hips, but was a bit snug around her waist.

Jeez, Viravia was a bombshell.

Pushing aside her self-consciousness, Miranda went to the door and cracked it open a bit.

"Where do you think she came from?"

Miranda paused.

"Quiet or she'll hear."

Mumbling followed, and she could no longer make out what was being said. Dang it. Miranda considered her options. She really *shouldn't* be nosy. She should be good and rejoin them all. But she'd never really been *that* good.

So, as a last ditch effort, Miranda pressed her ear to the crack in the door. And it worked. She could hear them.

"Do you think she was a traveling trader? Viravia, do you remember her from any of your travels?"

"No, I don't know her," Viravia said.

"We should remain vigilant," Maythra said. "Keep an eye on her."

Viravia's tone was hard. "She couldn't be of the Waking Order or she wouldn't have been able to cross the border into Rove Wood. The magical barrier is too strong."

"And Evythiken would have known, right?" Beleda asked. "He's a seer, after all."

Miranda could almost feel her ears perk up.

"Chief Ergoth confided in me that the seer hasn't been in his right mind. That is why he was dismissed from the overlord's service and sent to Karthoc," Maythra replied.

"It wouldn't hurt to have him examine her, though, right?" Savrah asked. Her quiet voice was hard to make out. "We could ask Chief Ergoth?"

*Was the seer here? In Rove Wood?* It kinda sounded like it. Miranda chewed her lip.

"I don't see why not. It's the least the seer could do while enjoying our hospitality," Maythra said. "I can ask our good chief. I'm sure he would do us the favor."

*So, he* was *here! The seer was* here!

"I don't think we need to go that far," Viravia said.

"I disagree," Maythra said.

"When I first came to this clan three seasons ago, you all welcomed me with open arms. Even though you knew nothing about me," Viravia responded. "But now you meet a newcomer with such suspicion."

Maythra snapped at Viravia. "After what happened to your mate, I would think you would be the most reserved. And besides, when *you* arrived here, you were already mated to our beloved Tavggol. The trusted and respected heir to this clan. This woman is involved with *Govek* of all orcs. Of course, she'll be met with suspicion."

Miranda's stomach twisted at how they referred to Govek. He'd told her he wasn't on good terms with the clan, but it was still jarring to hear the venom in Maythra's tone.

"I think she might be *imprinted* to Govek," Savrah said.

There was a brief silence.

Beleda's shocked tone came first. "What? That cannot be."

"I overheard him say that if she called him, he would hear her and come."

"You must be mistaken. They couldn't have known each other for more than a few days. That's far too fast for any imprint to form. Even Tavggol took a moon with Viravia, right?" Beleda asked.

"R-Right," Viravia hesitantly confirmed.

"And that was considered very fast."

Maythra cut in. "Anything is possible with that monster. It's possible his break from Yerina has made Govek obsessive. We all know how he treated her."

Miranda clenched her fists. Where the heck did she get off calling Govek a *monster*? And who was this Yerina? Govek's ex?

"Watch your tongue, Maythra," Viravia's voice was clipped. "What transpired between Yerina and Govek is rumor, and imprints are born from care and trust, not obsession and control."

"Perhaps for other orcs it is about love and care, but Govek is an *abomination*."

Okay, *wow*.

"You know what he did at Clairton."

"Maythra," Viravia warned again.

Beleda piped up. "Maybe Govek has known Miranda for longer than we think? His break from Yerina is a full season past now. And his hunts often took him to distant places. Perhaps he met her elsewhere and has been wooing her for a while."

"Govek doesn't hunt outside the Rove Woods. He might be fueled by rage, but he isn't stupid. And Oakwall is the only human village within these woods," Maythra countered. "No, I'm certain he must have stolen her. Just look at her condition."

"She is in rough shape," Savrah said so softly Miranda almost couldn't make it out. "Do you think she might have been a slave? I overheard one of the warlord's warriors talking about how the Waking Order forces men and women who refuse to join their gospel into labor. They treat them like animals."

"If she was, then Govek didn't *steal* her. He *saved* her," Viravia replied.

"Ha, rather he took her to be his own slave," Maythra said.

"That's too far." Viravia said. "I will not have you speaking so ill of my kin."

Miranda pressed her ear to the crack to hear better. What did Viravia mean by her kin? Were . . . were they *related*?

"You still call him kin after what he did at Clairton?"

"We weren't there, Maythra. We don't know what happened."

"We weren't, but it is our good chief who told us of Govek's transgressions."

"Transgressions he was forced to commit in order to retrieve his brother's remains."

"So, you *are* trying to justify Govek's horrors?"

"All I am saying is that we should look upon his loss of sanity with compassion. I know how *I* felt when Tavggol's remains were returned in that state. As his brother, Govek must have been utterly devastated."

*Oh wait, hold on now.* Tavggol *was Govek's* brother. *And Viravia was Tavggol's mate. So Viravia was Govek's* sister-in-law? *And the baby was Govek's* nephew?

"I think Chief Ergoth should have more grief over this than *any of us*, Viravia. He lost *both* his sons at Clairton that day. Tavggol in spirit and Govek in mind."

*He lost both his sons?* Govek *is the son of the* chief?

"I think the only one who truly lost his mind was Chief Ergoth when he sent his only remaining son to Estwill." Viravia snapped.

What was this about Estwill? Hadn't Govek been going to war? Was the war at Estwill? Miranda's heart thundered in her ears, and she tried to calm it so she could keep listening.

"How dare you? Chief Ergoth is our steady leader. I know him better than any in this clan. I am his only true confidant, and I can assure you he was torn to bits over his decision to send his only living son to Estwill. Even with how vile Govek can be."

"Insult Govek so blatantly again and I will no longer welcome you in my home." Viravia's clipped tone sent a shiver down Miranda's spine.

And still, Maythra found the gall to argue. "I speak only the truth."

"You speak cruelty toward the male who may well become the next chief of Rove Wood Clan."

*By god,* the punches just kept hitting.

"Ergoth would never *formally* name Govek as his heir. That brute will never be chief of this clan," Maythra said loudly enough that Miranda could move away from the door slightly and still hear her. "Fades help us if he bears a child upon this new woman, he's stolen from blast knows where."

"Maythra," Viravia snapped, her tone hushed. "Quiet!"

"Don't you try to silence the truth! We all know what will come if he bears a son. With our beloved Tavggol gone, Govek's offspring would be able to vie for the place of chief within this clan. Do you truly want Tavggol's son to have to compete for his rightful place against Govek's monstrous spawn? Do you really want to see our peaceful clan ripped apart by such strife?"

Miranda's hand clenched at her lower stomach and fury boiled hot in her veins.

A pounding sounded at the door.

"Wh-who is it?" Beleda asked, her voice a mere squeak. Apparently, Miranda wasn't the only one disheveled from listening to Maythra and Viravia go at it.

There was a brief pause. The patter of shoes going to the door.

"It's Govek."

# CHAPTER
# FIVE

*MIRANDA*

M iranda rushed out of the bathroom to everyone scattering.

"Miranda, let me find you more clothes before you go. Maythra, come help me, please," Viravia said, halfway up the steps already.

"Beleda can do that," Maythra said from the front door. Her hand was on the handle, but she hadn't opened it yet.

"I-I'll help." Savrah's voice held a tremor and her eyes were wide as she nearly bolted up the stairs after Viravia. Beleda followed suit, eyes skittering from the door to the stairwell. She was far less terrified than Savrah but obviously wary.

"D-Do you think he could have heard us?" Savrah whispered too loudly to Viravia as she followed the pregnant woman up the stairs.

"Miranda," Maythra said, chin high. "I will tell him to go.

There are many homes within our clan that you can stay in. None as grand as this, but still very nice."

"I'm going with Govek," Miranda said, fumbling to knot the neckline of her cloak as she moved to the exit. "Step aside."

"You don't know him, Miranda. He may have hidden his nature for a few days, could well hide it for a few moons, but soon you will learn what he truly is and will regret not heeding my warning," Maythra said coldly, her fingers clenching the handle.

"Is that a threat, Maythra?"

"It's a warning. One you would do well to heed. I have lived in this clan since I was mated at a mere eighteen years of age, and have known Govek since the day he was born, and I know better than any how vile—"

"I get to decide who I think is *vile*, Maythra. Now *step aside*."

"Fine. But know that I will be watching. You are foolish, but I won't abandon you. I am on *your* side, Miranda."

"All right. I heard you."

Maythra's gray eyes narrowed at Miranda for another moment before she finally moved out of the way. "I sincerely hope that you do not end up like *Yerina*."

She was trying to goad Miranda into asking questions, and Miranda *was* curious, but she also wasn't keen on hearing any of Maythra's biased answers. "Tell Viravia that I'll come back for the clothes later. Have a good night."

As Maythra sputtered, dumbfounded that none of her obvious manipulation worked, Miranda pulled the door open.

A wave of sage billowed out as she slammed the door behind her and ran right into Govek, who was perched on the top step.

"Oh gosh!" He caught her by the arms. "Jeez, for some

reason, I thought this stoop was bigger. Or I guess it's just cause you're big, huh?"

"Miranda," Govek said, his eyes dark and brooding. "What are you doing here?"

"Uh—" Oh shoot. He was big—*big* mad. But before Miranda could find a way to quell his anger, she noticed the sound of hacking from behind him and craned her neck to find there was another large orc standing on the path having some kind of asthma attack.

This orc looked *much* more like Govek, with more accentuated muscles and a much larger frame. That Rogeth orc from earlier looked like a twig by comparison—a very uptight twig.

"Is your friend okay?" Miranda asked, as the muscular orc coughed and wheezed. Waving his hand in front of his face as he moved away from Viravia's house. "What's going on? Does he need a doctor?"

"Fucking *sage*," the male croaked. "Get over here. Both of you."

Govek gripped Miranda's arm and led her over to the male. The orc was a darker green than Govek and not quite as tall, but had almost as much muscle. And what he lacked in strength he made up for in scars. The guy was literally *covered* with them. His arms were cross-hatched. There was a particularly gruesome one on his forehead, right under his cropped hairline. It cut through his eyebrow, stopping just above his eye.

He was also shirtless and wore a pair of shorts just as skimpy as Govek's. It was no wonder the others hadn't reacted to Govek's lack of attire when they were freaking out about hers. They must all walk around half naked. Did orcs not feel the cold?

When the gasping male wiped the tears out of his eyes

and looked up at them, Miranda could see an instant resemblance to Govek. Their eyes were the same shape though this new orc lacked the gorgeous gold flecks that Govek's eyes had.

The orc opened his mouth to speak and started hacking again.

"Are you going to be okay?" Miranda asked, noting how the question made Govek's grip on her arm tighten. "Lighten up, please."

Govek's expression flashed to chagrin, and he instantly released her.

*Oh yeah.* So *dangerous and out of control.*

The coughing male cursed loudly between gasps and rubbed his face.

"Seriously, dude. You need help?"

"I'm fine, woman. Fuck. It's just the blasted sage. Fades curse me," he said before turning his eyes on Miranda again. He scrutinized her. Those dark eyes flashed from the hem of her slightly too long skirt to the top of her unbrushed head.

Govek didn't grab her again, but she could feel him step closer. The warmth of his torso against her back was kinda nice. The chill of the night made her cheeks sting.

"Fuck, Govek, don't you feed her?"

Govek growled.

"He feeds me plenty," Miranda said, wantonly leaning into Govek so she could feel the rumble against her back. "I'm Miranda. And *you* are?"

"Karthoc. Cousin to Govek. Warlord of Baelrok Forge."

Miranda's breath hitched. "Karthoc? Really?"

The male's eyes flashed to Govek as he rose a brow. "Yes. What has Govek told you of me?"

"Oh uh. Lots of stuff about your home. He said we were

going to live with you. Or"—she looked up at Govek—"that's still the plan, right?"

Govek's expression was set with a deep scowl, and his glower made a shiver course through her.

Oh, shit a brick. He was actually *really* mad she didn't go straight to his house.

She'd have to make it up to him later. "Karthoc, the seer is in your company right? Could I talk to him?"

"*She's* the one who had questions for Evythiken?" Karthoc asked.

"Yes," Govek whispered. Miranda turned to get a good look and found him twitching, fists curled, arms poised to strike, fierce eyes on Karthoc.

*What the heck?*

"Govek, what's wrong with you?"

He flinched and looked away.

"He's a possessive idiot, that's what's wrong," Karthoc said, his tone laced with amusement. "For fuck's sake, Govek, I'm not going to take your woman. Get control of yourself."

Miranda blinked. Govek had indicated a jealous streak, but she hadn't thought it would be *this* bad. "Govek, he's your *cousin*, for crying out loud. You're this upset because I'm talking to your *cousin*?"

Govek raked a hand through his hair but still said nothing.

"There will be another time to discuss the seer. Best we part ways now," Karthoc said, already turning away. "I will see you at the hall for the announcement tomorrow. Do not be late."

"Announcement?" Miranda asked as Karthoc disappeared up the path.

"Why are you *here*, Miranda?"

The tension in Govek's voice made her bristle. "You said I should get clothes."

"I said they were to bring the clothes to you. At my home," he growled, spearing heat into her stomach. Dang it, why did his rumbly voice always have to cue her up?

"Well, they didn't. That Maythra woman is bossy as heck. But your *sister-in-law* is nice. Learned all about that. And a *bunch* of other stuff, too. I see now why you didn't want me getting all social with your clan here. Why didn't you tell me you were the chief's son? And why were you . . .?"

Miranda trailed off as Govek's expression paled, and the harsh reality hit her—his *brother* had been killed recently.

"Govek . . . about your brother, I'm really sorry—"

"We're going," Govek snarled. He gripped her arm and pulled her down the path. "Now."

"Oh, heck no. You let go." His hold wasn't tight enough to hurt, but she still would not tolerate him dragging her around. "Govek, let me go."

He froze in an instant, and his eyes flashed. He released her and stalked away, yanking at his hair with both hands.

It only took a few steps for him to stop. Turn. Open his mouth to speak and snap it shut. He had his jaw all tucked up again. It looked so uncomfortable.

"Come, *please.*"

The tone made her chest ache and she nodded, falling into step beside him. She examined his tense face, his rolling muscles, the tick in his jaw. She should let him calm down before interrogating him. *Really.*

"Govek, are you *really* the chief's son?"

He picked up the pace slightly, shoulders bunched.

"Govek, hold on! That's too fast."

"Yes." The word came out strangled but he did slow his pace.

"Yes?"

"Yes, I am the chief's son."

She paused and caught her breath. "And . . . then you left to go to war?"

The look he sent her was so dark and pained she forced herself to drop it.

"Viravia was nice," Miranda said, grabbing a topic right out of the icy air. "She makes soaps? She must really like the scent of sage because *oof.* Even her tea was sage. I guess it was fine, a bit overwhelming. At least I'm not allergic like your poor cousin—"

Govek let out a low growl so deadly it actually straightened Miranda's spine.

Oops. Probably best not to mention other guys right at this moment. "On Earth, I had lots of different soaps. They came in all kinds of scents. I liked the natural ones best which is all you guys have here, huh?"

God, what was wrong with her? All the shit going on and she was blathering about soap and sage.

"Miranda."

She looked up and he let out a ragged sigh, raked a hand through his hair, and swallowed hard.

Some of her toddlers liked a cuddle when they were having a rough time.

She reached out and took his arm, holding it tight to her chest. He let out a long breath and didn't pull away from her.

"I'm sorry I didn't insist they take me back to your home."

He said nothing but she could feel the tension release in his arm.

She reached up and stroked his jaw. "Why don't you untuck your teeth? We're alone now."

He snapped his gaze to her face a moment, and his throat worked.

Then he did.

"That's better," she assured him, gentling her touch.

His eyes flickered down her body. "Do you like my dress?" she asked.

Govek continued to stare, throat working in a slight gulp.

"It doesn't fit very well. Viravia must have been a total hottie. Not that she isn't hot stuff now that she's pregnant, just . . ."

Govek's eyes got large.

*Shoot, was he jealous of women too? Was she making it worse?* "Anyway. It was really nice of her to let me wear her clothes. Even if I don't do them justice."

"Miranda."

"Yeah?"

"You are beautiful."

Heat bloomed in her cheeks and stomach and Miranda finally found the strength to go quiet. Instead, she distracted herself looking at the tree houses as they passed. The paths were vacant, and the homes were dim. She wondered where everyone was.

The tree houses were *amazing.* She couldn't wait to see Govek's home.

"How much farther?" Miranda finally asked. They were surrounded by woods now with not a single house in sight. The paths were much more overgrown and there weren't any lanterns. It was so dark she was glad she had Govek's arm to help her. Only his glowing green eyes were visible in the night.

"There." Govek pointed to a tree about fifty yards away. It had taken quite a bit longer to get to his home than she expected. It was fairly small compared to some of the others they'd passed but it was too dark to really judge. As they drew nearer, she could make out the porch. Three steps led to a front door.

A front door which was half off its hinges.

"Er. Did you get robbed?"

Govek shot her a confused look before noting where her eyes were. "No. I'll mend it tonight."

"Not tonight. We should just relax tonight."

"You wouldn't rather be sure you don't get eaten alive while you sleep?"

She quirked a smile. "We both know the only creature I could be eaten by right now is *you*." He tensed again and Miranda straightened. "That was a sex joke, Govek. I don't think you're actually going to eat me."

He didn't respond and her gut twisted.

"Govek, how many members of your clan think you'd really hurt me?"

There was a deadly silence. "All of them."

Miranda was struck dumb by the sincerity of his tone as he led her up the steps and into the dark room. She could hear him walking around, a cabinet opened with a squeak and clattered shut.

"Viravia didn't seem to think that badly of you."

"She has only lived in these woods for three seasons."

Light burst in the room and she blinked rapidly, willing her eyes to adjust. Torchlight from several lanterns had all lit at the same time.

She was in a kitchen. A much nicer one than Viravia's. There was ample counter space, an actual sink near the window, and a massive wood stove filled the entire opposite end. There were cabinets and drawers, and cooking utensils hung from most of the available wall space.

"This is great," Miranda said, fingering the intricate leaf

and vine detailing carved into the cabinet doors. "Viravia's house didn't have anything like this." When he didn't respond, she pressed, "Do you like to cook?"

He was standing in a rounded entry. Behind him she could see flickering firelight illuminating a living room with a couch and two chairs.

"No."

Her brow furrowed. "No?"

"No, I do not like to cook."

Her lips pursed. "Then . . . why so much cooking stuff?"

He looked away, fists still bunched up at his sides. If he tightened up anymore he might cut himself with his claws.

"Govek, talk to me. Why do you have a full kitchen if you don't like to cook?"

Had it been for his other woman? Yerina, right?

Her chest tightened and the excitement at seeing such a familiar space dimmed. Apparently, Govek wasn't the only one with jealousy issues.

"I am not welcome in the hall."

"What?" She blinked, but he still wasn't meeting her eyes.

"The hall is where the clan has their meals. I am not welcome there."

"Why?"

Ignoring her question, Govek turned on his heel and stormed into the living room. She scampered after him, watching as he methodically lit all the candles in the room using a short twig with a tiny flame at the end. It took a while, there were ten or more candles all over the space.

This living room was much smaller than Viravia's but felt cozy. The gray cushions looked more worn but soft. The carpets were plain, dark brown, but lush. The rich brown wood walls were decorated with vine carvings and the shadows caused by the candlelight made their intricate detailing more pronounced.

It was truly beautiful.

But that beauty was dimmed by Govek's continued silence.

"Come *on*, Govek," Miranda pleaded, throwing her head back in frustration. He'd had that *whole* walk to calm down and it wasn't enough? "Work with me here. Talk to me."

*"You should stay with the other women."* His voice was a low, deadly grumble that flooded Miranda with equal parts heat and worry.

"What? What do you mean?"

He stalked toward a tall door with a rounded top at the back of the house. It was at the center of the far wall of the living room. She could see the forest through the window next to it, deep and dark and swallowing up the light. He trembled on the precipice. As if he were about to bolt.

Terrified he might, Miranda stepped into the living room but stopped herself from grabbing him. "Don't you dare leave right now, Govek."

"It is not safe for you."

"Govek—"

"If you knew what I was thinking right now . . ." he started with a snarl, whirling to face her. His eyes were pricks in the bright light. *"You are not safe with me."*

Miranda's brow furrowed. After growing up in a group home, she had ample experience dealing with dangerous people and knew when one shouldn't be messed with.

But Govek wasn't giving off that vibe.

"Why?" Miranda asked, and his expression flashed with confusion. "Tell me exactly why I'm not safe and I'll decide if I should leave."

"When you looked at Karthoc, I wanted to rip his *fucking* head off."

Miranda rose her brows.

Govek continued raging. "I want to burn the fucking clan to the ground rather than have your eyes stray from me. I want to render every male that might turn your head to cinders. I want to rip every tongue from every mouth so they do not have a chance to turn you before I can win you. I want to hide you away, so you don't have any chance to seek another male—"

"Wait, stop. Hold on," Miranda interrupted. "You think *I'm* going to seek out other men?"

"Why would you not? *Look* at you!"

Red hot anger flashed behind her eyes. "Sit down, right there on the couch."

Govek froze, hand still on the back door. His other hand clenched tight. Red blood was seeping out from between his fingers.

"Oh, for crying out loud. Govek, you cut yourself. *Sit down*. Right now or I really am going to get mad at you. Your ears will be bleeding too, from the length of the lecture."

Govek blinked at her, his eyes shifted from the couch and then back to her. "Did you not *hear* me? I am not *safe*."

"God, yes, I heard you. You're jealous and accusing me of things I would *never* do. *Now sit down*."

"But—"

"*Sit*," Miranda said using her best do-not-test-me voice. Govek's eyes went as round as her babies' eyes used too. "And tell me where your medical ointments are."

She stormed into the kitchen not waiting for his response, she'd seen a rag in there, hanging next to the sink. She tried to quell her anger but wasn't successful. Usually, she would force a smile and take some calming breaths but that was for her babies and Govek was a grown-ass man.

So, when she turned back and found him still standing, mostly unresponsive, she let loose. "Sit. Down. For pity's sake! To think you're *this* upset because I greeted your cousin. Do you really think so low of me that I would *cheat* on you with your family member? Really? What kind of woman do you think I am? Why would you even want to *be* with a woman like that?"

He attempted a meek reply as she snatched the rag off the hook and stomped back into the living room. Govek was very *very* lucky he'd obeyed her order and sat down on the edge of the massive, fur-lined couch.

"Give me your hand," she demanded, holding her palm open, waiting, but Govek hesitated. She looked him dead in the eyes and got mad all over again. "Let's get one thing clear, right now. I am not a cheater. I would never even *consider* cheating on you. If I don't want to be with you anymore, I'm going to make it *very clear* long before I try to mess around with someone else. And I will *never* get with your family members, and I will *never* get with your friends, and for crying out loud, stop looking at me like I'm the crazy one here. *You're* the one who thought I would cheat after fricking glancing at your effing cousin!"

Govek simply sat there with wide, blinking eyes.

She needed to calm the eff down or she was going to start spewing venom. She looked around the room again, taking in the comfortable space. "Your walls are pretty," she mustered.

"My . . . what?"

"Your walls. I'm trying to distract myself here. I don't want to fight with you. Lord knows I had enough of that shit when I was growing up."

There was a long pause before Govek ventured. "Who did you fight with in your youth, Miranda?"

"A lot of people. I was raised in a group home. No one gets put in a group home because they have good role models for parents. Uncurl your fingers. I'm not scared of your claws."

He finally obeyed and she dabbed at the cuts with the cloth. They were shallow and already seemed to be scabbing over, but she didn't want to let him go just yet. "Though to be fair, I never had role models at all. My parents died in a car accident when I was three."

"I am sorry, Miranda."

She let the apology roll around in her head for a moment, soothing the worst of the burning rage. "Sorry about my parents, or for accusing me of cheating?"

"Both."

A ragged sigh left her lips as she continued to stroke his now healed palm. Dang, orcs healed fast. Or maybe just Govek did.

"I truly did not intend to insult you. I am . . ." He was so quiet she could barely make out the tremor in the tone.

"You are . . .?"

"I am not in control."

"You keep saying that, but you seem pretty controlled to me." He met her eyes again. "You could have ripped Viravia's house apart looking for me, but you didn't. You could have attacked your cousin for saying hi, but you stopped yourself. You're clearly being eaten alive right now, but you haven't done much more than get all growly and threaten to bolt. *And* hurt yourself, which I'm pretty peeved about."

His hands began to tremble in hers.

"Govek, what makes you think you aren't in control?"

"I don't think it. I *know*."

"*How* do you know? Tell me." She clutched his hands, careful to avoid his claws.

"I have committed many atrocities in the past, Miranda. Far more than you could possibly imagine. Things that are unforgivable. Things that would make you despise me."

"Is that why you wanted to keep away from the clan? Cause you didn't want me to find out about all these *atrocities*." She searched his haunted eyes. "Well, that ship has sailed. It's way off over the horizon right now. You might as well tell me before they do."

His face contorted and he looked away. "What would you have me speak on, Miranda? What would you have me say? That I am at constant war with my own fury? That this whole fucking clan is *right* about me? I'm a dangerous wretch whose magic is built on chaos and rage. I fucking drove away my own . . ."

He stopped short, wrenching out of her grasp and stalking back across the room. His hands ripped at his hair.

"I don't fucking deserve to speak, Miranda. What could I say other than worthless excuses that do nothing to undo the damage I have done?"

"I still want to hear them."

Govek froze, shifted to look at her with half wild eyes. Beautiful eyes that glimmered gold in the firelight.

"I want to hear your thoughts, Govek. Because they aren't *excuses,* they're *reasons.*"

His hands dropped out of his hair.

"They are the *reasons* you acted the way you did. I'm not going to judge your actions until I can understand your perspective. Maybe I'll agree with your reasons, maybe I won't. But I ask that you trust me enough to tell me and let me come to my own conclusions."

Govek's throat worked. His eyes darted as if unsure he could speak, as if looking for someone or something to silence him.

Then he took a deep breath and said, "I've killed, Miranda. I've . . . *murdered* others."

Miranda sucked air sharply in through her nose to mask the jolt that confession shot through her. Her voice came out a little higher pitched. "Okay . . . who?"

"Why the fuck does that matter?"

"Because the circumstances behind *why* you murdered them matter," Miranda said, standing up. "You keep talking about control. Did you lose control and kill them?"

"Yes." Govek's eyes squeezed shut. "I went into a battle rage and my magic spiraled out of control."

"Battle rage. You were being attacked?"

"Yes."

"So, you were *in* a battle and killed people?" He nodded. "Civilians?"

His brows pinched together. "What?"

"People other than soldiers. Women, children, elderly?"

Govek swallowed hard, brows furrowing. Then he shook his head and she let out a breath of relief.

"So, you went battle crazy and killed *soldiers*?"

"Who they were does not matter. All lives are precious. Magic should *never* be used to cause harm. It should not even be *possible* to do so."

"Govek, if you lashed out because you were being attacked that is *completely* different from attacking someone unprovoked. You know that, right?"

"They weren't attacking me. They were trying to flee and I . . . I still . . ."

"You still what?"

His hands were back in his hair. "I lost my *mind*, Miranda! I blacked out. I *ravaged* them. By the time I came to they were fucking *pulp*."

Miranda managed to withhold a flinch at that mental image even as prickling coursed down her spine. "But *something* must have happened to make you do that. Something must have set you off. What was it?"

Govek's eyes were stricken and lost. He stalked away from her. Into the kitchen.

Why had he killed them so brutally? Was she safe with him?

"Govek, *tell* me. I. Want. To. Know. Your. *Reasons.*"

"They fucking *slaughtered him.*" Govek whirled around, eyes wild, muscles bulging, frame terrifyingly huge. Miranda would have bolted had she not been frozen to the spot.

"They flayed him. Stuck him on a spit. Fucking *cooked him alive.*"

Miranda sucked in a hard breath. She already knew the answer before she asked, but she needed to hear it from him. "Who?"

"My brother."

# CHAPTER
# SIX

*GOVEK*

The words felt like fire on his tongue. Choking him. Suffocating him.

And they would not stop coming.

"Tavggol was there to fucking *trade*. He *trusted* them— enough that he refused Karthoc's protection—and on the final meeting, they stole the boons he had brought in good faith and *butchered him like an animal.*"

Miranda's eyes went huge, her body flinched and shuddered, and she gripped her hands together about her chest.

*Fuck*, he should never have lost himself. Should never have spoken of this.

His hands trembled, worthless claws curling as he remembered that day. He could feel the soldiers' ticky blood. Their bones cracking, snapping like twigs with a satisfying crunch. Their gut-wrenching wails.

Spirals of magic had made his movements quick, his aim sure. Conjuring with the Fades made him even more deadly, helped him cut down every wretch faster and more brutally than any other warrior orc ever could.

He'd do it again in an *instant*.

He was a monster.

"Sit down here."

The order came crisp in his blistering mind, and he snapped up to find Miranda pointing to the couch. He gulped. He could not get close to her now. Not while his rage was so thick.

"Govek."

"Stay back," he snapped. He needed to leave, to escape, to run into the dark woods and vent his fury on logs and dirt until he was settled again. Until he could gain back control. Until he was certain his magic was soothed. He could already feel it burning hot in his chest, gripping around his thundering heart. The light of the Fades was growing at the back of his mind, threatening to blind him.

Tight warmth pressed into his torso.

Govek jerked backward, but Miranda's grip on him tightened. Her face was buried in his chest, her arms firm around his middle.

The fuck?

"Miranda, I'm not—"

"Sit down, *please*."

Her voice was thick and his ears rang from the sound. Her body was trembling.

"You're afraid," he said, wanting to pull her off him but unable to touch her with his clawed hands. At least the vile heat in his chest was soothing.

Soothed by Miranda's gentle warmth. He took a deep breath.

She looked up at him and his breath hitched at the sorrow

he saw in her face. Her eyes were flooding with tears, her red lips quivering.

*Fuck.*

"Sit," she said, as the word broke.

And he did.

She clung to him the whole way, and the moment he was seated, she crawled into his lap, straddled his thighs, pressed her chest into his, and wrapped her arms around his neck.

"I'm so sorry," she whispered. "That must have been . . . I'm so so sorry."

His eyes burned and he blinked rapidly, attempting to hide the unusual emotion.

The Fade light at the back of his mind dwindled away.

She ran her hands through his hair, stroking it. The soft touch was in such contrast to his usual ruthless pulling, it skittered goosebumps along his scalp.

"I think you did the right thing."

He lost his breath but managed a rough croak. "What?"

"Killing those men who tortured your brother to death." His mind stilled as he attempted to process her words. "I think that was the right thing to do. People who can torture others without remorse are too dangerous. By killing them, you saved every other person who would have been subjected to that fate."

No. That wasn't right. All lives were precious. Sacred. He was born under the Great Rove Tree. He could conjure the Fades magic. It should not be possible for him to kill *anyone.*

"Govek," she said softly, cupping his face in her warm hands. Her soft fingers grazed the side of his temples. "I am so *so* sorry that your brother died."

His throat constricted and her face grew blurry.

She pressed her forehead to his. "I'm sorry you had to see something so horrible. I'm sorry that you didn't make it to him in time. I'm sorry that those people stole him from you." She wrapped her arms around his neck and put her hands in his hair again. "But I'm *not* sorry you killed them. And you shouldn't be either." Her fingertips slid toward the back of his head. She pressed her fingers in slow circles at the base of his skull, just the way she had in the outer woods when she'd examined his countenance for the first time. When she'd looked deep into his face and accepted his appearance despite how loathsome most found it. Especially humans.

She was accepting him now in the same way. Accepting a wholly *different* part of him.

A part he never thought *anyone* would welcome.

Govek shuddered, closed his burning eyes. Let her gentle nature soak into him. He didn't deserve this kindness. He knew that. Not after all that he had done.

But . . . he couldn't bring himself to refuse it.

Miranda tucked her head into his shoulder, relaxing.

She wasn't going to move. She wouldn't leave him.

And that support forced him to drop the walls he'd built around his sorrow.

For what felt like an eternity, Govek grappled with the dark weight pressing down on him. Pulling him under. Burying him in the heat of rage and the icy grip of grief.

And eventually, that grip eased, and Miranda's gentle touch took its place.

He regained his senses. The fire in him ebbed to embers. His twisting guts settled. His claws slunk back into his fingers.

Miranda sat up, her face no longer blurred, her smile too sweet. And his heart skipped.

"Feel better?" she asked, and he could only blink and nod.

Fuck, he *did*. He actually *did*.

"Is there anything else you need right now?" she asked and *fuck*, his throat grew tight. He shook his head.

He just needed her to stay right here with him.

*Forever.*

She gave him another sweet smile before looking around.

"Your house is *so* pretty. Viravia's house didn't have all these carvings." She reached out and touched the leaf detailing he'd etched into the wooden arm of the couch.

His chest swelled with an unusual sensation he couldn't name. "I did them."

"What?"

The warmth in his chest bloomed, and he focused on it, using the sensation to drown out what remained of his rage and sorrow. He didn't want these first few moments in his home to be ruined by his own vile, uncontrolled nature. "I carved these. Took many years and a lot of patience." Working with the grain and the life of the tree was difficult. It required the use of magic to sense the tree's life and ensure it remained hale as the wood was chipped away.

"Govek, that's *amazing.* Wow, just . . . you did the walls too? And the detailing on the cabinets? And that coffee table?"

"Coffee?" Govek asked as Miranda moved from his lap to look closer at the detailing on the low ovular table in front of the couch.

Her head snapped up. "Oh no. You guys don't have *coffee*?"

"No."

"Oh, I'm gonna be in trouble in the morning. You must have *something* that helps you wake up?"

His brows furrowed. "There are many herbs that can aid with rousing when one is unconscious. Hovget, our healer, grows and stores them."

"That's not . . . oh gosh. We'll figure that out later. Is that your bedroom?"

"Our bedroom," he said without thinking.

She shot him a smile. "*Our* bedroom."

He followed her in, lighting the candles along the wall so she could examine the space.

She wasted no time flopping down on the bed with a huff.

"Oh, my god. A real bed! With a mattress and *everything*. I never thought I would be so happy to see a bed. Wow, this bed frame is incredible. Did you carve it too?"

"Yes." Her fingers traced the mountain scene he'd carved into the headboard. He felt guilty at how much he was enjoying her compliments. After everything he had confessed to her, he had yet to admit he deserved them.

He had committed a whole lifetime of wrongs. His furious outbursts of rage-laced magic had long been the reason his clan despised him.

How would Miranda react when she finally discovered the truth of all he had done? The clan knew of her now. There was no stopping her from speaking with them and no preventing them from warning her of his past atrocities.

He gulped past the lump in his throat. He needed to tell her everything but where should he even start?

What he had done at Clairton was certainly the most heinous act he'd ever committed. It made his other wrongs look trivial. But Miranda had embraced him after he'd admitted it. He could still feel her warmth and acceptance soothing away his deepest aches.

He had to work hard to keep from trembling under the force of such kindness. His knees were almost weak with relief.

As she rolled onto her side so she could more easily take in the image of the mountains and trees he'd carved, the cloak wrapped tight around her, accentuating the globe of her ass.

His blood heated.

Fuck, he really was a beast.

"Is that your only place to store stuff in here?" she asked, sitting up and pointing to the large trunk at the end of the bed.

"Yes." He barely had anything in it. What if she wanted a present? Perhaps he could quickly carve her something. She seemed to like that at least.

"You must not have much clothing. Not that I mind that."

Heat pooled in his gut, cutting off his worry as she passed him to go to the washroom. "What's in here?"

He went to light the torches so she could continue exploring. Her delight at everything had him almost relaxed.

Seeing her in his home, smiling as she discovered new things, caused an odd sensation in his chest. One that made his thoughts drift toward the future. A future where they could create a home *together*.

Warmth spread through him.

"Oh wow. This is pretty nice. It's bigger than Viravia's. Though she probably has two, huh? Since her house is two levels?"

"She does." He watched as she examined the wood sink that probably needed another sap treatment to keep it waterproof.

He used to use sap on Tavggol's sinks as well. His brother always forgot until it was long past due. Had Viravia done it recently? He wasn't certain how to ask to offer aid.

"So . . ." Miranda paused, searching his face. He tried to hide the remaining bits of his turmoil.

Judging from how her face fell, he wasn't successful.

"Come here, tough guy."

He gulped and went to her. She wrapped her arms around his neck and forced him to lean down close to her face.

The warmth of her lips collided with his. Her crisp honey scent swirled up into his senses, bursting in his mind. She teased his lips, nibbling.

Fuck, she felt so blasted good. He was about to scoop her up when she broke away with a little chuckle. "We need to teach you how to kiss."

"I'm not pleasing you?"

"Oh, you are. I just want you to please me *more*."

"I will do anything you ask, Miranda," Govek said, blood heating. "I will give you any boons you wish."

Her eyes softened, and he helplessly reached to cup her warm face in his hands. Her skin was so smooth, and her eyes were so gentle. Never in his wildest dreams had he imagined he could be looked upon with such gentleness.

He would do anything to keep her. *Anything.*

He gulped hard. "Just speak your desires, Miranda. I would move the whole of Faeda for your whims."

# CHAPTER
# SEVEN

*MIRANDA*

Oh shoot. He didn't actually *mean* that, did he? Cause what she *wanted* was to interrogate him about everything regarding this clan and his personal life until the sun came up. That or get him naked. It was hard to choose.

She glanced around the bathroom again. It really *was* nice, with smooth wood walls and a high ceiling. The torchlight illuminated the space more brightly than she would have thought three dim light sources could. Magic must have been at play, just as it had been with the twig match.

The tub was *enormous*, more than big enough for her and Govek to fit together.

She glanced at him and instantly knew that she needed to swallow down the bulk of her curiosity and give Govek a little pampering. He'd been through almost as much shit as she had.

His brother had been tortured to death. Burned alive.

Her stomach rolled. What he'd gone through was *horrible*. It was the absolute worst outcome.

The one that haunted at the back of her own mind. What if her babies . . .

*No, breathe.*

She did.

"Why don't we take a bath, Govek?"

He nodded. "You may go first."

"You don't want to take one with me? I feel like I owe you a hair wash."

His brows arched and her stomach dropped.

"Okay, if you tell me you *forgot* about the spring, I'm going to be very mad."

"I certainly did *not* forget. But you owe me nothing. Our exchange was mutual."

"Mutual." From her memory, the attention was completely one-sided. All centered on *her* pleasure.

"Yes." Govek's brow was furrowed and his eyes narrowed. "I gifted you the tincture to wash, and you allowed me to touch you."

Her gut warmed at the fact that he viewed pleasuring her as a *reward*, but she still protested. "Govek, we talked about this. I don't like thinking about our relationship as transactional."

He shifted and glanced away.

"I said this already, but I'll gladly say it again. I like you, Govek. I *want* to be with you. You don't need to give me anything in exchange for that."

"But . . ." He swallowed. "I hear you. And yet, this exchange is the only way I have ever known. Will you give me time . . . and guidance?"

"Yes, of course," Miranda said, breathing a sigh, a light smile playing at her lips. "That's not a problem at all. I'll just call you out whenever it feels like you're trying to give me gifts for the wrong reasons."

He nodded, shoulders sagging with clear relief even as she tensed again. Her thoughts went back to the woman at Viravia's house. To Maythra's warnings about *Yerina*.

Her stomach twisted and her mouth ran away with her. "Look, I know we've already covered *a lot* of traumatic stuff tonight, but like . . . I have to ask, did you do something . . . bad . . . to your ex? Yerina, right?"

His face constricted, and suddenly, she wasn't certain she wanted him to speak, so she talked right over him. "I'm not accusing you of anything, *really*. It's clear that Maythra is super biased against you, so I'm going to take everything she says with a healthy *bucket* of salt but like . . . we did *just* meet each other, and you *do* have this transactional quirk. Did you maybe read the room wrong with her and think that bringing her something fancy made you entitled to something she hadn't fully given her consent to—"

"Miranda."

"Y-yeah?" Oh frick, all of that came out *really* bad, didn't it?

Govek's eyes shut and his hand raked over his scalp as he let out a ragged sigh. "I did *not* harm her. And I gained full consent from her at every juncture before proceeding. Be that during rutting or any other time."

Miranda shifted, remembering his gloves and how he constantly asked for consent and how hesitant he was during almost the entire time they were intimate. "I believe you."

He nodded slowly.

Miranda shifted, unwilling to press him for more now that her anxiety had been quelled—for the most part. She searched the room. "How do you even fill that bathtub?"

Govek looked up. "What?"

"I don't see a faucet. Don't tell me you have to cart in the water by bucket."

Govek glanced from her to the tub and then crossed the room. He rapped hard on the ceiling twice and a long slender door fell open. A hollow bamboo pipe popped out.

She came over to his side and he tensed, so she stroked his arm, using it to steady herself as she went up on her toes and reached for the ceiling. Too high.

"I'mma have to get your help every time I want a bath, huh?"

He blinked, looking from her hand still resting on his bicep to the ceiling. "I . . . will find a way to lower it for you."

"You don't have to. We're still going to Karthoc's forge, right?" When he nodded, she said, "Then it's fine. It's only a couple of days, and I'd rather have baths with you, anyway. I'm sure we can both fit."

Govek gulped.

"What do you say?" She sidled close and grazed her fingers up his abs. His breath caught hard. "You want to have a bath with me?"

"Yes."

He hit the ceiling with the palm of his hand and water began to spill into the tub. The thundering drone was soothing. Steam rose, quickly heating the room.

He swung off his cloak before she realized what he was doing.

Holy hell, this guy was a *dreamboat*. Damn, was it possible to have this much muscle? To be this sculpted? Even the green coloring seemed to accentuate the lines and dips of his abs, the bulging of his calves, the thick cords in his thighs. *All* the way up.

He dropped his pants and her throat closed as his cock

sprang out, huge and ready. Her whole body ignited. A thrilled shiver raced from the tips of her toes to her scalp.

"Miranda."

She jumped and Govek snorted in amusement.

Then he bridged the gap between them and pulled off her cloak.

"Jeez, won't let me enjoy the view for a minute, will you?" She laughed at his impatience and unbuttoned the dress. He exhaled so hard she could feel it rustle her hair before a chilled shiver ran across her arms and stomach. Her dress pooled around her feet, and she looked up to see him examining her with just as much reverence as she had for him.

"Happy?" Her tone was breathless. She could feel his eyes trailing all the way up her legs before pausing at her breasts. Her thighs clenched.

"*Yes*," he grated. "Let me lift you in."

She nodded, and he scooped her up. His hot body felt delicious against her chilled skin, but he didn't linger for even a moment and brought them both into the water without preamble.

A throaty moan left her lips as he set her down in the hot water. She settled with her legs curled under her, the hot water lapped at them, and goosebumps broke out along her thighs.

It would take forever to fill a tub this size, but the wall of it was high enough that, once complete, it would cover her to her collarbone. She couldn't wait.

Govek turned away to take a place on the opposite end instead of sitting next to her. She pursed her lips, irritated at his retreat. She leaned forward and grazed her fingertips from the top of his firm ass all the way down his thigh.

Govek lost his balance and lurched forward into the stream

of hot water gushing out of the ceiling. He jerked away, sputtering and wiping at his face.

Miranda burst with laughter. She couldn't help it even as he shot her a glower and his cheeks darkened to a forest green. To quell the sting of embarrassment, Miranda moved around the stream toward him.

He slipped down onto his ass, blinking rapidly. She moved to straddle his legs and could hear him gulp over the rush of the water.

Lord, he felt incredible against her. His thighs were all hot and hard between hers. She wiped the water off his forehead and chin while his eyes fixed to her chest.

Her stomach warmed. "Like the view?"

His rumble of approval made her squirm, and he gripped her hips but hesitated to pull her in. She moved for him, pressing her stomach against his torso. She could feel his hard cock snug between her legs, and it made her pussy pulse. Her toes curled in the water.

"I don't want you to believe what the others say."

She snapped back to attention, realizing that Govek's expression had turned brooding, and he wouldn't meet her eyes.

"You mean . . . about what Maythra said? And others in the clan?"

"And Yerina's lies. I have no right to argue because some of what she shared with others *is* true. But . . . I still . . ."

"Please tell me, Govek," Miranda said, scratching at his damp scalp. "Like I said, I want to hear your side of things too."

He gulped as he looked at her chest again. "Can I rest my head here?"

"Yes?" Miranda said uncertainly, half expecting him to play

with her boobs. Instead, he brought his knees up so she was lifted higher, and he could more easily tuck his temple against her collarbone. His cheek rested between her breasts. His ear was right above her heart.

The warmth of him was staggering, and her heart skipped. She wondered if he could hear it.

"That last time with her was . . . awful." His voice was muffled. "I do not want to speak on it, but I will if you . . ."

"You don't have to." Miranda scratched his scalp again, and he shivered. She wasn't too eager to hear about him being with another woman. "You don't have to tell me anything you don't want to."

He nodded, hair tickling her sensitive flesh with each motion. "She . . . left. Rejected me. And I realized that nothing I could do would ever win her. I had done my absolute fucking *best* and she still . . ." His arms came around her middle and he squeezed gently.

"It's okay," Miranda said, leaning down to put her cheek against the top of his head.

"I lost my control, Miranda. Like fucking *always* and it ruined me. Us." His body went lax. "The message from Karthoc about my brother going missing arrived the very next morn, and I *left* without seeing or speaking to her. Nor did I send her a message. Even with her imprint still coursing in my veins."

Miranda's stomach twisted at the mention. Was . . . he still imprinted on her?

If he felt her tense, he didn't mention it. "She likely spread those lies out of hurt. There is some truth to them. There had been times that I was . . ." He shook his head against her. "I cannot overcome my nature. I am an uncontrolled wre—"

"*Stop* calling yourself a wretch, Govek."

He jerked away from her, looking into her face with wide eyes.

"You are *not* a wretch. Not to me. And a rough breakup doesn't give your ex the right to spread lies about you."

Govek looked back at her chest, clearly wanting to rest against her again. She pulled him back down, curling her hands around the back of his head and pressing him in to hold him gently.

If he wasn't brave enough to take what he wanted yet, then she would just give it to him. She could keep giving it to him until he gained his courage.

He sighed raggedly, though his tension eased. "It does not matter what the humans or orcs of Rove Wood say. We will be leaving, and I have no intention of interacting with Oakwall again."

"Oakwall?"

"The only human village within the Rove Woods. Our clan has been peaceful with them for centuries and meets with them to trade three times every moon."

"And that's where you met Yerina? Where she is now?"

"Yes. I met her at the trades. Her sister is the only decent baker in these woods."

Miranda snorted. "Is that why your bread is so awful?"

"I have never perfected the skill," he said flatly.

Miranda couldn't help laughing. "I'm sorry. Sorry," she said, stroking the top of his head. She curled around him. "Thank you for telling me all this, Govek. I know it wasn't easy."

He huffed.

"Can I ask you some more questions? Or have you reached your limit?"

His grumble rolled through her, but he nodded. "Ask."

"Are you still imprinted on Yerina?"

He pushed away from her again, looking aghast and confused. "No. Of course I am not, or I couldn't be imprinted on you. It broke at Clairton. A full season ago."

"Okay." She moved her hands down to tap at his chest, pursing her lips. "So, this imprint thing. How *exactly* does it work?"

Govek brought a hand down into the water to curl around her hip. The tub was three quarters full and suddenly the tap cut off on its own. The room plunged into silence. She glanced up just as the pipe retreated and the door in the ceiling clicked shut. Magic was amazing.

Govek remained silent, so she pressed, "The women at Viravia's . . . they made it sound like it took time. Like you needed to have pretty strong feelings for someone before you were imprinted."

His throat worked in a gulp.

"Do you . . . have strong feelings for me?"

Finally, he met her eyes. His lips were set in a tight line.

"It's okay if you do," Miranda assured him. "It's *good* if you do."

His brows went up.

"I have pretty strong feelings for you too, or I wouldn't be sitting naked in your lap right now." She stroked his chest, and he shuddered under her. "I was only asking because the women made it seem like it wasn't really *possible* for you to be imprinted on me so fast."

"It . . . is not."

She waited, let him gather his thoughts.

"I saw you fall from the sky, Miranda, and in that single moment, the imprint hit. There are children's stories of instant imprints, but I've never heard of it being real."

"Oh," Miranda said. Her gut twisted a little. "Are you sure that you actually *are* imprinted then?"

"Yes. Very." Govek wrapped his other hand around her hips now too.

"You mentioned before that you think the Fades did it?"

"I do."

Miranda hummed, unsure she liked the idea of him being *forced* into this. "So, what does this imprint mean for us? You?"

"It . . . drives me to care for you."

Miranda raised her brows.

"The imprint thrums when you are content and when you show me affection. It makes me want to offer you boons and protect you from harm."

"So, you are forced to like me?"

Govek snorted. "No. I *do* like you, and that makes the imprint stronger, and thus, I want to offer you even better care. If I had found you annoying or unpleasant, it would have faded out. It may have started strong, but it is growing *stronger* because I find you so . . ." He paused to think, and Miranda held her breath. "Radiant."

Miranda felt her heart filling up and flooding over with warmth. "Wow. You really know how to flatter, don't you?"

"It is not flattery. It is the truth."

Her face went hot, and she used her hands to cover her cheeks.

Govek chuckled, and she managed the bravery to look up at him, not wanting to miss seeing him laugh. Dang, he looked so handsome when he was smiling. The deep lines of his face smoothed. His eyes were bright and twinkling.

"Radiant and *adorable*," he said with such warmth that a whole-body flush rolled through her.

She would have ducked under the water in embarrassment had his expression not shifted. His brows loosened, his lips curled, and his eyes softened, making her want to swoon.

"Oh gosh, look at you," she sighed.

He tipped his head in confusion, eyes skittering away for half a second before she touched his face, drawing his attention to her. She trailed her fingers from his temples to his chin.

"Miranda . . . that feels . . ." His eyes were closed, and his whole body went slack.

"There you go. All relaxed," she said, scratching his scalp again. The cut was so uneven. "I wonder what you would look like with longer hair."

"I . . . don't know."

"You run your hands through it so much when you're upset, you'd probably end up ripping it out." She pursed her lips and examined his head. "I'm surprised you don't cut yourself."

"Long hair isn't practical for hunting—" His words cut off as she pulled one of his hands off her hips and looked at his palm.

"The wounds are gone." She traced where his claws had pricked. "Do orcs naturally heal fast or is it the magic?"

"We heal fast."

"Thank you." She leaned in close to his ear. His scent of pine was intoxicating. "For telling me all the things you didn't want to. And now we can do something much more fun for the both of us."

"Hmm?" He squirmed under her.

She smirked. "I'mma teach you how to kiss."

# CHAPTER
# EIGHT

*GOVEK*

His eyes popped back open just as she was leaning in. Her plump, hot lips pressed into his, fitting them between his fangs like a dream and coaxing a growl from his throat. She bathed him in her sweet scent, her gentleness. Her tongue licked the seam of his lips.

He jerked in shock, going rigid. Miranda pulled away with a giggle that brought both confusion and delight. She was so fucking gorgeous with a smile on her face he could hardly stand it.

She didn't pause her attention for long. "Open your mouth, Govek."

Open his mouth? What the fuck was she saying? He would shred her tender tongue to tatters.

But then her thumb pressed into his chin, unrelenting and swift, and it caught him so off guard that his jaw went slack.

And her tongue snaked into his mouth.

A choked sound escaped him as the taste of her registered. Honeyed and rich. It was like nothing his brain could fathom, like the most intoxicating drug, like sweetness transcended from the realm of the Fades. He wanted more.

Giving into his blasted urges, Govek gripped the back of Miranda's head and pulled her in deeper. He opened his mouth wider and touched his tongue to hers.

He wanted to clamp down on it, to nibble at her lips and drink her up. To bite her until she was marked by him, branded as his and unable to escape.

Govek jerked away, unsettled. He had to regain his control, but *fuck*, she tasted so blasted *good.*

"Mm, Govek . . ." Miranda cooed, sidling in closer. She grazed her teeth along his lips, and he lost all his breath. "I want more . . ."

He would never be able to deny her anything, especially this. He kept a firm hold on all his darker needs as he teased, licked, and sucked her mouth. Copying her motions, she showed him how unbelievably blissful kissing could be. And how badly it made him ache. His body felt taut like a rope, wound so tight it might snap.

"Miranda," he managed between dueling his tongue with hers. "This is making me crazed . . ."

As if she wanted him to go completely wild, Miranda spread her legs wider, right over his aching cock. He was throbbing and desperate, and he could feel her hot folds with every twitch.

And she continued massaging her tongue with his, teasing and thrusting and moaning at the back of her throat.

His hands became tight bands around her arms as he resisted the urge to grind himself between her silky folds.

"Am I too good at this?" she asked, pulling away just enough for him to feel every word against his burning lips.

Her eyes fluttered open, and she looked *right at him*.

"Fuck," he snarled, shaking with need. He wanted to keep kissing her but didn't want to risk destroying this. He couldn't let her see him. "Turn around."

"No."

Her denial felt like the slice of a whip across his aching flesh. "Miranda—"

"I want to face you." She licked his bottom lip. "I want to see you." She nibbled gently. "I want to see you crumble under me,"—she clamped down on his lower lip, sucking, then releasing him with a wet smack—"see your eyes roll back and your jaw tremble."

He lost his breath as she slid away, moving her hips so his cock dragged between her legs, grazing her thighs, stroking her core. Firey pleasure shot through his groin, and he hissed a breath between his teeth as his member popped out between them.

The scent of her arousal rolled off her. She wanted him. *Him.*

But how long would that last?

Miranda's fingers danced down his chest, tracing his muscles. "You're so sexy, Govek. I want to watch you lose your mind."

He should deny her but the sight of her pale hand against his green flesh as it dipped below the waterline made his throat close.

Lower, *lower* . . . almost there.

Her fingertips grazed the head of his cock and pleasure licked up his spine. His hips rolled, forcing her to grip his shoulder with her free hand to steady herself. The tight hold of her soft hand amplified the pleasure, electrifying him. She was clinging *to* him. Not leaving.

Her other hand fisted tight and pumped his cock from base to tip.

"*Fuck*," he breathed. It felt so blasted good he was shocked he could get words out. Her grip eased so she could tease the head, stroking around the rim, grazing his length. Her touches were fumbling, explorative.

Her hand firmly gripped around him again and he lost all his breath. His rational thoughts winked out.

"Dang, you're huge." Miranda's reverent tone skewered him. "I can't even close my fingers around you. You really do put all my toys to shame."

Fuck, *fuck*. His hand snaked between their bodies. He wanted to touch her, to ready her.

He wasn't wearing the gloves and after the turmoil of this night he could not trust his control.

Govek gripped her wrist, stopping her from stroking him any further even as it made him want to weep. "I need to . . . go get gloves."

"Hmm?" Her tone was breathy and deep.

Fuck, she was looking at him *again*. "Let me turn you around."

"Nope."

His gut twisted.

"Gimme that hand." Miranda took his wrist, brought it down over her stomach, past her thigh.

His blood boiled in his veins and all his fight left him.

She pushed two of his fingers between her hot slick folds. They glided effortlessly in her dripping wet sheath. The curls tickled at his palm as she lowered herself and increased the pressure.

Fuck, it was *so* much better without the gloves. Without thick leather blocking her softness from his touch. He could feel her pussy throbbing, feel the swelling nub at the top that made her breath catch and her hips thrust when he flicked it. He could not believe she was gifting this to him again.

She threw back her head and let out a moan that licked fire into every corner of his mind. His body quaked with need. His mouth watered and his tongue twitched, wanting to feel that beautiful slit under it. To rake over her little nub until she was screaming and writhing and begging for more.

An icy snap of dread sliced into his guts and agony flashed into his mind. Memories of having his mouth on Yerina made his stomach churn. He'd been so raw and hopeful when he'd finally *won* her.

And so devastated when he'd ruined it.

"Govek?"

"Fuck." He wasn't with Yerina. He needed to let that go. Right now. He was with Miranda.

"*Mirrranda.*"

"Ooh, say my name like that again."

His gaze snapped to the heat of hers. Her eyes were half-mast and misty, her red lips parted as she panted, her cheeks pink.

He'd never seen anything more beautiful in all his days.

His fingers twitched between her folds again and her eyes rolled, showing more of the white, flooding him with triumph. He grew brave and dipped his finger deeper into her opening. He gathered up some of her wetness in the water, slicking his digit before bringing it back up to the hard nub hidden in her folds.

He swirled around it and was rewarded with her breath hitching. Her body trembled all over. Goosebumps broke out along her shoulder and he leaned in to lick them, caressing the rough texture with his tongue.

"Oh fuck, *Govek.*"

Dark triumph blazed through his mind as she cursed. It was so sweet. Almost as sweet as her skin.

He swirled his finger around the nub and her hips bucked, thighs jerking and jittering against him. She ground down into his hand, wanting a firmer touch and he let her, going still as she took control of the pace.

Fades watching her use his hand to stroke her throbbing pussy was a pleasure he'd never known. It flooded him with such heat he could feel it pulsing in his chest, churning his mind up with need. He groaned, his voice going so low it felt like a quake in his gut, "*Mirrrhanda.*"

"Oh god, Govek! Do that again!"

Ah *fuck*! She sounded so good. Tingling blasted through his whole body.

"*Mirrrhanda,*" he repeated. Her hazelnut eyes flashed before squeezing shut.

"Govek, *yes.*"

"*Mirrrhanda.*" He snarled into her ear and she bounced on him, clutching his hand tight, and thrusting her hips.

"I want you," she breathed. Her sweet breath fanned his face. "I want your cock."

He growled and trembled. "Yes. Turn around."

"No, like this."

A zing of panic dimmed his bliss, and he gripped her hip, trying to force her around quickly, but she clung to him, resisting.

"No, Govek. I want to face you."

She couldn't. It would ruin *everything*. "No."

"Yes."

He tried to move her again, but her nails dug into his shoulders, stinging.

"Govek," she said, her voice less breathy, her eyes clearer as she examined his face. Looking too close, seeing too much. "Should we stop?"

Agony exploded in his chest, slicing deep into his veins. His hand retreated from her core and snaked around her hip to grip her ass, as if that might stop her from abandoning him.

If she wanted to go, there was *nothing* he could do to stop her. He squeezed his eyes shut, breath shuddering.

"Govek?" The bliss drenched tone was gone from her voice. This is where she would scorn him. "Hey, tough guy. Sweetheart." Her hands raked against his scalp, and she moved closer.

He opened his eyes.

Miranda looked down at him with concern. Her lips were still red and parted. Her eyes flashed with confusion. "Govek, I'm—"

"Don't leave." His grip on her ass tightened.

She blinked.

"Don't leave, *please*."

"Oh," her voice warbled. "Govek, I . . ."

He gulped, waiting.

"I'm not leaving. I swear I won't."

She moved in close again, pressing her breasts to his chest, sidling her hot core nearer to his cock. It jerked in response, desperate.

"I'm sorry. That isn't what I meant. I just thought that maybe you weren't ready. That you might want to stop for now. I'm not leaving." She vowed again, lips grazing his. His heart pounded so loud in his ears he almost couldn't hear her. "I'm staying right here. With you."

He let out a long breath, willing his tension to go with it.

"I want you so bad, Govek," she said between kisses and nibbles. Her tongue soothed the seam of his lips before he finally gave in and met it with his own. She tasted divine.

"You're so sexy. And hot. And I want to watch you come."

His stomach twisted and flipped. "*What*?"

"I want to watch you fall apart," she said, her lips brushing his with every word. "I want to watch your expression when you explode with pleasure. In me. I want to feel your thick cock pulsing inside me as you fill me up."

Oh fuck, *oh fuck*! He couldn't catch his breath.

"I want you see your jaw slack with bliss and watch your eyes roll back and your body quiver." She began to roll her hips up as she spread her thighs. His grip on her loosened so she could move freely.

"I want to stroke your face while you reel with ecstasy. I want to shower you with kisses just like this." She bathed his face with her nibbling, grazing her lips along his cheeks, his nose, between his tusks.

She lowered herself over him, and her pussy stretched over the head of his cock, parting her slit. The hot bliss shot delicious lightning up his spine.

"I want to see you, Govek. I want to know that it's *you*."

Fades help him, she lowered herself more. The head of his cock popped into the sweet softness of her core. The heat was incredible, and he lost all his breath as spikes of bliss radiated from his groin, up into his chest. He couldn't breathe.

"My big, sexy, handsome, tough guy. Tough *orc*."

*Fades.*

Pleasure exploded behind his eyes, raging through him. He

gripped her ass again, trembling, his mind fracturing. He wanted to plunge deep, to fill her up.

But he might hurt her. *Fuck.*

Miranda leaned back. She looked right at his face. *Right at him.*

And her eyes sparkled and her lips quirked. "*My orc.*"

Then she pushed her ass out of his grip and sank onto his cock, taking him all the way to the hilt.

His control shattered.

Govek roared, and thrust his hips upward, forcing his cock deep in her wet core before gripping her ass up and slamming in to her again.

Miranda's eyes closed and she moaned as she squeezed around his shaft, fluttering and rippling. He could feel every tiny twitch and it pushed him to the brink of his control. The honeyed scent of her burst in his nose, destroying his senses. He was enveloped by her heat, her desire *for him.*

Her eyes flashed open, and she met his gaze.

The pleasure was so intense it was mind bending but still his instincts screamed, and he tried to hide away.

She wrapped her arms around his head, pressing her hands into his forehead. She forced his head back, his neck to extend.

She wouldn't fucking look away from him. Her eyes raked reverently over his face, and bliss drenched him as he pounded her pussy. Rolling his hips, he panted. He was dizzy. He couldn't get enough air.

Miranda's cries swirled around him, her pleading moans and begging words. "Don't stop. Right there. Oh, *Govek!*"

His name on her lips was his undoing. Ecstasy reared hot and fierce, gripping his gut and made his thighs spasm. He didn't want to be first. He had to get her off.

But Fades be fucked! She snapped her hips just right and

her nails dug into his scalp, and she moaned his name again and ecstasy rolled up his spine, exploded in his groin, and burst in his head.

He roared so loud his ears were ringing. His mind shattered with the bliss.

Miranda screamed too. Her pussy squeezed around his cock. She looked right into the face of his orgasm and *came*.

*Watching him made her come.*

The pleasure of that nearly undid him. He couldn't fathom this. Couldn't imagine anything more intense. More incredible. Delight like he'd never known quivered in every limb.

He squeezed her tight, shivering, slowly coming down. He didn't want this to end. He wanted to stay here just like this. But Miranda was coming down too, and there was nothing he could do about it.

She collapsed on his chest, breathing hard. He tightened his hold on her, afraid she would come back to her senses and decide to leave.

All was silent but for Miranda's ragged breathing and the pounding in his head from his heartbeat.

She sat up, away from him, and he forced him to let her go.

She cupped his face, looking into his eyes, and leaned in to kiss him. It was so tender, so gentle. It made his throat tighten.

"That was wonderful," she lingered a hot, wet kiss on his lower lip before pressing her forehead to his.

His cock pulsed with pleasure at her praise and her thighs twitched in response. Fuck, she was so gorgeous. And generous.

He didn't deserve her.

"You . . . watched," he said dumbly. His voice was like gravel.

Miranda leaned back again. Her smile was radiant. Pure perfection. A gift from the Fades themselves.

"Yeah, I watched." She smoothed his scalp with her gentle fingertips—sharply contrasting the rough way he usually clawed at his head—easing away any lingering fear and hurt. "And I'm going to watch every time from here on."

# CHAPTER
# NINE

*MIRANDA*

"Has Ms. Smill come in with her deposit yet?" Mr. Barker asked Miranda and she stared at him. He had white hair, and wore a pressed gray suit today. Laugh lines creased his worried eyes.

Blackridge Bank swirled around her. Long teller desks, pillar lights, checkered marble floor.

*She couldn't be here. She wasn't here.*

"Miranda? Are you all right?"

*This wasn't right. The bank looked distorted. The floor was jagged. The wood desk was fuzzy. The work screen was blank.*

"Did you skip breakfast again, Miranda? I restocked the break room. Why don't you take yours early and get something to eat?"

Only the view out the front windows was clear. The busy city street visible with dreary skies—and cars and people.

So many people.

"We-we have to get out of here. We have to—"

The air raid sirens pierced through her, rolling around in her brain. She covered her head, squeezing her eyes shut.

She was in the vent.

The weight crushed her. The metal snapped and groaned. Searing heat blazed all around her, burning her. She couldn't get out. She couldn't escape. She would be cooked alive.

Blinding light pierced her mind and she screamed.

She screamed so loud.

And her babies screamed with her.

*Oh god! She couldn't save them!*

"Miranda!"

She gasped, scrambling out of the nightmare, clawing and sputtering.

Govek held her. "I've got you. You are with me."

"They're dying!" Her voice didn't sound like her own. "They're dying. We have to get them out! We have to help them."

"Miranda, it's a dream. Just a dream."

His voice was steady, firm, and it yanked her back to reality.

The reality that her babies weren't dying anymore. They were beyond help. They were already—

No. *No!* It wasn't true.

They hadn't suffered like she had. They hadn't been burned or crushed. Their parents had saved them. They'd made it to the ocean. To Faeda. Just like she had.

They *had*.

She pressed her head into Govek's chest, breathing in his rich pine scent, soaking up his warmth. She stroked the mattress under her fingers, moving them up to the mountain carving at the head of the bed. She traced the peak and breathed in the scent of the wood.

Clean air, no exhaust fumes or chemical undertones.

Govek's body felt a little tense under her as he pressed his mouth to the top of her head. She felt him gulp against her scalp.

Then he let out a very low, tender rumble.

The sound was like nothing she'd ever heard, like a buttery vibration easing away every drop of tension her muscles held. It rolled over her skin, wiped out all her thoughts and soothed her mind back into drowsy bliss.

"Thank you. That's good," she whispered, wanting him to keep it up. And he did. His body relaxed at her praise, and he growled again. "That feels good."

He let out a pleasure drenched huff, a chuckle of disbelief. He growled again, and she shut her eyes. They lay like that for a long while, but unlike the other three times she'd been woken from nightmares that night, her mind refused to slip back into slumber.

"I'll get your water," Govek finally said. His voice gruff from exhaustion.

"Not yet." She curled into him. She stroked his bare chest, and he huffed. "I'm sorry I've woken you up so many times tonight."

"It is fine, Miranda."

"Was I rescued by an orc or a saint?"

He didn't respond, only moved away slightly so he could reach the cup on the bedside table. She'd forgotten how big he was. How easily he could reach across the massive bed.

Morning light was barely breaking through the bedroom window. Massive dark trees loomed around them. A subtle breeze blew leaves past the glass. The crackle of the fire from the living room was soothing, dappling shadows on the wood walls. Everything was naturally built. No plastic. Barely any metal, even.

She took a sip of the crisp water. It tasted unreal. So pure it barely had any flavor to it.

Nothing like Earth.

She took a deep breath and tried to push the memories of desert waste and burning chemicals out of her mind. Even before the bombs dropped, water had to be triple filtered so it could be drinkable. Five times in the case of Riverside Daycare. It was one of their selling points. A twelve-stage filter —only the best for them. Her babies.

Her stomach rolled and her eyes burned, and she thought she might upchuck the water she'd just had.

"Miranda?"

Govek tipped her chin up, and she looked at his unearthly face. Green gold eyes, light emerald complexion, strong jaw with a slight underbite, pointed tipped ears. She grazed her fingers along one and he shivered.

He was not of Earth and that fact brought her endless comfort.

"I'm sorry," she said, withdrawing her hand. "I'm sorry I keep waking you up."

The nightmares just wouldn't stop. No matter how hard she tried to block out all her painful memories, they kept getting *worse*.

"All is well, Miranda. I do not mind."

She shot him a smile before resting her head on his chest.

He took the cup from her and set it on the table again. His pillows smelled of him, musky pine.

She chose to use his shoulder instead of the pillow. "How much time do we have left to sleep?"

"Not much. It's later than it seems. The day's grow short as winter comes in."

"Hmm." She glanced out at the quiet dawn. "Do you think the seer will be at the announcement?"

Govek hesitated slightly. "Perhaps."

"I just want to *know*," Miranda said slowly. "I'm certain he'll be able to help me recover my memories and tell me what happened to them. I know it's a long shot, but do you think . . . do you think maybe they lived? The babies I took care of?"

Govek tensed under her.

She looked up into his face and found his brow furrowed. "I know it's crazy. I know that. Really. But just like . . . it's possible, right? *I* lived. And there were those road signs. Someone must have gotten them working, so why couldn't it have been them? I'm pretty sure Josephine's dad even worked for the Highway Department. It could have been him and they could be here now. Lost in the woods like I was, just waiting for us to find them. And the seer would know where they are, right?"

It was insane. She knew that.

But . . . what if?

"Seer Evythiken's power is immeasurable," Govek finally said. "If anyone can unlock your lost memories and find other humans from Earth, it would be him."

"Yeah." Miranda said, trying to push her stupid hope out of her brain even as it sunk deeper. "Can we try to see him today? Even if he isn't at the announcement?"

"Yes. We should also see Hovget, the healer."

"I don't need a healer." Miranda said. "I'm not hurt."

"We need to ensure you're healthy, Miranda."

"I don't . . ." She chewed her lip. Being told she was healthy was almost more terrifying than being told she wasn't.

She should be irradiated, but she wasn't. She should have been burned alive, but she hadn't. She should have died from falling off that cliff, but she didn't.

Nothing made sense.

"He could also have something that might soothe your nightmares and allow you to rest well."

Guilt chewed at the edges of her mind as she looked into Govek's eyes, noting the dark green bags under them.

He needed rest too. He'd been her rock from the moment she'd fallen out of the sky.

She leaned in and kissed his warm cheek, right next to his tusk. "Thank you, Govek. For taking care of me. You really are a sweetheart."

He huffed out a laugh that rumbled through his chest under her ear. "Fuck, woman. The things you call me."

"What? You don't like sweetheart? Tough guy is better, huh?"

"At least tough guy is an accurate description."

She smiled. "I think that's the first time I've heard you give yourself a compliment."

He shifted uncomfortably even as he pulled her closer. He turned his head toward her, carefully lowering his nose into her hair. He tried to breathe deep without her noticing, but she *totally* did.

And it felt good. His attraction to her was so obvious all the time and it soothed that bone-deep wound from her childhood that had never fully healed. "Dang, years of therapy, and it turns out all I really needed was an orc who was magically stuck to me like Velcro."

There was a slight pause before Govek grumbled. "What do crows have to do with imprinting?"

Miranda gave into laughter so hearty, she actually had to sit up and wipe her eyes. "Oh my god, Govek. That's not . . . never mind."

"Are you . . . upset by the imprint?"

"No. Not at all. Not even a little bit. It's great actually. Quiets all those orphan abandonment issues that like to pop up from time to time. That's probably not healthy, is it? Liking that you're magically attached to me. But whatever. I've always *liked* clingy. That's why I worked with toddlers. They fall in love with you *instantly* for the simplest things and try to follow you, even into the bathroom. Not that I want you to watch me pee, that's not what I'm saying, I just—"

"Miranda?" Govek brushed the small of her back.

She collected her thoughts. "Anyway, what I'm saying is you can be clingy with me—as much as you want. If I don't like it, I'll tell you and we can work it out. Together. Okay?"

Govek's eyes widened, and she couldn't decide if his expression was one of surprise or wonder. Regardless, it was good, and she smiled, resting on him again.

"Miranda?"

"Yeah?"

"I will never abandon you."

He said this easily, as if he really meant it, and it was the simplest thing in the world to promise.

She looked into his eyes again and the sincerity there made her chest grow tight. She squeezed around Govek's middle and pressed a kiss to his cheek that she was certain didn't even come close to reciprocating how good he'd made her feel.

"You sure know how to say exactly the right thing," Miranda said, her eyes sliding shut as she listened to the steady drum of his heart under her ear.

A knock sounded from the living room.

"Someone's at the door?" Miranda asked, trying to sit up, but Govek quickly pulled her back down.

"Fuck them."

"The same way you fucked me last night?" she teased, forcing a chuckle out of him.

And then his breath caught. "You're bleeding."

"I'm bleeding?" She didn't feel hurt, only mildly sore around the thigh area and some achiness in her lower stomach that indicated she was about to—*oh, frick.*

"Uh," she forced him to let her sit up, looking down between her legs. She'd bled on his sheets. Dang it. "I'm so sorry. I can do the laundry. And do you know where I could find some pads or something?" Did they even have anything like that here?

Govek ripped the blanket off without preamble and she yelped as cold air blasted her.

The agonized expression on his face, joined by his claws slinking out and his body shuddering with withheld fury had her heart dropping. "I injured you."

"No," she insisted, quickly. "No, no. You did not. I'm just—"

Another harsh knock sounded. This time followed by the sound of a woman's voice.

"You are fucking bleeding, Miranda. Only I could have caused this."

Another harsh knock at the door.

"I'm on my period, Govek. That's all," Miranda assured him. "Who is that?" If it was one of the nicer women, then she could probably ask them for supplies.

"What the fuck is that?"

"What is *what*?" Miranda asked as the pounding became more insistent.

138

Govek got out of the bed, wrenched open the trunk, and threw the dress she'd gotten the night before at her. "We need to get you to a healer," Govek said, too loudly. "Put that on."

A muffled cry sounded at the door. "Govek, let me in."

"Is that Viravia?" Miranda asked, obeying his command to get dressed and starting for the doorway. "I can ask her for pads."

"Fuck," Govek raged, storming up behind her. "Fine." He passed her by and started for the front door, only to stop, frown with confusion and go to the back door instead.

He wrenched it open so hard Miranda suddenly knew how the front door had been ripped off its hinges.

Viravia scampered back, eyes wide in the bright morning light and her cloak hood tucked up tight around her hair. She held a wicker basket held tight in her arms. "G-Govek, where is Miranda?"

"I'm here," Miranda called as she entered the living room still buttoning her dress.

"Take her to the healer, Viravia," Govek demanded, walking all the way to the kitchen.

"Yes," Viravia said, rushing inside, putting down the basket on the couch. Her warm hands curled around Miranda's shoulders. The warmth of them soaked through the dress. "Come this way. It's all right."

"What?" Miranda shot her eyes back to Govek, who was looking pale and horror-stricken, and her stomach knotted. "What the—what is going on? I don't need a healer."

"I damaged you. Get her aid, Viravia."

"I'm not going anywhere without you," Miranda snapped, forcing the woman's hands off her shoulders. "And you didn't hurt me. I told you. I'm on my period."

"Period?" Viravia asked cautiously.

"Menstrual cycle. Monthly bleeding? Aunt Flow? Crimson tide? Govek didn't knock me up, so now my body is furious and intends to torture me for the next four or five days."

"Ah, yes, I understand," Viravia said quickly. "So, you *don't* need a healer."

"Not unless you've got pain killers or something cause the cramps are worse than a sledgehammer to the gut, but—"

"What the fuck are you talking about?" Govek demanded, looking between them. "You're bleeding, Miranda."

"For crying out loud"—Miranda pinched her nose—"it's too bloody early for a sex ed talk." She snorted, shaking her head. "Though I guess not too early to get all *bloody*."

No one laughed.

Viravia was pale, eyes averted, and Govek had his fists balled hard enough he was probably cutting himself again and Miranda groaned. "Oh my god. I'm *not* hurt, Govek. This is going to happen every month. I could get super detailed and complicated but I'mma save that for *after* I've had whatever equivalent of coffee you've got."

"Every month?" Govek asked carefully.

"Yes. For most women, it's a regular occurrence, and it's completely natural and I do *not* need help and you did *not* do anything to cause it. Other than, as I said, not get me pregnant. But that's a good thing where we're concerned."

He remained silent.

"Govek, if you had hurt me bad enough to make me bleed you would have noticed while we were cleaning up last night."

Realization flashed in his eyes, but he still shook his head and stammered. "But Yerina said that—" He looked away, wrenched his hand through his hair, but wouldn't meet her eyes.

What did his ex have to do with any of this?

Viravia, bless her, quickly changed the subject. "I brought you clothing, Miranda. And if Govek has fresh linen, I can show you how to fashion something to keep yourself clean."

"I'm assuming I just bundle up that linen and put it in my underwear?"

Viravia nodded.

"Then I'll be fine on my own." She sighed heavily. She'd never looked forward to her period before, but now she was *really* not looking forward to it.

"All right."

Then the woman just stood there.

"What else, Viravia?" Govek grated.

"Well, I . . . I heard about the announcement today," Viravia ventured, "Kar-er . . . the *warlord's* announcement. I just wanted to know if you knew what it was about."

Govek's eyes flashed nervously to Miranda. "I do not."

"Didn't you talk to him last night?"

"Yes, but all he said was that I must be there, which means we need to make ready. Now."

"Then, I'll go. Miranda, feel free to visit anytime if you need anything."

"Thank you."

Miranda waited until the door closed behind the woman before turning to Govek. "So, what exactly did your ex-girlfriend tell you about periods?"

"Nothing."

"She made you think they were *your* fault somehow? That you hurt her? If so, that's really *not* okay."

Govek said nothing but his expression revealed everything Miranda needed to know. Dang, no wonder the guy had so many hang-ups.

She crossed over to him and picked up one of his hands,

forcing it to uncurl. To his credit, he only tried to pull away once, even though his claws were out. Little pricks of blood dotted his palms.

"We're gonna break this habit of yours, Govek," Miranda muttered, reaching for another cloth on the counter even though the wounds were already closed. Dang, orcs healed fast.

"I am sorry."

"Lean down here."

He obeyed, and she planted a kiss on his lips. One that she'd *meant* to be quick and sweet but turned a little too heated. "Damn, Govek. You taste too good." She kissed his cheek and patted his chest. "How long do we have before we have to leave? Do you have any food?"

He grumbled a curse under his breath and looked around. "We will get you something at the hall."

"Okay. Let me get cleaned up a little. I need to pee."

She freshened in the bathroom and got her cloak on. By the time she was done, Govek had finished dressing and the sight of his tight button-down shirt and loose pants had her warring with herself.

"What?" Govek asked, brow furrowed.

"I honestly can't decide if I like you better shirtless or like this." She stroked his broad chest, and he huffed.

"This is the only shirt I have left. I will have to get more from the storeroom," he said as she pulled away. He went to the front door and was careful, but it snapped off the other hinge, anyway.

Miranda burst into laughter at his disgruntled expression. "Oh man, your brute strength is really getting the best of you now. You better be careful or the whole house will be rubble."

She hurried out, and he propped it in the doorway. "I promise to repair it."

"Eh, whatever. It doesn't look like anyone is going to rob us way out here." Miranda noted how far away the nearest homes were.

He fell into step beside her on the path, frost glittered in the sunlight, making the forest look like a glazed donut. Dang, she was hungry. She hoped the food in the hall would be good.

"Why is your house so far out here?"

He didn't respond, but his jaw was set, tucked all the way up again. She took his arm in hers and tipped her head up toward the sky.

Her breath caught from the sight above her head. "Govek, what is *that*?"

High above, the canopy of the huge trees blotted out most of the sunlight with their orange and red leaves. It was thick enough that it should have been impossible for the rays to get through, except some of the leaves weren't colored. They were *clear*, as if made of glass. Streams of sunlight cast through the clear leaves and brightened up the canopy until it appeared to glow.

"What are those?" Miranda asked in wonder, her eyes fixed to the sight. The leaves glittered, sparkling as they swayed.

"Those are the leaves of the Great Rove Tree," Govek said, pointing in the direction they were walking.

Miranda spied a truly massive trunk in the distance. So huge that it was almost difficult to comprehend among the rest of the forest. It stretched far above the others, breaking into thousands of branches and spiraling into the trees surrounding it. The glittering leaves reflected the bright red and yellow of the surrounding fall trees so vividly it looked like that area of the forest was on fire.

"Wow." Miranda breathed. Her throat constricted. "It's so . . . are they made of glass or . . ."

Govek studied her expression a moment before turning his attention to the canopy above. They'd just reached a more well-kept path and a few tree dwellings surrounded them. He moved away from her, and she thought he might be going to visit a neighbor. Instead, he selected a medium-sized tree without a house in it and shoved it. Hard.

The tree shook, swaying the branches, leaves rained down around them in a torrent. Miranda burst into laughter, covering her head from the onslaught.

Govek was back at her side a moment later, smiling lightly, and holding out one of the crystalline leaves for her to see.

She gasped, taking it gently, but it wasn't nearly as fragile as she thought. It felt like a leaf, was shaped like a leaf, but visually, it was like it was made of water. She could see her hands through it and her own blurry reflection on the outside.

"It's amazing."

"Yes," Govek agreed. She shot him a smile as he explained. "The Rove Tree's leaves don't fall in the autumn. They remain above to protect the clan from harsh weather. It was one of the Fades first creations."

Miranda looked up again, so drawn to the sight of the tree that she hardly noticed her surroundings until someone cleared their throat nearby.

She jerked to look, finding several orcs had left their homes and were watching intently.

They looked *very* different from Govek. Although they were similar in color, these orcs were slender, tall, and lacked the brawny muscles Govek sported. Almost like the difference between a male model and a construction worker. A scented candle versus a roaring bonfire. Flavored water next to a quad shot.

Miranda grinned. She'd always preferred buff over puff.

But all amusement died when a few of the orcs began openly whispering to one another and pointing. One even stepped in their direction.

Govek let out a growl of frustration so deep Miranda thought an earthquake might have been starting up.

And of course, the thrill shot right through her. Her thighs clenched as she squirmed. Damn, his grumbling, and its ability to get her all fired up.

In a flash, Govek's fury evaporated, and his head whipped toward her. His nostrils flared in a way that was far too telling.

"Oh, don't tell me," she gasped out, trying to stifle her arousal even as his hungry expression began to torture her. "Your sense of smell can't possibly be *that* good."

"It is," he confirmed, and she couldn't tell if she wanted to spontaneously combust or bury herself alive. "As it is for all orcs."

*All?* Her cheeks were rivaling the brightest of the leaves as her gaze shot to the orcs who'd been watching. She caught the tail end of their alarmed and shocked expressions before they bolted in the other direction.

Oh god. "Don't tell me they're also going to the hall?"

Govek's eyes narrowed. "They likely are."

She let out a ragged sigh. "Any chance they're going to forget about what they just smelled?"

"You are embarrassed?"

"Well, yeah. I'm gettin' all hot and bothered in public from just the sound of your voice. They're gonna think I can't control myself—which I can't—but still."

"You needn't be," Govek assured, placing his hot hand to the small of her back to get her moving again. "The scent of female arousal, in varying degrees, is quite common among our clan."

"If it's so common, then why did those guys look like they'd just been slapped with a salmon?"

Govek blinked before bursting with booming laughter that spread warmth all the way through her. "Fuck, woman. You are going to ruin me with your words."

"It will be the fun kind of ruining though, right?" she teased as he got himself under control. His laughter was wonderful, full and rich with a smile that completely transformed him. Her heart was going to burst right out of her chest if he kept looking at her the way he was now.

His laughter finally petered out as he looked up the path. She followed his gaze. Some of the orcs had stopped to openly gawk at them. Even at this distance, she could see that they were disapproving.

She was starting to understand why Govek had left.

# CHAPTER
# TEN

*GOVEK*

He looked down at Miranda, finding her brow furrowed and her lips pursed, as she watched the males mutter among themselves. She saw them look scornfully in his direction. Her eyes did not linger on any one in particular, but Govek inevitably felt rage burn away his humor at the thought that her affection might turn away from him and toward one of his brethren.

Before he could do anything foolish, she spoke. "So . . . I gotta ask, why *does* everyone here dislike you so much?"

He startled at the question, which he was certain he'd answered well enough the night before. "I have committed many atrocities, including the *murder* of humans, Miranda."

"Govek, you killed soldiers that tortured your brother to death. That's not the same as killing someone at random," Miranda said as if the murder of her own kind didn't unsettle her.

Just what kind of world had her Earth been?

"And isn't your cousin a *warlord*? Does he fight his war without killing? Don't other orc soldiers also kill in battle?"

She didn't understand, and why should she? She wasn't from this world. She did not know the will of the Fades.

Or what kind of abomination he was.

But she would find out. As much as it pained him to speak on this, Govek was determined that she hear it from his own lips rather than those of another.

"The clan of Rove Wood isn't like other orc clans. Those born under the Great Rove Tree are imbued with magic. Blessed. Chosen *specifically* by the Fades to conjure their power."

"I kinda noticed that." Miranda glanced briefly at the males who were walking ahead of them at a reasonable distance. They looked back often, ensuring Govek did not come too close. "They're a lot scrawnier."

Govek blinked. "Yes, they are. They fit the human ideals far better."

"Oh, I wouldn't say *that*. Maybe some women like a pretty boy, but I like my guys to have some meat."

As if to prove her words, she slid her hand beneath his shirt and stroked his abdomen, dipped her fingers between the accentuated bulges of his abs. He shivered. *Fuck!* Her touch felt good. It blazed through his mind like a balm and made him want to fall to his knees, babbling her praise.

"And Karthoc had *almost* as much muscle as you. He's your leader, right? So, don't try to tell me that having brawn is what makes your clan wary of you."

Fades help him! His blood boiled thinking about her noticing Karthoc's body. He managed to gulp down the embers burning in his throat. "The orcs of Rove Wood do not have as much muscle *because* they can use magic."

"So, they're built like pansies because they can do magic? Does magic suck up testosterone or something?"

Govek could not help snorting in amusement at the comparison between Rove Wood orcs and delicate flowers. "That is the Fades design. Orcs either have magic or strength, but not both. Both is dangerous, deadly."

"Oh," Miranda said slowly, looking up at him. "But you have both."

"Yes." He was a wretch for being so relieved that she didn't instantly understand how dangerous he was and bolt. Magic was powerful and should never be wielded by those who lacked control over their own violent rage.

"I have worked hard all my life to keep my magical gifts under control. My studies ended early in my youth when it became apparent I was growing like the warrior orcs, rather than taking the slender shape of those from Rove Wood. I have been kept away from group communions, where magical energy is thick, separated from celebrations where conjuring's would be performed, and given a home on the outskirts so that when I do lose control, it is less likely to cause irreparable destruction."

He'd worked so blasted hard to keep everyone in his clan safe over the many seasons, and *still* mistakes had been made. Orcs had been hurt by his fury. Chaos had been wrought by him. He could not be trusted.

"You've lost control before, right?" Miranda asked, her voice flat. "Or did they isolate you without just cause?"

Govek gulped. But she would hear this from *someone*. It may as well be him. "I have lost control *many* times. Not only am I far more prone to fighting, but the strikes I land are imbued with my magic, so they are more deadly. I have cracked tables in half with a single blow. Taken down trees.

Even my preference for hunting betrays my tendency toward violence." He swallowed hard as painful memories flooded his mind. "Once when I grew angry in the hall, I erupted soup boiling in the cauldrons and burned many in the process. That is why I am banned from eating there."

Miranda's face took on an oddly flat countenance and her voice was firm as she said, "If they had let you continue your magic studies, would you have better control over it?"

Govek blinked. "What?"

"They stopped you from learning, right? If they hadn't done that, hadn't isolated you . . ." Miranda shook her head.

"Miranda." He swallowed thickly but worked the words out. "My magic is not just *tainted* by my anger, it is caused by it."

Her brows rose and the calm reaction gave him strength to elaborate.

"Unlike my brethren, whose magic is sparked by meditation and serene control, *my* conjuring's are fueled by fury. To connect to the Fades, I must be in the throes of rage or grief. *This* is what makes my magic so dangerous and difficult to control."

He'd said it. He'd gotten it out. He watched Miranda's face, and his breath caught, stomach twisting. Waiting.

Her expression crumbled and shock spiked down his spine.

"Oh Govek. I'm so sorry. That's awful."

He sputtered, words catching on his tongue before he could push them out. "Why are *you* apologizing?"

Miranda wrapped her arms around his, and pressed her warm head against him as they walked. "Because I've had you do a bunch of magical favors for me. And in order to *do* them, you have to feel *bad*. I don't want you having to feel pain or anger just to make my life easier."

He blinked rapidly. "It's . . . fine, Miranda. I truly do not mind. I've been performing magic all of my life. It is unavoidable in this clan, as you saw by how many things within my home require magic to function. That is why I was given a home on the outskirts to begin with. It was for everyone's protection."

"So, you've been completely isolated from your clan almost your entire life because they didn't want to help you?"

"Help with *what*?"

"They could have found ways for you to live without having to use magic so much. And there are *loads* of ways to help anger issues, Govek. They could have helped you if they tried. Honestly, isolating you probably made it worse. It's pretty shitty that they made you live all the way out there and wouldn't even let you celebrate holidays with them."

He shook his head. She didn't understand. "My father did what he needed to do to keep the clan safe."

Her eyes flashed with anger and she came to a halt. "You mean the chief. Your dad, the *chief,* was the one that alienated you?"

"No," Govek said quickly. "No, it was my choice to keep myself separated."

"So, *you* picked that house at the edge of the clan?"

"No, my father assigned it, but I went willingly."

"And how old were you when you started living there?"

Govek's brow furrowed, not quite understanding why that was relevant. He had to think about it a moment because he honestly couldn't recall. "Seven summers or so."

The anger evaporated from her face, and he almost managed a breath until pain replaced it. "Seven. You were *seven* years old when you had to go live out there. Alone."

"Yes."

She shook her head. "You were a *baby*."

Govek jerked in shock. "I assure you I was not. I was twice the size of other Rove orcs my age."

Her lower lip trembled, and she stepped toward him. "Come here. Just . . . dang it."

Her voice broke as she wrapped her arms around his neck. Govek could not fathom why she was so upset by this information. "Orcs are not humans, Miranda. I was perfectly capable of taking care of myself."

"All orcs get their own homes at seven?"

"Well . . . no," he mumbled. "But it had to be done."

"Stop it," she said, squeezing harder. "Just . . . stop."

So, he did. He was enjoying the lush feel of her curled around him too much to speak anyway. Her honeyed scent and warm body and firm breasts pressed into his chest.

"I'm not going to argue about this with you right now, but damn." Miranda reached up to scratch at the base of his neck, and he nearly shivered. "Why the heck did you *stay* here? If they were treating you so badly, why did you *stay*?"

"They were not treating me badly," Govek insisted. "They have every right to be afraid."

"Karthoc didn't seem afraid of you. Why didn't you go live with him a long time ago?"

He wasn't. In fact, Karthoc's powerful warriors had accepted him into their fold when they had traveled to Clairton. But until then, Govek hadn't thought any other orcs would want to give him sanctuary. What chief would want to harbor a male so dangerous? Karthoc had invited him, but that did not mean the rest of the clan would accept him.

And aside from that. "Tavggol was here." His elder brother had been the only orc that Govek had considered a close confidant. Tavggol was the only one who came to visit regularly, brought him food, celebrated the seasonal shifts, foraged with him, fished with him, and even invited him to join his friends occasionally.

Miranda tightened her hold on him again, turning her face so she could nuzzle his cheek. He relished every gentle touch she gave him.

"If I had left, I would not have met you," he said before he realized the words were forming.

But before embarrassment at the telling statement could sink in, Miranda pulled him down by his arm and kissed him. She grazed her lips along his cheek and up the bridge of his nose before finding his lips and teasing him into growling.

Fuck, he wished he could open his mouth to taste her, but he couldn't risk lowering his jaw while they were still in the clan. He would have to wait.

"I'm glad I met you too, Govek. And it seems you had the perfect skill set to save me. The strength to protect me from that wild cat and the magical power to break us into the mines so we could escape that tornado."

He stilled. He had not thought of it that way.

"Govek!"

The scent of Hovget registered before Govek saw the male storming down the paths toward them. A few of the other males stopped to watch, and Govek could hardly blame them. Of all the orcs in Rove Wood, Hovget was one of the few with the courage to be blunt with him.

And judging from the healer's tense scowl, Hovget was certainly going to be blunt.

"Who's that?" Miranda asked as Govek released her from his grip.

"Hovget, the healer."

"No, the woman behind him? Is she friendly or . . .?"

153

Govek hadn't noticed that Hovget's mate, Wellia, had followed. The woman was a skilled healer as well, and quite a bit younger than Hovget, which had caused quite a stir when they began their relationship seven summers prior. Many still thought Wellia should be with a younger orc. One who was not too old to bear sons.

"Govek, what are you doing going to the hall? I expected you to come see me first. Blast, I expected you to show *last night*. Why didn't you allow the woman to come get checked by me or Wellia?"

Govek gritted his teeth, tucking his mouth up higher until his gums stung. There was no point in explaining his reasoning.

"He didn't stop me from doing anything. I didn't want to go. I still don't."

Hovget's sharp eyes landed on Miranda. He was one of the taller males, and though his slender form made him seem frail, Govek knew he had great strength. He'd seen Hovget haul an unconscious orc onto an exam table with little more than a heaving grunt.

"You did not want to be examined? Were you not traveling through the woods for multiple days?" Hovget asked with a scowl at Miranda that made Govek want to rip his graying hair out of his scalp.

"Well, yes, but Govek took care of me."

"You scent of blood," Hovget said, and Miranda instantly bristled.

"I'm menstruating. On my period," she turned to Wellia. "What do you guy's call it here cause I'm tired of the weird looks?"

"Do you mean . . . having your cycle?" Wellia asked, mostly whispering.

Govek felt flattened. So, this *was* a normal occurrence for women. He *hadn't* been too rough and injured Yerina every moon.

He hadn't needed to bend over backward offering the woman copious boons in apology or stay up night after night racked with guilt wondering what exactly he'd done to cause her harm so he could ensure never to do it again.

His fists curled.

"Right, I'm on my cycle," she said to Hovget rather loudly. "I'm Miranda, by the way. Perhaps you should tell me your name before you interrogate me?"

Hovget straightened, embarrassment spreading color into his green cheeks. "I . . . apologize. Newcomers are rare in these woods. I am Hovget, the healer for this clan."

"And I'm Wellia." The woman hurried forward, dark, curly hair bouncing with every step. "Welcome to Rove Wood. We're very glad to have you. Aren't we, Hovget?" She shot her mate a hard look.

"Yes." Hovget said quietly, looking at Govek again. "I am also sorry that the other women from Estwill didn't make it."

The accusation sunk deep into Govek's gut and stirred up fire.

"I'm not from Estwill and there were never any other women. I don't know what crazy rumors are going around, but Govek saved me," Miranda insisted. "And I don't want an exam. There's nothing wrong with me."

"Miranda, you should," Govek said as coaxingly as he could under the circumstances. She was so adamant, but blast it, she could be injured and not know it. Or become ill suddenly. Hovget's skills may catch something early.

"I'm. Fine," Miranda said so forcefully that Govek wondered what might actually have her so defensive. What were doctors like on Earth?

"It really won't take long at all," Wellia interjected, ringing her plump hands. "And we can do it right here. We don't have to go back to the healing house if you don't want to."

"You want to give me a physical in the middle of the street?"

"It's done with magic," Govek said, choosing his words carefully. "Hovget will only need to hover his hands over your head, and his conjuring will draw your condition to him."

"Magic, huh?" Miranda said softly. "And if something is wrong with me?"

Govek's gut twisted. "Then we will treat it."

Miranda looked a little more stricken. "And . . . if there isn't?"

Govek could not discern why being unwell was less upsetting than being well. "Miranda, you already think you are fine. Would this not just confirm that?"

She hummed softly, pursing her pink lips together and crossing her arms. The wind caught up her brown hair, displaying her neck.

She was so beautiful, he couldn't catch his breath.

What if she was sick?

"Please, Miranda?" Govek asked softly, ignoring the wide-eyed look his pleading earned from Hovget. "For me, will you?"

She groaned. "Fine. Okay. Just . . . whatever. It's okay."

Hovget approached and Govek tensed. "You need to release her, Govek, or you'll get muddled in."

Govek knew that, but he still hesitated a moment, his touch lingering on Miranda's back before finally stepping aside.

"I just stand here?" Miranda asked as Hovget raised his hands up.

"Yes," he said, closing his eyes.

For a long moment, the only sounds were the wind in the trees and the subtle muttering of nearby orcs. Govek's chest grew tight as he watched the waves of air shift around Miranda as Hovget's magic dipped into her body.

Had Govek been allowed to learn magic, he could conjure this himself. Or a minor version of it, at least.

Govek stilled, brow furrowed.

This was the first time he'd ever *wanted* to perform a magical skill.

"Done. She's well. No issues."

"A-are you sure?" Miranda asked.

"Yes."

"No radiation—er, I mean . . . poison?"

"Poison?" Wellia asked, approaching Miranda. "Were you also attacked by the boar?"

"You know about that?" Miranda tipped her head. "Man, gossip sure does fly here, doesn't it?"

"Yes. We have heard. Goblin poison attached to a boar's tusks, right?"

"Yes."

"I want a sample of your blood, Govek." Hovget was already reaching into his gray leather cloak for a vial. "Chief Ergoth said you would not consent, but I must insist on it."

"You're gonna take a sample of his blood right *here?*" Miranda asked, looking between them in shock.

"Yes," Hovget shot her a confused look.

"But it's not sterile."

"Sterile?" Wellia asked, coming even closer to Miranda now. "What do you mean by that? And where are you from, Miranda? Everyone says you come from Estwill."

"Oh, uh . . . that's a long story . . ." Miranda glanced at Govek, her expression tight.

157

"I found her lost in the woods. And I consent to give you some blood. Make it quick. Karthoc wanted us at the announcement."

Hovget uncorked his vial. "Hold still." He extended his index claw. Govek balled his fists to hide his own, which had unsheathed at the sight. Hovget wasn't a threat, but his worthless hands didn't seem to understand that.

"Wait, you're seriously just gonna cut him open right here?" Miranda shook her head.

"Yes," Hovget muttered as Govek lifted his shirt. "Looks like it left a small scar. How did you heal it?"

"Miranda brought water from the Spring of the Fades."

"Hmm. That should have healed it completely. There shouldn't be a remaining scar," Hovget said just before he slashed into Govek's hide.

Govek did not flinch, but Miranda did. She sucked in a hard breath and stepped to his side, taking his arm, rubbing it as if to offer comfort.

Govek soaked it up like the desperate wretch he was.

"There," Hovget said after collecting a full vial. "Done. Thank you."

Govek shrugged. "Can you use it to trace which faction of the Waking Order it comes from?"

"I don't know. I'm going to experiment. I might need more."

"Fine."

"It's already scabbed over," Miranda said, grazing her fingertips right near the wound. Govek worked not to shiver.

"That's all then. Wellia, let's return to the healing house before—"

"Wait." Miranda tightened her hold on his arm. "Do you

have . . . Do you have anything that could recover lost memories?"

"Lost memories?" Wellia asked, tipping her head.

Hovget tucked the vial of blood into his coat. "You have lost some of your memories?"

"Yeah, uh . . ." She looked to Govek for help.

"She's been through a trial. Some things that occurred during that trial have been lost to her mind."

"This isn't uncommon. Human minds are weaker and often strive to block unpleasant memories."

Miranda tensed, eyes narrowing when Hovget called her weak. Govek stifled his amused grin.

"I might be able to dislodge some of it with my magic. It might be painful."

"No," Govek said just as Miranda agreed. He snapped his gaze to his mate. "He said it would hurt you, Miranda."

"A little pain is worth remembering, Govek."

"The pain would not linger afterward," Hovget assured them. "Unless the memories recovered were incredibly painful."

Govek gritted his teeth, stomach rolling. He did not want to see his mate in *any* pain. No matter how short. And the Fades only knew what horrors Hovget would dredge up.

"I want to do it," Miranda said firmly, releasing Govek's arm, leaving him cold. "What do I need to do?"

"Miranda, no," Govek said. His guts were twisted about this, warning him. "This isn't the way."

"I have to at least try."

"No—"

"Govek," Miranda said, hard and clipped. Her eyes flashed with the kind of anger that made him ice over. "I'm doing this. You can either help me or step aside."

Fear snapped in his spine.

She would *leave him* over this?

He looked into her determined eyes and instantly knew he was not brave enough to take the risk.

"Fine." His voice came out strangled. "I stand with you, Miranda."

The hard expression fell away, and she gifted him a little smile. He wished it was enough to ease the turmoil rolling in his guts. The bitter, bone-deep warning that this was not the way.

Miranda stepped closer to Hovget. "What do I do?"

"Just stand here." Hovget rose his hands to the top of her head again. "We'll see. It is not a skill I have practiced."

Fuck. Govek's claws dug into his palms.

Wellia stepped closer to Miranda as if to offer support and Govek did the same, coming close but not touching her. Hovget's eyes shut and Govek watched Miranda's slack face.

For a moment, only the bird calls could be heard.

And then Miranda's face contorted, and her body quaked as if struck by lightning and her legs gave out from under her.

Govek snapped her up, catching her before she hit the ground. She wailed and it seared him through with agony.

"Oh god, oh god. Help!" she cried. Pleas that caused the imprint inside Govek's chest to blister. He clung to her and pulled her into his chest.

"I'm here, Miranda. I'm here with you. I will help you."

"God . . ." Miranda whimpered. "Oh god . . . Govek?"

"Yes," he said, lifting her a little higher as she pressed her palms to her forehead. "I am here. Are you in pain?"

"Yeah," she admitted, and it spiked fury behind his eyes.

"Help her." He ordered Hovget. Though now he saw the male was equally disheveled, bent over at the waist, clutching his own head. Wellia was holding his shoulder. Her brown eyes frantic as she peppered him with questions about his pain and symptoms.

"I'm okay," Miranda said, drawing Govek's attention back. Her eyes were red rimmed, her cheeks pale and sunken, and her body was shaking all over. "I'm okay. It almost . . . it almost worked. I saw things I didn't remember. Things from when I was inside the vent . . ." She pressed her fingers to her lips, face pale, skin clammy.

"Are you sure you're well?"

"It's just a little headache now. I'm fine," she assured him, patting his arm. "Put me down, Govek. I want to try again."

"No," Govek nearly snarled. Fuck, she wanted to do this *again*? It was ruining her. Ruining him too.

Why must she remember things that caused her such horrible agony?

"Govek," she said threateningly, and terror raged in him again. "I have to try. What if I remember something important?"

Fuck, was he fated to either watch her suffer or have her leave? To choose between her agony and her abandonment?

Abandonment was worse. So much worse. He could not let her go.

"No." Hovget's clipped refusal cut the air as he stood.

"Are you sure you're all right?" Wellia asked softly.

"I'm fine," Hovget assured her, patting her hand on his chest. "But I will not do that again. The pain you have, Miranda . . . it's too deep for my skill. You will have to find someone else. I'm sorry."

Miranda's shoulders slumped even as Govek was awash with relief so potent it loosened and warmed his chest.

"How do you feel, Miranda?" Hovget asked, coming close to look at her eyes. Govek held her tight. "How is your head?"

"It doesn't hurt anymore. It only hurt for a second—er, I mean, a moment."

Hovget hummed. "Perhaps, but even a moment more and there may have been permanent damage."

Miranda sagged in Govek's arms as he trembled. The damage could have been *permanent*?

"Thank you for trying." Miranda said, resigned.

Hovget nodded and stepped away. "We must return to the healing house before going to the hall. Otherwise, we would walk with you."

"It was good to meet you, Miranda," Wellia said, following Hovget as he walked away. "I hope we have time to talk more later."

"Yeah. Sure. I'll see you later."

Govek could not find his voice to offer farewells. The two healers walked away, and Miranda squiggled out of his grip.

"I guess the seer really is the only one who can recover my memories and help me figure out where my babies are," Miranda said and tension instantly closed Govek's throat. "Do you think he'll be at the hall?"

Govek gulped. "Miranda, I don't think it's a good idea. Hovget just said you could have been permanently damaged."

"Yeah, but he's the healer, not the seer. You said that the seer is more powerful," Miranda countered.

"He *is* but even he may not be powerful enough."

"*May* not," Miranda said. "So, there's a chance that he is. I have to at least talk to him."

"Miranda . . ." Govek's voice came out tight, strained.

"I have to at least *try*, Govek," Miranda said firmly. Each word cut deep, and he balled his fists. Her eyes narrowed on them before she met his gaze. "I'm going to try. If you don't want to help me, that's okay, I won't force you. I can figure it out on my own."

On her own?

Without him?

Fuck. *Fuck.*

He couldn't lose her.

"The . . . seer might be at the hall," Govek said quietly, holding out his hand to her. Desperate for her touch.

She took it without hesitation, gifting him with a smile. "All right, then. Let's go find him."

# CHAPTER
# ELEVEN

*MIRANDA*

"The hall is in the Great Rove Tree?" Miranda's eyes stung from the glittering light as they approached the center tree. It was literally the size of a skyscraper and towered over them. Its branches were as thick as houses and stretched further than she could see. Its crystalline leaves caused sun beams to ricochet off the lush browns and reds of the forest. It was so dazzling that Miranda was stunned speechless.

"Yes," Govek said tensely. His eyes flashed toward the groups of orcs who were all watching, whispering. Miranda tried to ignore it, but the task was becoming almost impossible as the crowd grew thicker.

She gulped. It was fine. She'd been in crowds many, *many* times. She'd lived in a major city, for crying out loud. And these people were far different from the screaming, panicking bodies she'd seen outside the bank windows before her boss had dragged her down into the vault.

One person had been trampled right outside the doors.

Govek squeezed her shoulder gently, leaning to meet her eyes. "Stay with me, Miranda." She breathed in his scent, focusing on what was above her. Branches and leaves and chilly breezes. As they got closer, she could see carved symbols etched into the surface of the trunk surrounding the massive main doors.

"What is that writing?" she asked, more to distract herself than anything.

"All the names of the members of Rove Wood Clan. They are carved there on the day of their birth."

"Really?" There must have been thousands, possibly tens of thousands. They stretched so high above that they faded out. "Where's yours?"

He didn't answer.

She pulled her gaze away from the tree and tapped his arm.

"My name is not among them."

Her brows shot up. "What? Why not?"

She'd thought the alienation had started when he was seven, when they'd found out his magic was powered by his negative emotions, so why wasn't his name on the tree?

What had happened on the day of his birth?

Before she had a chance to comment, they had breached the entry and all sense of comfort she'd had was snuffed out.

The space was overwhelming. It domed overhead with arches made out of branches. The crystalline leaves grew from each one in clumps almost like reflective clouds. The voices echoed off them, making the laughter and chatter seem like it was coming from above.

Three impossibly long wood tables spanned the room with few places to spare. Bonfires crackled between them. Some with massive pots hanging above the coals, others with hunks of meat on spits. Smoke wafted up and disappeared into the leaves.

The hall was packed with male bodies in all shades of green. Most of them were slender and tall.

Miranda's breath caught in her throat at the sudden, stark reminder that she was in a different world with a whole different species. Then she pushed her nerves to the back of her mind and straightened her spine.

Govek tucked her close to the wall, or rather the *trunk*, as they made their way around the perimeter. The walls were sanded smooth but followed the natural dips and grooves of the tree's outermost rings. The floor was solid wood with each huge ring shining below and continuing to circle all the way to the center of the room. If she counted each one, she could probably figure out exactly how old this tree was, but judging from what she could see from her vantage point, there were likely thousands.

The edge where they were walking was dark but for a few strategically placed torches. At the center, hidden among the clear leaves, she spied a dozen or more wood chandeliers covered with white taper candles. The candlelight was reflected off the crystal foliage and cast the room in a bright, warm light.

Most of the orcs were milling about, chatting with others, or fetching food and drink from around the huge bonfires. The atmosphere was friendly, almost inviting.

But every group she and Govek passed by went silent and watched them pensively. Their faces ranged from curiosity to contempt.

After how they'd treated him on the walk here, she couldn't bring herself to even be surprised.

She didn't care about them anyway. "What does the seer look like?"

"He is almost white. And blind."

He was blind?

Miranda searched the room again, but it was no use. She was so short compared to all the orcs here. But if she could get up a little higher, a white orc would be easy to pick out. Most of the orcs surrounding her were bright or dark green.

She gave up for the moment but determined to ask Govek to lift her onto his shoulders later. She tucked herself into his side and wrapped her arm around his.

Govek let out a content huff that had her looking up at him again. His eyes focused on her face as he breathed, "Thank you."

She blinked, tipped her head. "What for? For matching your pace? Cause I think you're matching mine really. I'd have to run to keep up with your natural gait. I guess it would be a good way to get a workout in." She popped her lips. "Though, I can think of much *better* ways to get a workout in."

Govek's eyes widened.

"Oh god." She covered her face with her palm. "Why do you let me ramble on like this? You *know* I always end up saying things I regret."

"I enjoy your rambles, Miranda," he said, perhaps for the millionth time and it warmed her the same as always. "*Especially* the ones you regret."

"Jerk," she said, though she softened the blow with a stroke to his hand and he chuckled. "Oh, what's that?"

Ahead, attached to the trunk, was an embroidered tapestry that spanned thirty feet both up and across. They were too close to the edge for her to get a good look.

Govek hesitated before pulling her away from the wall, into the crowd. The orcs that had been milling about gave him a wide berth and she tried to ignore their staring and concentrate on the incredible imagery before her.

It was of the Rove Tree. The trunk spiraling up in the center and arching over the top. The creators must have used the leaves to make thread because, just like the real thing, the canopy glittered and reflected the hall behind them.

Beneath were hundreds of orcs all performing various tasks. Those closest to the tree were mixing potions, meditating, growing plants, and filtering water into barrels from a bright blue stream that Miranda thought might actually be the spring Govek had taken her to.

"It is one segment from the Oracle of the Fades," Govek said, resting a hand on her shoulder.

"Oracle of the Fades?"

"Yes. The Oracle depicts all that was, all that is, and all that *should* be. It was the last gift given before the Fades went into eternal sleep."

"This is just one part?"

"The original work is said to be at the Sylph Tower on Mount Vythor. A place only traveled to by flight."

"Flight? Do you guys have planes?"

Govek's brow furrowed. "Like fields of grass?"

That answered that.

"How do you get to it? The Sylph Tower?"

"We don't."

*Oh.* Miranda turned back to the tapestry. "It's really amazing."

The orcs in the center were clearly of Rove Wood. They seemed regal, mindful. Their hands were clean and their actions were passive, but these only made up a small number. Perhaps ten percent of the whole. Most of the orcs were brawny. They ripped up trees, herded animals, and trudged in knee-deep mud to unblock rivers. One was tackling a wild cat, claws bared, teeth glittering, muscles bulging. Miranda was so struck with the comparison to the real life event, she didn't notice that the orcs at the end of the table behind her were whispering loud enough to hear, until one of them cried out. "Rogeth, get back here."

Miranda turned to look. They were all young, likely in their late teens or twenties. One was yanking his friend back down into his seat. She recognized Rogeth but none of the others. "Don't be *stupid*."

"But he's—"

"Vunek is right. It won't work."

"He'll go into a rampage."

"We have to be smart. There will be another time."

"But what if we're too late?"

Miranda looked between the still chattering orcs and Govek, trying to piece together what exactly was going on. Govek seemed set on completely ignoring them, but the more broken sentences Miranda made out, the more worried she got.

"Govek?" she whispered.

"I won't do anything," Govek said, though she could see his throat working, and his hands trembling, and she felt the tension rolling off him in waves that crashed around her, threatening to suck him down.

"I know you won't," Miranda said. "What are they talking about?"

"Saving you."

"Saving me?" She glanced back at the orcs, who were still watching. "But you're not doing anything."

"That does not matter. I am not safe," Govek said through his teeth. Miranda tightened her hold on his arm.

"You heard him," one of the orcs snapped. "I'm going to get her."

Govek ripped away from her, moving toward the males at the table. He took a single booming step forward as they all clamored to their feet. Bowls and soup and meat splattered to the wood floor.

"Whoa, whoa, whoa!" Miranda yanked his hand, dug her nails into his wrist. Forced him back around. "Govek, don't!"

Dang it, how could she even begin to stop him? He was so much stronger than her. There was just no way.

But her words were enough for now, at least. He whirled back toward her, heaving for breath, shaking for control.

"It's okay," she soothed. Her stupid brain was unable to think of anything better to say.

"My *son*."

The loud call came from her right, and when she turned, she was faced with the sight of a wood platform, like a stage, nestled right up against the wall of the tree trunk. It was around four feet high off the ground and likely more than twenty feet square. There were no railings or carvings and the only furniture on it was a single, high-backed chair placed at the center.

An older orc stood in front of it. From the distance, she couldn't make out much other than his wrinkled face and white hair.

And that he had his attention trained on them.

Govek jerked to his full height, away from the males he'd been about to fight. His muscles bunched, his back straightened, his tucked jaw quivered as if he were about to bear his fangs.

Then he moved her toward the platform, his hot hand tense at her lower back. As they drew near, the older male's features grew clearer. His frail limbs were covered by intricately embroidered robes, and he had white hair in detailed braids. He had a long nose and sharp eyes and a mouth set in a firm, unhappy line. His jaw was tucked up, like all the other orcs in this room, but it didn't look uncomfortable on them like it did on Govek. It didn't distort their features as much.

Probably because their teeth were much smaller.

"Govek," the orc said loudly, even though he and Miranda were drawing nearer by the moment. Many of the orcs around that weren't already watching turned their heads to look. "This is a happy occasion. There is no need for such *violence* here. Can you not withhold for even the length of a meal?"

Govek's jaw worked. His eyes fell to the floor. "I apologize, my chief."

The chief. Miranda had suspected this was his father.

They didn't look anything alike at all.

"Your apologies would be better served to the males who you frightened just now."

Govek turned and faced the younger, still glowering, orcs. "I apologize."

None seemed very receptive. In fact, Rogeth's glower seemed to get hotter.

"Good. Now come here. Bring the newest member of our clan. I wish to meet her."

Govek was so rigid he was trembling, but he tugged Miranda the rest of the way over to the platform. Everyone around them was silent, watching. The hair stood up on the back of her neck.

"Fair woman, I apologize for my son's lack of decorum," the older orc said, still talking too loudly, still standing on top of his platform. The chair, or rather the *throne*, behind him was done up in intricate carvings she hadn't noticed at the prior

172

distance. The red wood and elegant vine patterns glistened in the dappled light of the hall.

"Govek, release her. Don't drag her about. You are rendering her bruised."

Govek let her go and Miranda blinked with shock, chest tightening at the fact that he could release her by someone else's command so easily.

"Come, child," the orc said, his voice smooth and coaxing. He gestured toward the stairs near the back of the stage. "Join me here so we may converse more easily. You have nothing to fear. We will not allow harm to come to you."

"I wasn't worried about that. Govek does a good job of protecting me." Miranda tried to take back Govek's hand, but he had balled it into a tight fist and her stomach twisted. "Hey, uncurl, don't cut yourself."

Govek ignored her and the chief continued. "What's this? He's cut you? Fades, Agol, call Hovget to my throne. We need to get her injury seen to."

"What? No, I'm perfectly fine," Miranda said, even as a somewhat muscular orc she hadn't noticed before left his post at the back of the stage, descended the five steps, and disappeared into the ever-watching crowd. "I was talking about *Govek*—"

"Hovget, good, you are here. Bring Miranda to the stage."

They were back *already*? "Hold on, time out. I don't want to—"

"You should go."

Govek's strained rumble caught all her attention. "Govek, I'm fine with you."

"I'm not . . ." He raked a hand through his hair, eyes darting back to where the orcs he'd almost brawled with were still sitting and talking animatedly. "I need a moment."

Miranda let out a long breath, not wanting to leave him but . . .

The platform was taller. Would she be able to see the seer from up there? "Okay. I'll go up, but don't bolt on me. I don't know how to get back to your house."

"We would be happy to find you a home closer to the hall," the chief said. "Hovget, she's just here. Guide her up."

The doctor orc appeared on her left and gestured toward the stairs without touching her. "Miranda."

"Hi," she said to the male with a nod before brushing Govek's still clenched hand. "I'll be right back, tough guy."

Her pet name seemed to soothe him slightly. She would have given him a quick kiss to calm him further if the doctor hadn't been ushering her up so quickly, sticking close to her back.

"Don't mention the blood." Hovget hissed into her ear as they ascended the steps onto the platform. They were a little taller than she was used to and she had to concentrate on each one to keep from tripping.

"Excuse me?" Miranda said.

"Govek's blood," Hovget said. "Don't tell the chief I took some."

What the . . .? She didn't have time to question it because a second later she was being presented to the opulent orc whose wide smile and tucked away teeth were far more unsettling than Govek's sharp rows.

"Welcome, welcome. Come, tell me your name. Hovget, examine her wound. We don't want to leave her bleeding," he said exuberantly, waving Miranda forward.

Was he talking about her period? Jeez, could every orc smell it? "I'm really not hurt."

"She isn't," Hovget assured, passing her on toward the chief. "Can I go?"

"If there is nothing more you can do for her, then yes, Hovget, by all means, return to your mate. Come here, child. Let me look at you. My, you do look a state. We'll get you some better treatment now that you've arrived."

"I've been treated well by Govek." Miranda was getting tired of repeating this.

"What are you called? I am Chief Ergoth of this clan. You may come to me if you are in need of anything."

"You can call me Miranda," she said, looking out over the crowd of orcs. Most of them were now seated, which made it easy to search for the seer.

"Miranda," the chief said smoothly. "That is quite lovely and unusual. You are most welcome here, Miranda. We are glad to have you. It is very rare for us to have a woman from outside Rove Wood join us. Most come from Oakwall Village, you see. A community of humans we are quite peaceful with. All orcs of Rove Wood Clan are welcoming to humans. I'm sure you have enjoyed some of their hospitality so far, yes? Have you made any friends?"

"Uh, we just got here."

"But you visited with Maythra and Viravia last night, did you not? They spoke very highly of you. I'll make sure you can visit with them again. And that you can meet all the women who have chosen to make our clan their home. Them and their mates. We would be happy to host you here at the hall for all of your meals."

"Thank you." Miranda managed, blinking. Dang, and she thought *she* could talk fast.

"I'm sure being surrounded by so many orc males feels a might daunting. Do not fear. I will make sure only a few come to make their acquaintance at a time. And if *you* see any males you would like to become friendly with, please let me know and I'll ensure a meeting can take place."

What was this—a meat market?

"I was told your clothing was taken from you."

"That isn't—"

"Please be assured that we can get you anything you need. We don't have much in the way of women's clothes here, but our trade with Oakwall is only a few days hence. I'm certain you will find everything you need there."

"Oh, yeah, going to the trade would be good." Miranda glanced out over the crowd again. The faster she found the seer, the faster she could get down.

"Excellent. I will get Maythra to be your guide. As the oldest woman in our clan, she has much more experience and would be happy to impart it to you."

Oh, heck no. "That's nice, but I'm sure Govek can be my guide."

The chief looked momentarily stricken. "Ah, that may be difficult. My son has not gone to the trade for many moons."

"Oh?" Miranda asked, looking down at where Govek was. His hands were bunched, and his shoulders were slumped, and his dark eyes were brooding as they burned right through her. "Why is that?"

"There are . . . many reasons," the chief said, gesturing for her to follow him over to his throne. "Why don't you sit, Miranda? You're most welcome to, and I'm sure you are tired from walking for so many days."

"Oh, no. I'm good." The only place to sit was the fricking *throne*.

But the position the chief had moved her into, right near the center at the front of the platform, was much better for searching. She began scanning again. Dang, this room was huge. And packed full. There was only one stretch of the furthest table near the far back that was empty. Probably because there was a massive branch right above the blotted out the light from the chandeliers.

"Of course. Whatever makes you most comfortable. Your comfort here is paramount to me. As is the comfort of all within my clan. It is my duty to protect everyone within the boundaries of the Rove Woods."

"Thanks," Miranda said quickly. Gosh, there were *so* many faces. All slender and dressed in loose cotton garb. She would have thought with the varying skin colors it would have been easy to find one that was white, but now she noted that there were plenty of very light-skinned orcs.

"I only want you to be happy with your new home, so *please*, I urge you to let me know if there is anything or anyone troubling you. Also, you can help yourself to anything you like from the storeroom. There are many empty homes for you to choose from, as well."

"Thank you," Miranda said, only half listening. She'd found a stretch of table where a group of women were seated with their orc mates. It was a wonder she could find them at all in the sea of huge green bodies.

There were close to ten women in total and they seemed to come from all kinds of nationalities. What was the human demographic like on Faeda? How big was Faeda? Was it all one continent or many? The map Govek had showed her only covered this corner of the world.

The chief lowered his voice. "And there are many in this clan who would also readily offer you protection. Agol, my lead guard, has a son, who is equally as mighty. I would be glad to assign him to you."

"What? Oh, no. That's not . . . no. No, thank you," she said, noting now that there weren't any kids. Where were all the children? Had they just not been invited to this announcement?

"I understand. After what you have gone through, I can imagine that the company of any orc would be off-putting."

She really wanted to find the seer, but it didn't look like he was here. Actually, Karthoc wasn't here either and none of the burly warriors Govek had described. All the seated orcs were slender. The most muscular one was that Agol guy who'd fetched the doctor and even he only had a third the mass Govek boasted.

"But I must assure you that the other males of Rove Wood are not like my son."

Ergoth's words had her brows furrowing and her gaze turning to Govek. Poor thing looked so uncomfortable. Everyone's eyes were on him. She should get down now.

"You need not stay with him out of fear, Miranda. I swear I will never allow him to take advantage of your vulnerability again."

Miranda turned, all her attention suddenly on the chief. "Excuse me?"

"You don't need to feel embarrassed. You were lost, hurt. It is shameful that my son would take advantage of that."

*Oh shit.* "No, no. That's not—no. Govek didn't—"

"You don't need to defend him, my dear. I believe you. I know my son better than anyone."

"Govek didn't—"

"Please sit," the chief said, gesturing Miranda back. She realized suddenly that he'd herded her far away from the edge of the podium and now her calves were bumping against the seat of his throne. "Rest. Be at ease."

Why did he want her to sit in his chair so bad? Did it have

some kind of double meaning? She would not take the risk and find out.

"I want to get down now," Miranda insisted, moving to the side to escape the chair.

The chief's eyes flashed with an emotion she couldn't place and it made her stomach knot. "Have I done something to upset you? If so, I sincerely apologize."

"I just . . . I want to go back to Govek."

"You don't have to return to him, Miranda. We can protect you."

"I don't need protecting from him." Miranda's voice came out clipped. She was getting tired of repeating this. She looked past the chief and back down to where Govek should have been.

He wasn't there.

Her stomach dropped. "Where is—?"

She was suddenly wrenched away from the chief and his throne and into a hard wall of pine-scented muscle.

Thank god!

"Get away from her!"

Oh shit.

"Govek, control yourself," Chief Ergoth ordered firmly. "My son, this is *unseemly.* You've hurt her arm."

"No, he has—"

"Let her go, Govek." Another snarling male had come up behind them. Agol. He looked like he was going to try to brawl with Govek over this. Brawl and lose badly.

Govek growled but his grip loosened as if he were going to obey.

"The fuck is happening here?"

The roar came from the entry and Miranda turned to find

Karthoc had arrived with ten other warriors in tow. All battle scarred. All brawny and thick.

Not one of them was the seer. Damn it.

"Ergoth, what the fuck are you doing parading Miranda about on your blasted stage like she's some prize?" Karthoc stormed across the room, his booming voice reaching every corner.

"I was only getting acquainted with her, my young nephew. She is the newest member of my clan. I wanted her to feel welcome."

The warriors lined up at the trunk wall, watching silently as their much smaller counterparts glowered at them, whispering scornfully.

"You offer welcome by taking her up there for all your orcs to see, while her male is forced to stand by and allow her to be gawked at like a trinket?"

Hit the nail right on the head with that.

"She willingly came up to greet me," the chief countered, as Karthoc pounded up onto the stage. "Didn't you, Miranda?"

Did he expect her to agree? "I very clearly told you I wanted to get down, and you blocked my path. That's the only reason Govek ran up here, right?"

Govek kept his head lowered but his grip on her arm firmed again.

The chief's gold eyes went wide and then he fell into a sweeping bow that left Miranda flustered. "I sincerely apologize. I should have let you leave the moment you requested it, but I was afraid you felt coerced into staying at Govek's side."

"He saved her from the perils of the woods," Karthoc said, crossing his burly arms over his wide chest. "Of course, she would want to stay with him."

That he had. Govek had protected her and fed her and dragged her back to sanity after she'd fallen apart and not complained about it once.

"He's wrenched her by the arm," the chief said to Karthoc, eyes narrowed. "She should not be pulled around so harshly by a male so much stronger than her. It is clear intimidation and will make her feel like she is not allowed to leave him should she want to."

Govek flinched and released her, left her feeling cold after his warm touch.

"Leave him for another orc, you mean? Are you trying to spark a challenge between your males? You want to watch your precious conjurers be cut down by Govek's prowess?"

Miranda slipped her hand down Govek's arm and took his balled fist. She felt a hot sticky wetness between his fingers and her chest tightened with dismay.

"That is not how we do things here in Rove Wood Clan. We do not have vile, bloody fights among one another," Chief Ergoth said with his chin high. "Women are not belongings to be carted about. They can go where they wish. Speak to whomever they like."

"Well, I want to go with and speak to Govek," Miranda said firmly.

"There!" Karthoc said. "It's done. Now both of you can go join the rest."

Govek led her down in an instant. Miranda had never been so relieved to get off a stage in her life.

"Fuck, Ergoth. What's this precious little thing? A blasted *throne*? Like one of those prissy little human Highman? You're so frail you can't even get through your own blathering without needing to squat?"

Laughter bubbled up in Miranda's chest. She couldn't help it. But at least it was quiet enough that only Govek heard.

He jerked, startled, and snapped his eyes to her face. Seeing her smile seemed to put him more at ease and as he guided her away from the platform, he spoke. "I'm sorry, Miranda."

"You didn't do anything wrong," she said, giving his hand a squeeze. "Thanks for coming up to get me."

He nodded tensely and led her to privacy at the back of the hall.

# CHAPTER
# TWELVE

*GOVEK*

I t took every drop of Govek's will to not pick Miranda up into his arms and leave the hall.

His skin prickled, his jaw clamped, and his claws refused to sheath themselves. They threatened to rip through every male who thought about approaching Miranda. Even his own father.

He was a fucking horror. He wasn't safe for her. She should have gone with his father. With Maythra, or Agol, or his son Wolvc. With *anyone* else.

And yet the idea of her being taken from him made Govek want to rip the whole Rove Tree to the ground, tear through his clansman like they were overripe berries, and crush them to a pulp in his grip.

"Don't do that." Miranda touched his hands without the slightest hesitation, and he was so shocked his muscles bunched and he froze. Her skin was so warm and soft as she pried his fists apart and stroked the cuts he'd made. "I thought we were getting a little better," she chided gently, moving to use the hem of her cloak to dab at the blood. He quickly pulled away before she could.

"I am sorry," he managed, his voice thick.

Fuck, was he really going to keep her with him while he couldn't even think rationally?

But Fades help him. Was he going to be able to let her go?

"Don't be sorry," she said firmly. "You don't need to be. Your dad is the one who should be sorry."

Confusion blunted some of Govek's irrational anger. "He was only trying to aid you. To offer protection."

"I don't need protection from *you*. You *are* protecting me," Miranda said, causing more confusion to roll in. "But I'm not going to fight with you over it. Why don't we go get that food? Or would being around other orcs be too much right now? We could go somewhere quiet if you need to calm down a bit more."

Govek swallowed hard, working past the burning instincts to lock her away in his home and not allow anyone to look upon her ever again. He glanced toward the table where the women always sat with their mates. If he could not leave her with his father, perhaps he could let her be with the other women.

His father was right. She did not deserve to be dragged around like an animal. She did not deserve to have her choices snuffed out and her vulnerabilities preyed upon by his worthless instincts. The instincts that drove him to care for her and cleave to her would be the reason he lost her.

Her brow furrowed. "What are you thinking? Don't you dare tell me to go sit with them. I'm staying with *you*."

Her words soothed away some of his rage. "I'm not—"

"I get to decide what I want to do, Govek. And who I want to spend my time with." Miranda looked toward the table.

Every eye in the room was on her, but those of the humans burned the brightest. "*Maythra* is over there, and I don't see Viravia."

Govek let out a long breath, agony rippling over him at the thought. Without Viravia, it was likely that every woman in attendance would be quickly drawn into tales of all his past transgressions. Not that it would matter. There was truly nothing he could say to paint his past actions in a better light.

He raked a hand over his face, trying to find the correct path through this.

"Hey." Miranda was suddenly very near, her chest almost brushing him, her hands cupping the sides of his face. "You wanna just leave and go knock down a few trees?"

He blinked, shook his head. "*What?*"

"Could be a good way to vent frustration, right?" She hummed, tapping her chin. The sly smile she gifted him was so fucking lovely he almost choked. "And after it's down, you could, ya know, bend me over it?"

This time, he did choke.

Miranda grinned as his thoughts spiraled. "That's better. Why don't you think about it while we get some food?"

Think about it? While walking through the hall? While every single eye of his clansman and Karthoc's warriors were upon them? Was she being serious?

He supposed her little plan had worked because before he knew it, he was fetching her a bowl and guiding her over to one of the stewpots. He couldn't help noticing how close she remained to his side, how her gaze rarely left him and never once lingered on any of his brethren, how her expression only brightened when their eyes made contact.

Fuck, he was so lost to her. His instincts roared with

pleasure and the burning need to haul her over his shoulder and carry her back to the depths of his home eased away.

"Where's yours?" Miranda asked as he handed the bowl of fish stew to her and began to guide her to a quieter spot in the hall.

"I am not having any."

"Dude, you're all muscle. You probably have the metabolism of a sports car. You've gotta eat."

Govek huffed, mostly with amusement. "I did not understand a single word you just said."

"I could get you to eat if I wanted to," she threatened, forcing his mirth higher.

"I'd like to see you make the attempt."

"*Okay*, but I'm going to be using the same methods I used to 'handle' you yesterday before we got to the butchery."

Pleasure burst up his spine, especially when he noted a few of the nearby orcs close enough to hear had turned to look. "Fuck, woman. I thought these things embarrassed you."

She leaned up a little and whispered, "Being *smelled* and flirting are two completely different things, Govek." She looked around then, her eyes scanning the room. "Though I suppose I shouldn't if there are kids around. Where are all the kids? Were they not invited to this?"

"The sons are with their families and instructors deep in the Rove Woods." Miranda's curious smile prompted him. "Every orc son, from the time of their birth, goes to commune with the seasonal shifts in summer and winter. That is when the Rove magic is at its peak and the best time for teaching. They will not return for another half moon."

"Oh, that's pretty cool. Kinda like a field trip?" She didn't wait for him to answer. "Must be pretty fun."

Govek shrugged.

"You didn't like it?"

"I was not allowed to attend."

He shouldn't have said it so casually, because the expression that crossed his mate's face was anything but casual. "What do you mean? Why not? I thought you said they weren't wary of your magic until you were seven."

His stomach twisted as he realized his blunder. How could he tell her one of the darkest tales of his past? The one that caused his father to take drastic, necessary action to separate him for the protection of all in Rove Wood Clan?

"Hey," Miranda touched his jaw, working at the tension with her tender fingers. Her brow was furrowed. "It's okay."

Govek looked into her earnest face as his promise to speak his truths stabbed into the back of his mind. Right where her imprint was raging. Steeling himself, he guided her to one of the darkened corners at the very back of the hall, nestled between the grooves of the tree.

Her brows rose, and the words tumbled from his lips. "I only went once in my youth, and during that time, I flew into a rage and destroyed the encampment."

Miranda's eyes widened, and she asked a question he did not expect. "You said that the children started going from their birth. So how did you, as a *baby*, fly into a rage so crazy you destroyed things?"

Govek swallowed. "I was not allowed to attend until I was seven summers. And by then, I was so blasted behind in my learning I had no hope of catching up."

"Why weren't you allowed to attend before then?"

He forced himself to shrug. "The father must attend with their child for the first few years, but my father was unable to because of pressing matters within the clan."

"Why didn't he have someone else go with you then?"

"That is not done."

"What about Tavggol? Who went with him?"

"Tavggol was five summers my senior and a prodigy. By the time I was born, he did not need my father's guidance as he had already mastered the basics and was taking private lessons from Gogvi, the elder instructor."

She hummed to herself, thinking. "You must have been a pretty big kid to destroy the whole camp."

"I was large for my age, but the camp was built under a rock ledge, and we took our lessons atop it. When I failed to perform as expected, I grew angry, and my magic spiraled out of control. I destroyed the support, crushing the camp beneath."

Miranda shocked him again by huffing out a laugh. "Oh my god, are you serious? You must have been a wicked smart seven-year-old to come up with that."

"It . . . was not my intent at the time. The support was simply the closest pile of rock to vent my fury on." He looked away, toward the tapestry on the wall, toward the orcs in the center who kept their race whole with their magic. "If any had been in the camp at the time, they would have been crushed to death."

Her humor died, and the truth of his transgression became clear. He held his breath, preparing for her harsh reaction, for her rejection. His claws began to slice through his palms.

"So . . . you were expelled from your schooling because you *accidentally* destroyed the camp?"

Govek blinked.

"Honestly, if a seven-year-old could use magic to crumble the rocks and take out the whole camp so easily, it should have *never* been put under there in the first place. That was a bad decision on the adult's part. Who decided that was a good spot?" Miranda's expression darkened, and he gulped. "Was it your dad?"

Confusion forced him to tip his head. "I . . . do not know. I do not believe he contributed to the decision." Though Govek supposed, as chief, he may have. "Those rocks could not have been moved by any orcs in Rove Wood or by Karthoc's warriors. It is only with the combination of my strength *and* magic that I was able to budge them. That is why I am not . . . safe. It was that event that brought to light how my magic functions and how dangerous it is. It was that event that was the catalyst that led to my being assigned a home on the outskirts."

"I see," Miranda said casually, as if his admission meant nothing to her. And perhaps it didn't. She was not even of this world. She did not understand.

Her arms crossed as she narrowed her eyes at his father, who was still squabbling with Karthoc on top of the platform. The two had never gotten along and Govek suspected that was the reason Karthoc rarely came to Rove Wood Clan.

"One of the little girls at the daycare, Karla, was a bit of a spitfire."

Govek turned to face Miranda once more.

"She could get into the *worst* shit, but she was also super smart and a natural-born leader." Miranda's eyes grew misty, but before Govek could think of how to aid, she recovered, wiping the tears away. "Once she used leverage with the wall and knocked over one of the big bookcases we had into the sleeping nook. Destroyed the shelf, the tables, some of the bedding, and a lot of the books."

Where was Miranda going with this?

"She got in pretty big trouble. She could have hurt someone if they'd been sleeping." Miranda cast him a half smile, then gave her bowl of soup a quick stir. "Had to sing the 'sorry song' in front of the whole class and clean up the mess with only one aid for help. Her mom had to pay for all the damages. But all of us adults understood Karla hadn't *meant* to hurt anyone or realized how much damage pushing the bookshelf would do."

Miranda scooped up a large piece of fish from the bowl and pressed it to Govek's lips. The aroma flooded his nose with the scent of thyme and cooked trout. His stomach grumbled, and he helplessly obeyed her silent order, taking the salty bite and chewing it slowly.

"Karla's mom had just had a new baby. Becoming a big sister was quite an adjustment for her." Miranda scooped up another bite and gifted it to him.

"Govek, sometimes, kids react badly to change, but that doesn't mean they're bad kids. And it doesn't mean they're going to grow up to be bad adults."

Govek stopped chewing as the words filtered through him, leaving him thunderstruck.

Had she not heard him? Was he not explaining the situation clearly? Pushing over a single shelf was nothing compared to destroying an entire camp.

But a lump had grown in his throat and a pang of uncertainty was growing in the back of his mind. His eyes slid to his father on his mighty platform next to his gilded throne, arguing with the warlord as if he had any right to do so.

Govek shook his head, trying to dislodge the unsettling thoughts. He met Miranda's gaze again, soaked up her gentle smile, allowed himself a few moments to bask in her gracious judgment.

The comfort did not last long. Perhaps this transgression

could be forgiven in her eyes, but there were many more. *So many.*

Confusion passed over her features. "Govek—"

"My clan!"

The chief's bellow instantly cut off Miranda's response.

"My conjurers and communers, you who are set above with your prowess and gifted magic by the Great Rove Tree, it has been my privilege to lead this clan almost one hundred and forty wonderful seasons. Many trials have—"

"For blast's sake, Ergoth, get on with it," Karthoc said, earning tense silence from the Rove Wood Clan and chuckles from his warriors, who now lined the far wall, clearly having been refused seating just as Govek.

Ergoth continued, though with a hint of tension in his tone. "The Great Rove Tree, conjured by the Fades themselves, imbued with their light and power, has given grand magic to us.

"We acknowledge Sythcol, our great conjurer, whose skills outmatch any other, Hovget, the best healer Rove Wood has ever known, Caveskil, who calls the rains as if they are his kin, Ravtogh . . ."

The list continued, on and on, sinking Govek into the ground. Down to where the Fades slept so they could mock him in their slumber. Never once had Govek been acknowledged in the list of those who were blessed by the Fades. Never once had his clan had reason to give him more notice than a glance of distrust.

When he was younger, hunters were called and praised for their prowess. Govek had been in awe of their strength and strived to uphold their mantle. But they were praised no longer. With so many blighted beasts, there was no honor in killing those that were healthy, even when those kills meant their clan did not starve. The hunters he'd admired had all abandoned the Rove Woods for the war or had taken up a more suitable role within the clan.

"Let us honor the Fades. Praise them for their gifts to us," Chief Ergoth said, raising his wood goblet high, beginning a chant. Low calls rumbled as the whole clan spoke in unison. Even a few of the woman joined.

Govek remained silent. He'd never been taught this prayer.

"And now, my young nephew, Warlord Karthoc, would like to address us in good tiding." Ergoth stepped to the side, but not away.

"I will not drivel on," Karthoc said with a pointed look to Chief Ergoth as he took up the center of the platform. "The war is not going well. The Waking Order's numbers seem to grow with each passing day, and they have razed four clans south of Hexlin. There were no survivors and no warning before these attacks."

Govek went ice cold in an instant. Fuck! *Four* clans destroyed? Was the war going that badly?

Would . . . Karthoc's forge even be safe for Miranda?

"They come over the Wyin Mountains in droves. Despite the perilous passage and the legions guarding the borders, they continue to break into our lands. It is only a matter of time before they come to Rove."

A clamor rose from the clan, voices high and outraged. Chief Ergoth stepped forward.

"The edge of the Rove Woods is yet two full days of travel from here. Even if they breached the outer forest, they would not make it past the barriers that my conjurers have created."

"They would," Karthoc said, his voice flat. "It is foolhardy to believe they would not. The Waking Order is both cunning and *growing*. Their numbers outrank my own, three to one."

*Three to one?* Bile rose in Govek's throat.

"We will forge more defenses. Sythcol, come up, explain to the warlord what your plans are."

Sythcol stood up from his place at the head of the conjurers' table. He was only a little older than Govek but the deep-set lines in his face and his faded pale-green hair made him appear much older. His hands had long gone black from many seasons of endless conjuring. Creating magical healing remedies to send to Karthoc's warriors to aid in the war.

A war that they were losing, despite all efforts.

"Sit down, conjurer. None of your words will sway me. My decision is final," Karthoc said, waving Sythcol back. "And that decision . . ."

Karthoc trailed his eyes across the room until they met with Govek's.

"That decision is to merge Rove Wood Clan with Baelrok."

A dreaded silence descended. The harsh intake of air before chaos reigned.

And reign it did. Rove Wood Clan erupted. The cacophony of voices rose to dizzying heights, roaring into the branches of the Great Rove Tree, and spilled discontent and anguish into the air so thick Govek had trouble catching his breath.

Karthoc was going to merge Rove Wood with his forge.

The whole fucking clan would be there.

With Govek and his new mate.

*Fuck.*

"Karthoc, you must be jesting!" Chief Ergoth's voice carried above the others and quieted the fervor. "You cannot possibly mean for my clan to leave Rove Wood—"

"I am your warlord, and my decision is final. You will come with me to Baelrok."

"What of the tinctures you so desperately need? What of

the healing magic you require to keep the Waking Order at bay?"

"You will make them at my forge."

"They will never have the same potency. The Great Rove Tree is required to keep our magic hale. And what of future generations? No orcs will be born with magic if they are not conceived and carried within these woods!"

The smug smile plastered to Karthoc's face and forced Govek to gulp. The warlord's eyes snapped to Govek once before returning to the chief. "In the past that was true, *uncle*, but something has shifted in our race. In the last four seasons, we have found seventeen orcs who can wield magic. Warrior orcs born far outside Rove Wood that have no connection to this great tree."

*What?* Govek went cold as shock twisted into his gut and the blood drained from his face.

"That isn't . . . that isn't possible," Ergoth said with a shaking breath. Govek could only just make it out. "Only my clan can produce conjurers. Mine alone."

"Why such shock, uncle? Your own *son* was born a warrior with magic."

"Yes, and Govek is—" Ergoth's mouth snapped shut, and his fists curled.

Govek's heart thundered in his chest as agony gripped him.

"Govek is *what*, uncle? Speak full what you would like to say of my cousin. Your only living son of whom you should be proud. Govek is *strong*, just as the magic wielders we have discovered are. These males could win us the war. Their power could overthrow the Waking Order and yet you regard them with scorn."

"I would not scorn them," Ergoth stammered.

"You have rejected your own *son*, refused to train him in

his skills. Govek could be the most powerful male in my legions if you had not forced him into squalor at the edges of your clan."

"Govek is a different case. You do not know him as I—"

"I know enough. Enough to be assured that I cannot trust you to treat these other seventeen males with fairness. They need to be trained, and I cannot trust you, Ergoth of Rove Wood, to follow through on that. So, you will join me in Baelrok, where I can oversee their treatment myself."

"Of course, I wouldn't . . ." Chief Ergoth stood tall. "You are unreasonable, Warlord. Surely only a few of my conjurers would be needed to train them. Why, I would send Sythcol to see that the work is done well."

Govek saw the lead conjurer tense in his seat.

"Forcing us all to leave when only a few are needed is preposterous."

"*All* will come." Karthoc's voice held no room for argument. "I will not have this clan fractured apart, as I know well how being in groups enhances the magic. And being outside the Rove Woods will already stifle the training enough as is."

"If you know that, then allow them to come *here* to train," Chief Ergoth said desperately over the swelling voices of the crowd. "This place under the Great Rove Tree holds the strongest magic. The closest connection to the Fades. It is where the seasons themselves are birthed. Why, our sons are out communing in winter as we speak. Denying these conjurers of yours access to Rove's gifts will only stunt them."

"Yes, I agree," Karthoc said. Govek was flummoxed.

Ergoth breathed deep. "Then you will send them here."

"Only on one condition will I consider it."

The whispers began again.

"Name it," Ergoth said.

"If you want me to send the conjurers here, a score of my warriors will join to protect them."

"Of course," Ergoth said with an instant nod. "Of course, my nephew. We would welcome them warmly, just as we would welcome these new conjurers."

"I'm not done." Karthoc found Govek's eyes again. "I will send my warriors and *Govek* will be named the chief of Rove Wood Clan. He will lead them—them *and* you."

Govek's ears rang, his stomach dropped and his eyes blurred as he tried to comprehend the words spewing from his cousin's tongue. He could not discern if the roaring was from the voices of the clan or his own blood rushing through his veins.

"Silence!" Karthoc roared, though his demands did almost nothing this time. "Govek is the only male who understands what it means to wield strength and magic together. The only one who could understand their struggle. The only one who I can trust to follow my orders fully. It is that, or when I leave here to return to my forge, the whole of your clan will return with me."

Govek rose from his seat, ignoring the onslaught of voices and orders and harsh rebukes. Ignoring even the screaming logic in his head that demanded he confront Karthoc and force him to undo this horror.

He needed to think. To catch his breath. To fucking *escape*.

He never should have come back.

He was dimly aware that Miranda, his precious mate, had grabbed his arm as he turned to go. The worry in her intense gaze skewered him.

And then she blessed him with firm words. "I'll follow you."

# CHAPTER
# THIRTEEN

*MIRANDA*

"Where are we going?"

Govek's steps were heavy, his breathing was hard. She couldn't see his face, but based on how tense his back was, Miranda suspected his expression was impressive.

"I can see sparks coming out of your ears, Govek," she said, a desperate and failed attempt to lighten the mood as she struggled to keep up with his gait. "Govek, your house is that way, so what are we—"

"Not my fucking house anymore," he snarled, even as his steps slowed for her. She managed to catch her breath as he said, "We're going to the fucking storeroom and taking every Fades-blasted thing and leaving this wretched place."

"Okay. You sure we should make that decision right now?" Miranda asked, catching up to his side so she could see his expression. His eyes glittered with unchecked fury, jaw still tight around his tusks, a muscle in his cheek twitched. "Where would we go?"

"I don't fucking know," he admitted with a pain wrecked snarl that made her chest ache. "But it won't be anywhere near this clan or my father or my cousin. I'll build you a house near the mists and we'll cut ties with every blasted—*fuck!*"

"Near the mists?" Miranda pressed, but he didn't answer, only slowed his steps further. "Govek, tell me more. Talk to me."

He finally looked at her full on and the desperation in his eyes made her stop. She pulled at his hand and forced him to stop with her. "Govek . . ."

"They ordered me to my fucking death, Miranda."

Her stomach churned, but she managed to stay silent.

"My father ordered me to Estwill to retrieve women who he claimed wanted to live *here* even after I told him it would get me *slaughtered*. Even after I explained how wretched Estwill had become. That human city is a *stronghold* for the Waking Order now, and he expected me to just walk up to them without any aid. I would have been killed on sight at best. Brutally tortured at worst. And not one of the males in this clan gave a single shit. Not one of them said a *word* in my defense."

Miranda squeezed his hand tight.

He looked down at her hand in his grip. "And why should they have? I've done nothing but cause strife and fear. They were likely *thankful* I was gone. And now Karthoc wants me to fucking *lead* them? He thinks I could be capable? He's insane for believing that they would ever follow a single Fades-fucked thing I ever said."

Miranda reached up to soothe his jaw, massaging it into relaxing. Govek squeezed his eyes shut. "And if I don't, what then? Rove Wood Clan disbands? They are forced to join Karthoc's forge because of me? Thousands of years of peace and power all destroyed because of *me*?"

He looked so shattered it broke her. Miranda placed her hands to the side of his head, stroked his face. She didn't know how else to soothe him.

"I must be fucking *fated* to bring ruin to this clan," Govek said, his voice hollow. "An abomination of the Fades who brings naught but destruction."

"Govek!"

The roar had them both looking up, and the warlord was barreling toward them so fast that Miranda had the sudden urge to flee.

"Fuck, Govek," Karthoc spat. "I didn't expect you to *bolt*. What in Fades?"

"What were you thinking, Karthoc?" Govek snarled.

"For fuck's sake, you already knew this mantel would fall upon you when we found Tavggol's—" Karthoc stopped, straightening his spine as Govek balled his fists. "You want to challenge me, Govek? Cousin or not, I will accept."

Miranda started to panic. She had no idea what to do. She didn't want to leave Govek's side but she didn't want to be caught between the massive brawling inhuman males either.

Thankfully, Govek cooled off at that. "I want nothing from you, Karthoc," Govek snapped, turning on his heel, snatching up Miranda's hand and pulling her along.

"For fuck's sake, Govek. I thought you would *want* this!" Karthoc stormed after them, "Those miserable wretches have looked down on your talents all your life, this is your chance to—"

"What *talents*?" Govek snarled, still not slowing, though he glanced to check on Miranda. She worked to keep her breathing steady, not particularly wanting to slow down either. "The ones that make me a fucking *blight* on this clan?"

"What kind of blight provides more than half the meat?

What blight protects the clan from ruthless predators? What blight seeks retribution for an honored member? No other member of this fucking clan had the balls to join my forces and return Tavggol's body."

Govek was like a glass under a boulder, shuddering, cracking, ready to shatter. And Miranda wasn't certain she could put him back together after he was crushed to dust.

"Your strength and magic make you *mighty*. They make you stronger and better than anyone else here," Karthoc raged. "More than half of my warriors can no longer commune with the Fades! The other half hardly bear it. And now the Fades have gifted us warrior males who can not only commune but can *conjure*. Who can *wield* the Fades gifts for the better! Who can fight against the Waking Order and render them asunder once and for all."

"So, I'm to be a weapon for you, then?" Govek raged, whirling about to face his cousin again. "You intend to use me and *all* these males for your own gains?"

"For the gain of all orcs!" Karthoc roared, making Miranda jump and skitter behind Govek. "This war threatens us all!"

"You're blustering fools."

The words cut like a slice of lightning through Miranda's brain, but when she released Govek's arm the sensation evaporated leaving an odd numbness at the corners of her thoughts. Her panic over the fight had ebbed slightly.

It ebbed more when she saw that Govek and Karthoc were no longer at each other's throats. They staggered away from each other, palms to foreheads.

Karthoc recovered first and rounded on the orc who had approached them. "Use that magic on me again, Evythiken, and I will slaughter you where you stand, seer or no."

"I'd like to see you make the attempt," the orc said without the intensity, but Miranda was still struck dumb.

Though he couldn't have been any older than Govek, this male gave off an intense aura and was not like any of the others she'd seen.

He was white, or at least extremely pale green. He had no hair, just a smooth bald head. His jaw was untucked, and his teeth were long, sharper than the burley Karthoc's or even Govek's. His frame was slender beneath deep violet robes. And his eyes were white. Not a hint of a pupil. Blind.

This was the seer.

"I came to tell you that Chief Ergoth is spouting off in the hall, Karthoc. You're going to want to do something about it, or it's going to lead to chaos."

"Fuck," Karthoc snarled, glancing at Govek. "I'm not through with this."

"You should be," the seer said firmly. "You're not getting any further with him today."

"I know how to handle my own kin, Seer," Karthoc snarled.

Miranda gulped hard, wrung her hands, and withheld the urge to bombard the seer with questions.

"Go much further and Govek is going to leave."

"What the fuck are you talking about? Govek, what is he saying?"

Govek said nothing, but a muscle in his jaw ticked.

"He plans to take his woman and go. Into the woods somewhere. You *will not* be able to find him. His skills as a hunter are fueled by his magic and are far superior to anything you or your warriors could track."

"Is this true, Govek? You plan to abandon your clan and kin?"

The seer snorted. "Can't abandon wretches who gave you up first."

There was an unsettling silence that followed as Govek curled in on himself and Karthoc registered the information.

The tension was so thick that Miranda turned her eyes away. She wanted to look at the seer, but his intensity was too much. He was like the blinding rays of the sun, warm and inviting from a distance but too hot to look at directly.

Instead, she turned toward a large building on her left. Half of it was carved into the tree and the other half was a log cabin structure built along the outside. Windows lined the edges, and the door was only twenty feet away.

It opened and Viravia stepped out.

Miranda only had enough time to see the pregnant woman's eyes go huge as she took in the sight of the three orcs conversing before fleeing back into the room. She shut the door silently behind her.

Miranda quirked an amused smile.

"Fine," Karthoc said slowly. "I will let this be for *now*. But don't go doing anything stupid, Govek. If you leave, if you refuse the position you were *born* to take, you will regret it."

"Is that a challenge, Karthoc?" Govek snarled, his voice so deep Miranda felt it rumbling in her soul.

"No," Karthoc said. "Not a challenge, simply fair warning. If you leave before we speak again, I will tell every orc clan this side of the mountains not to harbor you. You will find no friends, no aid, not even a fucking *scrap* of food will be thrown your way. I will see to it that if you abandon this clan, the rest of your kind will abandon you too."

Miranda's stomach twisted and Govek went so tense next to her his body was quaking.

"You have a quarter moon to decide. That is as long as I

can stomach these miserable woods," Karthoc snarled. "I suggest you make the right choice."

Then Karthoc pushed past them, storming off loudly toward the hall.

"Who are you?"

All the hair on Miranda's body stood up and her eyes ripped to the seer. He regarded her with his milky, unseeing eyes and she couldn't find her breath let alone her voice. Finaly he said, "You seem... out of place."

"Yeah, I'm . . ." Her throat closed. "I need your help."

"My help?" The seer tipped his head, his white eyes striking and swirling up her thoughts. "Yes. I suppose you do."

"Miranda," Govek said warningly, squeezing her upper arm.

But the seer had outstretched his hand and the burning, overwhelming urge to take it slammed into her.

"Miranda, wait."

She didn't. She took the seers hand.

Her sight exploded with light.

And her consciousness winked out.

# CHAPTER
# FOURTEEN

*GOVEK*

"What the *fuck* is she?" Evythiken's voice was jagged. Sharp glass slicing through Govek's mind. He held Miranda tight in his arms and stepped away.

"Miranda," Govek rasped, shaking her slightly.

Fuck, she was gone.

Her body was limp, her eyes closed. He was trembling too hard to tell if she was breathing.

*Gone.*

Fades help him.

"Get her away from me," Evythiken said, gripping his head, half doubled over. He staggered toward the far edge of the path.

The seer's voice blistered through him like a red-hot poker and Govek managed a few more steps away, fighting between keeping Miranda in his grip and the trembling agony burning through him.

"Away!" Evythiken nearly roared. "I've enough of my own

agonies. I need not hers too. Get her away. Do not come near me again."

Fuck, *fuck*. An order from the seer was higher even than Karthoc's and still Govek grappled, caring only for his mate, who was now lifeless and still in his arms.

He had to get her to the healer. To shelter.

The storeroom.

Govek backed away from the seer and the bubble of agony popped around him the moment he was out of the male's mental reach. He glanced back only once to find Evythiken limping into the forest, head still in his hands. Fighting his own terrors.

Or Miranda's.

He nearly wrenched the door to the storeroom off its hinges and slammed it hard behind him as he entered. Inside, all was still, quiet. No one was here.

He staggered to the bags of stacked grain on the opposite wall and laid Miranda down, checking her breathing.

She was alive.

He fell to his knees next to her, his heart pounding, his blood coursing sharp terror through his veins. "Miranda, come back to me."

Her eyes fluttered slightly, and he gripped her hands. They were so tiny in his. So warm. Red streaks from his own bloodied palms marred them.

"Govek."

A croaking gasp left his throat as his mate's eyes opened. He ducked his head to hide the gripping tide of emotions flooding through him.

"Govek. What . . . where are we?"

He couldn't speak. He pressed her hands to his forehead.

He wanted to rake his claws along his scalp, but refused to let her go.

"Govek, where are we? What happened? There was a bright light and . . ." She shifted her weight, eyes clearing, breathing steadily.

She was all right. She'd recovered.

*Fuck*, he couldn't get his heart to stop pounding. His hands shook in hers.

"Govek? It's okay." She pulled her hands from his grip and grazed her gentle fingers along his scalp. Her soothing touch rolled over him like a balm. "I remember a bright light and . . . oh, the seer! Where's the seer?"

Fuck the seer. "Gone."

"What? Gone where?"

"Into the woods."

"But I need to talk to him. Let me up, Govek. I want to go find him."

The fuck? "No," Govek snarled, snapping his gaze up to hers. She jolted, hands falling from his hair to his chest. He worked to ease his fury but could not find the power in him to change his mind. "*No*, Miranda."

"But I need to talk to him. I need to—"

"You were *gone*, Miranda."

"What do you mean gone? I'm fine now. Let me up."

Did she not hear herself? Did she not see how insane this was? "*No,* Miranda. You are not well. He hurt you."

"Govek."

"No."

She pulled her hands away from him and it felt like his blood was icing over. She searched his face a long moment before saying, "Govek, I *need* to know where my babies are."

He opened his mouth to argue with her, but no words came out. He *knew* how important this was to her. He *knew*.

But she was important to him too. He couldn't lose her.

"I *have* to talk to him, Govek. I have to at least *try*." She took a deep breath. "The light in my head . . . it was because I touched him, I think. Which means I can just ask him questions without touching him. I really don't know why I grabbed his hand to begin with. It was so odd, like a magnetic pull."

She examined the hand that the seer had touched, rubbing it gently.

"Dredging," Govek said thickly.

Her eyes met his again. "What?"

"He was dredging . . . pulling things up from the darkest depths of your mind." It was one of the most intimate and unsettling conjuring's the seer could perform.

"Dredging . . ." she said to herself. Her hands were shaking, eyes wide, and his stomach rolled. "I need to try again, Govek."

"No." His refusal shuddered through him.

"Govek, you don't understand. I *need* to do this. I can feel it."

Fuck! The image of her shivering and collapsing bellowed through his mind. "Miranda, dredging can cause *irreparable* harm, if not done carefully. Your mind may never recover if you try again."

Her brows knitted. "But . . . what if it's the only way? What if I won't be able to find my babies any other way?"

"That's not impor—"

"Govek, don't you *dare* tell me that my babies aren't important," she said so forcefully he felt the snap of it blister down every limb.

Anger rose up, balling in his chest, vibrating his hands. The light of the Fades began to glow at the back of his mind.

Why couldn't she see this was not worth the risk?

Why couldn't she see what this was doing to him?

*He couldn't lose her.*

"Govek, I *have* to try again. *I have to.*"

He gritted his teeth, anger blazing in his gut and pulling his magic to the front of his mind. He fought it back.

"I can *feel* it, Govek." Miranda touched the middle of her chest. "I can just . . . *tell* that this is what I'm supposed to do, that this is the only way to find them. You believe me, right? I know it sounds so crazy."

It didn't. When the pull to dredge was birthed by the Fades, it was like a *compulsion.*

But he couldn't let her. *He couldn't.*

*He would lose her.*

"Govek?" Miranda's voice felt distant. Distorted. He bowed his head and took heaving breaths as everything pounded into his mind at once.

How *dare* Karthoc try to force his hand? How *dare* the seer touch his woman and birth this madness? How *dare* the Fades push his woman to do something that may *kill her*?

His anger was growing, flaming, *alive.* The Fades light was raging, swallowing him up. Threatening to burst.

His fingertips tingled with the force of his withheld magic.

He needed to leave. To get out of here and away from Miranda before he lost control and *hurt her.*

*He couldn't control it.*

Hands slipped up his cheeks and into his hair.

His breath caught in his throat as she swirled gentle circles around the base of his skull, massaged the hinge of his jaw.

He met her gaze and was unsettled to find her expression

tight. "Govek . . . if you don't want to help me with this, you don't have to."

*What?*

"I can do it on my own," Miranda said softly, and she may as well have *screamed* it into his ear. Burst apart his eardrums with it.

"This is something I have to do, but you aren't obligated to help me, Govek. You've helped me *more* than enough already. I'll never be able to repay you for everything you've done for me. So, it's okay. I won't blame you for bowing out entirely."

Bow out entirely.

She meant *leave* him.

She would *leave* him over this.

And all the anger evaporated out of his chest to make room for *terror*. The magic snuffed out, and he reached to grip her sides, wrapping his fingers around her middle, as if that might stop her from going without him.

He couldn't let her go. *He couldn't.*

"Govek?" Her voice held concern. Concern for *him*. Fuck, he did not deserve her gentle kindness.

"I'll help you," he managed past the lump in his throat. "I will, just . . . *fuck*."

But she'd *passed out*. Even the seer felt it was wrong.

Govek gulped hard. "The seer asked you to leave him alone."

"He . . . what? No, that doesn't make sense." Her brows knitted in confusion. Her hands left his face so she could rub the middle of her chest again.

What he would give to read her mind in this moment, to feel what she was feeling.

"Can you help me find him so I can ask? It's not that I don't believe you, it's just that . . . that . . ." She chewed her lip.

He gulped hard, mouth so dry it felt like sun baked sand. "The seer asked to be left alone and his orders are higher than the Warlord's. Going against them could get us banished from his presence permanently."

"Then . . . then what do I do? What do I do now?"

His eyes fixed on her chest, and he gulped hard. "We . . . must wait for him to make the first move."

Fades, he hoped the male never would.

"What do you mean wait?" She let out a dry laugh. "I don't think I can do that, Govek. Every *second* we aren't searching for my babies is another second they could be hurt. What if I'm too late? What if I'm too late to save them?"

Did she *really* think it was possible for her toddlers to have escaped like she did? It went against all logic and reason.

And yet, he didn't have the energy nor the desire to fight her on it. He'd almost lost her moments ago. He could *not* risk losing her again. No matter how his gut screamed that this path would end in disaster.

If he lost her, he would lose *everything*.

Including his sanity.

He took deep, cleansing breaths. "Miranda, the Fades will ensure things play out exactly as they want them to. They hold the power here."

"It's hard for me, Govek," she said, hugging herself and looking away. "The Fades are your gods, not mine."

"But they saved you just the same."

Her eyes shot to his, going wide.

"Can you trust them for now, Miranda?" he asked. "Just for a few days?"

She looked deep into his eyes and searched his face.

"Okay," she said softly. "For now."

He wanted to collapse from relief, but Miranda collapsed

first, falling against his chest, wrapping her arms around his neck, hugging him tight. Embracing him. He closed his eyes and crushed her in return.

"Gosh, dang. Today has been . . ." Miranda murmured, her breath warming his cheek. "You're right, Govek. We need a little break after all that."

He let out a long breath.

"That fight with Karthoc was really intense. Are you okay?"

He certainly was not *okay*, but he was better now that they were alone. "I will be fine."

"Yeah, you will." Miranda stroked his head and down his back. "I'm gonna make sure you are."

His breath caught.

"Ooh, did your heart just skip?"

Heat radiated in his cheeks, but he didn't have the strength to push her away yet.

"Okay," she said slowly. "So, I do have something else to hit you with."

He tensed, bracing for a stinging slap. He should have known that the hit would come from her words instead.

"Were you *seriously* going to just haul me off into the woods without getting my say on the matter at all? Really? And be careful what you say here, because the seer totally gave all your plans about bolting away already." She pushed back, leveling him with hard eyes.

He gulped. "I just . . . could not stand to be here."

She pressed her finger into the middle of his chest, poking him with all her strength. He barely felt it. "Don't you *ever* start making life-altering decisions like that without my input. Especially when you're as wound up as a fish on a line."

"I apologize, Miranda. I vow not to do anything like this again."

"Good," she muttered, wrapping her arms around his waist again. He curled around her, breathing her in.

"And another thing, for pity's sake, next time you want to fight somebody as buff as your cousin, you gotta at least put me somewhere out of the way. Somewhere I can see. Maybe get some mud and find me a camera. You guys make speedos here?"

What in Fades was she talking about?

Then she smoothed her palm over his shoulder. "Okay. I feel better."

He continued to hold her lightly even as she began to look about.

"Wow," Miranda whispered as she scanned the shelves and boxes. Everything in excess was stored here from canned preserves to bear traps. It was all neatly organized as well. Not a single item unaccounted for or out of place.

Chief Ergoth prided himself that his orcs didn't have to fight over scraps like some of the other clans. His father felt no sympathy for the orc warriors whose inability to connect to the Fades was leading their clans to famine.

Govek raked a hand over his face as Miranda stepped further into the room. Fuck, he was honestly supposed to lead these males when he did not even understand them? He'd witnessed how they grumbled over the prospect of being forced to reduce their own supplies so others did not starve to death. He'd not been present for the votes where the Rove Wood orcs denied aid to struggling clans, but he'd heard them proudly discussing the decision afterward.

Thinking about it now made him want to challenge them,

brawl until they saw reason, and slug his fist into their jaws until their complaints were silenced.

But that was not the way of Rove Wood Clan. The way here was to call for judgments, to discuss and vote and dole punishments that were so much worse than the momentary wounds from a challenge.

He was *not* fit to be chief.

"Viravia? Are you in here?"

Pulled from his thoughts, he watched Miranda search each aisle and corner. "What are you doing?"

"I saw Viravia in here a few minutes ago."

Govek frowned and sniffed the air. "She is not here." Nor did her scent linger enough to indicate she had been here within the last few days.

"But I saw her. Is there another way out?" Miranda continued to look around, peeping into every nook.

"There are two larger doors at the back that are locked." Govek plucked the linen scroll off the table at the entry and waved her over to his side. "Everyone comes in through this door to ensure they do not forget to register what they took or contributed."

He flicked through the scrolls, distracting himself from darker thoughts by explaining where his allotment was, what the things inside the storeroom were roughly worth by trade, and how to reduce his share after she took something. He could tell from her expression that she was finding it rather complicated, but couldn't help thinking the level of concentration on her face was adorable.

"Why is the elk you brought in yesterday worth less than the dozen rabbits this guy caught?" Miranda asked, pointing out the clear discrepancy.

Govek did not have an answer. He rolled up the scroll

quickly, wanting so badly to keep his irritation at bay. "I play no role in the allocation. Chief Ergoth is in charge of this."

"Your dad." Miranda pursed her lips. He nodded. "He gives you less on purpose?"

Govek's brow furrowed. "No. I simply don't need much. And the less time I spend in the clan, the better. The less interaction I have with other orcs, the less I will be drawn to violence against them."

She hummed in thought. "Fighting seems to be second nature to your cousin. Karthoc almost fought you right outside, and he didn't seem too shocked and horrified by the prospect of it."

"The warrior orcs of Faeda are not the same as the orcs of Rove Wood Clan. I was born of Rove. I should have control. It should not be possible to goad me into violence so easily."

"You were born here, but it's clear you don't belong."

His face contorted as agony gripped his chest at the truth of her words.

It hurt even more when her own expression crumbled. "Oh gosh, me and my mouth. I didn't mean it like—come here."

He went to her readily, falling into her embrace, breathing in her crisp honeyed scent, and letting it soothe him. Fuck, she felt so good.

"I meant you don't seem to belong *here*. You look like your cousin. Like the other warriors. There's a picture on that tapestry in the hall of an orc fighting a wildcat that looks *just* like you."

He blinked. He'd never noticed that.

"You don't seem to belong in the Rove Woods, but you certainly belong on Faeda. I'm just surprised you didn't leave to find a better place for yourself a long time ago. Even if your brother was here."

Govek said nothing, because truthfully, he did not understand it either. But there was no undoing the past, regardless.

"Okay. Let's move on to less heavy stuff. After taking care of me for so long, I think you deserve some pampering."

"Pampering?"

"Don't grumble at me. I felt your heart go all fluttery when I mentioned taking care of you." His cheeks began to burn again, but she just shot him a smile and began to search the shelves. "I'm going to—wait, are these usually open?"

Frowning, Govek went to examine the window she'd indicated. In the summer, they were occasionally left cracked, but not during the winter when damp could easily get in. There was also a stack of blankets on top of a barrel beneath the window that seemed to have been knocked over.

"Do you think . . . Viravia went out that way? She's awfully pregnant . . . she would have had to be desperate." Miranda picked up some of the wool blankets and stacked them back up.

"I still do not . . ." He paused and took in another deep breath. Viravia's scent was not present, but the scent of sage *was* a little stronger than usual and he knew the woman had an affinity for that herb. "I am not sure. We could find her and ask if you would like."

"No, no. I'm going to cook for you."

His heart began thundering again. "Cook for me?"

She raised her eyebrows. "You haven't had anyone make you a meal before, have you?"

"Tavggol would occasionally bring me a plate of what was left after seasonal celebrations or larger meals at the hall."

"Ooh, that's not the same at all." She grinned. "I'm excited. What do you like to eat?"

*You.* "Meat."

"I should have guessed that." She laughed and her delight soothed away a significant chunk of his tension. "Hmm . . . let's see. I'm not a very *good* cook but I'm sure I can make something you'd really enjoy. Do you guys have cheese in here? And butter?"

Govek followed her deeper into the storeroom until she came across the vegetables.

"Oh, these aren't in season, are they?" she asked, picking up a basket of strawberries.

"Anything can be grown with enough magic."

"Ah, right." She put it back down with a smile that tore at him. "Do you have a skillet in that kitchen of yours?"

"Yes."

"Cool. How about the oven? How does it work? Can I control the temperature easily?"

"Yes. It's controlled by magic and is quite precise."

"Magic coming in for the win again," she said, gathering up onions and peppers. "We need a basket. Is there bread around here?"

He fetched the basket, growing more excited by the moment. "What kind of bread?"

"Like, rolls? Oh, those would work." She picked up some fist-sized rounds of sourdough. "How many do you think you could eat? Two, three?"

"Of *those*? Likely twenty."

Miranda laughed again, and it lit his whole world. "We'll take *four*. Cause I'm gonna put stuff on them."

"On them?" But they were round, wouldn't it fall off?

"Yup. I've got you all confused, don't I? I'mma keep what I'm making a secret." She shot him a smile that had him relaxing. Despite all the turmoil of this afternoon, Miranda's babbling had soothed him.

After a few moments, she finally paused, tapping her chin. "You know, it is a shame to leave behind your kitchen. It's really nice. And your house too. You clearly spent a lot of time on it."

*Only because he had nothing else to do.* "Yes."

"I wonder"—she fiddled with a head of lettuce—"Couldn't we just . . ." She shrugged. "Live here?"

His fists balled. "Live *here*?"

"Yeah. I mean, if you don't become the chief, the rest of the clan will have to leave the Rove Woods, right? That means the whole place will be abandoned." She chuckled. "We could start our own little commune with my babies. We'd turn Rove Wood Clan into a membership of twenty, instead of two hundred. I mean, *technically,* you wouldn't have *ruined* your clan, just *reduced* it."

His mind reeled.

"We just have to find my babies first. Once the seer tells us where they are, it shouldn't take *too* long, right? I mean, I landed right near the Rove Woods. Maybe they did too?"

His stomach started twisting to the point he was no longer excited about her food.

She still wanted to go searching for them. She would *insist* on this.

Karthoc's threat spiraled through his mind. *"You will find no friends, no aid, not even a fucking* scrap *of food will be thrown your way. I will see to it that if you abandon this clan, the rest of your kind will abandon you too."*

The world outside of the Rove Woods was already dangerous. Between blight and war, there were few safe places to go. And those safe places were all orc clans and settlements.

Clans and settlements that would no longer harbor them after they got Karthoc's orders.

Fear laced his every limb and quaked in his mind.

It was too fucking dangerous.

What were they going to do?

"And we could be friends with Oakwall Village too, right? Trade with them and winter over with them, if need be. They'll have doctors and schools and all that . . ."

Fuck. Yet another snag. Though, arguably, this one was not nearly as dire. "I . . . am not sure." Miranda rose a brow, and he forced himself to say, "I may not be welcome at Oakwall."

"Because of what happened with your ex? I thought you said you didn't hurt her."

"I did not." Of that, at least, he was certain. "But many from Oakwall believe that I did and will not welcome my presence."

"Then why not just set them straight?" Miranda insisted, as if doing so was that easy. She must have read his expression because her own fell. "Govek, for a tough guy, you sure don't know how to defend yourself."

"The reason I cannot is *because* I am tough, Miranda. I am too aggressive. Too uncontrolled. Speaking my truths only ends in violence."

"You mean like today in the hall when Rogeth tried to snatch me?"

Govek's brow screwed up. "He was trying to *save* you."

"The difference between being saved and snatched is perspective. From my view, as someone who did *not* want to leave you and doesn't feel unsafe with you, it was snatched." Miranda reached up and pulled down a shriveled haga root.

"Don't use that."

"Why? Is it poisonous?"

"The taste is abhorrent. Like half rotten tomato with the texture of charcoal."

"If it tastes so bad, then why keep it?"

"It is very good for health and keeps for a long time." He was certain the ones in that basket were at least two summers old.

"It can't be that bad," Miranda scoffed and took a bite before he could warn her further.

Her face instantly paled and Govek had to use every ounce of his will not to burst with laughter. "Oh my god. That's *horrible.*"

Her voice was so shrill Govek was unable to hold back his mirth and nearly doubled over with it.

"You're so mean!" Miranda snapped making his laughter seize in his throat. Her words split him until she grabbed the back of his neck and pulled him down. "I'll have to punish you."

He froze as she planted a hot kiss on his lips. Her tongue pushed into his mouth and his groan was both from pleasure and disgust. She tasted so strongly of haga root and yet he wanted to delve deeper.

He'd had no idea that dueling with a woman's tongue could bring so much intense pleasure.

He growled, lifting her off the ground by gripping her under her tight ass. She wrapped her legs around his waist, bunching the skirt around her hips.

Fuck, he was lost. The taste of the root was forgotten as Govek drank her up. He sucked her tongue into his mouth and nibbled on her lips. In his haste, he accidentally prickled her soft skin with his teeth, but it only made her moan and squirm. The pleasure she brought to him was stark and consuming.

She broke off the kiss, panting, and looked around the floor. "We're making a mess."

He realized he'd shoved her against one of the shelves of

sewing supplies and most of the contents had fallen around their feet.

"I'm prepared to make a real mess." Govek lapped at the little bumps that had appeared on the side of her neck. "I want to take you here."

It was a foolish idea. Anyone could walk by the windows and see. But the truth of it was that he *wanted* the clan to know this woman was submitting to him. That she enjoyed his presence and eagerly accepted his cock.

"You can't," she whispered mournfully. "My period."

He gulped involuntarily as the truth of it brought him back to his senses. He adjusted her carefully so he could put a hot hand over her abdomen. "How is your pain? You mentioned cramping."

"Oh, it's fine. No cramps right now." She kissed his cheek, right at the corner of his mouth, teasing with her tongue. "It's just a bloody mess."

Govek tipped her chin to examine her face skeptically. He'd ripped the throat out of a blighted boar with his teeth a few days before and she worried about bloodying his cock?

But before he could argue an eagerness flooded her features and his gut pitched into want. "You know, on Earth, we call this time blowjob week."

His brows furrowed in confusion. "What?"

She snickered and then kissed his jaw. Then his neck. He shivered as she licked right over his pulse. "Let me show you what else humans like to do with their mouths."

She squirmed out of his grasp and pushed at him until he was half sitting, half leaning against a barrel of ale in one of the darker corners. A place that couldn't be seen from the windows. Her hands moved down his chest to the tie of his pants.

He let out a long exhale as she stroked over his member, tingling pleasure danced through his gut. His cock sprang free the instant she'd undone the closure.

"Oh man, you are happy to see me, huh?"

He huffed with amusement.

She smiled and then, inexplicably, went to her knees. His eyes bulged. "What are you doing?"

Her smile turned sly, and it raked a spike of confusion down his spine. "Like I said, showing you what else humans do with their mouths."

She couldn't possibly mean—

She held his cock in her soft, warm hand and dragged her tongue along the shaft, licking him from base to head.

Pleasure so brutal it was almost painful rocked through him and he lost his breath. He hardly had a chance to catch up before her wet tongue stroked him again. Sliding along his length and swirling around his tip.

His hands dug into the barrel, threatening to splinter the wood under his grip. She seemed to not understand how stretched his control was as she continued to torture him with slow, almost leisurely laps of her tongue.

"Govek, hush, or someone might find us," she chided gently, her lips close enough they brushed the head of his cock when she spoke. His mouth dried up.

Govek rested a trembling hand on the back of her head, desperate to ensure she didn't leave him yet.

He watched as her lips spread, and she took the head of his cock into her sweet mouth. Sharp, tingling pleasure barreled through his limbs. The urge to thrust deeper blistered through his veins, making him jitter and squirm to fight the urge. He was loath to hurt her.

He was too big for her. In every way. He *was* going to hurt her. The thoughts gave him back a tiny snippet of control.

Then she used her hands to stroke the hard length from the head all the way to the base. Her soft fingers sent torrents of pleasure through his stomach. Everything became tight. He felt inconceivable ecstasy, and he could feel nothing but Miranda everywhere. He dragged her honeyed scent into his lungs. Her soft fingers stroked the base of his cock. Her warm, wet mouth wrapped around the tip. She swirled her tongue at the head. Pressure mounted.

"Fades, Miranda, I'm going to—I can't hold—"

His warning went unheeded, and she doubled her efforts. He lost the battle against being quiet and let out a strangled cry. Ecstasy burst as he came. Pleasure danced up his loins, trembling through his spine. Flooding him. Filling him up. His sanity left him, and his hips thrust into her soft mouth against his will as the rapture pulsed on and on and *on.*

As the scattered remains of his sanity fell back around him and he heaved in breaths, his gaze jerked to the woman nestled between his legs. Her lips popped off his cock and her gorgeous eyes speared him right through the chest.

Her throat worked as she swallowed down his seed.

Fuck, the sight was too good, too right. Miranda was perfection. His deepest fantasy made real. Better. Even in his greatest dreams, he could not have imagined a woman more radiant than her.

He hadn't realized he had spasmed again until her tongue came out to lap at his cock. The gentle touch was too much, and his hips jerked away, desperate for reprieve. He gripped tight under her chin and used his thumb to wipe her sopping lips clean.

"I take it you liked that then?" she said softly, as if there could be any question. As if any male in this fucking world wouldn't prostrate themselves before a woman willing to give them this kind of pleasure.

He would worship her.

The sharp honeyed scent of her own arousal flooded his senses then, and he was struck by the knowledge that performing this gracious, selfless act had pleasured her too. Govek found his sanity, scooped his woman up, and planted a feverish kiss to her lips. The taste of himself on them made him more determined.

"What are you doing?" Miranda asked as he lifted her skirts.

"Returning the favor."

# CHAPTER
# FIFTEEN

*MIRANDA*

"Y-you can't!" Miranda said breathlessly, bracing against his chest as he hauled her up and plopped her down on the barrel he'd just vacated.

Damn, sucking him off had been way hotter than she'd imagined, and now she wasn't sure she had the willpower to hold him off.

"You think I give a blasted fuck about a little blood after your mouth was on me, Miranda?" he rasped into her ear, looming over her.

Miranda shivered and moaned and fought to clear her head. God, why did he have to be so good at working her up? Why couldn't she think when he was all hot and close and gripping her hair tight? He forced her head back, delving his tongue into her mouth, and pushed reason right out of her head.

She groaned around his tongue as his hands moved down and flicked her nipples beneath the rough wool dress. "But . . . but it will make a mess."

It was a shoddy argument, and they both knew it.

"I'm an *orc,* Miranda. I would sooner devour you than balk at your *mess.*"

"Oh god." She shivered. His rumbling voice vibrated through her stomach, pooling delicious heat between her legs, making her throb and squirm against his rough fingers as they stroked up her thigh.

His hands caressed their way under her skirt. They were so hot against her sensitive skin, and she was panting. "Tell me no," he grated. He swirled his thumbs closer to her pussy.

"Forget the mess." She breathed. "I want you."

"Good," he growled so low, right into her neck. She was still half out of her mind when he yanked her underwear down and slicked his fingers into her slit without hesitation. Excitement warmed her at his obvious confidence.

And then his fingers flicked right against her swollen, throbbing clit and she lost her breath.

"G-Govek," she whimpered, clinging to his chest, legs trembling.

He continued to stroke her. She was so wet. So slick. There was no resistance. He used his palm to press hard into her clit, and she ground into him mindlessly. "You smell *divine.* I can scent the need on you. You want me, don't you?"

Oh *fuck.*

His fingers went still. *"Don't you?"*

"Yes, yes." She jerked her hips. "Yes, I want you."

He growled with pleasure as a thick finger sank deep into her, forcing her to thrust and writhe. He pumped in and out, and she couldn't manage words even as she tried to beg for more.

He must have been able to read her mind because he

speared another finger into her, spread them apart, stretching her until the delicious sting made her eyes cross.

"Come for me, Miranda," Govek demanded against the top of her head. "Relent."

And she did, helplessly. Ecstasy exploded behind her eyes and rolled through her stomach. He made her take more and drove her mad as her brain flooded with deep, quaking bliss so powerful she saw stars.

She clung to him so hard it must be bruising him. She wrapped her legs around his calves and dug her heels into the back of his knees, shivering and gasping as her pleasure faded.

He held his hand up to her view, drenched and reddened from her orgasm. His face was a mask of brutal desire, all teeth and piercing golden eyes. "Now tell me, Miranda, should I wash or lick this clean?"

"*Fuck.*" She gasped as another shot of pleasure rocked through her, making her twitch. She should be demanding he go clean up, but instead she curled into him. Her core pulsing with delicious aftershocks and her mouth going dry with a desire to kiss him again.

He chuckled, the deep rumble warming her gut as he pressed his nose into her hair, right next to her ear. He dragged her scent into his lungs as if he were trying to breathe in her essence. "Fuck, Miranda. The things you make me want to do to you."

"Like what?" She managed passed her own gasping, only to lose her voice again as his laughter rumbled. It vibrated through her, causing tingling over her skin.

He scooped her up off the barrel, grinning. "Allow me to take you home and I will show you."

∾

"I'm supposed to be showing you the things I want to do to you, not watching you slave over my stove."

The kitchen was a complete mess of ingredients. She'd burned about half of what she'd tried to make. Almost every one of his dishes had been dirtied and Miranda couldn't help being frustrated at how inefficient she was at preparing food this new way.

And Govek was getting impatient.

She couldn't blame him.

"Here, taste this next," Miranda said, holding a fork of fried onions up to his lips.

His irritation abated, and he took the fork into his mouth without hesitation. His eyes shuttered closed, and he chewed slowly as if that might make the tiny bite she'd given him last longer. As if she wouldn't give him another one in less than five minutes.

"Does it need more salt?" she asked after he'd finally swallowed.

"No," he said, voice somewhat hushed. He lingered next to her, clearly wanting more, but not wanting to ask.

She'd run out of ingredients before she put everything together if she wasn't careful. Two pans of onions were still smoking and charred. Govek had said he'd eat them anyway, but she wanted to get this right for him.

He said he didn't like cooking, so she fully intended to take the job over. Even if heating the wood fire stove with different types of magic-laced kindling was nearly impossible to comprehend.

She fiddled with one of the twigs nearest her, wondering if she should add more heat.

"Don't use that one."

She looked at him. "Will I light the house on fire?"

"No, but your onions will burn. Again."

She sighed heavily. "This is impossible. It's so hard to tell them apart."

"That's only because you cannot see the magic within them," Govek said. "You need not do this, Miranda. I am happy to cook for you."

"I want to do it," Miranda said, reaching up to scratch at his hairline. "And you've barely eaten anything today."

He stilled, brows pinched.

"Let's get you refueled a little before you show me all the lavish things you want to do in the bedroom. Or on the couches. Or the table."

His eyes lit and darted to the small table on the opposite side of the room. "It would likely snap."

"Ooh," she hummed as heat spiked her through. "Honey, that sounds like a challenge."

But her teasing fell a little flat as he quirked a brow. "*Honey?*"

"You really want me sticking with tough guy, huh?" She ruffled his hair.

He leaned into her touch, closing his eyes. "Call me what you will, Miranda, but *honey* suits you far better than me. It is what you smell of."

"I smell like honey?"

His eyes opened and heated her. He bridged the gap between them, pulling her away from the stove and slanting his mouth over hers.

Pounding sounded at the door.

Miranda jumped and her cheek collided with Govek's nose. He grunted and jerked back.

"Oh gosh, I'm so sorry!" she said reaching up to rub at the

bridge of his nose. "Are you okay? I didn't hurt you too bad, did I?"

Amusement flooded Govek's features, and her worry drained away. "No, Miranda. You did not hurt me. It is doubtful that you could cause me any damage even if you headbutted me with your full force."

"Hey, I'm not that weak." This earned a dubious expression from him that made her huff. "I can take you down just fine without bruising your bits, and you know it."

He leaned in close, lips against her ear, hot breath stirring her hair, and growled, "*That,* I believe."

A delicious shudder rocked down her spine.

The pounding thundered again.

"Who the heck is that?"

"I'll get rid of them." Govek set her down and stalked to the door. It snapped off entirely in his hand.

Miranda covered her mouth to hide her laugh as Govek grumbled. They'd both forgotten it was broken. All humor died a second later.

Rogeth stood there all blustery and puffed up. He tried to fill out the doorway, but he was too slender for that, and his two male counterparts could easily be seen in the background.

All three looked ready for a fight, but Miranda doubted even their combined muscle could match Govek's.

Rogeth shot Govek a look of pure scorn. "Where is she?"

Govek growled and Miranda rolled her eyes. "Are you talking about me?"

"What are you doing to her? Are you forcing her to cook?" Rogeth snapped, stepping into the house and Govek instantly extended his claws, opened his jaw, and took a hard step toward the male.

"Hey, hey," Miranda said, taking her onions off the heat

and rushing over to Govek. "I thought I told you no brawling until after you get naked and get me to a safe place to watch."

Her words snapped them all right out of their near rampage and Govek snarled down at her. "*What?*"

She grinned, winked, and took his hand in hers. His low growl of pleasure had her sighing with relief.

"Govek, let Miranda go."

It was Maythra. Of course it was.

Miranda hadn't noticed her behind the burly orcs. Maythra pushed past her three comrades crowding the stoop and stomped into the house like she owned the place. Her sharp gray eyes flashed with disdain. "Oh dear, this is where you have been keeping her? Miranda, please, allow us to find you better accommodations."

"Thanks, but I'm good here." Miranda gripped Govek's hand. He was shaking with his attempts to control himself.

"Miranda," Maythra said, stepping toward her. "I know you have been through quite an ordeal. But I promise you, the pain is over. Govek cannot hurt you again."

"Again? He hasn't hurt me at all."

"Our wise chief told us you were lost, afraid. In a bad way. I know you feel you owe Govek for saving your life but—"

"Whoa whoa. Hold on there. I don't feel—"

"Govek, come out. Now."

"More visitors?" Miranda looked up at Govek and found his face stricken. "Hey, let's just tell them all to leave."

"No." Another familiar orc pounded up from behind the two already crowding the stoop, forced both of them *and* Rogeth into the tiny kitchen. Miranda suddenly felt like a worm surrounded by gulls. Dang orcs were *tall.*

"Govek." It was Agol and another younger orc who was

basically a carbon copy of him. Maybe with a tad more muscle. "Chief Ergoth has demanded your presence."

Govek tensed under her fingers and Miranda instantly clung tighter. "We're about to eat right now, so he'll have to go later."

"Miranda, I have plenty of delicious food at my home that I would love to share with you," Maythra said, stepping closer with her hands still extended. "Please, come enjoy my hospitality. We can eat and discuss your new lodgings."

"I don't want new lodgings, and I've got food here," Miranda said as Govek began to pull away. "Where are you going?"

"My father has ordered my presence."

"So, you *have* to go? Couldn't you go later?"

"Do not keep the chief waiting, Govek," Agol said.

"Rogeth, why don't you join us for a meal at my home? I'm sure Miranda would enjoy the added protection and you can get to know one another better."

"I don't need extra protection. And I'm not going with you." Govek worked his hand out of hers. "Govek, stop it. I'm not going."

"I must go, Miranda."

"Why?"

"Miranda, please, let us care for you. This is for the best," Maythra said. "Rogeth is a fine male."

Govek went still, a rumble in his throat.

"No, he isn't," Miranda snapped, keeping her eyes on Govek as his eye began to twitch, "I don't want anything to do with Rogeth."

There was a sharp intake of breath and Miranda's eyes only flickered to Rogeth long enough to see him looking affronted.

"That is perfectly fine, Miranda," Maythra said with a wave

of her hand. "You needn't bother with him if he isn't to your liking. There are many males. Why, Wolvc is also here. He would be glad to offer you his aid, I am sure."

"What the heck? Is this a meat market?" Miranda snapped, gripping Govek by the wrist since he'd balled his hands. "Look, I've already got a prime cut and he's keeping me extra stuffed and satisfied so you can all just skedaddle."

There was an instant stillness from the group before Govek broke it.

With bellowing laughter.

"For the will of Fades," Govek managed, covering his eyes with his hand. "Miranda, *fuck*."

"You need some water, tough guy?" Miranda asked, tension evaporating as Govek worked to recover.

Then Maythra ruined it. "Miranda, you are confused but we understand. You are *only* with him because you feel indebted to him for rescuing you. But you are safe now. We can care for you far better than this dangerous male ever could."

"Wow. Bold of you to assume that. You don't even know me."

"I know *Govek*. I know what he is capable of. Please, trust me. I don't want you to end up like Yerina."

Govek visibly flinched.

"He did tell you of Yerina, did he not? Of what he *did* to her? Of the abuse she suffered at his hands?"

"It's time for you to go. Where's the broom?"

"Govek, you must come with us," Agol said. "Now."

Miranda had just found the broom when Govek began following the male out the door.

"Hold on there! Govek, don't you dare!"

He froze in the doorway.

"Let him go, Miranda. It's for your own good."

"Govek." Miranda looked into his eyes. All the laughter that had once been there was gone. "Do you *want* to go to your father?"

His eyes flashed, hands twitched and bunched, shoulders hunched.

That was a clear no.

"Come back over here." Miranda waved him back in and he did so without hesitation. "All right, time to sweep y'all out."

"*Excuse* me—"

Miranda cut Maythra off by smacking the bottom of her legs with the bristles of the broom. The woman scrambled away. "Out! Begone demons!"

"Stop that!" Maythra said, trying to wave her away, but Miranda continued to smack her until the woman was on the stoop. All the males scrambled out without resistance, only offering wide-eyed looks as they stumbled down the stairs and onto the path.

"Govek, get the door."

The male Miranda assumed was Wolvc found his voice. "Govek, you dare ignore the orders of your chief?"

Miranda scoffed. "Chief? Sure."

"He is your chief too," Maythra said, her voice slow and deadly as she patted down her skirts. There were a few dust bunnies stuck to the wool. "You would do well not to forget who is harboring you."

"The way I see it," Miranda said slowly. "Either *Govek* is going to be made chief, or y'all are going to join Karthoc and *he's* going to be your new leader. Ergoth's days in power are numbered."

Tension rolled off the group. Obviously, this was something they hadn't quite put together on their own.

Before anyone could speak, movement up the path caught

Miranda's attention. Another group of orcs were walking toward them.

She didn't know what they wanted, and she certainly didn't want to find out. "You all had better fuck off or you're going to get the broom too!"

The males froze, confused and uncertain.

"Govek will *never* become chief of this clan," Maythra said, drawing Miranda's attention again.

Miranda rolled her eyes. "Just leave already."

"You will come to your senses soon, Miranda," Maythra said, clipped and focused. "You will realize this male has taken advantage of your dire state and see reason. And when you do, know that I will be here, ready with open arms."

"Cool. Govek, shut the door." Miranda went back into the kitchen. Govek obeyed, thudding the broken door back into place behind her. It sat precariously. "We really need to get that fixed." Govek pulled a chair over and wedged the entry shut.

"Oh my god. That was crazy. Does shit like that happen to you all the time?" Miranda asked, pressing her palm to her forehead.

"No."

His clipped tone had her glancing at his tense expression.

"Well . . . I guess that's good? I'm glad you don't get accosted in your house all the time." She put the broom back in the corner and went to the stove. Everything was done. She might as well serve.

She wondered if Govek even had an appetite still. Maythra's words banged around in her head, bruising and goading her into anger all over again. "Where do they all get off trying to drag us around like that? Demanding I go with her to her house. She likes to make it sound like it's in *my* best interest, but it's really just what *she* wants."

She piled her makeshift french fries, which had been cooked far too long, onto Govek's plate before starting to slice a roll in half. "I made my choice. I've been very *clear* on my choice, haven't I?"

Miranda caught Govek's eye again. He was tense, fists bunched.

"I chose *you*," she said sternly, forcing Govek to blink as if even he were shocked. "Dang, *you* don't even want to believe it. Everyone's so determined to give me a choice as long as I don't pick *you*. That's not a choice at all. That's manipulation."

She spread her makeshift ketchup and mustard on the bun before plopping on veggies. The onions were done enough. Everything else was raw. The meat patty was *huge*. Beef burgers always shrunk down a bunch when you cooked them, but whatever this meat Govek had gotten them from the butchery certainly hadn't.

God, she hoped it tasted good. The look Govek had given her when she'd asked him to turn the meat into pulp so she could make the patties had her tension easing into amusement. He was so funny when he was shocked.

"Sit down, tough guy," she said, and he did so slowly, still tense, still watching her close. Miranda sighed. "I swear half of our relationship is you supporting me through my absolute worst moments and the other half is me convincing you I would *never* willingly give up that support."

His throat worked in a gulp.

"I chose *you*, Govek," she repeated. "I'm not changing my mind."

"You . . . aren't?" he asked, not even glancing at the monstrosity of meat and bread she set down before him.

"Just pause for a minute and do a mental inventory of everything you've *done* for me, Govek. Saved my life multiple times. Carried me through the woods. You gave me all your food. You haven't gotten any solid sleep because you keep waking up to comfort me when I have nightmares. And through all that, you've never complained even *once*."

She moved her hands up to his face, massaging the corners of his jaw until it fell back into place.

"And aside from that," she said, still caressing gently. "You're funny and supportive and fun to talk to. We haven't known each other for very long, but what I've seen so far, I *like*, Govek. Which is saying something, 'cause I never found anyone I liked on Earth."

"I'm not leaving, Miranda."

His vow eased the last few drops of irritation right out of her, and she plucked a kiss to his forehead. "Go ahead and eat before someone else shows up to ruin our day. Next time they try, why don't you live up to your tough guy standards and give them what for? You keep saying you're out of control, but I haven't seen you lose control even once since I met you."

He looked stricken. "I . . . don't want to frighten you, Miranda."

"So, you're making the active *choice* not to attack because you don't want to scare me?" He nodded slowly, and she rolled her eyes, exasperation lacing her tone. "Govek, that's what control *is*."

His eyes widened, and he blinked. His fingers raked across his scalp.

A lifetime of conditioning wasn't going to change overnight. Miranda knew that and she had no qualms with chipping away at his insecurities one compliment at a time.

Govek turned his attention to the food and his brows screwed up adorably in confusion.

"It's called a hamburger on Earth. This is a very loose interpretation of one, but should still be good."

"It smells incredible. Where is yours?"

"I'll get it in a minute." She was fairly full since she'd been tasting things as she cooked.

She held her breath as he lifted the burger, took a bite, and began to chew.

His eyes closed and the groan that left his lips shivered right through her. Every trial she went through to make this for him was suddenly worth it a thousand times over.

"I'm totally going to be doing all the cooking from now on," she said as Govek devoured the burger in minutes. She got up to fix him another.

"Is . . . there more?" he asked, and she shot him a grin, delighted beyond words.

"Oh yeah. There's plenty."

"I'm going to become a glutton," Govek said as she heaped toppings onto the bun.

"Oh, don't worry. I won't let you get fat." She brought the new plate over. "I have *lots* of ideas on how to burn off the calories. I bet you have a bunch, too."

He growled low, lingering a hand down her back as she drew near and set down the plate.

"You gonna have me for dessert?" she asked, and his eyes lit with hunger that had nothing to do with the food.

Then a pounding came from the door.

"Oh, no," Miranda moaned. "Who is it now?"

Govek pushed her to the side and walked to the kitchen window, throwing it open to snarl. "Get the fuck off my porch!"

Miranda burst with laughter, suddenly knowing exactly what kind of old curmudgeon Govek might eventually become.

An orc voice stammered. "We mean no offense. We only wish to ask if you plan to stop the merger—"

Govek slammed the window shut and the voices could be heard outside, bickering back and forth about trying to knock again as he made his way back to the table.

"We're gonna have to find somewhere else to hang out, aren't we?" Miranda asked.

"Likely." He picked up his burger and chewed for a few long moments, relishing it. "Do you enjoy waterfalls?"

# CHAPTER
# SIXTEEN

*GOVEK*

"I'm not going to change my mind about going to find them, Govek."

Miranda's clipped tone made Govek's gut clench as he rose with his breakfast bowl and carried it to the sink. Three days of Miranda's cooking and he still couldn't believe how good it was.

Nor could he believe anyone would go to such effort to please him.

"I'll pack the rest of that," Govek said, nodding to the skillet of peppers, potatoes, and onions Miranda had diced up and fried in butter. His stomach was full, but his mouth watered. "We can take it to the falls and have it with the fish I'm going to catch. Unless you want to pick a new spot."

Miranda sighed heavily, crossing her arms, and glared at him. He could feel that glower all the way to the pit of his stomach. "You're changing the subject again."

Of course, he was. He had no desire to fight with her.

They'd been going in circles for *days*, and no amount of logic and reason could turn Miranda to his side. He'd truly hoped in time she would come around.

But she hadn't. Instead, she seemed even *more* convinced that the children she'd cared for on Earth had somehow made it to Faeda.

And she was determined to find them despite all odds.

"Govek." Miranda leaned heavily against the tabletop. "Tell me what you're thinking."

"I'm thinking . . ." He paused to examine her. The heavy bags under her eyes, the slope of her shoulders, the slow way she carried herself. "I'm thinking that you need more sleep."

Her body sagged, and she looked away. "We both do, don't we? I'm sorry I keep waking you up."

That wasn't the issue for him. It was the wailing. The crying and shuddering. The babbling about being trapped and crushed and *burned.*

Horrible images flashed in his mind of what had happened to Tavggol. The idea of Miranda going through something even remotely similar made him want to vomit. It made the imprint roar and quake with a desperate need to protect her at all costs.

He would not be able to protect her outside of the Rove Woods. Not without aid from his fellow orcs.

And Karthoc would ensure that he never got that aid.

"Hey."

Miranda's voice was hard, and he followed her gaze down to where his hands were balled into tight fists. Red blood oozed between his green fingertips.

Fuck, she hated when he cut himself. "Sorry."

Instead of censuring him, she pushed away from the table, got a cloth from the hook on the wall, and sidled up close to him. He could feel her warmth soaking deep into his frame as she lifted his hand to her view, and turned it over gently. She dabbed at his palm with such tenderness that he barely felt the sting. "We'll table this *for now*."

His brow furrowed. "You . . . want to put our discussion on the table?" How would one do that?

Miranda let out a laugh that evaporated nearly every drop of tension he carried. "Oh gosh. No. It's an expression. I just mean we'll talk about it later."

He let out a sigh of relief and nodded.

"Thank you," he said quietly as she finished cleaning the blood and stepped away. He turned to the kitchen, trying to decide where to start cleaning.

"Sorry, I made a pretty big mess this time, didn't I?"

"The aftermath of a Fade storm would have been more manageable," he teased.

She laughed again, the sound bright and clear and flooding the room with her light. His heart thundered.

A knock sounded at the door.

"Fades spit," Govek seethed. "It's *dawn*."

"They're really getting desperate since we've been hiding out in the woods," Miranda murmured with a chuckle. "Who is it?"

"Not sure." The scents from Miranda's cooking were too potent to get a good whiff, but he knew it must be someone from the clan. The scent of his brethren had been strong each night when they returned. They lingered outside the door, hammering away, wanting to talk to him, to drag him to the hall, to convince him to solve this merger problem that never should have been his to begin with.

Fuck Karthoc for forcing this into his lap.

"How long do you think they'll knock before going away? I'll bet you a kiss it's five minutes."

Govek's blood warmed, and he smirked.

She tapped her chin. "Or I could just drag you off to our bedroom and we could, very loudly, pretend that we can't hear them knocking."

A barking laugh left his throat and his tension eased significantly. She certainly had a knack for knowing just what to say to extinguish his tension.

The knocking stopped.

"Do you think they heard me?" Miranda laughed. "Just the prospect of overhearing us getting down and dirty is enough for them to turn tail."

Govek chuckled and went to the door. He inhaled sharply near the crack. Rogeth's pungent scent came through, but it was fading. "He left."

"Guess we should take this window of opportunity to escape," Miranda said. "Unless you think we have time for a quickie."

"I would much rather take my time with you at the falls." Govek kept his voice low and was rewarded when Miranda shivered.

"Ooh, let's hurry up then. Do you still want the breakfast leftovers?"

"Yes," he said, cleaning up what he could before they left. "And the bread—"

"Not the bread," Miranda groaned, forcing another chuckle out of him. There hadn't been any in the storeroom when they'd snuck over the day prior, so he'd made his usual recipe over the campfire at the falls, which used many nutritious roots and herbs.

And Miranda despised it.

"You liked it well enough when I fed it to you the first day."

"Yeah, only because I was *starving.*"

"It will keep you hale, Miranda." He would have been insulted but watching her try to gnaw on the hardened loaf was far too entertaining.

"My jaw can't handle *another* workout this morning. It's sore enough."

The devious image of his woman's lips wrapped around his cock flashed into his mind's eye and his blood boiled even before her words registered and iced him over. "Woman, you needn't go to such lengths to pleasure me."

"I absolutely should," she insisted.

"If the act causes you *pain,* then I don't want—"

Miranda crossed the room and gripped his chin before he could finish. "You know very well it doesn't cause me *pain,* Govek." She stroked his cheek as he huffed with pleasure. "But I'm still not eating anymore of that bread."

He grumbled half-heartedly as she leaned into him, fluttering her soft lips right over his thundering heart, flooding him with contentment so deep it pulsed through his veins.

"Let's finish getting ready," she said, moving to pack and pick up the living room, quietly taking on half of the tasks, working in tandem with him.

It felt incredible. Govek had never imagined having someone live with him could be so pleasant.

"Don't pack the bread," Miranda groaned, just as they were finishing up. "I *beg* you."

"You should save your *begging* for later, woman," he teased before shoving the bread into the pack and moving over to the back exit.

She hit his arm, and he chuckled, delighted by her boldness.

Miranda walked out into the icy morning, leaving him to

bar the door. The forest was still quite dark and glittered in the heavy frost.

A parchment stuck to the door caught his attention. He hesitated, noting that it smelled strongly of sage. Like it had been doused in the plant's oil.

"Oh, what's that?" Miranda asked, coming over. Govek pulled the note free. "Was it on the door?"

"Yes."

She looked over his arm. "I still don't understand how I can *speak* your language, but not *read* it."

"The Fades work in odd ways," Govek said absently, earning a scoff from her. "It's to you. From Viravia."

"Viravia? What does she say?"

"She has invited you to spend time with her in her home tonight."

"Really? Does it say for what?"

"No."

"Will you read it?"

"*Miranda, I would enjoy your company at my home tonight after the evening meal. From Viravia.*"

"That's it?"

"Yes."

Miranda puffed out an irritated breath. "But that could mean just her, or it could mean *all* the women, right?"

"It did say 'I,'" Govek said, instantly understanding Miranda's concern. "It's doubtful that Maythra will be there, and even if she is, you could leave." Maythra had come by more times than any other, even more often than Rogeth.

"That's true," Miranda mumbled as they began up the trail. The autumn chill wasn't bad this morn. The sun was warm and melted every spec of frost it touched. The dappled light was lovely as it played over Miranda's rich, brown hair and soft features. He watched her cheeks grow pink from exertion as they climbed the steep path.

So far, none of their unwelcome visitors had bothered following their scent up the hill behind his home, and Govek hoped that trend would continue. The constant slew of orcs at their door had long grown insufferable.

It was especially infuriating when they came late at night or early in the morning. Miranda was weary enough from her constant nightmares. Hovget was the only male that hadn't tried to bother them in the last few days, and the only one Govek would have welcomed since it meant he could finally retrieve the sleeping tincture for Miranda.

Miranda tipped her head to the bright sky, hazelnut eyes twinkling. Her breath made fog around her face.

She was so beautiful it made his whole body flood with warmth. This gorgeous woman was happily following him up a trail, ready to make camp in the cold with only him for company all day. Content to warm up by sitting in his lap and jabber until he was left with no illusion to what she really thought.

And what she thought was so *wonderful*. Delight at the scenery, pleasure over the food.

Compliments for him. Constant, endless touches and sweet words that made him ache.

How had he gotten so fucking *lucky*?

He couldn't lose her.

She shot him a sly grin that made his heart thunder. "Wanna race?"

Govek blinked slowly. "You want to *what*?"

Miranda burst into laughter. "Govek, you make it sound like I just asked you to chop your hand off."

"I cannot decide if you are delusional enough to honestly

think the match would be fair," he muttered, though his irritation lightened at her continued laughter. "You would stand no chance in this."

"Well, then how about you give a girl a break and let me have a head start?"

His eyes narrowed. "A head start?"

"Yeah, I'll start running and you count to like thirty or something before—"

"Counting to a hundred would not be enough," he snorted. "Perhaps not even to a thousand."

She smacked his arm, and he grinned helplessly at her courage. "Hey, I'm not *that* slow."

"You are, Miranda. I have seen tree slugs that—"

"If you compare me to a tree slug, you are going to *thoroughly* regret it."

"As I was saying, I have seen unbelievably gorgeous butterflies that could flutter faster than you."

"Better, but seriously, it could be fun. I mean, worst-case scenario, you catch up to me in half a breath and maybe we could play a little game. I could be the butterfly and you could be the hawk chasing me down."

The comparison made his blood simmer even as he worked for calm. "Miranda, hawks *eat* butterflies."

"Even better." She smoothed her hand up his chest, forcing him to stumble to a stop. "I think I'd like being eaten by you."

Tension shot through Govek so quickly, Miranda tensed with him.

She blinked. "What's wrong?"

"Nothing." He wrenched the worthless memories of his last encounter with Yerina out of his mind. He had lost control with her, but he would *not* make the same mistake with Miranda. He *could* not.

He would never forgive himself if he drove Miranda away.

"Govek, I was only teasing," Miranda said, brows pinched. "If you aren't into giving oral, that's okay. I'm not going to pressure you into doing anything you don't want to."

He growled low, raked his hand through his hair. Fuck! Her words were *torture*. He wanted to taste her so badly it was almost painful. His mouth watered and his tongue tingled. Fangs clenched with the desire to bite.

He couldn't. He would lose control and *ruin* this.

"Govek?" Miranda pressed, and he opened his eyes, met the confusion in her face full on.

"Let's go." She didn't argue, just linked her arm with his and followed him in unusual silence.

The trip to the overlook where Govek had built them a camp was quick, and Miranda let him go so she could take in the view of the falls. Her reverence at the crisp blue water plummeting down the cliffside into a massive pool below them even after three days here still took his breath. Her red lips parted, her hazelnut eyes widened, and her hair glistened from the damp.

"Not too close," he censured, earning a dark look from her. She liked to sit on the large log right near the cliff and it drove him crazy.

"If you're so nervous, then why don't you come join me? Hold me steady."

Fades he wanted to, but there were chores to be done. "I need to make you a fire," Govek said, and blessedly, Miranda followed him over and helped carry kindling from the edges of the clearing. The little camp they'd made was covered with damp leaves, but the sky was clear. Once the sun dappled light through the trees, they would dry out.

He pulled a saber cat fur out of his pack and arranged it on top of the leaves Miranda had gathered into a pile right near the fire. Her little makeshift chair.

She only sat there when she wasn't sitting in his lap.

He lit the fire easily using two striking stones. In reaction, Miranda came over to give him a quick kiss on the cheek. Pleasure tingled through him. The tiny bit of extra effort it took to light the fire without magic was worth the praise Miranda gave him for it.

*"If it makes you upset to use magic, Govek, then maybe you should try not to. Not that I'm afraid of your temper, because I certainly am not. I just don't like the idea of you hurting to make my life easier."*

*Fuck*, she made him feel good.

Miranda was settling down next to the crackling blaze, and he leaned in to nuzzle the side of her neck with his nose and tusks. Her sweet honey scent poured into him, flooding him with contentment.

She laughed, chiding him. "Govek that tickles," but she placed a lingering kiss on his cheek. "I could live up here."

Govek exhaled softly, glad his woman shared his love of the forest.

"There's something about this place, right? Or these woods, in general? That happy tingling from the goblin mines is gone now, but it still feels *good* here. Or maybe I'm just crazy."

"You are not crazy. Most orcs feel at peace within the Rove Woods because of its connection to the Fades."

"But it's weird for a human to feel that, isn't it?" she asked, gazing out toward the falls again. The sorrow in her expression cut him deep. "I don't belong here."

"That isn't true." His chest tightened as she turned to search his face. "You are just as natural as all the other creations, Miranda."

She quirked a smile that did not meet her eyes. "That's a nice thought."

"It is a true thought. The Fades created humans just as they did the rest of Faeda."

She hummed. "I think . . . there's more to it than that."

"What do you mean?"

"I don't know . . . do you think the seer might?" she asked hesitantly and every muscle in his body tensed at the cursed memory of her touching the seer's hand and falling in a boneless heap. He'd barely managed to catch her before she hit the ground.

She had been *gone*. The feel of her limp body in his arms, the sight of her closed eyes, and the clammy cool of her skin, it thundered in his veins and pooled dread into the pit of his stomach.

The seer had done that. And Miranda wanted to do it again.

"Govek?"

Fuck, it was getting too hard to hide his feelings on this topic. And he knew where she stood with it. She'd made her position clear. There was no use arguing with her. She would do this on her own if he didn't aid her.

She would *leave* him.

He could not risk that. No matter how his instincts screamed, he could not bring himself to start an argument that may result in her rejecting him the way he had been so many times before.

"I should get the fishing done, Miranda." Govek moved to stand.

"Hey."

She gripped his wrist and pulled him down and lingered a gentle kiss to his lips. Bliss radiated through his entire frame.

251

She broke off the kiss far too soon and he asked, "Do you want to wait here or come down to the pool with me?"

"I'll wait here."

His disappointment was stifled as she kissed him again. It took far too much effort to leave her, but he had to, or they would have no lunch.

He gathered his spear, tied it to his back, and began the slow climb down the cliffside.

# CHAPTER
# SEVENTEEN

*MIRANDA*

Miranda waited until Govek was out of sight before going to the edge to watch him, then she breathed a sigh of relief when she saw him drop onto the slim bank far below. Safe and sound. She ducked back before Govek could look up and see how close she'd gotten to the ledge. He *hated* when she got close.

But the view was absolutely *stunning*, and it was difficult for her not to linger.

The positioning of the falls where they'd made their camp *was* a little dangerous. They were on a cliffside halfway up the waterfall. The glittering crystalline water plummeted from a ledge twenty feet above her and crashed into a deep pool nearly forty feet below. The cliffside seemed stable enough, Govek had examined it to make sure, but mist from the falls made everything around a little slick.

That mist also sprayed up, casting rainbows in almost every patch of sunlight that streamed through the trees. Gray-blue rocks covered with bright green moss framed the banks. They were offset by the bright red foliage of the trees surrounding them.

The rushing water itself was rapid, vivid, and *loud*. It helped clear her mind and eased her into relaxing.

Govek had built them a makeshift camp, and they had come up here from dawn till dusk for the last three days. He'd created a lean-to using sticks and animal furs, so they had a dry place to protect from the wind and falling leaves. The campfire had a tall wall of stones circling it to keep loose embers at bay. He'd even collected some of the moss into thick piles and covered them with soft deer hides so they had beds to nap on. And do other things . . .

Her chest warmed, and she suddenly wished he would hurry with the fishing.

The number of fish they'd eaten was out of hand. She almost felt bad about it. Govek's skills with a spear would single-handedly cause the small trout to be extinct.

And yet, every day he would climb back up the cliff with a dozen more, like it was nothing. Green abs glistening from mist and sweat. Damp shirt sticking to his skin, accentuating his arms. Eyes glistening with pleasure when he saw her waiting.

He really was the best distraction.

"Fades have *mercy*."

Miranda jolted to her feet and whirled around, scampering further away from the edge of the cliff just to be certain she wouldn't slip.

And closer to the newcomer.

A bald white orc with misty eyes and a slender build stood at the edge of the tree line, scowling and muttering.

The seer. The seer was here. At their camp.

He let out another foul curse and then turned back to the woods.

"W-wait!" Miranda hurried toward the white male before he could escape. "Seer, wait!"

"Get away from me. I told you, you're too *much*."

"Too much what?" She'd been waiting for a chance to find her way back into the clan for *days* just so she could find this male and now here he was. Right in front of her! "Please, can't you tell me? I could fix it."

"There's nothing to *fix*. You aren't supposed to be here."

Before Miranda could stop him, he turned and disappeared back into the forest. Her mind worked rapidly. Govek would *fume* if she went after the seer right now, but dang it, she *needed* to talk to him.

Making Govek upset would just have to be the price she paid.

Before she could even reach the tree line, the seer was walking back into the clearing. He froze, white eyes blinking slowly.

"I'm back, aren't I?"

"Yeah, you are," Miranda said, somewhat breathlessly.

"*Fuck*." The seer nearly snarled making his way over to the fire. "Give me some food."

"Uh . . ." Miranda went to Govek's bag and dug through it, producing the hardened bread. "Here."

"Set it there," the seer muttered, pointing to a rock nearby.

"Can you . . . see?" Miranda asked as she sat it down.

What *were* the extent of the seer's powers?

Would he really be able to tell her what happened to the children at Riverside Daycare?

She wrung her hands. Her desperation for answers gripped her so hard that she saw stars.

255

"Did you honestly just ask me if I could *see?*" the male asked, voice clipped. Then he cursed, snapping his hands to his bare head, gripping hard enough to bruise.

"Are you okay?" Miranda said, hurrying over, but she was careful not to touch him.

"What do you think?" the male snapped. Miranda somehow managed to stay silent.

Silence seemed to be the right approach because the seer snatched up the bread and took a bite. His shoulders relaxed. His palm pressed into his forehead. "This is horrible."

"Yeah, sorry. Govek is catching fish right now. We'd be happy to let you stay and eat."

"I don't want to be around you one split of a moment longer."

Her stomach dropped, "What did I do wrong? Can you tell me that much at least?"

The seer paused, fingers digging into the lump of bread, white eyes lingering toward the fire. She wondered if he could see the light of it or maybe he just felt the warmth. He finally sighed, long and hard.

"I *apologize.* Things with that blasted fool of a warlord aren't—thank you for the bread. I won't be finishing it. Do you want it back?"

"No, it's fine. You can keep it."

"Are you certain? You could likely use this as a weapon. Use it to fend off those desperate fools pining and plotting away in the hall. Though I suppose Govek does that for you, doesn't he?"

Miranda straightened. "Wait, what? What do you mean, *plotting?*"

"I'm sure you *noticed.* Most of the Rove Wood fools are desperate for new women. All they have are those humans from Oakwall who've known them their entire lives. Why do you think Tavggol took the risk of sparking peace with Clairton?"

Miranda's brow furrowed. "Are you saying that the Rove Wood orcs are plotting to separate me and Govek?"

"Do birds squawk?" the seer muttered. "Some are too scared, and some are smart enough not to try, but there are a few shallow idiots that think themselves so lofty you would never refuse them."

"Which ones?" Miranda asked, wanting to avoid them.

"I'll tell you if you let me go."

"Let you go? I'm not holding you here."

"Your desperation to *dredge* is," he muttered, tossing away the hunk of bread.

"Really?" Miranda inched a little closer.

"Oh no, you don't. You sit *there*."

Miranda glanced to where he was pointing. "Uh . . . that's off the cliff."

"We're next to a *cliff?*"

"Yeah, the falls are over—"

"I'm blind, not deaf. I can hear the falls. I thought we were at the *bottom*. For fuck's sake, are the Fades *trying* to kill me?" The seer stalked back toward the tree line, and this time, Miranda stayed put. "All I want is to get to that blasted hall so I can have a half-decent meal and the Fades tip me around and put me *here*. They want me to be in agony *and* starve to death is that—"

He broke off with a hiss. Doubled over.

Miranda hurried forward. "Are you okay? Do you need—?"

"I'm fucking *blistering,*" the seer raged. "*Get*—wait. Don't move."

Miranda froze.

"Just . . . wait." He took a hesitant step forward and breathed deep. Miranda chewed her lip.

He continued moving toward her. Each step made tension grow in her chest. She watched the male's hands, her own shaking as they continued to wring her skirt.

*Just a touch and this would be over.*

Her lip trembled. She didn't know how she was so certain touching this male would solve the problem, but she *did*. And god, it was everything she could do not to run forward and grasp hold until she finally found out what had happened to her babies.

The seer hissed sharply and began to walk away, then froze again, groaned.

"For *fuck's* sake, get yourself under *control*."

Miranda stepped toward him. "W-what do you mean?"

"Your *grief*. It's maddening. Muddling. You must *stop*."

Her grief? "I . . . can try. If I can be distracted, I'll—"

The male hissed again. "Fine. *Fine.* I admit there is something, but I cannot dredge it *now*. You aren't ready."

"What do I have to do to get ready?"

"I don't blasted know." He gripped his head again. "They won't stop screaming long enough for me to figure it the fuck out."

"Screaming? Who's screaming?"

"*The Fades.*"

The . . . Fades? But weren't they supposed to be asleep?

"Ha! I wish they slept. Would give me a reprieve from their endless wailing."

Her eyes widened, shock making her cold. "Can you read *minds*?"

"I read what the Fades allow." He slumped further. "And right now, that is mostly constant agonizing screams."

Miranda's chest tightened as she wondered what it was like to be constantly hearing tortured screams in your head.

"Your pity is kind, but you should save it for your male. Sit down there, Miranda. And clear up your mind."

"Clear my mind? Of what?"

"Of *everything*. I need it cleared so I can *dredge*, so the Fades will let me fucking go to the hall and get breakfast."

Oh. Miranda chewed her lip. She had no idea how to do that. The memories of Earth were *constant*. Endless. Even when she was distracted by a task, they hovered in the back of her brain, ready to pounce. To grind her up into a pile of useless mush. To drown her in her fear and regret and horrible *guilt*.

"*Hush.*"

Miranda's back went straight. The seer's hum sounded so much like Govek it was almost terrifying.

"I was trying to soothe, not *startle*. This isn't going to work. It's too thick. I can't clear it. You have to."

"But . . ." Miranda didn't know what to do. Nothing made sense.

How was she supposed to overcome the horrors of Earth on her own? The *seer* was supposed to be the one helping her with that. *He* was the one that would show her what happened to her babies. Tell her they'd survived. That they were okay with their parents. Unhurt. Wandering Faeda and waiting for her to find them.

"Ah, that was it then." The seer stood.

"What?" Miranda scrambled to her feet as he began to walk away. "Wait, where are you going?"

"That is what I was meant to say here. You need to clear your mind. Until then, I cannot help you."

"But I don't know how to do that." Miranda's stomach twisted.

"That isn't my problem," he said, and Miranda almost crumbled, begging, when he paused. His brow smoothed. His expression eased.

The seer looked so *young*. He couldn't have been much older than her, but there were dark bags under his eyes, his cheeks were hollow, and his body was too thin.

He'd clearly weathered horrible storms.

Just how long had he been riddled by agony? Used as a tool of the Fades? Was there even a light at the end of the tunnel for him, or was death going to be his only reprieve?

His expression softened more. "You are far too *kind*, Miranda. Be careful who you offer it to."

"Do you mean Govek?"

"Fades, no. That male came back *here* for you. He deserves every scrap of kindness you willingly throw his way. I mean, the males in the clan. The ones who would see your kindness and twist it into what they want."

"Who?" Miranda asked.

"Best I not say. It will muddle things."

"Muddle what?"

But the seer only turned away again. "My task here is done and your male is approaching. We'll cross paths again, Miranda. Fades be."

The male walked off into the woods and disappeared just before Govek burst up from the edge of the cliff, no spear in hand, his face a mask of anger.

"Where the fuck is he?"

"He's gone," Miranda said, seeing no reason to deny it. You can't hide smell. "He went that way."

Govek almost bounded into the woods before Miranda interrupted his charge. "You really going to leave me alone?"

He stopped short. Breathed hard. Stormed back over to her side. "Come here."

She let him pick her up and plunk her down on a boulder. His hands stroked her limbs. "Did he hurt you?"

"No. I would have screamed if he'd tried."

Govek took a few deep breaths.

"Govek, I didn't call the seer here. He showed up on his own."

Govek raked a hand through his hair and squeezed his eyes shut.

"He somehow found me out here, even though he was headed for the hall. That says something, doesn't it?" She cupped Govek's face. "It's what I'm supposed to do, but you still have doubts somehow, don't you?"

"It's *dangerous*, Miranda," Govek rumbled, leaning in, caging her.

"You think *everything* is dangerous where I'm concerned." She scratched gently at his scalp, relishing the warm, pine scent of him. "Even *you*."

"I *am* dangerous, Miranda."

"But dangerous things can also be *necessary*," Miranda pointed out, willingly barreling right into the topic that had been a constant form of strife for days. "Like finding my babies and bringing them back here to Rove Wood Clan."

Govek growled low in his throat. "Miranda."

"I'm not going to stop arguing about this, Govek," she said firmly, "I understand you think it's not safe to leave the Rove Woods—"

"It *isn't*."

Miranda took a deep breath. "I only want to leave long enough to find my babies."

"Leaving for *any* amount of time is too risky, Miranda."

She huffed out a breath of irritation. "Look, I *know* I sound crazy. I really do. I know I have no proof that they're even out there. But my *gut* is telling me that the seer knows *something* about them. Something that will . . . help."

Something that would take away the agony of wondering if they were screaming for her. Something that would stop her mind from getting stuck on the image of them suffering, crushed and burned. Something that would ease the horrific, bone-gnawing, gut-heaving *guilt* that *she* had been the one to live.

And they had—

No. They *hadn't*.

They were here. On Faeda. She just had to find them.

"What if we got someone else to go?" Govek asked softly, breaking her out of her thoughts.

Her brow furrowed. "Someone else? What do you mean? I thought you said none of the orcs or humans here ever leave. And I highly doubt Karthoc or his warriors are going to help unless you become the chief."

Govek sighed heavily, looking off into the woods so he wouldn't have to meet her eyes, and then said. "Viravia used to be a traveling trader."

"Oh yeah. I think I remember that being mentioned when I was at her house." Miranda tapped her chin. "So, you think she might know someone willing to help find my babies?"

"Not help." He breathed deep, and she felt the exhale rustling her hair, tickling. "With enough boons, I believe we could convince someone to fetch them for us while we stayed here."

"Govek," Miranda said warningly. "That's *not* going to work. What if he gets the wrong ones? I'm the only one who would recognize any of them. And I'm the only one they would know to trust."

"You could give the tracker information that only you would know. And describe the children to them so he knows he has the right ones."

"But that's—"

"Miranda, I do not believe you are comprehending just how *insurmountable* it will be to find them with both the humans *and* orcs working against us. And although I have the maps, I have never been further out than Clairton. I have no allies, no knowledge of the terrain, no idea where there is even solid hunting or foraging ground."

Miranda shifted uncomfortably, mind quailing against his logic. "But . . . they are *my* responsibility. I'm supposed to find them."

"Miranda, you said before that you feel you are supposed to *save* them. Part of saving them is also preparing Rove Wood Clan for their arrival, yes? How can you do that when you are searching all of Faeda for them? You'll bring them back here to an abandoned clan that has not been maintained over the harsh winter."

She hated that he had a point and hit a low blow in retaliation. "An abandoned clan and a village of humans *you're* on bad terms with."

Govek growled and looked away again. "I don't *need* to be on good terms with Oakwall."

"For the last time, Govek you *do*. You absolutely do. You need community too. What if you got hurt and needed a healer?" He gave her a dubious look, and she amended. "Fine, what if *I* got hurt, and you tried to get me help and the residents of Oakwall turned you away at the gate?"

His expression turned stricken. It should not have made her feel so triumphant.

Govek looked away. Into the woods. Only the slight rustling of the wind in the crisp autumn leaves broke the tension as he thought.

She *had* to change his mind. She didn't want to do this without him. She didn't want to face the prospect of leaving him to find her babies.

But she would have to if he didn't come around.

"A compromise then."

Her heart thundered.

Govek met her gaze. "I will go to the trade with you in two days' time and try to mend the bridge with Oakwall *if* you agree to ask Viravia if she knows a tracker who could help find your Earth children for us."

Miranda's heart was skittering all over itself and her guts twisted up so harshly she thought she might vomit. "How can you be sure that Viravia would even *know* anyone? How do you know we could trust them if she does?"

"Viravia has never betrayed this clan. She never would. The life of her son depends on the stability of these woods."

His voice was cold and quiet and reminded Miranda that the clan was now facing a merger. She knew it weighed on Govek greatly, thinking about his nephew growing up at Baelrok.

But he'd also never once said he'd be willing to take on the role of chief to prevent that from happening.

She pressed a palm to her forehead. Things were so fricking *complicated*.

"Do we have a deal, Miranda?"

Did they? Her head ached as she went over all the moving parts.

There was no guarantee that Viravia would know a tracker. If she *did*, Miranda could still find a way to convince Govek to let her go with him to find her babies when the time came.

And they *needed* to get on friendly terms with Oakwall, regardless.

"Okay." Miranda nodded. "We have a deal."

Govek's relief was so clear on his face that it *transformed* him. It smoothed out all the stress lines between his eyes, loosened his jaw. A wide, devilish grin broke across his face that made her stomach flip. Warmth spread through her, and she leaned into kiss his nose, his cheeks, his soft lips.

His expression had turned tender when she pulled away and it made her want to melt.

"Okay," Miranda said softly. "So, first step I guess is having dinner with Viravia tonight and asking her if she knows someone who can help find my babies."

Govek nodded slowly.

"And then day after tomorrow we go to the trade. Do you have anything you want to do to prepare? Should you hunt for it, so we have a peace offering?"

All the contentment in Govek's expression fell away, and he was back to looking stricken. He raked a hand through his hair and sat back away from her.

"Govek, it's okay. I know this isn't going to be easy for you. I'll do everything I can to support you."

"Thank you," he said softly. A quirked smile played at his lips. "It's . . . odd to have someone on my side in this. I never have before."

Her heart fluttered even as her stomach twisted.

"We will have to be *very* careful with how we proceed," he

explained. "They have the leverage necessary to issue a judgment against me. And if they do that . . . it will bring the worst upon us."

"A judgment?"

Govek took a deep breath. "That is how Rove Wood Clan deals with disputes. They hold judgments, where the clan votes on the guilt of the transgressor and decides on a punishment."

"Sounds a bit like what we did on Earth."

"If Oakwall calls for a judgment over the accusations against Yerina, I would be severely punished."

"Only if you're found guilty, right?" He blinked in surprise, and she said slowly, "You said you didn't hurt her."

"I did not. But I have *never* been found innocent, Miranda."

She went cold. "Never? How many times have you been the transgressor of these judgments?"

"Many times."

"And . . . how many times were you found guilty when you were innocent?"

"It doesn't matter."

Anger flashed to cover her pity. "Govek, it absolutely does. I can't believe they would find you guilty of things you didn't do."

"I technically did all the things that I was called to face judgment for." He looked away. "Just not to the extent that was described during the hearing."

"So, what? You threaten someone and then they say you actually attacked?" Govek's eyes told her everything she needed to know. She sucked in a hard breath. "And then what? You mentioned punishment."

"Typically, it was a period of banishment and binding. My home was already on the outskirts, so I was magically bound against any violence and not allowed to step foot in the clan for a few seasons," Govek admitted.

Miranda shook her head. "A few seasons? If you couldn't commit any violent acts, how did you hunt?"

"I . . . didn't."

"Then how did you get food, Govek? Since you weren't allowed in the clan, you weren't able to get to the storeroom . . ." she broke off thinking of the bread.

He made it entirely of things he foraged out here in the woods.

Miranda's stomach dropped, and her chest tightened. She clutched the loose fabric of Govek's pants and forced him to step closer to the boulder, to lean down so she could wrap her arms around his neck in a tight hug.

He sagged against her, wrapping her up in return. He squeezed slightly before trailing his hands down her back and cupping under her ass, lifting her off the boulder so he could hold her close. He pressed his forehead to hers. His eyes were squeezed shut and her chest felt like a hollow pit.

"I'm so sorry, Govek," she whispered, cupping his face in her hands, stroking the hinge of his jaw.

"It is my fault, Miranda. I should not have threatened violence. It is not the way of Rove Wood Clan."

No, the way of Rove Wood Clan was to alienate and pass judgment, to place blame without knowing all the facts, and to look down on others simply for the way they looked or how they were born.

It sounded far too close to Earth's atrocities. The purpose behind Earth's *wars*.

She would not let them get away with it.

"We should ask Viravia about the trade tonight."

"What do you mean?"

Miranda leaned back to look Govek in the eye. "We're going to ask her how *exactly* Oakwall feels about you. I don't believe that everyone thinks you hurt Yerina."

"Miranda—"

"Govek, they had a whole *season* to pass judgment on you and they didn't. That has to mean *something,* right?"

Govek said nothing, but his expression was doubtful.

"We're going to ask her. It can't hurt," Miranda said. "And then we'll just have to do our best at the trade. If the clan wants to hold a judgment against you, then so be it. They can't banish you if they aren't here to uphold it, anyway."

Govek paused. "That's . . . true." He met her eyes with a nod. "We will ask and I will try."

Triumph burst in Miranda's chest, and she kissed him hard. "Thank you, Govek. I promise it will be worth it."

He nuzzled against her cheek and took another deep breath. "It already is."

# CHAPTER
# EIGHTEEN

*GOVEK*

"You're seriously not going in with me?"

Govek leaned against a tree part way into the woods where they could not be easily seen, arms crossed, eyes fixed to the dwelling before him. The ancient home that had always belonged to the heir of this clan. The massive, multi-level structure he'd last been in when Tavggol was still . . .

"No," he said slowly. "I'm not going in."

Tavggol was no longer within. He had no ties to this place now.

"Govek." Miranda crossed her arms over her chest and leveled him with a hard look. It was too dark for her to see his scowl clearly, but she certainly could make out the glow of his eyes.

"Miranda, I was not invited."

"What do you mean you weren't invited?"

"The missive did not mention me in it."

"Govek, we're a *couple,* and she's your sister-in-law."

"I highly doubt she sees me as such," Govek muttered, looking toward the darkened windows again. The scent of sage was overpowering so he could not scent Viravia within and her home appeared shuttered. He scrutinized the windows for movement, but saw nothing.

Was she even there? Why would she invite them and then leave?

"She doesn't see you like a brother?" Miranda's brow screwed up.

"No," Govek said honestly, wondering why his mate was so unsettled by that fact. "Viravia was not from Oakwall originally, so we did not have the time to grow familial bonds."

"Did . . . you grow *any* bonds? Like, just as family?" Miranda asked. "She defended you in front of Maythra."

"Viravia has always been kind." Too kind. She was his brother's *mate* and yet she cast Govek constant smiles and tried to draw him into frivolous conversation.

Admittedly, Tavggol had never seemed affronted by her shows of affection. At the time, Govek thought nothing of it, but now that he had Miranda . . .

If Miranda had cast easy smiles at Tavggol, Govek knew he would likely be goaded into violence. Brother or no.

"What's wrong? Out with it. Don't be so quiet."

"I'm always quiet."

"You're really not," Miranda muttered, but softened the blow by taking his hand in both of hers. "Tell me what's on your mind."

Unwilling to admit *imagined* jealousy toward his own brother, he said, "The house is dark, and I have not seen movement."

"Oh." Miranda looked at the house again. "Do you think she's not in there? Maybe she went to the hall?"

"I . . . don't know. I can't scent her past the sage."

Miranda searched his face for a long moment.

"If you're worried about her, then *come on*," Miranda tugged his hand, and he allowed her to lead him across the path and onto Viravia's stoop. She knocked without preamble and Govek held his breath.

They heard a slight rustling within. The curtain next to the door moved slightly and an eye peeped through. That eye widened at the sight of them and disappeared back into the darkened home.

Then light flickered brighter, and the door sprang open.

"Well, good evening," Viravia said quickly, glancing between the two of them. Her bright blue eyes flashed in the dim light, her dark hair glistened. "How are you two? Please come in."

Govek hesitated, struck a little dumb by this oddly warm welcome. He only crossed the threshold when Miranda placed a hand at his back and gave a light shove.

The home was the same as he remembered, and Govek was struck in the gut by that. The furniture was in the same place. Tavggol's favorite chair was nestled in the corner. The rugs and wall hangings hadn't budged. Viravia had not even switched out the glassware for smaller, more manageable items.

It felt as if at any moment Tavggol would walk down those steps. His eyes would widen at Govek's sudden appearance. He'd laugh and tease him about never wanting to visit in the clan and then force Govek to sit by his fire and talk until the sun brightened the windows.

"Are you all right, Govek?" Viravia asked, soft and pressing.

Govek swallowed hard, working to find words.

271

"Why don't you let me make you some tea?" Miranda suggested softly. "Let him have a moment."

"No," Govek said swiftly, the familiar bubbling of anger rising in the back of his throat. "No. I don't need a moment."

They hadn't come here for him. He was being a fool.

"Govek," Viravia started, but he just shot her a hard look and she sucked in a breath. "Why don't you both come sit down?"

"I was only here to bring Miranda. I do not want to intrude."

"You could never be an intruder here," Viravia said, rubbing her belly. His eyes fixed to the swell of it. The lump in his throat grew anew. "Here." She pulled out a chair at the kitchen table. "Sit."

He should have left, stormed out the door and gone back to his home on the outskirts. He should not be standing here pretending that everything was well and that his own lack of action hadn't led to his brother's demise.

"Govek."

The call was strong. Firm. He looked into Viravia's eyes and saw the strength that his brother must have fallen for.

"Set it aside," Viravia demanded, and his gut pitched. "There has been more than enough guilt in the last season. It was not your fault."

It was not his fault? She should be raging at him, casting him out, calling him vile.

He'd *known* that the trade deal with Clairton felt off, that there was something *wrong*, but he'd let the matter drop in the face of Tavggol's determination. He'd been too distracted with Yerina's endless demands and had let Tavggol leave.

And his brother had never come back.

"It's not your fault," Viravia said softly, and the words

cracked at something in Govek's chest. She turned away as if she hadn't just shattered him with her forgiveness.

"I'll make tea, Miranda. It's no trouble," Viravia said, waving Miranda into a chair. "How have you been? I hear things haven't been exactly . . . *easy* in the clan."

Miranda settled into the large wood chair. The back was too tall for her. "Yeah, we've been spending a lot of time in the woods. Basically, only going back to the house to sleep right now. Seems like everyone and their mother is trying to talk to Govek."

"I'm sure," Viravia said, trundling into the kitchen area. She seemed to get around easily enough, but there was bedding stacked on the end of the couch as if she was sleeping there.

"Are you unable to get up the steps?" Govek asked, voice still tight.

Viravia shot him a wide-eyed look before murmuring, "You're as observant as Tavggol. Yes, it's been a chore recently."

"Oh gosh," Miranda said. "I'm so sorry I didn't notice. Do you need help? I'm happy to do any cleaning or cooking you have. Or we can move some of your stuff downstairs?"

"That's so sweet, but the women have already got me covered. I almost always have someone here nagging me to keep off my feet. Especially now that I can't make it to the hall for meals." She shot Miranda a smile. "Nice to have a different kind of visit for a change."

Miranda smiled back and Govek felt his tension ebb.

"Most of the clan is still buzzing about the announcement," Viravia said, placing sage leaves in the kettle. "Have you spoken to the warlord since?"

"No," Miranda said. "Only members of the clan come to bang on our door. As far as we know, anyway."

Viravia nodded, looking pensively down at her herbs.

"Was there something you wanted to know about him?" Miranda asked, casting Govek a look that indicated she thought this might have been the reason Viravia had invited her over.

"Oh no. Just . . ." Tension rose in the woman's back, but when she turned, she was forcing a smile. "No. You came here to visit. Let's talk of more pleasant things."

She was hoping for information about the merger, Govek was certain. About whether he was going to pick up his father's mantle. The prospect of moving must have been daunting with the babe in her stomach so large.

Quite unbidden, Govek was struck by the flash of an entirely new image. A vision of Miranda with her own swollen stomach. Her ability to move stolen by the mass of an orc son growing and faced with the challenge of losing her home.

Conflicting emotions abraded against his raw senses, and he rose from his chair, moving to take the tray of cups and tea from Viravia.

Her eyes grew wide. "Oh, *thank you*, Govek."

He nodded gruffly and went back to his place, setting the large cups down in front of the chairs.

Viravia walked over with no hesitation in her stride and sat, patting her stomach tenderly. Yet he knew she must feel some pain if she could not get up her steps. "You are a strong woman, Viravia."

"O-oh." Color came into the woman's cheeks as her eyes darted away, and her lips quirked in a little smile. "That's nice of you to say."

Govek took a hard breath as he turned her mug, so the handle faced her. Viravia would be fine. They would let her ride in a cart. Hovget and Wellia would leave with them, with all their medical tinctures. Wellia had birthed many orc sons both here for the mates and for the conquests at Oakwall Village.

Miranda would have none of those luxuries. They would be here. Alone. With only the Oakwall midwife to attend her. A woman Govek had never even met properly.

He shook the disconcerting thought away, but it stuck in the back of his mind. Like an itch he couldn't quite reach.

Was staying here alone truly the right way?

# CHAPTER

# NINETEEN

*MIRANDA*

Miranda was a complete jealous idiot.

She fixated on every soft gaze Govek shot Viravia's way. The way his eyes lingered on her as she walked. The kind gestures, even turning her mug so she could pick it up easily. That random, unprompted compliment . . .

Damn it all, he *wasn't* flirting. He was just being nice. She was his *sister*-in-law.

*"We did not have the time to grow familial bonds."*

God, why did that get under her skin so bad?

"Um . . ." Miranda mumbled, and Govek snapped his gaze away from Viravia. There was an awkward pause. "I'm really sorry the pregnancy has been so hard."

"I-It's all right," Viravia said, skittering her gaze from Govek to her. "I signed up for it, after all. And I would go through anything for this little one to be healthy and whole."

Miranda sagged, forcing tension out. "Have you picked a name yet?"

"Not yet," Viravia said, before rolling her eyes. "Maythra has been *very* pushy about her favorites, though. She hasn't been bothering you too badly, has she? I've tried to get her to stop but . . ."

Miranda snorted. "Girl, that's nice of you, but you've got enough going on, and I can fight my own battles."

Viravia relaxed slightly and sat back. "Maythra has been a part of this clan the longest of all the women. She feels a sense of entitlement and leadership and likes to wield it around. But there are a few of us who don't bow to her bluster. Savili is one of them. You'll like her very much, Miranda. She and my other friends will all give you a warm welcome when they return from the seasonal communion."

Govek tensed beside her, and Miranda glanced to find his expression flat. His eyes lowered as if lost in thought.

"They'll be here soon, actually. The seasonal communion is being cut short because of the warlord's idiotic"—Viravia pressed fingers to her lips—"Sorry. I don't mean to insult. It's just . . . to *merge* Rove Wood Clan! He's absolutely . . ."

Miranda leaned in, curiosity getting the better of her. "He's what? You can be open."

Viravia flashed a look at Govek. "I have no warmth toward my cousin at the moment. State your peace."

"He's an absolute ass," Viravia unleashed, throwing her hands up. "To think that he would be stupid enough to even *consider* merging this clan with his forge. Which is in the center of the *war,* mind you. And he thinks the healing tinctures will be of better quality? Ha, perhaps the distribution will be easier, but there is no *magic* outside these woods. The Fades have truly abandoned this world. Every part but *here.*" She stroked her pregnant belly and looked out into the dark autumn.

"You talk like you know it really well," Miranda said, heat from the mug stung her palms. "Out there, I mean."

"Before I became a mate, I was a traveling trader. With my . . . father." Viravia's face grew haunted. What things lurked in this woman's past? "The world outside Rove Wood is harsh and unyielding. This is the only truly safe place."

"It's . . . really that bad?" Miranda asked, glancing at Govek.

Viravia looked between them. "Are . . . Don't tell me you are thinking of *leaving*?"

"No," Govek said quickly, before Miranda could even consider telling Viravia their plans.

"Good," she said, slumping in her seat. "Govek, I know that many here think you would not be suited as our chief, but I—"

"I wish not to speak on this tonight, Viravia."

Viravia pursed her lips as if she were about to argue.

"Actually," Miranda cut in. "About you being a trader . . ." Her gut pitched as she considered her words. Her mind quailed thinking about not being the one to go and find her babies. And yet . . . she glanced out the window into the woods, gut twisting, thoughts blanking, warmth flooding her veins.

Govek was right. She didn't want to leave these woods either, and she had *no* wilderness skills. There was no harm in asking. "Viravia, do you know someone who could help me . . . find my family."

Viravia straightened, blinking. "Your family?"

Miranda's throat closed. Frick, it was *hard* to get this out. "Yes, we were uh . . . separated. I have no idea where they could be. I was going to talk to the seer and see if he could tell me where they were. But then, once I finally know where they are, there's the trouble of actually *getting* to them."

Viravia's eyes were alight with curiosity.

"I was hoping you might know someone who could help be a guide. Someone from your trading days," Miranda finished.

"I see." Viravia tapped her slender fingers against her mug, thinking, and then cast her eyes on Govek. "You know, if you took the role of chief, you would technically be a higher rank than the warriors. You could order warrior orcs to find them for her. You could even send messages to all the clans for aid."

Was that true? Miranda's gut twisted, and she shot her eyes toward Govek. Unfortunately, he wouldn't meet her gaze.

And she knew *exactly* why. She'd seen how he was treated. Knew how he felt about this clan. Asking him to take up the mantle of chief just so she could order orcs to find her babies was . . . it was too much to ask. She couldn't put this on him, no matter how desperate she was.

"That might work, but for now, things between Govek and Karthoc are a little tense. Do you know of anyone else who could help?"

She felt Govek's warm hand brush her leg, and she glanced up at his face to find his eyes soft with gratitude. Her heart picked up the pace, and she gave him a light smile, wishing she could kiss him instead.

Viravia was awash with disappointment, but she tried to hide it by straightening her back. "I . . . may know a few who could help. But contacting them would be a difficult task. Unless I can convince Chief Ergoth to let me use an enchanted bird . . . let me think on it."

Miranda sagged with relief. "Thank you, Viravia. So much. *Really.*"

"Of course." Viravia's eyes were still alight with curiosity, but she was kind enough not to press. It made Miranda want to open up about *everything*. Her babies, Earth, the war . . .

But no . . . putting all her horrors on Viravia would be incredibly cruel. Especially after the woman was being so kind and helpful.

So, she simply moved into the next important topic. "Viravia, we were also hoping to know how *Oakwall* feels about Govek."

Viravia blinked, perking up again. "Oh? Did they contact you, Govek?"

"No."

Her shoulders slumped. "I see. Chief Ergoth hasn't wanted to tell them much, especially about the merger, but he has been telling everyone in the clan that he fully intends to keep control over the trade relations and peace with Oakwall. I have no idea what Kar—the *warlord* is going to say when he finds out. He wants you to be the full chief, Govek. He doesn't want Ergoth to have any power here anymore."

"Do you think Oakwall would be open to Govek being in charge of the trade?" Miranda broached.

"Well, yes, of course," Viravia said without the slightest hesitation. She glanced at Govek. "You . . . don't agree, Govek? This isn't about Yerina, is it?"

"My father has made it clear that Oakwall would not be comfortable with my presence."

"Your father is looking out for the good of the clan, but he *rarely* looks out for *your* good," Viravia said, and a smile quirked Miranda's lips. "I'll be blunt. There are a good number of Oakwall residents, *as well as* orcs here, that like to speak ill of you, but *most* know that Yerina is full of boar shit. Her story changes every blasted trade. Only the imbeciles who thrive on drama truly listen to her tales now."

Miranda's smile widened. Seeing someone finally go to bat for Govek was so refreshing. She shot Govek a triumphant look that softened when she found him looking relieved.

"You might get a few odd looks, but I doubt anyone would be brave enough to be openly hostile, especially knowing you are going to be the next chief of Rove Wood Clan."

Govek's expression darkened, and Viravia saw it just as well as Miranda.

Viravia was about to ask, so Miranda cut in. "The trade is day after tomorrow, right? Will you be going too?"

"I . . . yes, I will," Viravia said, reluctantly allowing the shift. "I have some things that I need to pick up from some artisans of Oakwall. For the baby."

"Oh yeah?" Genuine interest flooded Miranda. "What kind of things?"

"Things for feeding him, mostly," Viravia said, stroking her belly again. "Women in my family have always struggled with feeding at the breast. Sorry. I'm sure you don't want to listen to me blather on about that."

"Oh, I don't mind. I used to work with young kids before I . . . came here."

"You did?" Viravia asked. "As an instructor?"

"Uh, well, kinda? More like I would watch them when their parents were busy. Some of them were still being bottle fed, so I have experience with it."

Viravia's eyes brightened. "Interesting. You fed babies milk? Without being a wet nurse?"

"Oh yeah. All the time."

"In that case"—Viravia got up and hurried to her cabinet, pulling out a basket—"could you give an opinion on these? I had the glassmaker at Oakwall construct them and then another artisan made the tops from leather and tree gum."

She set them down in front of Miranda and excitement danced in her. "Nipples for bottles?"

"Yes. I'd seen them used at one of the larger villages only once in my childhood. Replicating what I saw has been quite a challenge."

"You got the shape right," Miranda said, fitting the top onto the glass jar. It was nice and snug. "But the hole is too big for a newborn."

"Hold on." Viravia went to fetch a parchment and quill. "Do you mind if I take notes?"

"Of course not," Miranda said with a smile.

And take notes she did. Viravia wrote down almost every word Miranda said. It felt odd to be treated like such an authority on the matter. Odd, but good.

Halfway through, Miranda glanced at Govek, wondering if he was getting bored and found him brooding, lost in thought. His eyes slid from Viravia's rounded stomach and back to his massive hands.

Was he thinking about holding her baby? Miranda's mind tipped toward the idea of Govek cradling a newborn and her heart thundered.

How would he be with her babies once she'd saved them? Gruff and overprotective and kind. Her chest warmed at the thought.

How . . . might he be with *their* children? If they decided to have them.

Her heart fluttered and she shook her head, concentrating on Viravia. "Your baby is lucky to have you."

Viravia's cheeks colored even as she smiled. "I certainly hope so. I was never around any babies growing up. My father was a traveling merchant, so we moved around a lot. You must have learned so much from your village. There must have been many babies to care for there."

"Oh yeah, uh, it was . . . huge." Her throat closed. Dang it, the woman had asked a simple question, and she couldn't even bring herself to answer.

Warmth covered her fingers, and she found that Govek had engulfed her hand with his own and gave a comforting squeeze. Miranda relaxed, soaking up his strength and letting him soothe her like he always did.

Then Viravia cast her an easy smile. "I'm sorry, Miranda. I didn't mean to pry. We all harbor things in our pasts. I'm certain that we will get to know each other well in time." She rose from her seat. "Could you favor me by calling a messenger to take this to Gladen at Oakwall, Govek? If I send it tonight, he might have time to adjust the bottles before the trade."

Call a messenger?

Viravia went to her window and opened it just as Govek whistled low.

A little robin flew in a moment later, glided across the room, and landed on Govek's outstretched finger.

"Oh my gosh!" Miranda gushed, heart hammering. The bird was so tiny and cute sitting on Govek's hand. "That's so cool! You can call birds? You're like Snow White."

"What is a Snow White?" Viravia asked, coming over with a string and a much smaller note she'd made.

"She's a princess," Miranda said with a smirk. Did they have princesses here?

Apparently, they did, because Govek's face darkened into a scowl and Viravia burst into laughter.

Govek snapped his gaze to Viravia's face. Watching her close.

Viravia patted Govek's hand affectionately. "Well, you do look as pretty as a princess."

Miranda's stomach churned again.

She was being *stupid*. They *weren't* flirting. Govek wasn't dumb enough to do something so horrible, and Viravia was *nice*. Really nice. Miranda liked her.

Which made watching the two of them smile at each other even more difficult.

He was finally making *friends*. Miranda felt like a complete ass for putting a downer on that. What was wrong with her?

"Are you well?"

Govek asked, and her guilt mounted that he'd noticed. "Yeah. Yeah, I'm fine." Goddamn, she couldn't even make herself *sound* fine.

This was so stupid. *She* was so stupid.

"You two seem quite close with your teasing," Viravia said, pointedly, making Miranda's cheeks heat. "Tavggol was wonderful too. He really helped me feel comfortable here. I could never imagine a better partner."

Miranda sagged. "I'm so sorry for your loss, Viravia."

Viravia's eyes fell, and she stroked her stomach. "It is hard. But I have many fond memories. And some not so fond. Does Govek slam doors and stomp his feet as loudly as his kin?"

"Maybe?" Miranda wasn't sure where this was going.

"Well, I have advice on how to fix that." Viravia grinned. "I make these perfumes, you see. Very fragrant. *Very* effective as discipline."

Miranda half gasped. "No. You didn't."

Viravia shrugged, her smile widening. "They have these nice little dispersers on the tops so you can spray them. Hiding behind the door was usually a good location. That way you can spritz the moment they err."

Miranda burst into laughter. "Oh my god. That's genius."

"Miranda," Govek said warningly. She shot him a grin.

"And if they don't learn the first few times, you can aim for the eyes."

Miranda laughed even more, tears flooding her own eyes in her mirth. "So, you have some, right? I'm sure I can find a way to repay you."

"Miranda," Govek repeated, but Miranda only shot him a sly grin.

And then a hard knock sounded at the door.

# TWENTY

*GOVEK*

V iravia rose. "Who could that—"

"Maythra," Govek said, and Viravia's expression went dark.

She muttered. "I'll get rid of her."

Govek moved closer to Miranda so he couldn't be seen as Viravia opened the door. "Maythra, hello. You already brought food by earlier. I don't need this."

The scent of barley and fish wafted from the door.

"Yes, well, I wanted to make sure you're eating enough. Tavggol's son won't be healthy if you don't eat properly."

"I told you already, I'm fine."

"How can we be sure our next chief is hale if you do not eat what I provide?"

"Wellia has assured me I'm healthy."

"Pah, that youngling."

"She's very experienced under her mate's guidance, or are you saying that Hovget isn't knowledgeable enough?"

"Of course, I'm not saying that. Here, just take it." There was jostling as Maythra handed over the bowl of fish soup. Viravia began to close the door when Maythra said, "You have a guest?"

Viravia was thrown off. As was Govek, since they had been silent and could not be seen from where Maythra stood behind the door. "I'm very tired. I'm not up for entertaining more visitors."

Maythra scoffed and pushed Viravia's door open fully, barely noticing that it knocked the soup bowl. Some of the liquid sloshed onto the floor. "I am not a *visitor.* I am mother to all in this clan. I am family."

Govek rose to his feet just as Maythra's lofty features fell. "What are *you* doing here?"

Miranda took Govek's hand as he withheld his irritation.

"Come away from him, dear." Maythra waved at Miranda as if she were a child in need of direction. "I want to check your condition *without* this male looming over you."

"I'm perfectly fine."

"Honestly, if something I did a few days ago offended you, I apologize. We were all rather out of sorts from the announcement, but it's past us now. Our chief is handling it. There's no reason to turn away from the clan who has embraced you out of fear this male might retaliate."

"Wow." Miranda snorted.

"Come here. Now. We can protect you."

"Govek protects me just fine." Miranda took Govek's hand, and her touch eased the sharpest stings of his blooming anger.

And besides, he had no right to be angry with Maythra. Her fear for his mate was valid, and her reasons for despising him were sound.

But Miranda's continued refusal caused the woman's face

to contort. Her nose scrunched as if she smelled something foul and her body puffed up like a hen readying to fight.

"Fades mercy, you were meant to come *alone*. But of course, this male could never let a woman he's imprinted on out of his sight for a moment. You realize how dangerous he is? What must I do to convince you?"

Viravia stepped in front of the woman and herded her back toward the stoop. "Maythra, *you* invited her to *my* house?"

"I did what I had to." Maythra tried to resist but the threat of getting soup sloshed onto her had her backing back out the door. "Look at her. She's completely beguiled."

"Govek would never hurt a woman, Maythra," Viravia said sternly. "Certainly not one he feels strongly for."

Maythra's eyes flashed between them all for a moment before a vicious gleam settled and she planted her feet, refusing to go down the steps. "Is that why you've always trusted him? Because you knew his feelings for you would prevent him from doing you harm?"

"What?"

The tone of Miranda's single word spiked a torrent of shivers down Govek's spine.

"Maythra," Viravia gasped. "That is *not* true."

"Of course, it is true. And you must reciprocate, since you were the one that suggested he take you on as his mate."

Viravia stammered. "Th-that—that was for the good of the *clan*. For my son to have a father figure in his life and to stop Govek from dying at Estwill. It was not due to anything between Govek and me."

Maythra snorted. "A father figure like *him*? There are far better models in Rove Wood. You could have had your pick, you know."

Tightness gripped Govek's chest.

Maythra stared hard at Miranda. "As could you, and you *should* choose another. Or do you truly want to be with a male that is so vile he—"

"Leave, Maythra!" Viravia yelled, causing them all to jump at her volume. "Now. And take your wicked tongue and disgusting slop with you."

"I won't go. Not until I can ensure this new dear is *safe*."

Viravia took the bowl Maythra had given her and shoved it into the woman's chest. Stew splattered all over her dress and coated the stoop. Maythra staggered back, screeching as if she'd been burned though the meal was clearly cold. Her foot slid in the muck and she toppled, ass hitting the top step hard before she bumped her way down to the ground, shrieking with indignation but clearly unharmed as she got back to her feet.

"How *dare* you!" Maythra screamed, wiping the brown stew off the front of her gown. "You may be carrying the next heir, but *I* am the matriarch of this clan, and our chief will hear of this."

Govek took this moment to quickly haul Miranda down the steps, intent on carrying her home. Thankfully Maythra was too busy wiping herself to notice as he passed her.

Fuck, he'd *known* coming into the clan might be a bad idea, but he hadn't expected *this.*

Viravia laughed. "Oh Fades, are you *actually* calling yourself the matriarch out loud now? I thought you were delusional, and this proves it. Chief Ergoth doesn't even acknowledge that you are together, let alone mated."

"I *will be* the matriarch," Maythra spat. "Chief Ergoth will announce it soon."

"Chief Ergoth has lost his power, Maythra. He's in no position to be creating *imaginary* titles. And if he truly intended to give you one, he would have done so a long time ago."

"He *will*. You'll see! He wants to atone for the wrong that was done to me and my poor Zayvor! To atone for the atrocity his own *son* caused!"

Govek's gut twisted at the mention of Maythra's lost mate.

Viravia stepped forward, careful not to slip in the stew, looming over Maythra with gleaming eyes. "If Ergoth wanted you for his mate, he would have taken you long ago. But he's nowhere near foolish enough to make such a ghastly choice. Now get the fuck out of my sight."

"Holy shit."

Govek snapped his gaze to his mate, finding her wide eyed. He tightened his grip on her and swung back around toward the forest. "Let's go."

"Miranda!" Maythra screamed after them, clearly trying to follow, but Govek was already through the brush. "That monster will show his true face in time! You'll see! You'll wish you had obeyed me!"

Neither of them looked back as Govek continued carrying Miranda toward their home. He trembled under the force of the truths that Maythra had screamed into the night.

"Let me down."

Govek did so instantly, lowering Miranda to her feet. She turned away from him, heaving a sigh and muttered a dark curse under her breath.

"I . . . I did not want it to come out this way." Every one of Maythra's words spiraled through his mind, and he didn't even know where to begin. Fuck, Miranda had been so *determined* to avoid the vile woman that he hadn't prepared what to say.

Perhaps now was the time to tell Miranda the truth of his

birth. Of the reasons Maythra, and many of the older members of the clan, despised him so greatly.

If not for him, Maythra's mate, Zayvor, one of the greatest conjurers this clan had ever known, would not be dead. It would not be such a struggle to keep up with the production of healing tinctures. The blight in the Rove Woods may not have grown so swiftly. Some said that Zayvor, at the height of his power, had even been capable of holding back winter for half a *moon*. There was no doubt Rove Wood Clan would have been far more bountiful had Govek never been born. He swallowed down his pride and worked for the words to explain this atrocity to Miranda.

"So, how long were you going to let me hang out with Viravia before you told me you were supposed to become mated to her?"

*What?*

"For the love of—goddamn"—Miranda covered her eyes with her palms—"You really let me just . . . watch you two be all flirty."

Govek was so thunderstruck he could not make a sound. *Flirt* with Viravia? With his *brother's mate*? What was she talking about?

"And to think I had to find out from fucking *Maythra* of all people."

"Miranda, I was not—we were not—"

"Don't tell me I imagined it, Govek. I saw how you were looking at her!" Miranda skewered him with a glower that rocked him to the core. "Why are you even with me if you have *her* as an option? Is it because of your imprint on me? Does it force you to pick me when you really want her?"

"No, that's not—Viravia is *not* an option. She is my *brother's widow*."

"So, if she *wasn't*, then you would have her?"

What the actual fuck? "No. Miranda, I—"

"She's about twenty times prettier than me and *super* nice, and damn it!" Miranda scrubbed at her eyes, turning her back to him, and took a few steps into the woods. "Damn it . . . even *I* like her. I can't even *blame* you."

"You . . . you think I would leave you? For *Viravia*?" He could hardly grapple with the idea.

"Of course I do!" Miranda spat throwing up her hands. "And maybe not even *her*. There's a whole world out there, Govek. A whole world of people who don't have their brains all messed up and wouldn't wake you up from screaming nightmares a million times a night. And who don't feel like their chests are going to implode every time they think about the babies they—they—"

Her eyes flooded even as she wiped them, and it tore at his chest. Govek moved toward her, endlessly grateful that she did not continue to back away. His control was in ribbons, and he wasn't certain what he would do if she ran from him now.

"You think *I* might leave *you*. You think that someone else could be better suited for me than *you*?" The imprint was absolutely *raging*. It blasted heat through his veins with every beat of his heart.

"Govek, we've only known each other for like a week. Of *course,* someone out there might be better suited for you."

Govek choked, laughing half hysterically.

"What the heck?" Miranda said, though his misbegotten mirth had her tears drying as fury took their place. "Why are you *laughing* at this?"

"I apologize, Miranda. Truly. Because what you suggest is so completely ludicrous, I could not maintain my composure.

And that of all things, *this* has you so upset." It pleased him to no end. He truly was a beast.

"If that's the case, then why were you looking at her like . . . like she had the fricking messiah in her belly?" Miranda was furious, and the only way he could think to quell it was with the truth.

"I was envisioning *you* with child."

Miranda's face went slack, and all the anger drained away. "*What?*"

"It was you who I was imagining. Carrying . . . my child." Saying the words out loud caused a deep swell of yearning he could not explain. He'd never even considered having a son. Never thought himself worthy of such a thing. But now, with Miranda staring at him, her eyes blinking with wonder, he could not seem to shake the thought from his mind.

He stalked forward, feet and heart hammering. He got down on his knees in the icy dirt before his beautiful, foolish, misguided mate. "I would never be insane enough to even *consider* holding affection for a woman other than you, and imprints are *created* by romantic bonds. Not the other way around."

"But . . . we didn't have a romantic bond when you imprinted. You didn't even know me."

That was true, and he had no explanation for it, but he knew one very vital truth. "Yes, but with every moment I spend with you, your imprint grows stronger. Every laugh, every smile, every fucking glance you spare me. It makes me crave you."

She gulped and fidgeted.

So, he dug deeper for more words. "Every meal you cook for me, working hard to please me even though I would literally eat rotting scraps if you served them. Every naughty joke that makes me burn and howl with mirth. Every gentle touch and easy word and fucking *everything* about you. I long for you, Miranda. *Only you.*"

Her fingers grazed his hair, sending a torrent of shivers down his spine as she gently scratched.

"Viravia is *nothing* compared to you. I would throw her into the wastes if you willed it."

"Oh god," Miranda said, her tone finally lightening. "Don't do that."

He sighed, relief slamming him. "And I vow to you she does not hold *any* affection for me, either." Miranda looked dubious, so he rushed on. "And if she does, then I will squash it out. I will never speak another word to her."

"She's the mother of your nephew."

"I don't give a shit."

Miranda laughed, pressed her palm to her head. "God . . . this is such a mess." His heart squeezed and then she finally— *finally!*—leaned down to embrace him, tucked his head into her chest and bathed him in her warmth. All the tension flowed out of him.

"I'm sorry I'm acting crazy. Viravia is so nice and . . . it's just . . . I don't *share*," she said into his scalp.

He pulled back from her and took her face in his hands. "It is not possible for me to be imprinted upon any other woman, Miranda. You are it for me."

"You were imprinted on someone else before," Miranda mumbled.

"She was a fucking speck of dust next to your glory." He extended his fingers into her hair, splaying them out to cage her skull. She was *his*. He would never even glance at another woman for the remainder of his days. "*You are it for me.*"

"All right," Miranda finally relented. "Okay."

Okay. He buried his face in her chest, surrounded himself in her sweet honey scent. Fuck, to think she'd been mad about something like *this* after all the horrors that were revealed tonight. The idea of losing him was what had her the most worried. He would ride the high of it for decades.

He would do *anything* to keep her safe and hale.

And that started with making peace with Oakwall.

"Come, Miranda, if we are going to go to the trade day after tomorrow, we will need plenty of rest."

She smiled as he rose to his feet. "You know, I think the only thing that could go wrong now is someone preventing you from going to the trade at all."

Fuck. She was right.

"Govek?" Miranda said warningly, clearly seeing the alarm on his face. "Is there someone who *could* stop you?"

He took a deep breath. "Let's go home, Miranda. We'll need to be prepared for tomorrow."

"What's tomorrow?" Miranda asked, allowing him to scoop her up.

"We're going to see my father."

# CHAPTER
# TWENTY-ONE

*MIRANDA*

"Are you sure we really need permission to go to the trade? Your dad already invited me, and you said you weren't banned or anything . . ." Miranda kept her voice quiet. The sunset was to her back and the massive hall was before her. The Rove Tree's crystalline leaves glittered as the dimming sunlight burst pinks and reds all over the sky.

Govek had paused outside the doors of the hall, unwilling to touch them. He'd been warring with himself internally *all* day. She could see it in his quiet scowling, his bunched fists, the tight set of his shoulders that no amount of rubbing could release.

"I must ask, Miranda. I have not attended for a long time. My father may want to warn the village headman that I'll be there."

"Okay." Miranda took his free hand in hers. She'd brought up a million alternatives to this already. They could sneak over to the trade without anyone noticing, or show up later before anyone could stop them, or even send a message to Oakwall's headman themselves. Govek had shot them all down. He truly thought speaking with his father on the matter was the only option.

She sighed, wishing her gut thought this was the best option, too. "I'll follow you."

Govek shot her a grateful look and pushed open the door. The warmth of the hall roared over them like the smothering of a forest fire. Miranda fought for air.

But that initial anxiety gave way when no one noticed them entering. The hall was busy, but not nearly as crowded as it had been on the day of Karthoc's announcement. Its long tables had large gaps between groups. The pots above each fire were unmanned. Miranda couldn't tell if they were early or late, but either way, they hadn't come at a busy time.

Govek worked hard to keep them unseen. He tucked her close to his side and shut the door gently so it wouldn't make any noise. He kept to the perimeter, using the dark and distance from the tables as a shield.

Miranda looked past him into the room, noting that most of the orcs were laughing, chatting amicably, clearly enjoying their meal. The doors behind them opened again and the male who entered immediately called out to his friends and went to join them.

Miranda scanned pensively but thankfully Maythra didn't appear to be there.

With how desperate the orcs had been to talk to Govek, she'd expected complete chaos the moment they crossed into the hall. It dawned on her that Govek was able to sneak in like this because he had *practice*.

How many times had he slunk into this hall, trying to remain unseen and avoid withering glares, while everyone else was welcomed exuberantly? How many times had he stood at the outskirts going hungry and watching others eat?

Her stomach twisted up, and she hugged his burly arm, resting her head on the firm muscle. She felt his tension ease.

"I'll get you some food first," Govek said quietly, moving her toward the outermost fire where an elk was set on a spit off to one side. There were carving knives below it and bowls on a small table so it could be divided out.

Miranda suspected it was the elk Govek had taken down. There were puncture wounds on its flank that she remembered. The memory of watching him get bucked around lightened her tension.

As they drew nearer it became obvious that there were deep cuts in the hide, all along the side and back, long and jagged.

"Wow, what happened to it?" Miranda asked as soon as she realized that the cuts in the meat were not meant to be there. Govek said nothing but his shoulders tensed slightly as he sliced some of the meat from the elk and placed it in a bowl for her.

It wasn't until he turned, and she raised her brows, that he finally relented. "My father . . . prefers my larger kills to go to more novice butchers. It is good practice."

Miranda wasn't the least surprised. "Wow, seriously?" It was clear they'd tried to salvage parts of the meat, but some of the cuts had been too deep and the edges burned black.

Her stomach twisted as Govek's expression went flat. He'd worked so dang hard to make that a clean kill, and his dad threw it to some rookie like it was garbage.

Govek finished filling her dish with roasted vegetables and fruits from another table nearby. All the ones she liked best. Her anger had dimmed by the time he handed it to her.

But then he did nothing. He just stood there. With his hand

on her shoulder, and his tense frame looming, and his gold eyes flickering around the room as if waiting for someone to try to swoop in and start harassing him.

"I . . . need to go speak with my father now."

"I'll go sit over there." Miranda pointed to one of the darker, empty sections of table. They'd talked about how he wanted to speak to his father alone.

"You should sit with the other women. No unmated orcs are allowed to approach you there."

Miranda glanced toward the table of humans and their mates. Still no Maythra, but that didn't mean much. She knew how most of them felt about Govek. But she also knew Govek was on a wire's edge and having to worry about her while he was trying to concentrate on his conversation with his dad wasn't ideal.

"I . . . uh . . . I can take her over."

The meek voice caused them both to jump and spin around. Beleda stood there, half hidden behind a tense orc Miranda hadn't met yet. The orc was slender and short, with intricate braids along his scalp.

Govek's grip on her shoulder tightened, looking hard at the orc Beleda clung to. "Tayveth."

The male orc's dark green eyes only narrowed slightly.

Oh, for crying out loud. This guy wanted to fight? Govek would *flatten* him.

And it wasn't the best idea. Their low profile had been destroyed by Beleda's address and most people in the hall were now looking in their direction, craning around each other to watch. Some were even getting to their feet.

So much for hiding in the corner.

"Miranda, it's good to see you again," Beleda said, her voice shaking a little.

300

"It's good to see you too, Beleda," Miranda said, glancing at the angry orc behind her.

Beleda hurried on. "This is my mate, Tayveth. We're all eager to meet you. Would you like to eat with us?"

She heard Govek gulp.

To help ease the tension, Miranda turned to Govek, stroking down his cheek. "I'll be all right with her." She carried her touch down to his chest and gave a little shove. "The faster you have your convo, the faster we can go home."

Govek's jaw worked, and his eyes flashed from hers to Tayveth's.

Miranda hooked a finger into the collar of his shirt and pulled him down to whisper. "Dude, you'd *eviscerate* that guy. He's got the muscles of a toddler. *I* could take him for crying out loud. Ain't no way I'm leaving this"—she stroked Govek's bulging bicep—"for that twig."

Govek's heated chuckle shot triumph down Miranda's spine and forced her to grin, helplessly. He buried his face in her hair a moment, nuzzling the top of her head. "Fuck, woman. You and your comparisons."

He released her and addressed an angry looking Tayveth. Clearly, he'd heard Miranda's insult, but thankfully Beleda hadn't. "Keep her safe."

Tayveth snorted. "As if *I'm* the one—"

"We will," Beleda quickly interrupted, putting a hand on her mate. The male huffed but relented.

Miranda watched pensively as Govek moved off toward his father's platform.

He'd be gone for a couple minutes. Nothing bad could happen in a couple minutes.

And Maythra wasn't here. It would be fine.

"Come this way, Miranda," Beleda said, gesturing for her

to follow. Miranda tried not to get all antsy about the way Tayveth followed close behind her, as if he were herding her along. "We've been hoping you would join us for a while. We wanted to see how you are, uh . . . settling in."

"I'm settling in great," Miranda assured them. "Govek has been treating me really well."

"Of course," Beleda said with a light smile just as they arrived at the table. As they did, all the orcs got up and went to sit elsewhere.

"Oh, they—they don't have to leave on my account," Miranda said, even as they were already gone.

Beleda fidgeted. "It's not you, it's . . ." She glanced toward where Govek stood. He'd paused half way to the platform and was watching.

Ah. Miranda understood then. None of these guys wanted to get into a punching match.

"Sit down here by me," Beleda said, gesturing Miranda to one of the bench seats. "Let me introduce everyone."

There were ten women seated at the table, and every one of them had the same expression on their face—pale shock and brow-pinched pity. Two-thirds of them were younger, around her age, and the rest were much older. She realized that all the middle-aged women were probably with their children at the seasonal communion.

Beleda rattled off their names so fast Miranda's head spun.

"I swear I'll try really hard to remember all of your names." Miranda cast them a smile that she hoped didn't reveal how tense she was.

One of the older women chuckled. "Just call everyone dear. That's what I do."

"You saying you don't remember my name, Glenna?" another elderly woman replied.

"I have better use for my memory, *dear*," Glenna teased, but then she looked at Miranda. "I'll remember your name, though." Miranda tensed as she finished. "Miranda is an odd one."

"I hope odd isn't bad."

"Certainly not," one of the younger women, Renni, said. She had cropped short black hair and very dark brown eyes. "In fact, it's better. Adds variety."

"And it is very pretty," the woman on her opposite, Aviah, said. She had tanned skin and large brown eyes and a smooth voice. "Is it a family name?"

"Oh, uh. I'm not sure," Miranda said. "My family died when I was little."

"Oh, I'm so sorry," Glenna said with genuine concern.

"It's okay," Miranda assured them. "I was only three. I barely remember it."

"Well, we're happy to be your family now. I am Hilva. It's an easy one, so I am sure you will remember," the youngest at the table said. Her sharp, pale eyes kept shifting to an orc at the opposite table and Miranda assumed he was her mate.

"Thank you for the welcome, Hilva," Miranda said carefully, uncertain about the inflection the young blonde woman had used. To test it, she continued, "Govek has made me feel like family already."

Hilva's expression pinched, confirming Miranda's suspicion.

Beleda quickly changed the subject. "Are you coming with us to the trade tomorrow?"

"Uh, yeah, I think so. Govek is telling the chief now," Miranda replied absently as an orc approached Hilva and whispered something in her ear that made the girl gasp.

"Do you mean . . . Govek isn't coming too, is he?" one of the other women asked, drawing her attention away.

All eyes were suddenly on her, and the whispering stopped.

"That's the plan," Miranda said quietly.

Murmurs shot up from the adjoining tables, but before the women could do anything but gasp, Beleda said, "Oakwall will be glad to trade with Govek again. He typically takes hunting requests. I've heard a few people talk about missing them."

Miranda's tension eased slightly at that, even though Hilva was back to whispering.

"In fact, if you want, Govek could linger behind and I could be a guide to you. Show you where the best wares are. Then you could take the hunting orders back to him when we return from the trade," Beleda offered.

"That's a fine idea," Aviah said with a relieved smile.

"Oh, uh, no. I don't think—" Miranda glanced between Hilva, who had just spouted something like "we have to tell her," and Beleda, who was now rigid.

Miranda had enough.

"Look, either tell me what you're whispering about or knock it off."

Hilva did not hesitate, thank god, "He lied to you."

"Hilva!" Beleda cut in.

"He did!" Hilva said, her cheeks reddening. "We're really going to just let him *get away* with it?"

"It isn't our place to interfere."

"Welp, ladies, that ship has sailed. You've interfered," Miranda said. "So, you'd better get on with spilling the rest of those beans."

The women looked between each other, clearly not quite understanding.

"Just tell me."

Finally, Beleda sighed and spoke up. "He told you that a *butcher* cut that meat."

It took Miranda a second to realize what they were talking about. They meant the elk. "Okay, go on."

"The butchers would never do such horrible work. The meat came to them like that. Already cut up."

"What are you saying?" Miranda went cold as the other women avoided her gaze.

Hilva rose to her feet, skewering Miranda with her sharp, angry eyes. Her voice rose high enough to echo off the crystalline leaves of the Great Rove Tree, raining poison down around them all as she said.

"Govek caused those marks. He *tortures* animals as he kills them."

# CHAPTER
# TWENTY-TWO

*GOVEK*

G ovek found his father where he usually was—on his throne atop the platform, surveying the meal with sharp eyes.

Govek sucked in a deep breath, knowing what this conversation would entail. His father would not let the trade be their only topic. The merger would be brought up.

His father would never allow him to be chief, of that Govek was certain, but Ergoth likely expected Govek to find a way to change Karthoc's mind. To stop the merger by other means.

His gut twisted as he tried to imagine what demands his father might make.

Helplessly, he scanned the crowd and found Miranda being led over to the women's table. The other males were getting up to give his mate a wide berth.

*Good.*

"Govek."

He turned around and found Karthoc, tense and glancing into the crowd as if looking for someone.

"Warlord," Govek said quietly.

"You don't scent Evythiken, do you?" Karthoc said, still searching the crowd.

"No."

"Blasted male has a habit of popping up where he's least wanted," Karthoc said. "And he'll skin my scalp if he finds me talking to you. Come over here."

Govek hesitated. It was unwise to ignore an order from the warlord but he was unwilling to be interrogated if he could avoid it.

Karthoc scowled at Govek's reluctance. "I'm not here to beat you down about becoming chief. I'm here to talk about the trade."

The trade?

After a deep breath, Govek followed Karthoc into a darkened corner of the hall. "You are going to the trade, right?"

Govek furrowed his brow. "I planned to. I'm here to speak to Chief Ergoth about it."

"Good. I need you to do me a favor and distract him so we can follow."

Govek went cold. "*What?*"

"Don't look so Fades-stricken. I just need to speak to the headman. I don't have much choice after Brovdir . . ."

"What did Brovdir do?"

"I'll tell you if you get us to the trade *without* your precious father finding out."

Govek's mind reeled. What had mild-mannered Brovdir done to muck up relations with Oakwall?

Did this mean Oakwall knew about the upcoming merger?

Govek turned slightly to search out Miranda in the crowd,

using her presence to aid his addled thoughts. She seemed well chatting with the other women.

"I can tell you how to find it and you could arrive early."

"Wouldn't your father scent our trail?"

"How many males are you planning to take with you?"

"All of them."

What the . . . "That's too many, Karthoc. Just take three or four."

"There's no time to work a challenge, and with how badly my males want to go, I'd likely have three or four *dead* by the end of the fighting." Karthoc glanced toward the platform where Govek's father was still seated. The chief hadn't spotted them.

"Viravia makes scented oils," Govek said, recalling the brief conversation from the night prior that had Miranda cackling with glee. "They might cover your tracks."

"Tavggol's widow? I've not even been introduced to her yet. You think she'd give me anything without complaint?" Karthoc asked, narrowing his eyes on the women seated across the room.

"Viravia isn't like the other women. She won't chase you out."

Karthoc grunted. "Let's hope the women of Oakwall share that sentiment."

Govek's eyes widened.

He was taking all fifty of his warriors to the trade to find *conquests*? No wonder he didn't want Chief Ergoth to find out.

"Govek, what are you doing over there?"

A shiver went up Govek's spine at his father's call, and he turned to face him.

Ergoth's golden eyes narrowed with suspicion as they landed on him and Karthoc. "Come over here, my son. *Now*."

"Do not tell him," Karthoc hissed before giving Govek a sharp pat on the shoulder and walking away.

"Karthoc," Govek called, words slipping quietly from his lips unbidden. His cousin turned back. "Do you really have . . . seventeen?"

He'd been choosing not to think about this. It didn't matter. The warriors who could wield magic were at Baelrok Forge, and he and Miranda would be here in the Rove Woods.

And yet . . .

"Yes," Karthoc said with a sure nod and a rush of heat flooded Govek.

Seventeen other orcs like him. Seventeen warrior males who could conjure magic.

Govek curled his fists to fight the rising tide of emotions. It didn't matter. It changed nothing.

He turned to make his way to his father.

Agol and Wolvc stood at the bottom of the platform, chests puffed, but they allowed Govek to climb the few steps onto the wood stage and into his father's daunting presence.

"My son. Finally escaped from the woods, I see. What were you speaking on with Karthoc?" Ergoth asked, still seated comfortably upon his thrown, barely bothering to look Govek's way.

"He asked for directions to the best hunting grounds."

Ergoth flashed him a scowl, obviously suspicious, but instead of prying, he scooped up a cup of mead from the thick arm of his chair and took a long swig.

Govek paused, watching as his father, a male in constant control, gulped a large sum of the mind addling drink. There were dark bags under his father's eyes. His cheeks were slightly hollow and the wrinkles on his brow were a little more prominent.

Chief Ergoth rose from his throne. "The woman you brought looks well with the others. You should allow her to come here more often."

Govek's chest tightened and his fists balled as he gazed at Miranda. "It was her choice to stay away."

His father shot him a skeptical look before straightening his robes. His gaze turned scrutinizing.

"She is attractive, isn't she?" Ergoth said, and to his shame, Govek's claws slunk out against his will and a rumble threatened to burst from his lips. "The Fades must smile on us to have such a lovely new member join our clan."

The growl escaped.

"Govek, this is a happy night," Ergoth said too loudly. "Why bring anger here?"

Many eyes turned and Govek balled his fists tighter. Thankfully, it seemed Miranda had not heard. She remained unaware of how horrible her mate was at controlling his vile nature.

*"Easy there, tough guy."* That's what she would say. And she would take his hands and rub them, soothing him into releasing his fists. He forced them to unclench on his own. She would be upset if he cut himself.

Sufficiently calmed, Govek looked to his father only to find him watching Govek with a flat expression, but the odd tension was wiped clean in a flash. "I am glad you finally relented your grip. She looks happy there, mingling with the others. You'll drive her to resent you if you keep her isolated."

"As I said, *she* was the one who chose to stay away."

His father only scoffed and before Govek could refute him he continued. "She should come to the trade with the other women tomorrow. It would be good for her to have some time with the others and I'm certain she has many needs to be fulfilled."

Govek's urge to keep his mate to himself roared ugly in his mind even as logic fought him. "I agree. In fact, I am—"

"Chief."

The interruption came from Wolvc and, judging from Agol's harsh look, he had no idea why his son was cutting in.

Ergoth did, though. He took to his feet, nodding to the young guard. Wolvc hurried off toward the exit even as Agol's confusion deepened.

His father began toward the back of the stage. "We should not be muddying the meal with our conversation. Come, my son."

Sharp dismay closed around Govek's gut as his father waited for him at the entry into the deeper parts of the tree. The chief's private study—where Govek had never been. He paused to look at Miranda, finding her addressing the youngest woman in the clan. He could only see her back and could not make out her words, but the tension in the tone strung him up. It made the imprint ache and burn in his chest.

"Govek," his father snapped. "Come. Now."

Govek's spine straightened at his father's harsh tone and Govek forced himself to look away, convincing himself that his mate would be well. What could happen within the Rove Tree? Surrounded by the other human mates?

So, against all better judgment, Govek ignored his violent impulses and followed his father into the dark.

# CHAPTER
# TWENTY-THREE

*MIRANDA*

Miranda's stomach dropped at Hilva's wild accusation. Govek tortured animals? What was she saying?

Why did no one at any of the tables say anything to refute the woman's mad claims? In fact, all of them looked . . . Miranda's stomach twisted.

They looked at her with *pity*.

"Calm down, Hilva," Beleda demanded, gesturing for the woman to sit. "Let's not make a scene."

Too late for that. The room had already hushed, listening in. Some even blatantly turned to watch.

The only solace was that Govek was nowhere to be seen. The platform with the wood throne was vacant, but for that one older guard standing at attention next to the stairs.

Govek must have already been meeting with his father somewhere in private. Thank god. She didn't want him to have to hear these horrible lies.

"No. Why should I? Why shouldn't we speak of it? It's horrible. He's *horrible*," Hilva said, shaking off the hand of the woman so she could remain standing. "He might have hidden it from you for a few days, but he can't hide it forever. He *tortures* animals for his own pleasure. No natural orc would *ever* hurt one of Faeda's creatures like that. His magic is twisted and foul."

Miranda gripped her bowl of hot stew so tight it was a wonder it didn't shatter. "You saw him do that?"

The woman's expression contorted. "He's kept you secluded for *days,* so of course you'd be on his side. But mark my words, the truth will come out, and then you'll—"

"*You've seen him torture animals?*" Miranda demanded again, her voice solid and low. The young woman glanced at Beleda, clearly shaken by Miranda's harsh tone.

Beleda spoke carefully. "No. No one is allowed to watch him hunt. He's too dangerous. He could go into a battle lust."

"I've watched him," Miranda said. "And he never tortured anything."

Hilva scoffed, crossing her arms. "He is hiding it from you, then. I know it's hard to believe, but—"

"I've watched him take down *every* animal he's hunted since he got back here, *including* that elk," Miranda said loud enough for all the listeners to hear her clearly. "And he gave every single one a clean, easy death. He never even *considered* torturing them."

A few of the women at the table looked between each other, but Miranda could tell most didn't believe her.

"You don't have to defend him, Miranda," Hilva said. "We know what he's like, and we know he's deranged. You're just making yourself look foolish with these lies."

"You're calling me a *liar*?" Miranda didn't realize her voice could go so deep and chilling. Hilva flinched.

"Of course, she isn't," Beleda said quickly, gesturing for Miranda to sit again, but she wasn't going to sit down until Hilva did. "That isn't what we mean. We're all just confused."

"I am not confused," Miranda said carefully. She turned to look around the room. She didn't know who had butchered the animal, but she could be fairly sure her words would get back to them. "No one else here can hunt elk but Govek, right?"

The room was so quiet it prickled along her skin like nettles.

"When he wrapped it up in the butcher cloth, it only had two injuries—a snapped neck and punctures on its flank, where he initially grabbed it. There was not a single other cut or wound on it."

"I don't believe you," Hilva said haughtily, even as one of the other women snapped at her under her breath and tried to pull her down.

"I honestly don't give a rat's ass if you believe me," Miranda snapped. She was so fucking tired of all this bullshit. "But before you continue passing judgment on things you haven't even seen with your own eyes, why don't you ask the butcher who skinned the animal what parts of its fur were bloody?"

Hilva blinked, clearly confused. As were most of the faces watching her.

Miranda called upon every crime scene show she'd watched on Earth. "Animals don't *bleed* after they die. If Govek tortured it while it was still alive, it's fur would be stained around the marks just as it was around the punctures in his back."

315

Whispers sounded from the crowd, and one unknown voice broke out. "He-he could have washed it."

Miranda glanced but couldn't see which orc had spoken in the crowd. "He washed the *slashes* but not the punctures? For pity's sake, do you even hear yourself?"

"He could have," Hilva insisted.

There was clearly no changing anyone's mind.

Miranda threw up her hands in surrender and muttered under her breath, "Fuck all of you. I'm leaving."

Her steps were heavy and hard as she made her way to the doors and out into the chilly night. No one got in her way or called out to stop her.

The doors slammed behind her, and the icy woods cooled away her anger so fast, she lost her breath. The exhalation came out shaky, and her eyes prickled.

Damn, it was no *wonder* Govek had left for the war. *She* wanted to leave after that. There was no reasoning with those assholes. She hoped the conversation he was having with his father was going better than *her* conversation had.

More like a fight than a conversation.

She sighed, scrubbing her eyes and walking over to stand to the left of the doors so she could wait for Govek to come out. He'd be able to find her by her smell, she was sure. Hopefully, he wouldn't go ballistic when he found out she'd left without him. Or maybe she hoped he would. They deserved it.

Miranda collapsed against the Great Rove Tree. Exhausted. *They* deserved it, but Govek didn't. And lashing out would only cement their awful opinions about him.

He couldn't defend himself. There was no one on his side.

No wonder he'd stayed silent.

The tears she'd been trying to hold back slid down her

cheeks in icy tracks and dripped onto the cloak Govek had made for her.

Light burst to her left.

On a gasp, Miranda straightened up and looked into the now almost pitch-black woods. The sun had set, taking its beautiful colors with it.

But in the darkness of the forest there was a glow.

The soft light flickered between the trees, casting eerie shadows on the damp, icy ground. The leaves were colored oddly in the dim, a sea of deep maroon. Her stomach twisted.

And the light grew brighter. Shining from deep within the foliage.

It felt . . . *familiar*.

Miranda got to her feet. It was stupid. She shouldn't go into the woods alone.

She *shouldn't*.

But the light grew higher, and her curiosity overcame her sense of reason.

Govek would find her if she got into trouble. All she had to do was call him.

She drew away from the hall. Her hand slipped from the rough bark, leaving the grounding texture of the Great Rove Tree behind as she stepped onto the stone path. Wandering nearer to the light until she was as close as she could get while still staying within the light of the lamps illuminating the pathway.

At her feet, the warm yellow glow from the firelight mingled with the odd, bright white glow from the woods. They didn't have lights this color on Faeda. All their illumination came from *natural* sources.

This light was crisp and white and *breathtaking*.

*And oh, so familiar.*

She stood on the precipice between the protection of the clan and the unknown of the woods. Grappling. Debating. Warring in her mind.

And then, on a deep breath, she stepped off the path into the white.

# CHAPTER
# TWENTY-FOUR

*GOVEK*

G ovek was surprised to find that within the dim room
behind the platform there was yet another opening, one
that led to spiraling stairs. His father began the climb without a
word, holding up his luxurious robes so they wouldn't catch
under his feet.

Govek loped after him. The wooden stairs creaked under
his weight and the walls brushed his shoulders.

It was a fair distance to travel, far up into the Rove Tree.
Govek could feel the life within it thrumming with every step.
He closed his eyes and used the magic within the tree to calm
himself.

When he opened them again, he had reached the top and
was breathless.

The room was large and circular, with a massive round
table in the center. Twenty or more chairs surrounded it. High
above the room was a thick canopy of *mirror leaves*, as

Miranda liked to call them. They reflected the torchlight and illuminated the space, dappling the light on all the surfaces.

The surround was open to the air with a branch railing encircling the room. Govek moved to the edge, taking in the view.

Fades, it was *incredible*. He could see most of the clan from this spot. All the homes twinkling in the twilight as their fires crackled. Karthoc's camp was visible off to the right and he could hear loud cheering and garbled mirth, as if they were having a brawling match.

"What racket," Ergoth muttered, glaring toward the camp. "The *warriors* have no concept of what is proper within the Rove Woods."

Govek said nothing, only tightened his hands on the wood railing.

"You've refused my direct order to come to the hall for four days, Govek."

Govek swallowed and faced his father. "I was in no position to leave my woman."

"Stand down, Govek. I did not bring you here to chastise. But you must also see, don't you? That things cannot carry on the way they have before. Between us—and you," his father said, his slender frame poised in the dim light. His chin rose and his gold eyes gleamed.

Unsure what to say in the face of such words, Govek was silent.

"I wanted to apologize, Govek. About Estwill."

Govek's jaw dropped.

"Only after you were gone did, I realize the letters from Corine were forgeries. I should have seen it long before, but I was blind by my sorrow, and the will of this clan is not easily pushed aside."

His father set down his cup on the railing and faced Govek head on. "They have called for me to ensure the clan's stability. We were all badly shaken by the death of Tavggol, but I should not have listened. I should have remembered that you are my son, and my loyalty should be as strong to you as it is to the clan. I am truly remorseful over my choice, Govek, and it will not happen again."

A heavy, searing weight lifted from Govek. From his mind. From his chest. He breathed in the crisp night air, tinged with the sweet smell of frost and roasting meat.

"I hope from now on, we can be a united front. We are each other's only kin, after all. The clan may want to divide us, but we are still of the same blood," Ergoth continued, a light smile playing at his lips. "I hope we can both try to listen and be more reasonable with each other."

Fades, was this reality? Govek pondered that he may have eaten some foul rotten fruit, and he was having a fevered delusion. His father had *never* apologized to him. For *anything*.

"I hear you fought with Karthoc after the announcement. I saw you storm from the hall and I regret being unable to follow. You understand, don't you? The clan was in a full uproar. We had to use Sythcol's clearing magic just to get everyone to settle down."

Govek nodded slowly, only slightly surprised. The clearing was typically used during judgments, but it did have a calming effect.

"Karthoc refuses to speak about your argument. Your cousin doesn't trust me. That's obvious by his choice to unseat me from my position." Govek's father looked back toward the camp so Govek couldn't see his expression and his tone wasn't telling. "He is too thickheaded to see anything but his own drive for control. I know not how to deal with such violence and strife. It isn't in my nature the way it is yours."

Govek's gut, which had just begun to loosen, twisted into knots again.

"I trust you to deal with him, Govek."

Govek blinked, knocked flat, completely flummoxed.

"You can handle Karthoc and the warriors he leaves here, and I will aid you with the clan, and together, we will ensure that prosperity remains within the Rove Woods. That is all we have ever wanted, isn't it, Govek? To ensure that *our* clan continues with its good work."

"You . . . you *want* me to take on the role of chief?"

Ergoth blinked slowly. His eyelid twitched slightly, but he recovered. "Of course, Govek."

His father *wanted* him to take command of the clan? He *wanted* Govek to lead?

His father . . . trusted him with such an important task?

Something deep within Govek's gut ached. Something warm and thick with yearning. An emotion he'd forced himself to push away long ago. In his youth. Before he was abandoned at the outskirts.

"Govek, you don't have to be afraid. I can help you lead this clan. I will advise you on every decision. Why, I could simply continue as always. All you will need to do is communicate with Karthoc and deal with the warriors he leaves behind to guard us."

All the pleasure that Govek had gained from his father's perceived confidence was popped in an instant.

*This* was his father's plan. To simply put Govek up as a front to deceive Karthoc. He should have known. He shouldn't have been surprised.

"Karthoc's demand is quite resolute. I have tried to

negotiate, and believe me, he will not fold. Our *only* option is to move forward with his orders. It is the fastest way to recover from this interruption to our usual bliss."

The word "bliss" struck something hard at the base of Govek's spine. It reverberated into his mind and cast clear the stark differences between his life now, and the one he had lived a single season ago.

The blissful world his father had created in this clan had been nothing but a nightmare for him. He had not even realized how bleak his existence was until Miranda came with her light and warmth.

Truly, now, he lived in bliss, and he would not go back. He *could* not go back. Not to blindly follow his father's orders *or* Karthoc's.

"No."

"No?" Ergoth said quietly. "No what, Govek?"

"No, I cannot take command of this clan."

Ergoth froze in his place and Govek found himself working to keep from retreating. Did he truly need to ask his father for permission to go to the trade? Perhaps he should just leave now.

"You must be jesting," Ergoth said. "Be logical. You cannot *possibly* want to be the reason our perfect clan is disbanded after centuries of prosperity?"

Govek's gut twisted. This was a truth he grappled with almost constantly. Usually, Miranda was there to soothe the ache and distract him from the worst of his burning guilt, but there was no reprieve for him now.

"And what of all the thousands of orcs that will die without the tinctures and healing magic we provide? You want their deaths to bloody your hands?"

Govek took a breath. "The conjurers can continue their work from Karthoc's forge."

"That isn't known for certain, Govek," Ergoth spat. "None of our conjurers have ever worked outside the canopy of the Great Rove Tree. Most have not even stepped foot outside of the Rove Woods."

Govek had already considered this. But *he'd* managed to conjure up hot water in the outer woods. If he, an orc with almost no magical training, could manage it, the mighty workers of this clan could too.

"And even if we can," Ergoth continued. "The few weeks of travel will put a massive strain on our already dwindling supplies. We cannot create tinctures while hiking through harsh winter conditions. And what of the time settling in at the forge? We may not ever recover, and thousands will die because of it."

His father's words were smooth, rehearsed. Chief Ergoth had clearly used them on Karthoc, and considering it had not swayed the warlord, Govek could only conclude that meant Karthoc had thought of a solution already.

"And think further, my son, of these new conjurers who need to be taught our ways."

Govek went rigid.

"These poor males with magic who have never experienced the joy of living within the Rove Woods, of conjuring under the canopy of the Great Rove Tree," Ergoth continued. "How will they ever hope to be properly trained without my guidance? Who would teach them the ways of communing with the Fades without the blessings of our Great Rove Tree?"

Govek's mouth was dry. "*You* would train them?"

"Of course, I would, Govek," Chief Ergoth said, leveling him with a hard look. "You, of all, should understand how dangerous it is to have magic without the discipline to use it properly."

Govek went very still. He did know that. He knew it better than any.

But after Miranda's conversations with him, Govek wondered . . . was it truly *his* fault he had not properly learned how to wield his magic? Was it really his own lack of discipline and control that had caused him to be banned?

He swallowed hard. "Father, if that is true, why was I never trained—"

"Are you *questioning* my past decisions as chief, Govek?" Ergoth's tone was laced with venom so potent Govek could feel it prickling his skin. "You *know* what you have done. What you still *could* do. I did what was necessary to protect this clan. What's done is *done*. I see no reason for you to speak on matters of the past now."

Govek's tongue felt as dry as sand on a hot summer day and he bit it hard enough to taste metal.

He'd grown so accustomed to Miranda listening to everything he had to say, to her attentive eyes taking in every word, to conversing openly without judgment.

He'd nearly forgotten that the orcs of this clan, his father included, did not want to hear his wretched excuses or words of defense.

*"They aren't excuses, they're reasons."*

His fists balled and his blood simmered, and the oddest thought crossed his mind.

Was it really their right to silence him? Were his words truly worth less than theirs?

"Govek, this *is* what is best for you too. All your past atrocities could be wiped clean with this. I can *help* you wipe them all clean. Give you a fresh slate. All you have to do is follow my directives as you lead the clan, and I will ensure you are forgiven."

Pain jolted through Govek's whole frame. Rattling his bones. Twisting up his guts.

How many nights had he laid awake in his bed, on the outskirts, alone and hungry with the agonizing burn of a magical binding blistering his veins, *wishing* his father would extend his hand like this? That the great Chief Ergoth might offer aid and help Govek find his place within the clan? That he could find a way to be forgiven?

Miranda's smiling face flooded his mind's eye. The harsh memories of the burning faded.

Did he . . . need to be forgiven?

Did he even *want* that?

What would forgiveness from his clan even offer? Why did it *matter*?

He had Miranda now.

"And think of your woman," Ergoth said. "How would she fair in such war-torn lands? To say nothing of the perilous journey there. In the dead of winter."

Govek agreed with that wholeheartedly. That was the reason he did not want her to leave here, even to find other humans from Earth.

"And I'm *certain* her head is turned by the idea of becoming matriarch of this clan. She must be thrilled at the prospect of the power she'll have being the chief's woman."

Govek snorted in amusement at the thought. Miranda completely supported his decision not to become chief. She'd never once indicated that becoming matriarch was something she wanted. All she wanted was to live a peaceful, secure life. Away from war. With a family.

With *him*.

Words slipped out before he could think better of it. "She has suggested to me she'd rather live separately from the clan."

"You cannot be serious."

Govek went cold with regret and jerked his gaze up to his father's blazing eyes as Ergoth raged. "She cannot possibly be so *foolish* as to *support* your decision not to take lead of this clan."

Anger blazed in Govek's spine at the insult toward Miranda. "It is a decision we have made *together*."

"Well, her decision to keep you from taking on the role of chief is supremely ignorant," Ergoth spat. "She must know that there is no place more comfortable or peaceful than the Rove Woods. She must know that there is no better clan than this. I will speak with her. I guarantee that with a few moments alone, I will have her mind changed—"

"You will not be alone with her." Govek almost snarled.

Ergoth's eyes went wide as he examined Govek from top to bottom. "So, this is your plan, then? You will forsake the only family you have ever known for a woman you've barely met? You would betray us for someone who could very well be deceiving you?"

"Miranda is not—"

"How could you know? How do you know anything about a woman you found wandering in the middle of the woods? Wandering about days away from any human settlements."

"I know, I've—"

"You cannot know. It is not possible for you to know. Don't try to skew things in your favor. Cast aside your selfish needs. This woman is clearly not good for you. Can you not see how our clan will *fall* if you do not do exactly as I tell you?"

"I will not give Miranda up," Govek raged, his control slipping.

"Even if it means saving your kin?" Ergoth raged back, flattening out some of Govek's anger as shock took its place. "I *raised* you. I gave you *everything*. I could have cast you out and left you to starve, but instead I kept you. And *this* is how you thank me? By ruining everything I have worked so hard to achieve? All for some blasted human who will only betray you in the end?"

There was a wildness to Ergoth's tone, a craze to his eyes. The wind caught in his hair and tangled it up, disheveling him.

Govek had never seen the like in his father's face before. *Never.*

"I have worked too fucking hard to have *everything* crumble because some ill-faded woman has turned your head." Ergoth's voice was cold as ice.

Shock closed in around Govek's chest and smothered out the anger. Ergoth's heavy breathing was the only sound in his ears. His father did not trust Miranda. This should not have been surprising. And yet, it sparked a flame of terror in the dark pit where Govek's fury dwelled.

"I will not betray you, Father," Govek said slowly, his skin prickling with the need to remove the target from his lovely mate's back. He chose his words carefully. "I have no intention of leaving these woods."

Ergoth's face went flat, but he was still breathing hard.

"I will stay out of the way, as I always have," he said carefully, working to placate. "I will follow your judgment."

His father's eyes flashed with triumph before shifting to something dark, something that made Govek's blood chill and his gut quiver. His instincts to hide away in his home, or better yet, run into the forest rang out.

He could not fight his father. The great Chief Ergoth was

too cunning and wise for the likes of Govek. The best he could do was give Ergoth what he wanted and retreat.

"Good." His father went over to his cup, still sitting on the railing, and downed the thing in a single swig. "Good. I am glad we are on the same page about this."

Ergoth's motions were jerky as he swirled the empty goblet in his hand. His dark eyes were calculating. "Tell me, my son, where *does* this woman of yours come from? You seem so certain it is not a settlement of the Waking Order."

"She comes from a place far from here," Govek said, wanting to swing the conversation back to the trade so he could leave. "Father, I came to talk to you about—"

"What of family, then? She must have kin."

"She has no family. She was an orphan."

Ergoth snorted. "Even orphans have people who cared for them in their childhood, Govek. Even the most unworthy."

"She had no one person set to the task," Govek said, forcing down the heat rising in his throat and instead thinking on the many tales Miranda had told him of her life growing up. Of s'mores, and camping trips, and birthday parties with streamers and cakes. Most of them were happy memories, even without parents to care for her. They often left him overthinking on his own childhood, trying to find similarities. He always came up short. "She was raised in a group of likened young."

"Ah," Ergoth said knowingly, looking back out over the dazzling view. "That makes sense then."

A chill at his father's unsettling perceptiveness shivered down Govek's spine. "What makes sense?"

"Children who are abandoned cleave to the first being who gives them any attention." Ergoth slid his gaze to Govek. "Even if that source isn't a fit choice."

Govek clenched his teeth, anger burning in his gut and forcing a growl from his throat at his father's implication. Miranda had not chosen to stay with him only because he was the first male to want her. His chest puffed slightly as he forced in a breath.

"Control yourself, Govek. For the sake of the Fades, *must* you defile every sanctuary with your anger? You cannot even set it aside in this holy place?"

Govek swallowed thickly. "I apologize."

"Apologies only have worth if actions follow them," Ergoth said. "I have always aspired to aid you in this. Ever since you were a small child, I have tried endlessly. You're a grown male now, Govek. How is it possible that you *still* prick to anger so easily? Even when you *know* how dangerous your anger is. Do you feel no shame?"

Govek gnashed his teeth.

Ergoth sighed as if the fate of Faeda were on his back. "What I say about the ways of orcs and women isn't anything *new*, even if it is vile. Many warrior orcs have manipulated their partner's desperation in order to win themselves conquests. Most must resort to playing upon the human's dire circumstances to coerce the woman into their beds."

"I have not coerced Miranda," Govek said so low and threatening the words felt like blades in his throat

"Of course not, Govek. You are misconstruing my words," Ergoth said with a frustrated shake of his head. "I speak *generally*. Of the *warrior* kind. It works quite well for them. The woman is so blinded by her need to be wanted or saved she can overlook *anything*. At least, for a time."

"Miranda is *not* going to—"

"I am not speaking of *you*, Govek. Can you not see past your own selfishness?" Ergoth snapped. "Why do you constantly misinterpret what I tell you? Do you *want* us to be at odds? I try so hard to understand you, to *help* you, and you constantly battle with me, despite my efforts."

Govek bowed his head to hide the fury blazing behind his eyes. He just needed to find a way out of here. An opening to leave. Fuck asking his father about Oakwall. They'd just sneak over or show up late, like Miranda suggested they should.

"And here you are again withdrawing, refusing my advice. It truly is impossible with you, Govek. I do not know why I continue to try."

"I have always listened to your advice, Father."

"And never taken it."

"It . . . it does not come easy for me," he began slowly, picturing Miranda's open and accepting face in his mind's eye. "I—"

"Most things have not come easy for you, Govek. I know this better than anyone. I am your *father*," Ergoth said with a shake of his head. "That is why you *must* let me help you when Karthoc forces you to be chief. You must allow me to guide your hand. Promise me this."

Govek's jaw twitched. "I vow it."

"Good," Ergoth said, moving swiftly across the room to a cabinet next to the stairs. He threw open the doors and pulled out a new jug of mead.

"Govek, I have always worked in your best interests. Even the order to Estwill was done out of my care. I know how *badly* you wanted a woman. How badly *all* the orcs do. Think of your youngest cousin. Poor Brovdir has fallen to the plot of preying on a woman in need many times. Karthoc said he has attempted with over a *dozen* conquests. Some abused, some half starved. None of them fulfilled their duty in the end."

Govek ached for his cousin.

"And who could blame them? I certainly do not," Ergoth said without even a sliver of sympathy. The mead jug glugged loudly as he poured it into his glass. "Why, as soon as the threat of *death* is gone, one opens their eyes, don't they? It makes sense that these women would leave once the cloud of trauma has lifted."

The working of Govek's heart grew louder in his ears as his father's truths simmered in his veins.

Would Miranda leave him if she was presented other options? Once her need for constant support was eased, would she abandon his side for a more pleasant male?

The idea made his muscles bunch. He wanted to tear apart every male that glanced Miranda's way, to remove every threat that might try to lure her from his grasp.

"Govek," his father said slowly. "Calm down. I'm not insinuating that Miranda will leave you for another male."

"No other orc will come *near* my woman."

His father shot him a darkly amused look. "Govek, they already *are*. You left her in the hall, remember? But I'm sure it will be fine. The males here in the Rove Woods aren't beasts. Well, I suppose Karthoc's warriors might be considered as such. Why those males are so frantic for women, they even threatened to storm *Oakwall*. Blessedly, I was able to convince them to keep their distance. Our clan would be devastated if our peace with Oakwall was ruined by their single-minded lust."

Govek gnashed his teeth, took deep breaths. Calm. He had to remain calm.

"You've been with Miranda long enough now. She must be carrying your babe." Ergoth took a long gulp. The sweet scent of the brew was making Govek ill. Fermented honey. Ergoth lowered his glass. "She *is* carrying, isn't she?"

"Miranda has been through a trial. She is not ready yet."

"As have we all," Ergoth said, slow and sweet as the drink tainted his lips. "But we still fulfill our duties, don't we? We still find a way to persevere even in the face of tragedy. Tell me, Govek, does Miranda simply not want to have children or is there a good reason for her to refuse you?"

"It was—" Govek swallowed thickly. "It was a *mutual* choice to abstain."

"I see." Ergoth took another sip, his eyes shimmering above the cup as he continued to watch Govek. "Well, since it was mutual, I'm sure you have nothing to worry about."

Govek gulped, clenching his hands. Miranda had given him no reason to worry. She'd been *adamant* she wanted no one else.

And yet, after his confession the night before about imagining her with his child, she had avoided the topic. She'd not mentioned it once. For all he knew, she wasn't thinking about it at all.

Fuck, why did the idea that she wasn't considering it hurt so blasted much? He'd never wanted children before now. He still shouldn't.

"Hmm, seems that Karthoc's chaos has slowed early tonight. That means they might be on their way to the hall to eat," Ergoth said. "I tried banning them, but Karthoc overruled it. We're fortunate our sons are away at the seasonal communion. These warriors are so desperate for a child, I wouldn't put it past them to *steal* one of our own."

Govek jolted at the horrid accusation. He couldn't even *fathom* that any orc might do something so vile. Especially one of the warriors under Karthoc's direct command. They were the best and bravest of their kind.

"Disgusting," Govek's father said under his breath and

Govek swallowed at the malice in the chief's eyes as they looked upon Karthoc's camp. "You know, perhaps you *do* have reason to worry. Who knows what level Karthoc's warriors would stoop to gain a woman?"

Govek blinked, prepared for the surge of jealousy to heat his chest and burst Fades light behind his eyes.

And . . . it didn't come. Instead, he saw Miranda's smile again. Miranda pouting with jealousy over Viravia. Miranda furious that he would think she'd been flirting with Karthoc. Miranda telling him over and over in both her actions and deeds that *he* was her choice. The only one she wanted. His tension eased.

And she called. He felt her speak his name. The spiderweb like strands of the imprint that connected her to him thrummed and prickled in his mind.

"You know, I believe I heard Miranda's name spoken by them once or twice. I can't be certain since they quieted when I drew near."

Govek barely heard his father as he strained his senses toward Miranda. Why had she said his name? She should be fine. Eating in the hall with the other women—

The tiny, muffled pang of Miranda calling once again blistered through him and his heart stopped in his chest.

*She was calling for help!*

His instincts roared to attention, terror burrowing deep, wringing him out.

"Perhaps . . . if you are truly worried about the males, you should return to your mate's side."

She was in pain! He could *feel* it in the tone. It sliced his mind to ribbons.

The light of the Fades exploded in his mind. Whirling up his magic in a surge that sent tingling rage to every part of him.

He could not control it.

He could not cool down.

*Miranda had been hurt!*

He barreled toward the stairs. Fists bunching, claws extended, fangs dripping.

Someone had hurt her, and he would *rip them apart.*

"Govek, try to calm! You haven't even seen if she's betrayed you yet," his father yelled after him. The voice carrying down the stairs as Govek slammed them, forcing his body through the narrow opening.

"Govek control yourself! Don't do something you'll regret!"

But it was too late. He was already lost to his rage.

# TWENTY-FIVE

*MIRANDA*

The woods were absolutely *oppressive.*

It was so dark. So quiet. So still and cold. Black trees loomed above her, caging her in. The wind had stilled, casting the forest into eerie silence. Her footsteps were muffled by the damp, fallen leaves.

Her throat closed and her fingers flexed. She reached around to hug herself around the waist, and she sucked in sharp breaths of the crisp night air through her teeth.

She was *not* on Earth. She was not in a vent or underground. This was a forest. A forest in a place called Faeda. That's all.

And she had to follow that light.

The bright white light in front of her illuminated the forest enough that she could see without tripping over any branches. The red and orange leaves were washed out and the muddy ground was reflective from the damp.

Miranda slowly followed, allowing the light to draw her in.

It was so unusual for this all-natural world. No fire could produce such crisp, perfect light.

So, what was it? And why did it feel like she'd seen it before?

*Because you have.*

She edged around a log and scoffed at herself. Of *course,* she had seen it before. On Earth. Earth had plenty of bright white lights.

But she wasn't on Earth. Earth was gone. It only lived in her nightmares now.

Was . . . this a nightmare?

Miranda looked up again, through the trees. Her heart seized in her chest.

This was certainly *not* Earth. Nor was it a nightmare.

A spring lay before her, crystalline and blue, outlined by moss-covered rocks and cream-colored sand. The ripples on the surface swayed melodically as if some unseen music beckoned. The trees around were illuminated, making their orange and red leaves seem to glow.

And the illumination came from the spring itself. Bright white light poured from the surface, flooding her, drowning her.

A deep sigh broke her wonder. "So, you found me then."

She blinked as an orc stood up, revealing himself. He'd been crouching behind a large boulder to her right. He was slender, white, bald, and his eyes were milky.

But not necessarily unseeing.

The seer.

The light dimmed, and Miranda's stomach churned with confusion and dismay. "W-wait, what was that light?"

The seer, who'd been brushing off his long gray cloak,

paused and tipped his head in her direction, a single eyebrow raised. "You could *see* that?"

"Yes," Miranda said, even as she took in the scene again. The crisp blue water was going black and the illuminated forest was slowly plunging back into darkness.

She couldn't be in the dark. Her mind quailed and her pulse quickened, and she wrung her hands, unsure of what to do.

"Strange that you are so afraid of the dark when that is how I have lived almost my entire life," the seer snorted, clearly amused.

But he raised a pale hand toward the spring and the light within brightened again, so bright this time there were hardly any shadows in the clearing surrounding them.

"What is that?" Miranda asked. "What kind of magic?"

"It is not magic. It is communion."

Communion? "You're . . . talking to the Fades?"

"In a way. It is a very one-sided conversation."

She nodded slowly. "They must have guided me here."

"Your *curiosity* guided you here, woman. Though, it is odd you can see the communion. I do not recall any other human ever being able to do so."

Miranda said nothing, just continued to watch the light as it rippled and swayed with the gentle flow of the water.

"How is it you can see it, Miranda? Tell me, from where do you truly come?"

She wrung her hands together, stomach sinking with anticipation and anxiety. She needed to find her babies. She *knew* they were here on Faeda and she needed to save them.

Only the seer could tell her where they were. "Do that dredge thing with me, and I'll tell you about where I'm from."

The seer snorted. "I'm blind, not dumb." Her stomach

dropped as he scrutinized her, eyes narrowed. "You still aren't ready."

A bubble of hope burst around her. One she hadn't even realized she'd built. "Can't we at least *try*—"

"No."

"But I have so many questions. Or, one *really* important one—"

"Yes, and you steadfastly refuse to even *think* about anything else. You work to bury yourself rather than heal."

"What do you mean?" Miranda asked softly, even though she knew. She absolutely knew.

But the seer spelled it out for her, regardless. "You have to stop *hiding* from your past, Miranda. The answers are in it. How do you think the dredge will work if you cannot even face the memories it will bring up?"

"But . . ." She didn't *need* to remember the horrors of Earth. She didn't *need* to remember the blank spots in her memory. She could let the mystery remain forever. As long as she was able to save her babies.

The seer needed to tell her where they *were*. That's it.

"It hurts. I know. And it's nice to sleep on your male and let him soothe and distract and care for you at every turn."

Her stomach twisted.

"He likes it too, Miranda, so stop with the guilt. He likes it *too* much. Govek has his arms so far open it's no wonder you fall into them at every opportunity. Not that he can be blamed for this. It is not his responsibility to deny you comfort. It is you who must put the work into healing."

"I don't . . . need to heal."

"What?" The seer's shock was almost palpable and, under alternative circumstances, it might have made her laugh.

"I don't need to remember what happened on Earth. I just need you to tell me how to find my family."

The seer's brow screwed up.

"*That's* why I'm here. Why I want to dredge with you. To find them. My . . ." Her throat closed and her eyes prickled, and her breaths came in short pants.

"Miranda, listen to me."

His voice sounded odd, like a vibration. Like two voices overlapped to create one. The sound of it rolled over her skin and made her arms break out with goosebumps. The light from the spring grew so bright she felt like it was absorbing into her.

"*Everything* is connected," the seer said slowly. "*Everything.* Your past, present, and future blend together to create the whole of your life. You cannot live that life in *parts*, Miranda. And I cannot *dredge* in parts."

"But . . . I only need you to tell me where they are."

"I can't do that," he said firmly, and her hopes were dashed, shattered like icy glass at her feet, slicing open her skin and making it difficult to breathe. "Not now."

Not now . . . that meant . . . later?

"What . . . what do I have to do?" Miranda straightened her back. She'd do *anything.*

And she *could* do anything. She'd healed from trauma before. In her childhood. After her family died in the car accident and she'd been left all alone. Sent to live with children that had come from much worse situations than she had. A place where adult attention was divided so thinly it felt like trying to drink water from a cup of dry sand. Where you could be surrounded by dozens of people and were still overlooked.

She'd spent her entire career working to make sure the babies at Riverside Daycare *never* felt like they were unwanted or unseen.

And then she'd abandoned them—

No! *No!* She hadn't. She knew she hadn't.

They were here. On Faeda. She'd do anything to find them. Even face the horror of what had happened on Earth.

"Please," she insisted. "Tell me what I have to do."

"It won't be easy," the seer said, turning back to the spring and brightening the water again. It was odd, but the light never hurt her eyes. Never felt blinding. Even as the tree trunks turned almost white from the bright illumination and the leaves went colorless and the sand glowed like the sun.

It was so bright. *So bright.*

And familiar.

"If you want your answers, you're going to have to sit with the horrors that you keep pushing away and accept them instead. You will need to work through your pain and shed light on the places of your mind you are trying to keep in the dark."

"But . . . every time I try to do that, I *panic.*" Miranda focused on the glowing water. "I can't move or breathe or even *think.* How am I supposed to heal when I'm so consumed by pain it makes me shut down?"

"As I said, it isn't easy."

"I don't even know where to start," Miranda whispered. On Earth, even with therapy, it took months. *Years.*

Was she going to be able to heal before the seer left the Rove Woods?

"You have time," the seer said as if reading her mind and, as unsettling as that was, Miranda couldn't help but feel soothed by his assurance. "I'm not going to be leaving Rove anytime soon. Unless that fool of a warlord does something incredibly daft."

"What do you mean?"

But the seer didn't answer, instead he pointed off into the dark forest. "Go that way."

"What?"

"Go that way and sit on a log."

"Go and . . . why?"

"You want to spark your healing. That's what you need to do. But mind, it's going to *hurt.*"

"Hurt? Will I be injured?" Miranda's stomach twisted up.

"That I cannot see. I cannot say what *exactly* will happen. I only know that something will. Something... initiating."

"Initiating." She said slowly.

"Yes. It would be much easier to take it slow and soothe naturally, but if you're insistent about pushing on, then..."

She gripped her hands. She didn't *have* time for this to go the natural way. She needed to dredge *now*. Her babies were somewhere in this world and she *needed* to find them. Before it was too late.

"So, I just sit and wait . . . over there?" She pointed to her right.

The seer snorted. "Ah, nothing like those sweeping gestures I cannot see." Miranda dropped her hand even as the seer raised his. "That way. Go. You don't have a lot of time."

She took a deep breath and nodded, "Thank you, seer."

"I'll see you again."

Her heart thundered at the confirmation. They *would* have another chance. She just had to put in the work first. That was fine. She'd done this work before. Her whole childhood was spent in and out of therapy appointments.

She said a quiet goodbye to the seer and turned away from the light of the glowing spring, turned her back on the comfort and security to face the pitch black of the woods.

Miranda took her steps carefully. Frost crunched under her

feet, but the damp leaves cushioned her stride. She could hardly see anything. Wet, chilly foliage kept brushing at her hands and cheeks. Her hair caught in a bramble once and yanked hard as she moved away.

Finally, she came upon a downed tree and sat atop it. The icy chill of the log soaked through her clothes, but at least she didn't get wet. The cloak Govek gave her was pretty well waterproof.

She hoped this was the right log. She didn't see any others nearby but...

She wondered if Govek would come for her soon. The dark was churning around in her like a stalking predator. She would have loved to lean into Govek, let him drown out the fear.

*"It is not his responsibility . . . It is you who must put the work into healing."*

The seer was right. She *had* to do this to move forward. She couldn't lean on Govek at every turn.

And he had his own demons to battle. He was battling one *right now*. Speaking with his father in a hall full of orcs who thought the worst of him.

They thought he tortured animals.

Someone, perhaps *many*, had *lied* to make Govek look like a monster.

How many other lies were discoloring Govek's reputation? How many other lies were forcing him to be an outcast?

And who had started them?

She waited. Brooding. In the quiet. In the dark. The rustling of leaves and the cracking of branches and the swirling terrors of her mind all made her flinch.

Feet pounded up right next to her so fast she couldn't even flinch.

Something wet and sticky splatted on her face and mouth.

Miranda yelped and staggered to her feet. Some of the liquid got on her tongue. It was pungent and bitter. She swiped it off, lost her footing, and tripped backward over the log.

Her head spun, her throat closed, and her body quaked.

She was no longer in the woods.

*To Be Continued . . .*

# MIRANDA AND GOVEK'S STORY CONCLUDES IN:

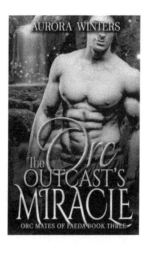

**The Orc Outcast's Miracle:**
Releasing August 2024

*With deadly secrets coming to light, will their love survive?*

**Miranda is resolved to create a new life on Faeda.**

And that new life is threatening to unravel before her very eyes.

With the ever pressing need to find her loved ones looming at the back of her mind, Miranda must now face the clan who is accusing Govek of a crime he did not commit.

And just when she thinks she finally has a foolproof plan, new evidence comes to light and the perfect future she imagined with Govek threatens to crumble beneath her feet.

**Govek has never triumphed before, but he is resolved to do it now.**

Standing accused is nothing new for Govek. He's been found guilty of so many atrocities he's long lost count. But this time, he refuses to simply roll over and accept whatever punishment his brethren dole out.

Because the punishment he faces is losing Miranda forever.

As their love begins to shine, Miranda is dealt devastating blows that threaten her sanity, and Govek must face the true reason he's been reviled his entire life. The mysteries of their pasts begin to unravel and fear of the unknown threatens to undo the trust and love they've worked so hard to build.

# WANT MORE NOW?

## The Orc Outcast Is All Tied Up

With the trauma of the tornado and goblin mines behind them and the arrival at Rove Wood Clan on the horizon, Miranda and Govek must make the best of their night.

For Govek that means tying Miranda up high in a tree so she doesn't get eaten by predators while she sleeps.

For Miranda… being tied to a tree means something *quite* a bit naughtier.

Follow this QR Code or go to https://www. aurorawintersromance.com/rm2-sign-up to subscribe to my newsletter and you'll get these free, spicy bonus chapters, as well as maps of the Rove Woods and Rove Wood Clan!

# LET'S KEEP IN TOUCH!

Sign up for my newsletter on my website,
www.AuroraWintersRomance.com
or follow me on Instagram @aurorawinters.romance.

# ACKNOWLEDGMENTS

Thank you so much for reading book two of my Orc Mates of Faeda series! I'm grateful to every one of you who continued following Govek and Miranda's story. If you want to go above and beyond you could head on over to Amazon and leave a review.

So many people helped to make this book possible. A special thank you to my husband for supporting me through all my writing woes and keeping the house afloat during crunch times when I was spending every spare moment at my keyboard.

To Daisy who spent countless hours helping me edit the books and giving feedback on video calls. The books would not be what they are today without your advice!

To Lacey Braziel at Lacey Braziel Edits for your expert line and copy editing. And to Cassie Weaver at Weaver Way Author Services for your awesome beta reading, proofreading, and formatting. You both rock!

And once again, thank you to all of my readers! I appreciate every single one of you.

# ABOUT AURORA WINTERS

Growing up in the Pacific Northwest meant many rainy days spent on indoor activities and from a young age one of my favorites has been creative writing. I was penning monster romance stories in high school between classes before I even realized it was a genre and still have many of those original drafts. (Which will never, ever see the light of day again because they are truly cringe worthy!)

It was only recently that my writing grew from a personal hobby into a dream of publishing. When I'm not obsessing over my writing, I can be found wandering through the woods with my daughter and husband, taking pictures of pretty leaves, and throwing sticks for my little dog, Dash.

Let's keep in touch! Join my newsletter at www.AuroraWintersRomance.com.